"He should have got the girl."

So he'd read the book she'd written to exorcise the ghosts of having loved him. Shay closed her eyes as Lyon's fingers traveled up the sides of her breasts.

"Page one hundred and twenty-three was our last night together, wasn't it?"

"Yes!" She tried to push his hands away. "And at the end of that night I felt the same loathing for you that my heroine felt for Leon de Coursey."

"You may be able to control the characters in your books, but you can't control me. I lost you once. It isn't going to happen a second time."

Shay looked at him coldly. "All you'll ever get from me is the contempt you deserve."

His hands stayed confidently in place. "And a response you can't deny."

Books by Carole Mortimer

HARLEQUIN PRESENTS

These books may be available at your local bookseller.

Don't miss any of our special offers. Write to us at the following address for information on our newest releases.

Harlequin Reader Service
901 Fuhrmann Blvd., P.O. Box 1397, Buffalo, NY 14240
Canadian address: P.O. Box 603,
Fort Erie, Ont. L2A 9Z9

Carole Mortimer

GYPSY

Harlequin Books

TORONTO • NEW YORK • LONDON
AMSTERDAM • PARIS • SYDNEY • HAMBURG
STOCKHOLM • ATHENS • TOKYO • MILAN

Harlequin Signature Edition published July 1986

ISBN 0-373-83202-8

Originally published in Great Britain in 1985

For my husband John,
My own inspirational hero!

CHAPTER ONE

'SHAY.'

She didn't turn at the sound of that voice, her gaze unwavering from the long wooden box being loaded on board the small jet in front of her, all that remained of her five years of marriage, the broken and twisted body of her husband Ricky being flown from America back to the Falconer estate for burial in the family plot.

'Shay.'

She didn't want to turn to the owner of that rich baritone voice, didn't want him here at all, interrupting a moment that belonged completely to Ricky and herself.

'For God's sake, Shay!'

For God's sake! She wanted to turn and shout at him that if it weren't for God she wouldn't be here now, that if it weren't for God Ricky wouldn't be still and lifeless inside that oblong box they were even now securing inside the plane, that he would be beside her as he had always been, the love they felt for each other their greatest happiness! But she didn't turn and say any of those things, knew that if she once gave in to that hysteria she would lose the one thing that was keeping her in one piece; her belief that even though life could be cruel, none of them had any choices, it was all, ultimately, decided for them.

7

She finally turned as the doors closed on Ricky's coffin, coolly facing the man she knew was responsible for dealing with the authorities and paperwork to get Ricky's body out of the country they had made their home for the last three years, and back to their native England; she certainly hadn't had anything to do with it, too numb to deal with details like that. No, she had known only Lyon Falconer could have managed such organisation in the few weeks it had been since they had found Ricky's body, had known he was in California somewhere using the indomitable Falconer influence to take his brother home in the family jet. She also knew the two of them had nothing to say to each other, had informed her lawyer that she didn't want to see Lyon when he had told her the other man was in the country.

Lyon Falconer. He hadn't changed at all in the last three years, lean and muscular despite being very close to his fortieth birthday, his tawny hair styled just over his ears and down to his collar in a way designed to look casual, that very casualness indicative of its expensive cut. His arrogantly harsh face was lean and craggy, dominated by narrowed tawny eyes, his nose long and straight, his unsmiling mouth a forbidding line, the squareness of his jaw as uncompromising as ever. The tailored, dark three-piece suit and cream silk shirt pronounced him for exactly what he was, a successful businessman, although its formality in no way detracted from his lean muscularity, his power not just of the physical, a single-word command from him having been known to daunt even his most powerful of adversaries. And Shay knew she was far from being that.

But she wasn't the unsophisticated Shay Flanagan from Dublin any longer, the young girl not good enough to become a member of his élite family. She had been a Falconer herself now for over five years, was this man's sister-in-law, had gained in confidence almost beyond recognition since this man had first noticed her ebony head among his London personnel. At least, she hoped she had, feeling the first stirrings of inadequacy she had known in a long time, a very long time.

Not that any of that showed as she and Lyon faced each other across the tarmac, the black silk dress adding height and slenderness to the already five feet nine inches she was in the high-heeled sandals. The soft ebony of her shoulder-length hair was hidden beneath the silk hat, the lace pulled down to partly obscure her face, the purple depths of her eyes unadorned by anything but naturally long black lashes. There were classical lines to her face; high cheekbones, small pert nose, generously wide mouth, the latter feeling as if she hadn't smiled in months. As indeed she hadn't!

And she didn't smile now, her gaze steady on that autocratic face. 'Lyon,' she greeted coldly.

'Shay, you look—'

'Like hell,' she drawled mockingly, wanting no insincere compliments from this man. She looked exactly what she was, a recently widowed woman.

Lyon looked momentarily annoyed, the emotion quickly controlled and masked. 'As usual, your presumption of what I was about to say was incorrect,' he bit out harshly.

'Really?' she derided, turning to walk up the steps that led into the luxurious interior of the waiting jet, knowing the crew were merely waiting for them to come aboard before they obtained clearance to take off.

'You've changed, Shay.'

She stiffened at the surprise in Lyon's voice, had known he would follow her up into the plane, the door even now being secured behind them, only the hostess Jenny stopping them from being completely alone, something Shay knew she would avoid whenever she could. She and Lyon Falconer had nothing to say to each other, they never had.

'I'm twenty-four now, Lyon, not eighteen,' she dryly stated the obvious, taking her seat in the lounge area, smoothly crossing one knee over the other, her legs long and silky, turning gently to smile her thanks to Jenny as she brought her a glass of iced tea, not questioning how the other woman knew of her preference; the Falconer staff were paid, very handsomely, to know the needs of the Falconer family before they were even aware of them themselves. Shay turned away with indifference as the small blonde woman lingered over giving Lyon his neat whisky; obviously Lyon still had the power to attract women in their droves!

Tawny eyes flashed with specks of green as Lyon angrily sensed her derision. 'I didn't just mean physically,' he rasped as Jenny disappeared into the galley.

She calmly reached up to remove her hat, placing it on the seat beside her, her neck long and slender, her hands equally so as she brailled the neatness of her severely-styled black hair. 'I grew up, Lyon, if that's what you mean,' she drawled dismissively, turning to look out of the window as the small jet began to taxi towards the runway. 'Marilyn isn't with you?' She arched perfectly curved brows at him, her slender hands, adorned only by her thin gold wedding band, folded neatly on top of her fastened seat-belt.

Lyon's mouth tightened. 'No, Marilyn isn't with me,' he bit out.

'I just thought, she is the family lawyer . . .'

'One of them,' he confirmed gratingly.

'And your wife,' Shay added tauntingly.

'Yes,' he acknowledged abruptly. 'But I'd really rather not discuss her right now.'

Navy eyes sharpened to purple. 'As you wish,' she nodded distantly. 'You came alone, then?'

'There was no reason for anyone to accompany me. Our lawyer in Los Angeles was able to deal with anything that had to be done.'

'Of course, David Anders,' she nodded again,

having worked closely with the American lawyer herself the last two months, coming to the airport today as per his instructions, knowing he had managed to secure the release of Ricky's body. She had hoped Lyon wouldn't be sharing the flight with her, although she had known it was a futile hope; the haughty head of the Falconer family wouldn't rest until his youngest brother was back in England where he felt he had always belonged, even if Ricky's body were now lifeless.

'He did a magnificent job,' Lyon said curtly, his mouth grim.

'Yes,' she acknowledged, her face suddenly looking stricken.

Lyon was alert to the sudden change in her. 'You still don't like flying?'

'I hate it,' she answered pleasantly, sipping her tea, not showing now even by a tremor of her hand how her senses lurched at the acceleration of the jet engines as they prepared for take-off.

'Perhaps it would have been better if you had remained in Los Angeles—'

'And not come to England?' Her eyes flashed her anger at the suggestion. 'Ricky may have been your brother, Lyon,' she said icily, 'but he was my husband, and I want to be there when you have him put in the ground!'

Lyon winced noticeably. 'The last two months of waiting have been a strain for you,' he bit out. 'This journey can only be causing you more pain.'

He didn't know the half of the pain she had suffered the past two months, she had made certain he wouldn't know, had remained alone in California after Ricky's plane had crashed in the mountains, all the time hoping that he had survived the crash, that by some miracle he had lived when the light plane he had been piloting had gone down during a freak thunderstorm in the mountains. It was the 'somewhere' that had caused all the pain, no one knowing exactly *where* the plane had gone down, Ricky and the plane remaining undetected until three weeks ago. Until that time she had lived with the hope, not sleeping, not eating, anxiously waiting for news from the people she had paid to continue searching for him after the authorities had given up. David Anders had informed her that Lyon had flown over briefly after the accident had been reported, that he had been convinced by the authorities that there was no way Ricky could have survived the crash in the area he had gone down. Shay had refused Lyon's request to see her then, would have refused to be with him now if it were in her power to do so. But it wasn't.

'I can cope,' she told him distantly.

'I'm sure you can,' Lyon nodded grimly. 'God, Shay!' He fumbled with the fastening of his seatbelt as her skin turned a sickly green as the plane parted with the ground, striding across the cabin to her side as the plane ascended dramatically.

She looked up at him with uncomprehending eyes. 'You aren't supposed to do that,' she said

dazedly as he came down on his haunches beside
her, her hands looking pale and delicate as he
took them into his warm, much larger ones.

'Are you going to faint?' he asked briskly.

Shay's eyes widened at the suggestion. 'No!'
she denied—and promptly did so!

She came round with a slow groan, turning
over to bury her face in the pillow as she lay on
the double bed in the converted bedroom off the
lounge area, Lyon standing with his back towards her, staring out of the small window as
they flew above the blanket of fluffy-white
clouds.

She had wanted to remain so composed, had
once sworn this man would never see any sign of
weakness in her again. Collapsing in the way she
had had definitely been weak! But she hadn't
cried when they told her Ricky's plane had gone
down, nor during the following two months, not
even when they finally found him still seated in
the crashed aircraft, his neck broken from the
impact with the ground; surely she was entitled
to one fainting fit? She just wished it hadn't been
Lyon who had been the one to witness it!

She swung her feet to the carpeted floor, her
shoes neatly beside the bed, putting up a trembling hand to her mussed hair, smoothing it before
Lyon turned suddenly, aware of her return to
consciousness, his eyes narrowing as her head
went back challengingly.

Shay could have no idea how vulnerable she
looked, would have been dismayed if she had

known, and Lyon was aware of that. Shay *had* grown up in the last six years, had grown more beautiful too, and he had to clench his hands at his sides to stop himself from reaching out for what had once so nearly been his. She had been his brother's wife since then, he hadn't seen her for three years, and yet he only had to think of her to ache with an unrequited desire, knew that he ached with that desire even now.

He could still remember the first time he had seen her, her long hair untamed, purple eyes alight with laughter as she giggled with some of the other typists before silence fell over the room as they realised the head of the company had walked in to their office with one of the directors. The other girls had quickly looked away and got on with their work, but purple eyes had remained on him curiously. Such open interest from one so young hadn't been something he had experienced before. God, he had already been thirty-three then, past the age of instant attraction, especially with such a child. Or so he had thought . . .

'I'm sorry,' she was saying now, her composure back in place. 'I've disliked flying even more since it was the way Ricky died.'

Lyon could feel the agony of jealousy over his young brother rip through him, hadn't known a day go by without feeling that same jealousy since Ricky had announced his intention of making Shay his wife. Ricky may be dead now, but Lyon still couldn't forgive his young brother for marrying the girl he—The girl *he* had wanted, damn it!

This beautifully elegant woman might not be that girl—but he *still* wanted her!

To Shay he looked as coldly remote as usual, none of the cauldron of emotions burning so hotly beneath that surface-cool exterior in evidence. He was a cold-hearted bastard, always had been and always would be. It was a pity he and Marilyn couldn't make more of a success of their eleven-year marriage, there was no doubt they made the perfect couple!

'I should have thought of that,' he murmured abruptly. 'This just seemed the quickest way . . .'

'And after waiting all this time I'm sure you just want to get Ricky home so that you can bury him!' She slid her slender feet into the black sandals before standing up, feeling at too much of a disadvantage sitting on the bed.

'Shay!' Lyon rasped.

'Sorry,' she drawled in a bored voice. 'But you and Ricky were never close, I just assumed . . .' She shrugged dismissively.

'Too damned much,' he scowled darkly. 'The whole family has been deeply shocked by Ricky's death.'

The 'whole family' consisted of two more brothers, Matthew and Neil, born between Lyon and Ricky, Lyon's wife Marilyn, and numerous aunts and uncles—and all of them looking up to, and ultimately guided by, Lyon. He was the unchallenged head of the Falconer empire, each member of the family working for that empire. Even Ricky, despite his differences with Lyon, had run the American office, that distance between the two brothers allowing a certain respite from the bitter arguments they used to have when Shay and Ricky lived with the rest of the brothers in the mansion the Falconer brothers called home.

'I'm sure they have,' she said dryly. 'Do you have the funeral arranged?'

His mouth tightened with irritation. 'I called Matthew yesterday and asked him to make the necessary arrangements,' he admitted grudgingly.

She nodded, as if she had never doubted he would have everything under control. There was only one thing he had never been able to control, and that had been his anger towards her. He had never been able to forgive her for marrying his younger brother and so becoming one of his prestigious family. No doubt, now that Ricky had finally been pronounced dead instead of merely missing, Lyon would see that she ceased being recognised as a member of his family. Only she didn't intend letting him do that to her, had no intention of bowing gracefully out of their lives.

'And Neil, how is he?' she enquired coolly, finding Neil, at thirty-two, very like Ricky, with his blond good looks and easy-going charm, Matthew's colouring slightly darker, and at thirty-five Ricky had told her he was becoming more like the eldest Falconer every day.

'We aren't here to exchange social pleasantries, Shay,' Lyon told her impatiently.

'I'm well aware of the reason we're both here, Lyon,' she rasped bitterly. 'And if you would rather we spent the next nine hours in silence then I can assure you I'm more than agreeable.'

'I'm sure you are,' he said with barely controlled violence. 'But it's been three years since we saw each other, do you really have nothing better to talk to me about than Neil and Matthew?'

'The weather?' she scorned.

Tawny-coloured eyes became like burnished gold. 'Hell, Shay, can't we even be polite to each other now?'

'Were we ever?' she derided in a bored voice.

'Once,' he muttered, his gaze suddenly intense.

If he expected to disarm her he was disappointed, one thing the School of Hard Knocks and Snubs had taught her was invincible poise, and she had learnt that lesson well, from his own family mainly. 'That was such a long time ago, Lyon,' she dismissed indifferently.

'And you've forgotten it?' he scowled. 'All of it?'

'Of course not,' she drawled. 'Didn't you ever read page one hundred and twenty-three of *Scarlet Lover*?'

'You put me in one of your damned books?' Lyon demanded incredulously.

'You didn't read it?' she reproved, moving through to the lounge as he didn't seem to be going to, knowing he would follow her. He did, standing gloweringly in the background as she smiled her thanks at Jenny for replenishing her glass of iced tea. 'You really should have done, Lyon.' She turned to mock him.

'So it would seem,' he bit out, glaring at the stewardess as she hovered in the room with them. 'Don't you have a meal to prepare? Or something?' he added darkly.

'Er—no. I mean, yes—sir.' Jenny looked taken aback, had worked for the Falconers for the last seven years, and not once before had Lyon lost his temper with her in this way. Of course, this was a sad occasion for the family, and everyone had always known of the friction that existed between Lyon and Ricky's wife, Shay. 'Excuse me.' She made a hasty retreat to the galley, closing the door behind her.

'Jenny doesn't appear to be accustomed to your bad humour,' Shay mocked, sinking gracefully down into one of the comfortable armchairs, once again crossing one elegant knee over the other, unconsciously emphasising the slender beauty of her legs as she did so.

'Meaning you are?' Lyon rasped, very aware of all of this woman's beauty, and despising himself for it. She had once made her dislike of him more than obvious, to want her now, *especially* now, was pure madness on his part.

'Oh yes,' she derided. 'Don't you remember?'

'I remember a lot of things that happened between us in the past—'

'Strangely, I don't,' Shay cut in firmly. 'You really should have read *Scarlet Lover*, Lyon; I was sure you would have recognised yourself.' She smiled briefly, inwardly, not at or with Lyon. 'Ricky felt sure you would want to sue me!'

'Could I have done?' he asked tightly.

'I doubt it,' dismissed Shay coolly, her humour gone as quickly as it had arisen. 'Of course the man's name was Leon de Coursey, and he did have blond hair and tawny eyes too, was about the same age—'

'And was he a despoiler of young maidens too?' Lyon rasped harshly.

'No.' Her mouth tightened. 'But he was married!'

'Shay—'

'You never did tell me how Neil is,' she interrupted his angry outburst.

'He's well,' Lyon dismissed curtly. 'But we were talking about one of your books—'

'Amazing, isn't it,' she said thoughtfully. 'At twenty-one I suddenly discovered I had a talent for writing.' She still found the fact that she was a best-selling author awe-inspiring.

'And making money,' Lyon put in derisively.

She looked at him unemotionally. 'That too, although it isn't as much as it might seem. But I must admit I like the look on people's faces when they realise I'm Shay Flanagan, the author of those historical sizzlers. I hope you're duly grateful about the fact that I didn't drag the Falconer name into my disreputable career,' she continued scornfully. 'Ricky assured me Grandfather Jonas would have turned in his grave!'

'Considering the fact that my father, his only child, was born illegitimately, I don't think Grandfather Jonas would have any right to criticise,' Lyon drawled. 'What happened on page one hundred and twenty-three in the book, Shay?'

She had known he wouldn't be diverted by the deviations in the conversation. 'I'll get you a copy,' she promised casually.

'I'd rather you told me now,' he insisted roughly.

Shay shook her head firmly. 'I never discuss my work with anyone.'

'But if I feature in one of your books—'

'I didn't say that you did,' she contradicted coldly. 'Page one hundred and twenty-three is a very explicit sex scene—and we once had a lot of those,' she added hardly.

'You were married to Ricky, couldn't you have used your—times, with him?' Lyon grated forbiddingly.

'I said it was a sex scene, Lyon, not a love scene,' Shay said crushingly. 'Now, if you wouldn't mind,' she stood up, 'I think I should like to go into the bedroom and rest for a while.'

'Shay . . . !' His hand snaked out and captured her wrist as she would have walked past him.

She looked at him unemotionally. 'Please, don't cause a scene, Lyon.'

'And if I do?' he challenged.

'You remember my Irish temper?' she said calmly.

The hand that wasn't holding her wrist moved up to the scar on his right temple. 'Vividly,' he drawled dryly.

Shay's gaze moved to the small white scar, remembering how she had once thrown a cup at him, a fine china missile that had smashed when it made contact with his head, blood dripping down his face from the gash it made. 'I can see that you do,' she said with satisfaction. 'Well, I may appear calm and collected to you,' she spoke pleasantly, 'but if you don't release me there are one or two glasses in here that I could use instead of the cup.'

Lyon looked at her sceptically, and then with grudging admiration as he saw she was in earnest, slowly released her arm. 'You little hell-cat,' he murmured in fascination.

She didn't show any emotion for the name he had once called her at more intimate moments in their past relationship. 'Ricky preferred to think of me as fiery.' She felt an inner satisfaction as Lyon's mouth tightened at the mention of her intimacy with his brother. 'I prefer to think of it as an aversion to being pushed around.' Shay stepped back from him. 'I won't be requiring any dinner,' she informed him coolly. 'Perhaps you could have Jenny wake me when we get to England?'

Tawny eyes narrowed. 'You intend sleeping for the next eight hours?'

Shay shrugged narrow shoulders. 'Why not?'

'I thought we could talk, become reacquainted,' he grated.

'Reacquainted, Lyon?' Her smile was one of genuine amusement. 'Were we ever *acquainted*?'

His mouth tightened at her mockery. 'We were lovers, damn it!'

'Is that what you would call it?' she scorned. 'After being married to, and in love with, Ricky, I have a much different name for what *we* once were. Now if you'll excuse me, I don't wish to be disturbed.' She walked past him into the bedroom, closing the door on his rage at being dismissed so autocratically, knowing he wouldn't disturb her, that he was too angry to follow her.

Now that she was alone, away from those all-seeing tawny eyes, she didn't have to keep up the pretence any more, sitting down heavily on the bed, wrapping her arms about herself as she shuddered with reaction.

Oh Ricky, she silently cried, why aren't you here to take care of me, to love me! Twenty-eight was too young to die, especially when he had so much to live for.

She knew her husband would have enjoyed this verbal sparring with Lyon, that he had revelled in their animosity, the clash of characters between the two brothers only becoming so heatedly intense after she and Ricky were married. They were all aware of that, the relationship between herself and Lyon no secret from the rest of the family. Ricky had never been angry about her and Lyon, only angry *for* her. Especially after reading *Scarlet Lover*.

She had written the manuscript during the days once Ricky had gone to work, hadn't told him about it, embarrassed at her own imagination, only allowing him to read it after it was completed. She had known the exact moment he reached page one hundred and twenty-three, had watched him anxiously, her breathing becoming constricted at how still he had suddenly become.

He was sitting cross-legged on their bed, the manuscript spread out in front of him, looking up at her with pained eyes. 'Leon de Coursey—'

'I'll change it.' She ran to him, stricken. 'I won't send it to a publisher. It's only rubbish, anyway,' she dismissed. 'It was just something for me to do while you were—'

'It isn't rubbish, you will send it to a publisher, and you won't change a thing,' Ricky told her intensely, his laughing blue eyes unusually serious. He cupped her face in his hands. 'That was what it was like between you and Lyon?'

'Lyon?' she hedged unconvincingly. 'I don't—'

'Darling, we've never lied to each other,' he encouraged gently. 'What we have together is—fantastic. What you had with Lyon, if de Coursey is him—and I believe he is—was something else entirely. It was primitive, savage—'

'Yes, it was both of those things,' she acknowledged bitterly. 'We seemed to bring out those qualities in each other. But it was also destructive.'

'It's all right, darling,' Ricky took her in his arms, holding her trembling body close against him, beginning to kiss her, the manuscript, and Leon de Coursey, or Lyon—the two had become confused in her mind by this time!—were forgotten in the heat of their passionate exchange.

But the next day Ricky had parcelled up the manuscript and sent it to a reputable publisher, and now the heated historical romances of Shay Flanagan were almost history themselves.

Just as her relationship with Lyon was also history, a painful part of her history she had tried to put behind her.

Damn it, what was she doing in there! Lyon shook with the rage of being instructed what to do as if he were one of the help. No one had ever, *ever*, spoken to him that way before! And all it had achieved was to make him want Shay more than ever.

More than anything he was curious about page one hundred and twenty-three of her book. Was Leon de Coursey the hero of her book or the villain? Knowing how Shay felt about him, de Coursey was the blackest villain there had ever been!

God, she had grown incredibly beautiful the last three years, he could feel his thighs tightening just at the thought of her. Had she undressed now that she was alone in the bedroom, was she naked even now, lying between those brown silk sheets, moving sensuously in her sleep as she always used to.

He had been haunted by those sounds she used to make as she slept, had woken up in a sweat more than once after imagining her there beside him, only to know the agonising disappointment of pent up desire when he found he was once again alone, that Shay now shared his brother Ricky's bed, giving him all the passion she had once so freely given him.

He had never forgotten the look on Ricky's face when he had first been introduced to Shay; his young brother had looked as if it were Christmas and New Year all rolled into one, with Shay the glittering angel on top of the tree. To her credit Shay hadn't looked at him the same way for several months, but finally it had come. Lyon could still feel the pain in his gut at knowing she was no longer his.

'Lyon?'

He turned sharply, scowling. 'What is it, Jenny?' he asked tersely.

She smiled engagingly. 'I wondered if there were anything I could do for you?'

He remembered other times he had received completely different offers from this beautiful woman, occasions when he hadn't been averse to her providing him with the physical relief he needed, even on the bed in the adjoining room once. 'A whisky,' he requested harshly, ignoring how hurt she looked at his coldness. 'And just keep them coming until we land.' He was going to need to be numb from the feet up to cope with knowing Shay was only feet away from him after imagining every woman in his bed was her for the last five years.

'And Mrs Falconer, can I get her anything?' Jenny recovered quickly from his snub.

'Nothing,' he bit out, staring broodingly at the closed door to the bedroom.

He was still staring broodingly at the door, Shay on the other side of it, when they touched down at Heathrow Airport hours later.

He had been drinking. She had known it the moment she came out of the bedroom to join him to leave the plane. Lyon wasn't offensive, didn't look or act drunk, but she knew he was one of those people who became more controlled after consuming alcohol, the tawny eyes narrowed, his mouth a compressed line of tension.

She spared him only a brief glance before turning to the mirror to put the hat back on her recently brushed hair, several tendrils having escaped as she lay sleepless on the bed. She had known she wouldn't really be able to sleep, hadn't slept without medical help since Ricky disappeared, but the thought of spending all that time alone with Lyon was abhorrent to her. But as she lay on the bed she had almost been able to feel his eyes burning her flesh through the closed door, and she clung to the sanctuary of the bedroom, preferring to save her energy—and emotional strength—for the ordeal of returning to Falconer House.

'We can leave now, if you're ready.' Lyon watched her gloweringly.

She pulled the black lace of her hat down over her face before turning to look at him, knowing by the scowl on his face that he disliked this partial shield to her emotions. The time when she gave a damn what Lyon liked or disliked was long gone!

She gave a haughty inclination of her head, as coolly composed as when they had faced each other in Los Angeles all those hours ago, ignoring the hand he put out to guide her down the steps to the waiting airport cars, one for them, the other for the coffin containing Ricky's lifeless body, the law deeming the funeral director with the car should take over now.

She bore the tedium of Lyon's dealing with the passport officials with a bored look on her face, secretly wondering how much longer she could keep up this cool façade as the man seemed to linger over clearing them. It was true that the shock of losing Ricky had numbed her, that her independent career from the Falconer empire had given her a confidence she had hitherto lacked, but this act of cool emotionalism was causing more of a strain than she felt able to cope with. But not for anything would she admit to Lyon how all this was affecting her.

'Could we hurry this up, please?' Lyon suddenly pressed as the man continued to linger over checking their passports. 'As I'm sure you can imagine, my sister-in-law is under severe strain.'

The man glanced sympathetically at Shay, receiving a wan smile in return, miraculously seeming to find no further delay with their documents.

Once out in the general flow of people at the airport, Shay felt her panic rising, flinching from the cameras as they clicked practically in her face as each newspaper representative tried to get the best picture of Richard Falconer's widow, questions coming at them from all directions, the hand that grasped her arm making her pull away.

'It's me, you little fool,' Lyon rasped, pushing his way through the reporters, pulling her along with him. 'Where the hell is the damned car?' he swore roughly as they emerged out into the English summer sunshine.

'Mr Falconer—'

'Thank God.' He turned to the chauffeur gratefully, guiding Shay to the waiting limousine, the windows discreetly darkened for privacy.

'I'm sorry about this, Mr Falconer.' The man preceded them. 'But there's been a bomb scare, and the police are—'

'Yes, yes,' Lyon dismissed tersely, still running the gauntlet of the press. 'Let's just get out of here.'

'Thank you, Jeffrey.' Shay smiled at the man as he opened the back door for her, sliding inside and across the seat as Lyon climbed in next to her, cameras still clicking, the questions still coming until Jeffrey firmly closed the door, enclosing them in cool, silent peace.

'I'd like to know how they found out when we were arriving,' Lyon scowled heavily.

Shay had a more resigned view, knew that the press were always able to find out what they wanted to know. She had been badgered by the worldwide media as soon as Ricky's plane went down, the last weeks a nightmare of trying to escape them, finally having to move from the apartment she had shared with Ricky the last three years and move into a hotel, security guards placed outside her room to protect her privacy and grief.

'Does it matter?' she sighed, the incident just another horror in the nightmare her life had become since Ricky's crash.

'Yes, it—No,' Lyon amended with controlled violence as he saw the unconscious vulnerability in deep purple eyes, the pale skin beneath those fathomless depths looking bruised and trans-lucent. 'No,' he sighed heavily. 'I don't suppose it does.'

Shay didn't even question the way Lyon had stepped down from his undoubted anger at their arrangements being known by the press, shut him out of her mind completely as they began the drive to the house, grateful for the self-discipline she had learnt from her writing, needing mental as well as physical control to maintain the daily schedule of work she set for herself in order to meet her deadlines. It would have been so easy to have sat back and lived on Ricky's wealth, to have treated her writing as a mere hobby to keep herself amused. But she hadn't wanted that, had made it into a career. She felt an inner peace now that she had.

God, why was she wandering in this way! They would be at Falconer House soon, the scene of her greatest happiness, greatest humiliation, and finally her greatest pain.

It was a huge house, big enough for several families to live in comfortably, but she still didn't know how she had managed to live there for two years after her marriage to Ricky, didn't know how she was going to visit there now. Because visiting was all she intended doing. She couldn't stay on there, not even if Lyon asked her to do so. And she knew that he was going to ask her to do just that, that it probably wouldn't even be a request but an order. It was one she would enjoy disobeying!

CHAPTER TWO

'GOOD grief, Matthew!' Shay's exclamation was instantaneous on seeing him. 'What have you been doing to yourself?' She looked askance at the sling supporting his immobile arm.

The awkwardness she had envisaged upon entering the Falconer house again was forgotten in her concern for Matthew. His wheelchair had moved silently across the hall carpet as he came to meet them in the entrance hall, Shay shocked to see how pale he was, almost as white as the bandage on his arm beneath the sling.

Matthew Falconer had been in a wheelchair when she had first been introduced to him six years before, an explanation for his incapacity never offered by any of his family, although she had heard from the office grapevine when she still worked for Lyon that Matthew had been injured in a skiing accident at the age of nineteen, his legs severely damaged, and had been in a wheelchair ever since.

She had also learnt, from experience, that Matthew's inability to walk in no way detracted from his masculinity, or his ability to put a person in their place with a few well-directed words! After a few minutes of being in Matthew's dynamic presence people tended to forget he *was* in a wheelchair, the electronically-operated machine having so many gadgets on it he could perform practically anything an able-bodied man could do—except, of course, walk.

'Can't you think of a better greeting than that after all this time, Gypsy?' he drawled wryly, pain having etched lines into his handsome face over the years that shouldn't really have been there on a man of only thirty-five.

Gypsy. It was a long time since she had heard that particular nickname, two long heart-breaking months! The three younger Falconer men had taken the space of one afternoon to come up with the name Gypsy for her; Lyon had instantly hated it, refusing to call her it. But Ricky had continued to use the name after they were married, and hearing it now brought tears to her eyes.

'Matthew.' She bent and kissed him warmly on one rigidly hard cheek.

He managed a tight-lipped smile. 'You always were an affectionate little thing,' he muttered. 'Too affectionate on occasion.' He shot a sly glance at the stone-faced Lyon.

She had forgotten Matthew's cryptic, sometimes cruel, sense of humour, holding back her own smile with effort; one thing the Falconer men could never be attributed with was tact!

Matthew turned fully to his older brother. 'The two of you came back alone?'

Shay turned in time to see Lyon's warning look, instantly feeling a ripple of apprehension down the straightness of her spine. Lyon was displeased with his brother for asking the question, and she had a feeling *she* was the reason for his annoyance with Matthew.

'Yes,' he replied tersely, dismissively. 'What happened to your arm, Matthew?'

The younger man shrugged. 'The controls of this stupid machine went haywire for a while and I hit the ground,' he told them with self-derision. 'It's nothing serious, just a sprain.'

'You didn't mention it when I telephoned yesterday,' Lyon scowled.

'I said it's only a sprain,' Matthew bit out tautly. 'I'm in a wheelchair, Lyon, not senile! I don't need you fussing over me like an old woman every time I accidentally cut myself shaving!' He looked at the older man challengingly.

Who would eventually have won the silent battle of wills Shay wasn't sure; Lyon was obviously the stronger-willed of the two, but Matthew had his pride on his side. Even feeling the interloper, as she did, she couldn't let the senseless battle go on.

'Could I have a cup of tea, do you think?' She cut across their tension. 'I'm feeling a little weary.' Her eyes hardened as she looked at Lyon. 'I think you might be better having coffee,' she told him with sarcasm. 'A whole pot of it!' she added before strolling through to what she knew was the main family lounge, the décor different from what she remembered, in green and cream now, but otherwise the room was just as elegantly comfortable as she remembered it.

Matthew was still chuckling as he followed her into her room. 'Been drinking, has he?' he mused.

'Just a little,' Shay drawled.

'You always did have a strange effect on my big brother.' He grinned his satisfaction with the fact.

'I don't care to be discussed as if I weren't present.' Lyon strode across the room to pour himself a glass of whisky from the cut-glass decanter.

'Oh, we know you're here,' Matthew taunted. 'But what about Neil?'

Lyon's mouth compressed into a thin line as he turned and rang for the maid. 'He'll be back tomorrow,' he supplied abruptly, turning to the young woman who entered the room so that he could order Shay's tea.

Once again Shay had sensed Lyon's reluctance to discuss Neil in front of her. 'Is Neil away?' she probed softly.

Matthew gave Lyon a censorious look. 'You haven't told her?'

'Obviously not,' he drawled. 'For God's sake, Matthew,' he scowled belligerently. 'It isn't the sort of thing you just blurt out in the middle of a flight that Shay was already finding such a strain!'

'Hell, Lyon, you've been in Los Angeles almost three weeks,' Matthew criticised.

'During which Shay flatly refused to see me,' Lyon rasped harshly.

Shay felt no regret for that decision, had no desire to spend any more time in his company than she needed to. 'Where is Neil?' she asked tautly. 'Has he been hurt in some way? God, he isn't dead too . . . ?' She gasped as that horrific thought occurred to her.

'No, of course he isn't dead,' Lyon snapped. 'Your fertile imagination is running riot!'

'Then why won't you tell me where he is?' she demanded impatiently. 'Why all the secrecy?'

'Because he's in Los Angeles,' Lyon muttered.

'Los Angeles . . . ? But—' She broke off, a cold stillness slowly creeping over her, her hands clenching at her sides, the long lacquerless nails digging into her palms. She didn't feel any pain from the wounds she was inflicting, knew another pain that far superseded it. 'He's running the Los Angeles office, isn't he.' It was a statement, not a question, the deep purple of her eyes her only show of emotion now.

'Shay—'

'Isn't he?' she directed the question at Lyon, ignoring Matthew's attempt to reason with her. 'Answer me, damn you!'

Tawny eyes darkened furiously at her dictatorial tone. 'Yes, he is—'

'You bastard!' Her hand unclenched long enough to move up and slap him hard across one arrogant cheek, the white fingermarks she left livid against his tanned flesh as he remained immobile after the attack.

'Shay!'

'You replaced Ricky with him,' she accused disgustedly, once again ignoring Matthew. 'One brother is dead, never mind, I have two more I can send in his place!' she said heatedly, bright spots of colour in her otherwise pale cheeks.

'Shay—'

'Excuse me,' she at last acknowledged Matthew's efforts to speak to her, 'I have to get out of here before I'm sick all over the Persian rug!' She swallowed convulsively, breathing deeply in an effort to hold in the nausea. 'I take it I've been given the suite I once shared with Ricky?' Her eyes flashed warningly at Matthew.

'It's always kept prepared in case you or Ricky came home for a visit,' he frowned. 'But I thought this time you might prefer—'

'I prefer the suite I shared with Ricky,' she told Matthew forcefully. 'It's one of the rare places in this house that holds no bad memories for me!' She hurried from the room, her head held high.

'Let her go,' Lyon instructed his brother as he would have followed her, his lips barely moving as he stood rigidly still, shifting suddenly, throwing the contents of his glass to the back of his throat before refilling it, welcoming the burning sensation as the alcohol hit his empty stomach.

'Haven't you had enough of that for one day?' Matthew watched him concernedly.

'Not nearly enough.' Lyon grimly drank the second glass straight down too.

'Getting drunk isn't going to help the situation,' his brother spoke soothingly, his hazel eyes troubled. 'And it's going to give you one hell of a headache in the morning!' he added derisively.

Lyon scowled. 'I'll worry about that then,' he bit out.

'Worry about it now, Lyon, and tell me what happened on the flight here; Shay was as taut as a violin string when she arrived.' Matthew shook his head.

'Nothing happened.' Lyon achingly recalled the hours he had sat feet away from Shay, only a thin door separating them physically; mentally it might as well have still been the Atlantic!

'Nothing?'

'No,' he confirmed abruptly. 'We barely talked to each other.'

'Then why was she—like that?' Matthew looked puzzled.

'Doesn't she have the right?' Lyon groaned. 'I *have* sent Neil to Los Angeles to replace Ricky—'

'What else could you do?' Matthew said impatiently. 'Shay is going to realise, once she calms down, that you had to send someone in his place to run the Los Angeles office.'

Lyon stared up the stairs Shay had so recently ascended, the scent of her elusive perfume still in the air. 'Someone, yes,' he acknowledged bitterly. 'But it didn't have to be another Falconer.'

'You make us sound like something contagious,' Matthew derided dryly.

'I think to Shay we are,' Lyon nodded, wondering if he would ever be able to shut out the agony of knowing Shay considered him to be the lowest creature on earth. It was there in her voice every time she spoke to him, in every glance she gave, and there was nothing, *nothing*, he could ever do to vindicate himself in her eyes. 'All except Ricky, of course,' he acknowledged tightly.

Ricky was dead, his own dear brother, although the twelve years' difference in their ages had meant they were never really as close as he and Matthew had always been. Still, Ricky had been his brother, and the only thing he could think of right now was that Shay was no longer married.

He had to be sick, or drunk, or both. Probably both. He would never have admitted these feelings, even to himself, if his defences hadn't been down. A man was dead, a brother he had loved, and all he could think about was how good it had once been to make love to the woman who was now his widow!

'Lyon?'

His tormented gaze focused on Matthew. 'She's more beautiful than ever!' he rasped.

'Yes,' Matthew agreed softly.

His mouth twisted with self-derision. 'I'd hoped that she wouldn't be.'

'Gypsy was destined to be always beautiful,' Matthew remarked thoughtfully. 'She's like a pure-bred racehorse; long supple lines and a glossy coat.' He grimaced at the description. 'Only Shay has ever been able to make me wax lyrical like that; I wonder if *we* have any Irish in us?'

'Shay brings out uncharacteristic emotions in most men,' Lyon remarked with bitterness.

Matthew's expression was mocking as he arched dark blond brows. 'What emotions does she still bring out in you, big brother?'

'None of your damned business!' Lyon scowled, not willing to admit to anyone the torment of knowing Shay was so close to him once again. He found himself wanting to keep reaching out and touching her just to see if she were real or a figment of his tortured imagination. And then those purple eyes would rake over him contemptuously, and he would *know* it wasn't all a dream!

'I had a feeling it wouldn't be,' his brother drawled derisively.

Damn Matthew, he always had been able to see and guess too much. Being in a wheelchair might have physically incapacitated him but his other senses worked overtime. Matthew saw, and understood, too much!

'Isn't it time you told me exactly what happened to your arm?' prompted Lyon determinedly.

Now it was Matthew's turn to scowl, his humour fading completely. 'I don't need reminding of the embarrassing episode,' he snapped. 'One of the maids found me sprawled out in the study, and I had to suffer the humiliation of being dragged back into my chair by Hopkins! I'd really rather not talk about it right now.'

Lyon could understand his brother's feeling of

helplessness at having their butler haul him back into his chair; Matthew had never accepted the restrictions of his incapacity well, had mastered everything for himself so that he never had to rely on other people. Lyon had no doubt that if it weren't for Matthew's injured wrist he would have managed to get himself back into the chair and wouldn't have mentioned the incident to anyone.

He walked to Matthew's side. 'Okay, we'll discuss the progress you've made on the Thorpe contract this last week—*then* we'll talk about your fall.'

His young brother glared at him. 'You're a determined bastard!'

Lyon grinned. 'I don't think there's anyone who would argue with that!'

The bastard, the lousy, unfeeling bastard!

The accusation resounded round and round in Shay's head all the way up the wide spiral staircase and along the hallway to the suite she and Ricky had shared for the first two years of their marriage. She stiffened as she entered, finding a young maid unpacking her suitcases for her; she had always taken care of the apartment herself in Los Angeles.

The young woman straightened, a pretty blonde with mischievous blue eyes, although she looked more than a little concerned at the moment. 'Are you all right, Mrs Falconer?'

'I'm fine—er—?' She looked at the other woman enquiringly.

'Patty,' she supplied absently. 'You look—ill,' the maid finished awkwardly.

'Could you possibly come back and do that later?' Shay ignored the query in the other woman's voice.

'Of course,' Patty agreed instantly. 'Is there anything I can get you before I go?' She still looked worried by how pale Shay was.

'I believe someone was getting me a pot of tea,' Shay managed steadily, wishing the other woman would just go—before she broke down.

Patty nodded. 'I'll bring it up to you.'

Shay nodded her gratitude, afraid to trust her voice again, standing straight and proud until the other woman had left the room, her shoulders drooping dejectedly as soon as she was alone. Damn Lyon, damn him to the hell he belonged in! How dare he replace Ricky as if he had been of no importance, and with Neil of all people. Not that she had anything against Neil, after Ricky he was by far the most uncomplicated, and likeable, of the Falconer men. But by putting him in Ricky's place he made Ricky seem of no consequence, as if he had already been forgotten by the Falconer family.

He would never be forgotten by her—he had been loving, honest, and open, the two of them friends as well as lovers. In fact, they had been friends first. How dare Lyon do this to Ricky's memory!

'Is it safe to come in?'

She spun round at the sound of that gentle voice, her stormy gaze locking with Matthew's mocking one. 'What do you think?' Shay muttered.

'I think a man, but particularly a Falconer, would have to be a fool to want to interrupt your privacy at this precise moment,' he drawled.

'And are you a fool?' she asked hardly.

'I think I must be.' Matthew propelled himself into the room with his uninjured hand at the controls. 'Although perhaps the fact that I've brought your tea up with me,' he indicated the tray balancing on his knees, 'will soften your heart towards me. I persuaded Patty to let me bring it up to you,' he explained.

'Come in, by all means.' Shay turned towards the dressing-table mirror, removing the hat, also taking out the single comb that held her hair in place, running her fingers through the feathered waves as it cascaded down past her shoulders. 'But don't expect a pot of tea to soften my attitude towards the Falconer men,' she advised sharply as she turned back to face him.

Matthew looked at her admiringly, completely undaunted by her harshness. 'You look magnificent when you're angry, Shay. Like a heroine from one of your own books,' he added challengingly, putting down the tray to pour tea for both of them, adding the milk but no sugar that he knew Shay preferred.

She frowned. 'You've read one of my books?'

'Not just one, all five of them,' he revealed with satisfaction.

She swallowed hard. 'I see,' Shay said tightly. 'Out of curiosity?' she challenged.

His mouth twisted. 'A person only needs to read one book by a particular author out of *curiosity*, five can only be read out of enjoyment.'

'You like historical romances?' she asked sceptically.

'I like yours.'

She gave him a scornful look. 'Don't think you have to say that; Lyon felt no compunction in telling me he's never even looked at one!'

'You should know me better than that, Shay,' Matthew reproved. 'I've never been known to waste my time on worthless compliments.'

It was a valid criticism; Matthew, like all the Falconer men, could be brutally honest. 'I'm sorry,' she said stiffly.

'No, you aren't,' he accepted good-naturedly. 'You're so damned angry at all of us at the moment you would like nothing better than to tell us all to go to hell.' His eyes narrowed. 'So why don't you?'

Shay looked at the gleam in his eyes, his expression of relish. 'You would like that, wouldn't you?' she slowly began to smile.

Matthew shrugged. 'It's been a long time since I've seen Lyon this—'

'I'd prefer not to discuss Lyon,' Shay cut in forcefully. 'I've done my best to forget his existence the last three years, and once—once all this is over, I shall endeavour to forget him again.'

'You might have done your best, Shay,' Matthew said gently. 'But it wasn't good enough.'

Her gaze sharpened. 'What do you mean?'

'I said I had read all of your books, Shay; *Scarlet Lover* was a written tribute to what you had with Lyon.'

'It was the story of a man who was never satisfied with one woman, who trampled over the feelings of all women! Damn it, that character wasn't the hero of the book!' Her eyes glittered emotionally.

'Maybe not,' Matthew conceded. 'But you left the readers wishing he were.'

She flushed. 'Only another man could consider that immoral alley-cat a hero!'

'Correct me if I'm wrong,' he said softly, 'but didn't your editor try to get you to change the end of the book so that de Coursey *did* get the heroine?'

Her eyes widened. 'How did you know that?' she demanded agitatedly.

'You may have avoided coming back here to visit us the last three years,' Matthew taunted, 'but Ricky came back alone a few times.'

'And he—he told you about the book?' It was true, her editor had tried to get her to rewrite the end of *Scarlet Lover*, to make Leon de Coursey the hero, but she had refused, only her threat to withdraw the manuscript altogether making her editor accept that decision. But she hadn't known Ricky had discussed it with anyone!

Matthew nodded. 'He told me a lot of other things too, but I don't think you're ready to hear them just yet. I'll leave you to drink your tea in peace.' He put down his empty cup. 'But, Shay,' he paused at the door, 'don't be too hard on Lyon, he misses Ricky too.'

'The two of them argued incessantly—'

'I argue with Lyon too,' Matthew insisted. 'A lot of brothers argue, most siblings do, it doesn't mean they don't love each other. Don't take out your anger and frustration on Lyon by making any assumptions concerning his emotions; I haven't met anyone yet who has been able to work them out correctly—and that includes me,' came his dry parting comment.

She had thought she knew Lyon's emotions very well once, had believed he was in love with her. But like the fictitious character she had created in his image, he hadn't cared about her feelings, or any other woman's for that matter.

After she had seen him that first time, in the typing pool, Shay had looked out for him everywhere. Not that it did her much good, to the lower echelon in which she included herself he was a pretty elusive figure, keeping to the executive upper floors when he wasn't travelling to his other offices in Europe and America; in fact she had a feeling his visit to the typing pool that day had been his first and his last. But he could occasionally be seen striding about the building with one of his executives, and Shay had made the most of those times, magnetised by the ruthlessness of his masculine beauty.

But she was only one of the many females who felt that way about the charismatic Lyon Falconer—almost every woman in the building, young and old alike, found him just as fascinating. In fact, visible employer or not, he was the main source of gossip among the female staff. It was from them that Shay learnt he was married, a fact, no matter how remote her own chances were of attracting him, that had caused her considerable pain. But the same grapevine had informed her that he and his wife were separated, that they had lived their lives separately for some time. All the women had agreed that a divorce took some time to effect, and that in the mean time Lyon Falconer was as good as single again, there for any woman brave enough to try and attract him.

Shay certainly wasn't brave enough. At eighteen she had only been in London just over a year, having been brought up in Ireland by her grandfather since she was ten, her parents killed in a car crash at that time. The soft Irish brogue she had acquired during her seven years in Ireland had made her the recipient of considerable teasing when she first moved to London and began working in the typing pool of the Falconer company, the diversities of their many interests, the considerable property they owned, making them a good company to work for.

The brogue had all but disappeared during the

next year, until it was just a lilt to her speech, giving her voice a charming sing-song effect. John Turner, one of the accountants for the company, claimed it was the magic of her voice that made him constantly hound her for a date. He was pleasant enough, blond and handsome, but he nevertheless didn't appeal to her, although he refused to take no for an answer. The Christmas party was almost her downfall as far as he was concerned—instead she had jumped from the frying pan into the flames of hell!

It was a noisy party held in the spacious and attractive cafeteria, plenty of food supplied by the company, drink too, and a lot too much flirting between people who had no right to be flirting at all. Shay ignored the food, stayed away from the drink, and avoided the flirting whenever she could. That was until John Turner cornered her in the kitchen.

'Well if it isn't my little Irish colleen,' he affected an amateurish Irish accent as he advanced on her.

She had escaped to the kitchen minutes earlier to get some air, the adjoining room smoke-filled and noisy as loud music played and everyone talked at once trying to be heard above it. 'I've told you before, I'm not Irish,' she said icily, pushing at hands that seemed to be everywhere at once.

'With a name like Shay Flanagan?' he scorned, managing to trap her hands against his chest as his arms held her immobile.

'My father was Irish,' she sighed. 'Will you please let me go?' The smell of the alcohol he had consumed made her feel nauseous.

'If you give me a kiss I might think about it,' he leered suggestively.

Shay grimaced her distaste of the idea, finding him only tolerable at the best of times, totally disgusted with his state of inebriation. 'Let me go, John,' she ordered in a firm voice.

'And just what are you going to do about it if I don't?' he taunted.

'Try me?' Shay challenged softly.

In answer his arms tightened about her, his whisky-smelling breath fast nearing her mouth. It took only a second to lift her foot, place her stiletto heel on his toes, and grind down.

'Why you little—'

'That will be enough, Turner. It is Turner, isn't it?' queried an icy voice.

They both turned guiltily, Shay paling as she saw who the witness to the embarrassing scene had been, John looking ashen as he hastily moved away from her and turned to face their employer.

'Yes—er—sir,' he swallowed hard. 'It was only a little harmless fun,' he whined defensively.

'I don't believe Miss Flanagan agrees with you.' He turned to her questioningly.

Shay was dumb-struck, had never been this close to Lyon Falconer before, the tawny eyes as yellow as a cat's, the ruthlessness she had sensed in him at first glance having given him lines of cynicism beside his nose and mouth, the latter faintly contemptuous as he took in her ruffled appearance.

'Miss Flanagan?' he prompted hardly at her silence. 'If you would like me to leave the two of you alone again, then just say so,' he taunted.

She blinked, recovering herself with effort. 'I'm sure John would like to rejoin the party,' she said quietly.

John looked disconcerted, frowning at her. 'Don't you want to come with me?'

Tawny eyes held her gaze, challenging her answer. 'I think I'll stay here for a while,' she answered John but it was to Lyon Falconer she looked as she spoke, their gazes locked.

Neither of them seemed consciously aware of John Turner leaving, although Shay shifted uncomfortably once she realised she was completely alone with the man she had been gazing at longingly for months now. What to say to him, what *could* she say that would hold his interest for longer than it would take him to excuse himself politely and leave!

'Would you like to dance?' he asked gruffly.

'Dance?' she repeated with forced nonchalance, certain he couldn't be serious. But surely the request was taking the bounds of politeness too far? Besides, she hadn't heard it was a quality he was known for!

His mouth twisted derisively. 'Or what passes for dancing out there right now,' he drawled.

She had seen for herself the erotic movements

of the few couples that were bothering to dance; it had been one of the reasons she had escaped to the adjoining room. She certainly couldn't imagine herself dancing with Lyon Falconer in that way! 'I don't think so,' she grimaced.

'No, possibly not,' he agreed dryly. 'A drink, then?'

'I don't drink.' She shook her head.

'Food?'

'I'm not hungry.'

He shrugged broad shoulders beneath the expensively tailored suit, its chocolate-brown colour making his hair look a light tawny colour. 'That would seem to take care of that.' He turned to leave.

Panic rose up within Shay at the thought of his going. So she didn't drink alcohol, and she wasn't hungry, she could have pretended, damn it! 'Mr Falconer!' Her frantic call stopped him and he turned back to her with mockingly raised brows. It was then that she realised he had been playing with her, that he knew all the time she wanted to be with him, to spend time with him. He knew exactly what effect he had on her, on all women! She moistened her lips. 'I just wanted to wish you a "Merry Christmas",' she lied, knowing she had been about to tell him she had changed her mind about the drink. But it was the fact that *he* knew it, that he had expected it, that made her contrarily change her mind.

He looked taken aback. 'Merry Christmas?' he repeated incredulously.

'Yes,' Shay confirmed brightly. 'You see, I have to be leaving now.'

He frowned, totally disconcerted. 'You have—someone, to go home to?'

She wasn't leaving for Ireland until the following day, but she still had her packing to complete. Besides, she didn't like to admit to this man how alone she was, somehow felt as if that were asking for his company. 'I'm going away tomorrow,' she smiled. 'I have some last-minute things to do.'

A shadow seemed to pass over Lyon Falconer's ruggedly handsome face. 'I'm going away for the holiday period myself,' he revealed abruptly.

Shay could imagine him on the ski-slopes of some exclusive resort, or possibly lazing on the beach of a South Sea island, or perhaps sailing the calm seas on a leisurely cruise. 'I doubt if your idea of going away for Christmas is the same as mine,' she drawled, her eyes aglow with humour.

His eyes narrowed, his mouth tightening at her derision. 'I'm going to Bermuda.'

She smiled at her second guess being the closest. 'And I'm going back to my grandfather's home in Ireland, a small cottage, a real fire instead of an electric one, and a tree that sheds its pine-needles all over the carpet!' It wasn't until she began talking about it that she realised how much she had missed her home this last year, and how much she was looking forward to seeing it again.

'You're homesick,' Lyon Falconer stated abruptly.

'Yes,' Shay confirmed huskily.

'If you miss it so much what are you doing in London?' he frowned.

'My grandfather didn't want me to marry Devlin Murphy,' she recalled with a smile.

'Devlin Murphy?' the man across the room from her repeated sharply.

She nodded. 'He lives next door to my grandfather.'

'And you were in love with him?'

'No.' She laughed at the idea. 'But my grandfather was afraid that I might be if I didn't get away and see something of the world other than Ireland.'

'And now that you've seen it?'

Her laughter faded, a sad look in deep purple eyes. 'Now I know that although I love the place I could never settle for a small cottage in Ireland for the rest of my life, even if it does have a real fire,' she admitted with a sigh of regret.

'Nice to visit but you don't want to live there,' Lyon Falconer derided.

She became conscious of exactly who it was she was revealing her inner feelings to, stiffening slightly. 'You're very cynical,' she told him without thinking, blushing fiery red when she did so.

'But correct,' he mocked.

'Yes,' she bit out. 'I hope you have a nice time in Bermuda.' Shay moved to brush past him as he still stood near the door.

He grasped her arm. 'Come for a drive with me,' he invited huskily.

'A—a drive?' She swallowed hard, his close-ness unnerving her.

'Yes.' His gaze held hers, purple captivated by yellow cat's eyes. 'You don't want to dance, you aren't hungry, and you don't drink, that only leaves going for a drive,' he drawled.

'But it's late . . .'

'Does that matter?' he encouraged throatily.

Of course it didn't matter! 'Where will we go?' asked Shay breathlessly.

'Wherever fate decides to take us,' he answered with surprising intensity. 'Shay . . . ?'

'Yes?' He was so close now their thighs were almost touching.

'Do you believe in fate?'

After tonight she believed in anything! 'I think so,' she nodded.

He gave a sudden grin, looking younger, his hand sliding down her wrist to capture hers. 'Then let's see what it holds in store for us!' He seemed to be challenging that fate, daring it to deny him something he wanted very much—and that something was Shay.

Shay should have known then not to become involved with a man who challenged life itself, who lived his life as if each moment were his last, should have run from him before he had the chance to hurt her. But she hadn't run, had allowed him to pull her through the crowded adjoining room, into the lift and out to his waiting car, filling her with the same recklessness that had possessed him.

They hadn't spoken as they drove, but there was none of the awkward silence between them that should have existed, the smiles Lyon sent her way filling her with a quiet glow of expectation.

He stopped the car near Regent Street, taking her hand to walk at her side down the dazzling street, the famous Christmas lights filling them both with a childish sense of the ridiculous, each picking out the unlikeliest items in the illuminated shop windows that they would like under their tree Christmas morning.

'But what I'd really like,' Lyon suddenly turned to growl, 'is an Irish pixie with purple eyes.'

Colour flooded her cheeks as he held her intimately against him, making no secret of his stirring arousal as he moved his thighs against hers. 'I'm too tall to be a pixie,' Shay told him awkwardly.

'One of the "little people" then,' Lyon mocked her.

'It's the same thing,' she said crossly. 'And on Christmas morning I intend being under my own tree in Ireland, opening my own presents!'

'Pity,' he drawled, swinging her away from him. 'What shall we do now?'

She pulled a face at the lateness of the hour. 'I'm usually in bed at two o'clock in the—' She broke off as she realised exactly what she was inviting with her thoughtlessly spoken words.

'What an excellent idea,' Lyon mocked. 'Your bed or mine?' He quirked dark blond brows.

'Neither,' Shay gasped. 'I may have impulsively left the party with you, Mr Falconer,' her Irish accent returned in her agitation, 'but that doesn't mean I'm willing to jump into bed with you!'

'Why not? You want me, don't you.' It was a statement not a question. 'I could see that you did the moment our eyes met across the typing pool that day.'

'You—you saw me then?' She looked up at him with startled eyes.

His mouth twisted. 'It isn't every day I encounter a purple-eyed pixie, especially one that looks at me so longingly, which was why I made it my business to find out your name. Did you like what you saw that day, Shay?'

She moistened her lips with the tip of her tongue, her cheeks becoming even redder as she saw the way he was watching the provocative movement.

'Do you like what you see tonight?' His gaze compelled her to answer.

'Mr Falconer, please—'

'I'd like to, Shay, I'd like to pleasure every silken inch of you, to taste you, to have you taste me in return.' His gaze was fixed on her lips as he slowly bent down to her.

His verbal lovemaking made her quiver with expectation, her lips already parted for the invasion of his kiss, and it was an invasion, the silken thrust of his tongue plundering deeper and deeper inside, inviting her to do the same to him. The lights, the softly falling snow, the noise of the people and traffic, all faded with the intensity of that kiss, Lyon finally the one to pull away.

'Shay, come home with me,' he invited hoarsely, his forehead resting on hers as they both trembled, his skin warm and damp.

'I can't.' She shook her head. 'I have to go home and finish packing, I leave for Dublin in the morning.'

'Don't go,' Lyon grated. 'Come to Bermuda with me!'

Her sceptical gaze found only deep seriousness in his expression. 'I can't do that,' Shay finally murmured. 'My grandfather is expecting me.'

'I want you with *me*,' Lyon told her arrogantly.

He sounded like someone who was never denied something he had decided he wanted! 'I'm sorry,' Shay refused stiltedly, 'but I promised my grandfather I would go home.'

'And what about me?' Lyon demanded harshly, the desire fading from those unusual eyes. 'Does what we have end here and now?'

'Not if you don't want it to.' Her voice was a soft apology. 'We could meet when you get back from Bermuda and I come home from Ireland.'

'So we could,' Lyon grated his displeasure. 'Well, I'd better get you home.'

She had known he was angry, that he was still angry when he left her at her home fifteen minutes later having made no arrangements to see her again after Christmas as she had suggested they should.

She had spent a miserable Christmas in Dublin with her grandfather, had sensed the elderly man's concern when she constantly assured him she was perfectly all right; he just wouldn't have understood if she had told him she was pining for a man like Lyon Falconer, a man who was still married and also fifteen years her senior.

She would have been much better off if Lyon had remained angry with her, if he hadn't telephoned down to her desk several weeks later and ordered her up to his office on the fourteenth floor!

CHAPTER THREE

'SHAY!' the excited male voice greeted. 'My God, Gypsy, no woman has the right to grow even more beautiful, the way you have!'

'Neil,' she greeted dryly, used to the exuberance of her youngest brother-in-law. But even she wasn't prepared for the way he burst into the room and swung her round in his arms. 'Neil, you fool, put me down,' she laughed breathlessly, pushing at his arms.

'I came up to warn Neil you were resting and didn't want to be disturbed,' Lyon remarked coldly from the doorway Neil had left open. 'But it seems only some members of this family disturb you,' he added icily.

Shay's smile faded as she slowly released herself from Neil's arms, straightening her black and white silk dress before answering. 'You don't disturb me, Lyon,' she looked at him haughtily, 'you disgust me!'

He sucked his breath into his lungs at the insult, a savage twist to his mouth as he turned on his heel and left the room, his back rigid.

Shay hadn't seen him since she had struck him so forcibly the day before, had refused dinner yesterday, and had eaten breakfast and lunch in her room today, asking the friendly Patty to tell the Falconer men she preferred to stay in her suite and rest, just wanting to be alone. She hadn't allowed for Neil's arrival today, or his determination to see her again.

She looked at him now, regretful that he should have witnessed that ugly scene. 'As you can see,' she grimaced, 'nothing changes.' She sought for lightness.

'You have.' Neil's eyes glowed with admiration. 'I can remember a time when you would simply have thrown something at Lyon rather than give him a verbal dressing down.'

'How are you, Neil?' Shay ignored the reference to her past, often stormy, relationship with Lyon. 'You're looking very well.'

'I am well,' he nodded, sobering. 'I'm really sorry about Ricky,' he added softly.

Neil was only a slightly older version of her husband—blond hair, blue eyes—and looking at him now caused a fresh ache in her chest for the man she had lost. 'So am I,' she sighed.

He flushed awkwardly. 'I'm sorry if I've intruded, if you would rather not talk about Ricky. Lyon told me—'

'Damn what Lyon told you!' Shay burst out in agitated anger. 'What does he know about how I feel, what did he ever *care*?' Now that the icy veneer was cracking she didn't seem able to stop the angry flow. 'I'd like to talk about Ricky, I'd like to share him with someone. But I can't!' Her face contorted with the agony of burying the memories of Ricky deep in her heart.

'You can share him with me, Gypsy.' Neil moved to take her in his arms. 'Talk to me about him; even though he was my brother I didn't see much of him the last few years.'

'That was my fault,' she groaned into his throat.

'Of course it wasn't,' Neil chided. 'God, we might all be brothers, but we don't have to live in each other's pockets! When I marry, *if* I marry,' he amended ruefully, 'I don't intend to stay in the family mausoleum either!'

Shay moved back to give him a watery smile. 'You always were good for me,' she said gratefully, taking the handkerchief he held out to her.

'Believe me, after being one of the middle of four boys, it's nice to have a sister I can tease and spoil.' He guided her over to the sofa as he spoke, sitting them both down, his arm about her shoulders as he held her at his side. 'I'd also like to be the brother you feel you can confide in,' he prompted softly.

'Neither Lyon nor Matthew exactly fit the role, hmm?' she derided.

He shook his head. 'Both as tough as old leather. Now me, I'm the easy-to-know-and-get-along-with brother,' he grinned encouragingly.

'Like Ricky,' she said sadly, having talked to her husband about anything and everything.

'Like Ricky,' Neil nodded.

Once she began to talk, Shay couldn't seem to stop, telling Neil everything that came into her mind, her head resting on his shoulder as she did so, feeling a closeness with him that she hadn't known since those last precious days with Ricky.

So he disgusted her, did he! He remembered a time when disgust was the last thing she felt towards him.

God, she had been incredibly sweet the night he rescued her from Turner's lecherous clutches. Although he doubted 'rescued' exactly described what had happened; the amount of alcohol Turner had consumed by that time meant that he would probably have passed out if he had tried any real physical exertion, such as making love. And Shay would probably have realised how far gone he was once he got over his anger at having his toes crushed by her shoe!

Which was why *he* had stepped in when he had. Shay had been suitably grateful for his interception, and it had stunned him when that gratitude had left him outside her door at the end of the evening instead of on the other side of it. He had decided then and there not to contact her again, that her naïvety had only confirmed her youth; and he was too old and too cynical to participate in such 'no touch' games.

Bermuda had been everything he had thought it would be, and worse. Family Christmases, especially in a family like his own, were destined to be a failure from the onset, for everyone involved. He found himself thinking of the 'Irish pixie with the purple eyes', wondering if she were enjoying her Christmas as much as she had seemed sure she would, and if Devlin Murphy were helping her enjoy it! God, the mere fact that he remembered the man's name had come as a shock to Lyon, that he envied Shay her 'little cottage, real fire, and pine-needle-shedding tree' when he had a villa on a private beach, miles of unspoilt coastline, the hot temperatures providing him with a deep sun-tan, and the ten-foot-high artificial tree in the lounge that wouldn't dare to shed anything, let alone pine-needles, had totally astounded him.

That the deep purple of dark-fringed eyes haunted him angered Lyon, throwing him into a whirl of parties and women once he returned to London after the holidays. And when they hadn't worked in banishing her from his mind he had decided to see Shay once again, to talk with her, to see if she really were as beautiful as he remembered. When she had entered his office on that Monday morning he had known his memory had played tricks on him; she was even more enchanting than he remembered, those huge violet eyes dominating her beautiful face.

That she was nervous of him, of his reasons for summoning her there, was obvious, her long slender hands clasped together to stop them from trembling. 'Why do you think I wanted to see you?' Lyon asked harshly, unable to resist the impulse to make her suffer a little for haunting him in the way that she had.

Her throat moved convulsively, a long creamy expanse of delicate flesh he wanted to caress with his lips and tongue. 'I—I have no idea,' she answered steadily enough after that initial hesitation.

Some devil possessed him, annoyed at her coolness. 'I want you to go down to your desk and get your things,' he ordered. 'You're leaving.'

Shay gasped, her small breasts moving beneath the thin silkiness of her pale lilac blouse, the aroused points of her nipples visible through the lace of her bra and the sheer material of her blouse. If just thinking about seeing him again could cause that reaction it promised much for their future together! He forced himself to dampen the elation and listen to what she was saying.

'You can't just sack me,' she claimed indignantly. 'I always do my share of the work, and I haven't missed a day or been late since I started working here. I'm not even the last one to be employed, Stacy came after me. Surely you have to have a good reason nowadays for sacking someone like this? I can't—'

Charming as he found the increased Irish lilt to her voice when she became angry, he was bored with the game he had started with her. 'I'm not sacking you,' Lyon calmly interrupted her tirade. 'I merely want you to get your coat and bag so that I can take you to lunch.'

'Take me—? But—I—You—' Her spluttering ceased as two bright spots of red colour entered her cheeks, her eyes two purple jewels. 'You aren't taking me anywhere, you arrogant swine!' She turned on her heel, her body moving gracefully as she walked.

'Shay!' Lyon was on his feet in seconds, realising he had seriously misjudged this Irish vixen, that the placid demeanour and violet eyes hid a fiery temper, an independence that wouldn't allow any man, even one as powerful as she must know him to be, to order her about. She was waiting for him when he crossed the room to her side, stiff with anger as he put his hands on her shoulders to turn her round. 'Will you have lunch with me?' he coaxed, trying to remember the last time he had had to persuade a woman to spend time with him. He couldn't.

'I don't—'

'*Please.*' He turned her fully into his arms, her perfume as elusive as the woman herself, feeling his body quicken with the same desire that had assailed him the last time he was with her. 'Shay?' he prompted cajolingly.

She tilted her head back to look at him, her young face challenging. 'Why?'

Why? God, what strange questions this woman-child asked! 'Because I want to be with you,' Lyon smiled.

'You haven't felt that same need the last three weeks,' she accused, seeming to bite her lip as she realised how much she had revealed in that candid statement.

And she had revealed a lot; it was exactly three weeks since they had all returned to work, when he had vaguely said he might get in touch with her again. This little vixen wasn't as immune to him as she wanted him to believe!

His gaze dropped to those revealing breasts, her breaths short and shallow, the nipples even more pronounced, showing darkly against the light material of her blouse. She wanted him as much as he wanted her! 'I wasn't sure if Devlin Murphy would have followed you back from Dublin,' he teased.

'Devlin leave his beloved Ireland?' Shay smiled at the thought. 'Never!'

Lyon sobered, knowing her anger was fading, that she was surrendering to the attraction she felt for him, that mischievous glow coming back into her eyes. 'Lunch, Shay?' he urged firmly.

Uncertainty flickered across her face. 'Wouldn't it look a little—odd?'

'Maybe, a little,' he acknowledged distantly. 'Do you care?'

A reckless light appeared in her eyes. 'No,' she replied happily. 'Not if you don't.'

'Why should I?' Lyon shrugged, not caring for his employees' opinion of his actions, and it was a long time since either he or Marilyn had been concerned with the marriage vows they had made over five years before.

'No reason,' Shay dismissed, her eyes glowing. 'I'll meet you downstairs once I've collected my things, shall I?' she suggested eagerly.

He was glad now he had decided to drive himself into work that morning, the custom-built

Porsche usually standing idle during the day at the underground parking at his apartment while his chauffeur, Jeffrey, drove him through the heavy traffic of early-morning London in the limousine; it saved on his own blood pressure, besides giving him the freedom to work in the back of the car during the journey. This morning he had aggressively wanted to challenge the traffic himself, daring anyone to get in his way, sexual tension making his mood volcanic.

As Shay climbed into the black vehicle beside him he thought how well she looked there, her fierce pride making her act as if she drove in fifty thousand pounds'-worth of car every day of her life. At that moment he had wanted her so badly he would have *given* her the car just to have one hour in bed with her. It might be a high price to pay, but he had a feeling, young though she was, the experience of making love to this woman would be worth it.

Lunch, what he had thought would be a tedious lead up to what he really wanted, became dinner too after they walked the afternoon away, the maître d' finally having to point out to them that it was after two in the morning, that all the other patrons had left, and that the staff were waiting to go home. Lyon had been stunned— delighted!—that Shay had so interested him as he listened to her attractively lilting voice that he hadn't been troubled by his usual malady when with a woman for any length of time, any woman—boredom. Shay had enchanted him with stories of her childhood, her grandfather, her beloved Ireland, and the fascination she felt for London, to such a point that the last fourteen hours had passed as if they were minutes. He could see by the shock in her candid purple eyes that she hadn't realised the passing of the time either, and that pleased him.

Shay's flat wasn't large, just four rooms; a lounge, a kitchen, a bathroom, and a bedroom, but the warmth of the décor, the obviously lovingly hand-painted furniture and soft feminine touches all made it seem like the warmth of Shay herself enveloped you as you entered.

And he wanted that warmth for his own, wanted all that she had to give, turning her into his arms as she looked up at him shyly, the sudden silence between them after hours of endless conversation doubly significant.

Her mouth tasted of brandy and honey, her body felt soft and warm as his hands wandered over her hips and back, the hard tips of her breasts pressed against his chest through his shirt. And he didn't want any barriers between them, his fingers deft on the buttons of her blouse.

'Lyon?' She frowned up at him uncertainly.

He was disappointed that she had returned to playing games, but if that was the way she wanted it he was willing to go along with it. He wanted her, any way he could get her. And if it couldn't be tonight he would leave her with an ache as deep as his own.

'I only want to touch you,' he coaxed softly. 'I'll stop any time you tell me to,' he promised, feeling satisfaction as she instantly relaxed in his arms.

It was that trust that was his undoing, and for the first time in years he knew he wasn't going to be able to control the outcome of this encounter. Shay caught fire as soon as he cupped her bared breasts, pulling him in to that fire until he craved the taste of her, wanting to know every silken inch of her.

She was no longer hesitant as he stripped her, clinging to him, the touch of her soft lips on his throat and chest making his blood burn in his veins, on fire at the kittenish moans emitted from her parted lips as he returned to them again and again.

God, he could taste the sweetness of her even now, feel her shuddering with released desire, see the bewilderment in purple eyes as she realised what had just happened to her. He hadn't meant things to go as far as they had, but when he saw the confusion in her face quickly followed by contrition, he was glad that they had, knew that the pleasure he had given her had been totally unexpected, that although she felt a certain amount of mortification about losing control in that complete way, she also felt guilt that her pleasure hadn't been a shared one, that Lyon's desire still throbbed and strained against her.

And although it had caused him an agony that took him to hell and back he had refused her

embarrassed offer to give him that pleasure, had
known, even though that denial cost him dearly,
that the next time they were together she would
be all the more eager to give him that satisfaction.

No, he hadn't disgusted her then—but if she
had known of his thoughts, of his devious
schemes to make her more compliant with his
desires, he probably would have done. God, he
disgusted himself!

Did every widow feel as she did, that she was
acting out a part in a play, as if the whole thing
had been some horrendous mistake, as if any
moment now her husband would come walking
through the door and laughingly demand to
know what she was doing in this stark black
dress, her face pale beneath the black lace of the
veil that drew over her from the small black hat
confining her riotous black hair.

God, how she wished Ricky *would* walk
through the door. Instead, she sat calmly waiting
for the cars to arrive that would take them to the
church where they would bury him. He would
occupy the grave next to his mother and father;
their youngest son, their baby, the first to join
them there. Shay could have seen him buried
nowhere else.

It had been left to Neil, dear kind Neil who sat
with her for hours at a time while she silently
lived within her grief, to tell her what time the
funeral was today. She had seen nothing of
Matthew and Lyon the last two days, had stayed

up here in her suite, eating little, sleeping even less, thinking incessantly.

And the thinking took her nowhere; Ricky was dead, she was here at Falconer House where she had sworn never to return again, and today they would put him beneath the ground for ever, where she would never be able to see or touch him again.

'Ready, darlin'?'

That voice, that dear kind *familiar* voice! But it couldn't be, illness prevented him from being here. Had grief and lack of sleep made her hallucinate now, or—

'I'm really here, Shay-me-love,' that gentle voice assured softly.

Only Grandy had ever called her Shay-me-love in that exact way. He had to be here! 'Grandy!' She turned and ran across the room into her grandfather's waiting arms, knowing as he gathered her in his bear-like hug that she *was* still alive, that she could still feel, that she was home in his arms! 'Oh, Grandy!' she choked again, burying her face against his chest.

'There, there now.' He awkwardly patted her shoulders a few minutes later when the tears hadn't abated. 'You'll make my jacket go all limp,' he complained teasingly.

She gave a choked laugh as she straightened, wiping her cheeks with trembling hands. 'I had no idea—Why didn't you tell me you were coming? Oh, I'm so glad you're here!' She looked with love at the man who had brought her up single-handedly after her parents had died. Patrick Flanagan hadn't changed much in all those years, his hair still a dark unruly mass of curls, his eyes still a deep twinkling blue in his kind, lined face, although over the years Shay's height had almost equalled his five-foot-eight frame. He was still an attractive man, despite being in his sixty-fourth year. 'You didn't mention it when we spoke on the telephone yesterday. In fact,' she added sternly, 'I distinctly remember telling you not to come.' The heart condition he had developed in recent years prevented him from doing too much travelling.

He raised dark brows at her. 'And since when have I taken orders from you, Shay Falconer?' he reproved.

Her mouth quirked. 'Never. But you should have told me you were coming, I could have met you at the airport.'

'Falconer sent his chauffeur—'

'Lyon?' she questioned sharply. 'Lyon knew you were coming here?'

Her grandfather nodded. 'You seemed so—so unlike my Shay when we spoke on the telephone yesterday, so cool and distant, so I called Falconer later that evening and asked him if he thought it a good idea if I came over for a few days. He thought it would,' he explained simply. 'So here I am.' His smile was reassuring.

Shay bit her lip to stop herself making the angry retort that sprang to her lips, wanting to question the fact that Lyon could speak with any authority on what was or wasn't good for her. But today, and now, was not the time to voice her resentment towards Lyon. For whatever reason, and she would never believe it to be out of genuine kindness—Lyon didn't have a heart to be kind with!—he had advised her grandfather to come here, and for that she mentally thanked him. Mentally, because she would never verbally acknowledge to Lyon how much having her grandfather here at this time meant to her.

'He's invited me to stay on for a few days,' her grandfather continued frowningly. 'But I haven't accepted yet; I don't know what your plans are.'

She was aware of the question in his tone, deliberately turning to the mirror to remove all trace of tears from her cheeks. 'I have to talk to you later,' she told him as she readjusted her veil. 'I was going to fly over to see you after the funeral.'

He cupped her elbow. 'Falconer seems to assume you'll be staying on here.'

Shay's mouth tightened. 'Lyon always did assume too much,' she bit out icily.

Grandy turned to her as they reached the suite door. 'Then you don't intend staying?'

She forced the tension from her body, needing desperately to talk to her grandfather, but knowing now was not the time. 'We'll talk about it later,' she assured him warmly. 'It's a little complicated.'

She was aware of his puzzled blue gaze on her,

although with his usual thoughtfulness he didn't pursue the matter when he could see she obviously didn't want to just yet. He had always been someone she could talk to, who she could go to with her problems, both as a child and a woman, and yet even he didn't know how extensively Lyon had hurt her, could have no real idea of how much just being in the same house with the other man upset her.

She hugged his arm to her side. 'I can't tell you how much having you here—now—means to me.' Tears glistened in her eyes once more.

He gently touched her cheek. 'I can see how much. I'm going to miss Ricky too.'

She gave him a grateful smile, knowing he had liked and approved of her husband, that the liking had been mutual, she and Ricky often visiting her grandfather in Ireland even if she refused to include Falconer House in those visits. Only Ricky's death had been able to force her back here.

'So tell me which of the family vultures are gathered downstairs to get a look at the grieving widow,' she invited bitterly.

'Shay!'

'Sorry.' She blushed a little, sorry that her grandfather had to be a witness to the bitterness she felt towards Ricky's family. 'What Falconer relatives are gathered downstairs?' she rephrased the question.

He shrugged. 'A couple of dozen assorted

uncles, aunts and cousins; I don't remember any of their names although I was introduced to them,' he grimaced. 'Then there's the three Falconer brothers. And Lyon's wife. And a rather good-looking young man whom I've never seen before.' Grandy frowned.

Shay also frowned at the mention of the latter; she was definitely not in the mood to meet a complete stranger. It was bad enough that she had the family to contend with without that. And Marilyn Falconer. It was years since she had seen the other woman, but as Lyon's wife Marilyn had been destined to take an instant dislike to Shay, and the feeling was mutual. Marilyn was everything that Shay wasn't, at thirty-five more Lyon's own age, sophisticated, petite, with glorious red hair and an incredibly beautiful face. And when they first met she had been Lyon's wife for over five years, a fact she had taken great pleasure in relating to Shay.

She had known she would have to see the other woman again while she was here, but it hadn't been something she welcomed for today. Or having to be with a man she had never met before. If she didn't know the man then Ricky probably hadn't either, and if the two men hadn't known each other he had no right to be at Ricky's funeral.

She could see the cars lining the driveway as she and Grandy walked down the stairs, feeling her heart lurch at the sight of them, her hand clutching tightly to her grandfather's arm as they entered the lounge together.

It wasn't so much a funeral as a social gathering, the 'assorted uncles, aunts and cousins' talking about the room in small groups, with the beautiful Marilyn playing the hostess as she flitted from group to group. Lyon, Matthew and Neil were together in front of the unlit fireplace, a tall dark-haired man whom she didn't recognise standing at Neil's side; obviously the man her grandfather had spoken of. Shay didn't know him she was sure of it, although he looked pleasant enough, and she dismissed him of being any threat to her peace of mind as she felt tawny eyes on her, Lyon much more of a threat than the innocuous stranger could ever be.

She turned coolly to meet Lyon's gaze, tensing as he spoke briefly to the other men before coming over to where she stood with her grandfather, the rest of the Falconer family too polite to stare openly, although she sensed quite a few of them giving her sideways glances.

'I hope it wasn't too much of a shock seeing your grandfather so suddenly,' Lyon spoke smoothly.

'It was a pleasant surprise,' she corrected. 'Although he really shouldn't have been encouraged to face the strain of travelling,' she added critically, Lyon as aware of her grandfather's condition as she was.

His mouth tightened at the rebuke. 'If you're ready to leave now . . . ?'

Shay nodded coldly, keeping her gaze averted from the rest of the people gathered in the room, although she knew several of them were openly watching her now. 'My grandfather will travel with me,' she announced curtly.

'Of course,' Lyon nodded, as if he had expected it to be no other way.

'Just my grandfather,' she added pointedly.

'Shay—'

'I trust you have no objections?' Shay met Lyon's gaze challengingly.

He looked as if he had plenty. 'Not if it's what you want,' he rasped.

'Oh, it is.' She ignored her grandfather's dismayed expression; not even for him could she be polite to this man she so despised. And the idea of revealing, in front of Lyon, the grief she felt whenever she thought of burying Ricky, was totally unacceptable to her. She wanted her grandfather at her side, no one else.

The drive to the church was made in silence, the ceremony brief and poignant, the small ceremony outside the greatest test of Shay's strength. And as the vicar's words began to slur into each other, and the ground began to rush blackly at her with alarming speed, she knew she wasn't going to make it.

And then strong hands grasped her shoulders, tilting the world back on its axis, and Shay turned to Lyon with blazing violet eyes. 'Take your hands off me!' she flared vehemently.

He seemed to pale, his hands slowly dropping back to his sides. 'I thought you were going to fall,' he muttered huskily.

She gave him a look that clearly told him she would have preferred that to having him touch her in any way, turning sharply to go to the graveside and make her silent goodbyes to Ricky, her walk back to the car made alone, her head back proudly as the tears fell.

'You've changed, Shay,' remarked a mocking voice.

She turned before reaching the door of the car that Jeffrey held open for her, her gaze cool on Marilyn Falconer, the other woman as beautiful as ever. 'Sorry?' She arched dark brows.

Marilyn looked beautiful in the clinging black gown designed to emphasise her voluptuous figure; the fullness of her breasts, her slender waist, and femininely curving hips. At her side was the man Shay didn't know. He smiled at her in an awkward way, seeming uncomfortable with the situation, and Shay wondered at the emotion from a complete stranger.

'As I remember it,' Marilyn drawled in her throaty voice, 'you never used to be averse to my husband's touch in that way!' Blue eyes glittered challengingly.

That the other woman had enjoyed witnessing the encounter between Shay and Lyon was obvious, that she took great pleasure in drawing attention to Shay's past relationship with Lyon, even at the funeral of Shay's own husband, showed that Marilyn hadn't changed at all in the last few years, that she was still a vindictive bitch.

'I really don't care to discuss it, Marilyn,' Shay

dismissed, looking pointedly at Marilyn's companion.

'Oh, don't mind Derrick,' Marilyn said airily. 'He's well aware of your past relationship with Lyon. I take it it is still in the past?' she added tauntingly.

Shay felt the colour drain from her face. 'Very much so,' she bit out, ignoring the listening Derrick as the other woman seemed inclined to do so. 'You're more than welcome to him!'

Marilyn's eyes widened. 'But, my dear Shay, I no longer want him. Didn't you know that?'

'I—'

'Time to go, Shay,' her grandfather spoke sternly at her side. 'If you'll excuse us?' He looked coldly at Marilyn and Derrick. 'What was that bitch saying to you?' he asked harshly once they were in the car as it moved smoothly down the narrow driveway to the road.

'Grandy!' she gasped.

He looked unperturbed at his uncharacteristic display of antagonism for a woman he barely knew. 'You went as white as a sheet as soon as she spoke to you,' he said grimly. 'I couldn't let that continue.'

Shay was still inwardly ricocheting from the shock of what Marilyn had just said. Oh, not the other woman's insensitivity in questioning the relationship between her and Lyon now; Marilyn had never been known for her diplomacy, especially where Lyon was concerned. What shocked her so much was the last claim

Marilyn made, about no longer wanting Lyon. Surely the other couple couldn't finally be going to divorce each other? Six years ago she had believed that would never be possible, Lyon had convinced her that it wouldn't.

The Falconer office grapevine had usually been correct, if sometimes slightly exaggerated in its information, but about the relationship between Lyon and his wife they had been completely wrong; the couple still lived together, were still married, and intended staying that way.

Shay hadn't been able to understand the sort of marriage they had. A 'modern arrangement', they called it, each having their own 'friends', bringing those friends to meet the rest of the family at Falconer House, even sleeping with those partners there, but neither having the intention or inclination to end their own marriage. Unfortunately, Shay hadn't discovered that until her love for Lyon had been such a fundamental part of her life that to rip him out of her heart had been to destroy herself.

And if the couple were finally to divorce, whose decision had it been to end their 'modern arrangement'? Lyon had made it plain six years ago that he would never make that choice.

'It was nothing, Grandy,' she dismissed as she realised her grandfather still looked concerned. 'Marilyn and I have never pretended to be friends.' Shay's tone was scornful, her composure back in place. 'We never could be.'

'Nevertheless—'

'Don't give it another thought, Grandy.' She squeezed his arm reassuringly. 'I'm not going to.'

He didn't look convinced by her dismissal of the other woman, but he wisely didn't pursue it any further. But he did stay close by her side once they arrived back at the house, glowering fiercely at any member of the Falconer family that dared to talk to her. Shay was amused by his protectiveness, grateful to have him there, knowing he had helped her get through a very difficult time.

Finally the guests began to leave, only the close family left; Shay and her grandfather, the three Falconer men, Marilyn, and finally the man Derrick. Shay had stopped feeling curious about him, the man was quite innocuous, in fact he barely spoke to anyone.

'Thank God that's over,' Marilyn said in a bored voice once the final relative had left. 'Perhaps now we can have something a little stronger to drink than sherry!' She moved to the extensive array of drinks on the side table.

'Isn't it a little early in the day for that, even for you?' Matthew drawled caustically.

She flashed him an angry look before turning to her husband. 'Lyon?' She snapped.

He gave a disinterested shrug. 'Help yourself,' he invited wearily.

She gave Matthew a triumphant smile. 'Anyone else?' she offered.

No one answered, and Marilyn helped herself to a liberal amount of whisky before making herself comfortable in one of the armchairs, crossing one silky leg over the other. 'Now isn't this cosy?' she said to no one in particular.

'I would hardly call it that.' Once again Matthew was the one to answer her.

'Civilised, then.' Marilyn sipped her whisky with enjoyment. 'Very civilised,' she repeated thoughtfully.

'Marilyn—'

'I mean,' she continued talking as if Lyon hadn't spoken, 'where else would you find a husband and wife, the wife's lover, and the husband's *ex*-lover all gathered in the same room?' She looked guilelessly about the room at the stunned people standing there.

The silence was deafening; Shay had always thought that a contradiction in terms, but at that moment she understood what it meant perfectly. The silence *was* deafening, everyone speechless after Marilyn's casually vindictive statement.

To Shay's surprise it was Neil who answered Marilyn this time. 'Your idea of civilisation would disgust even the animal kingdom!' he spat out contemptuously, striding from the room.

'One down, five to go,' Marilyn taunted unconcernedly.

Shay felt her grandfather stiffen at her side. 'Your behaviour, madam, at a time like this,' he spoke coldly to Marilyn, 'is enough to make a saint leave any room you occupy.'

'Marilyn—'

'Don't look so worried, darling,' she laughed lightly as the man called Derrick spoke warningly. 'Patrick won't really leave, will you?' She turned to Shay's grandfather. 'I don't believe you've been properly introduced to my fiancé,' she continued brightly without waiting for him to answer. 'Have you?' she challenged.

'No,' he replied tersely.

Shay finally had her answer as to exactly who the man Derrick was, although she had guessed a few minutes ago that he had to be the lover Marilyn had spoken about; it certainly wasn't Matthew or Neil! But she had had no idea of Derrick's existence, or that Marilyn and Lyon were at last to divorce; Ricky had never mentioned it to her. Although in the circumstances perhaps that was understandable, she had shown little interest in any member of his family over the last few years.

Marilyn introduced her fiancé as Derrick Stewartby, a fellow lawyer.

'We'll be married as soon as my divorce from Lyon is complete, some time in the new year,' she added with satisfaction. 'Although, of course, you won't still be here then, will you, Shay?'

'Won't I?' Shay returned stiffly, irritated at the other woman's almost triumphant tone.

Marilyn gave her a sharp look. 'Surely you'll be returning to America soon to resume your career?'

Shay wasn't fooled for a moment by the other woman's attempt at lightness; the thought that she might be here when Lyon was finally a free man bothered Marilyn very much. She needn't

have worried, Lyon could have been free years
ago and it wouldn't have mattered to Shay.

'I can write anywhere,' she said softly, sensing
that Marilyn was far from the only person in the
room that was tense as they waited for her
answer. But she looked at no one else but
Marilyn.

'You intend staying on here?' The other
woman frowned her displeasure at that idea.

'Not at the house, no,' Shay dismissed the idea
with a mental shudder. 'But in England, yes. You
see,' she added softly, 'I want my child to be born
here.'

CHAPTER FOUR

OH GOD, had she really told them there was to be a child! She hadn't meant to break the news of her pregnancy quite so bluntly, had wanted her grandfather to be the first to know, had intended telling him when they were alone later. But it was done now, an act of defensive retaliation because of Marilyn's condescending attitude, an emotion she was incapable of preventing even after all this time.

The reactions of the people in the room varied dramatically, and it would have been amusing if it weren't the child she and Ricky had created before his death that caused these mercurial reactions.

Her grandfather, she could tell, was ecstatic, Matthew looked pleased too, Derrick Stewartby seemed dazed by the whole conversation, although he was concerned at the pale fury in his fiancée's face. And lastly Lyon. Shay looked at him challengingly, stunned at how grey he had become, his eyes appearing a pure molten gold. And she knew the reason for his anger, her baby meaning she would remain an integral part of the Falconer family. But if Lyon believed she was any more enamoured of that idea than he was he was very much mistaken; she hated it. But at the same time she didn't intend to deny her child its birthright just because she detested its uncle.

'That's wonderful, darlin'.' Her grandfather was the first to recover from the shock of her announcement, hugging her tightly. 'I can't begin to tell you how pleased I am for you.'

She could see and feel his pleasure, returning his hug. 'Thank you,' she said tearfully.

'I'm happy for you too.' Matthew moved forward to squeeze her hand. 'Did Ricky know?' he asked gruffly.

Shay's smile gentled. 'We found out a few days before he disappeared. He was very excited at the prospect of becoming a father,' she assured his brother softly.

'Just when can we expect this—the baby to make an appearance?' Marilyn demanded sharply.

Shay sobered as she turned to the other woman. 'I expect the baby to be born in just over five months.' Her mouth twisted as Marilyn's gaze moved sceptically to the flatness of her stomach beneath the soft material of her black dress. 'I can assure you I am almost four months' pregnant,' she drawled derisively at the lack of subtlety.

The other woman flushed angrily. 'I wasn't questioning the validity of your pregnancy,' Marilyn snapped. 'Only the timing of it. After all, it's over two months since Ricky died —'

'Marilyn!' Lyon cut in harshly, speaking for the

first time since Shay had made her announcement, his voice gruff. 'For God's sake—'

'Don't be naïve, Lyon,' she scorned. 'By presenting us with Ricky's baby, Shay has effectively established a reason to hang on to Ricky's share in the company; no woman would deny her child that birthright!' She looked at Shay with dislike. 'I'd put a sure bet on it's being a late baby!' she sneered.

Shay didn't have the strength to hold back her furious grandfather, watching in horror as his hand made painful contact with Marilyn's face. Her grandfather wasn't normally a violent man, abhorred violence on any level, but the provocation had been extreme; Shay could have hit the other woman herself at that moment and felt no regret for the action.

'You, madam, have the filthiest mouth I've ever encountered,' Grandy bit out in disgust to accompany the blow. 'And if there weren't a lady present, *my granddaughter*, I would tell you in your own disgusting language exactly what I think of you!'

'Don't worry, Patrick,' Matthew spoke grimly, 'I'll do that for you—as I escort Marilyn to the door!' he added pointedly.

'Well I don't know why everyone is so angry with me,' Marilyn looked petulant. 'You have to admit, this baby is a little—convenient.'

Shay drew herself up to her full height. 'My baby isn't a convenience at all, Marilyn,' she bit out clearly. 'Ricky and I desperately wanted this child, had been trying to conceive one for several months, and I don't aim to see it harmed, not even by your caustic tongue, so I would advise you not to make your slanderous assumptions outside of this house. This baby will be mine, will be born in my home, the home I make for us in England, and I don't aim to let it be contaminated by the oppressive atmosphere of this so-called family,' she dismissed disgustedly. 'Now if you would all excuse me, I should like to go to my suite.'

Lyon watched her go, deaf to the heated conversation taking place between Matthew, Patrick and Marilyn. It hadn't occurred to him that Shay could be pregnant with Ricky's baby, he had put the fainting down to grief, although he realised now it was probably a combination of both things:

Shay was carrying Ricky's child. He tried to analyse how that made him feel, and couldn't. One thing he did know, she couldn't leave here now. Without paying attention to the heated argument going on in the room, he strode off after Shay.

Only Lyon and Derrick had refrained from making any comment about the baby, and as the latter was probably still totally bewildered by the significance of it he didn't really count. What had Lyon been thinking behind those golden eyes; she never had been able to tell. She had expected the angry outburst to come from him, knew from the lawyer in Los Angeles that Lyon had already had the papers drawn up to buy Ricky's share in the Falconer empire from her. As one of the family lawyers in England, Marilyn had been sure to know of that contract, had probably helped draw it up! As the other woman had guessed, the existence of her baby prevented Shay from accepting the more than generous offer; she owed it to Ricky to let his child claim, and know, its natural inheritance from him.

She was ecstatic about the baby, Ricky had been too, but she would be the first to admit that it also placed her in an awkward position, that of having to see Lyon when she would rather never set eyes on him again. Her only consolation was that he knew it too.

Without benefit of clothes, a soothing bath being run in the adjoining bathroom, she knew her pregnancy was much more noticeable, her reflection in the full-length mirror showing full breasts, the nipples turning a darker brown, the tips highly sensitised as they prepared for the baby, her stomach slightly rounded, a faint fluttering sensation there when she least expected it telling her that her pregnancy definitely wasn't a fantasy.

She secured her hair back loosely with a ribbon, relaxing back in the sunken bath, closing her eyes wearily as the scented water began to soothe her. It was all over, she could leave here now, find a

reliable lawyer who, for the most part, could deal
with Lyon. It was as if a weight had finally been
lifted from her shoulders, and she could breathe
again, could leave the stifling atmosphere of
Falconer House and look forward to her life with
her baby.

She was smiling gently to herself as she re-
entered the bedroom from taking her bath, her
hands halting in their task of tying the belt
around her robe as she saw Lyon slowly rising
from his sitting position on her bed, quickly
finishing the task as she straightened her shoulders challengingly. She was unaware of the forward thrust of her hard-tipped breasts beneath
the clinging silk of the black robe with its purple
flowered pattern that Ricky had brought back for
her from a trip he had made to Japan the previous
year.

'What are you doing in here?' Shay demanded
hardly, furious that he had dared to invade
her privacy in this way, no matter what he
considered the provocation to be.

He shook his head. 'When I came in here I had
no idea you were taking a bath.'

She gave him a scornful look. 'You don't seem
to have left even when you did realise.'

Lyon shrugged, his mouth twisting. 'I wanted
to talk to you.'

Her eyes flashed her anger. 'Do you also doubt
the length of my pregnancy?' Her hands clenched
about the tie-belt of her robe.

'Marilyn has the suspicious mind of a lawyer—'

'Marilyn has the mind and mouth of a sewer!' Shay spat out contemptuously.

'Those too,' he sighed ruefully. 'I just— Why didn't you tell us about the baby, Shay?' Lyon's eyes had darkened to a deep tawny colour.

She shot him a resentful glare, moving to the mirror to release her hair down her back, irritated that the smooth paleness of her face now lacked any make-up, feeling emotionally naked and exposed too. 'I did intend telling all of you.' She turned back to Lyon. 'There just hasn't been a suitable occasion,' she dismissed.

'You consider today was a suitable occasion?' Lyon mocked disbelievingly.

'I consider your wife's harassment just another of the nightmares I've had to endure in this house!' Shay snapped vehemently. 'Marilyn certainly excelled herself today!'

'Marilyn is no longer my wife,' Lyon reminded softly.

'You aren't divorced yet,' scorned Shay disbelievingly, sure there would be no divorce between this couple. 'Whose idea was it for you to separate?'

'Marilyn met Derrick and decided she would like to marry him,' Lyon revealed stiffly. 'He's a lawyer, too.'

'I didn't think it was your decision.' Her voice was bitter.

'Shay—'

'What do you want in here, Lyon?' she asked

wearily. 'It's been a traumatic day and I'd like to rest for a while now.'

'I wanted to—I need—' He came towards her blindly, his hands covering hers as they still rested on the tie of her belt. 'Let me see, Shay,' Lyon urged gruffly, his eyes pure gold.

Her shocked gaze clashed with his, paling before the heated colour flooded her gaunt cheeks. 'No . . . !' She groaned her protest, unable to move as his lean hands gently caressed hers.

'*Please,*' he encouraged throatily.

Shay stopped breathing completely as he moved her hands aside, holding them firmly at her sides before slowly releasing them and moving his own hands back to the belt at her waist. She wanted to stop him, her desperation evident in her panicked dark eyes, but she couldn't seem to move or speak, gasping for air as Lyon pulled the belt apart, smoothing the silk material back on to her shoulders, Shay's breathing becoming strangulated as the cool air brushed her hot flesh.

'Lyon—'

'Shay,' he moaned achingly as he looked hungrily at her gently swelling body. '*Shay!*' he groaned again, touching her with hands that were no longer steady.

She meant to push those questing hands away, but as Lyon gently cupped the heavily aching weight of both her breasts she could only watch him dazedly, mesmerised into stillness at those leanly tanned hands against her much whiter flesh.

His head bent suddenly and he guided the tip of one painfully sensitised breast into his mouth, easing the pressure there for a moment as he suckled the nipple moistly before moving on to its twin.

'Lyon, no . . . !' She shook her head in denial, the unfamiliar feel of his lips against her breasts making her feel dizzy.

'I *need* to,' he told her raggedly, looking down at the soft swell of her stomach now, a hand curving about the smoothness. 'Does it move, Shay?' he asked hoarsely. 'Do you feel your child inside you?'

'Yes. *Yes!*' she repeated forcefully as he stroked her stomach.

'You can't leave now, Shay.' He shook his head, watching the slow movements of his hand against her as if mesmerised himself. 'The baby has to be born here.'

'No—'

'Yes!' Lyon insisted heatedly, a fever in his eyes. 'Your child will one day inherit everything there is. I don't intend to marry again, Matthew won't marry at all, and if Neil is going to do so he's taking his sweet time about it! This child—' He once again touched the swell of her body. '*Your* child, will probably be the only Falconer heir. It has to be brought up here in its father's home.'

'You don't doubt that the baby is Ricky's?'

'No,' he stated emphatically.

Shay shook her head. 'I can't live here.'

'You have to—'

'I don't *have* to do anything,' she told him haughtily. 'Not any more.'

His mouth tightened as he held back what he had been about to say with effort. 'At least stay until the baby is born,' he urged evenly.

'No, I—'

'Shay?' A knock on the door accompanied Neil's calling of her name. 'Matthew just told me the good news; can I come in?'

Shay looked down at Lyon's hands still on her stomach and hip, horror gripping her as she realised she was still blatantly exposed to his touch and the heat of his gaze, pulling sharply away from him to refasten tightly the belt of her robe. 'Get out of here,' she snarled. 'And don't let Neil in as you leave; I couldn't face anyone right now!' She turned away from him, her head bowed, unable to stop the trembling of her body.

'Shay—'

'*Get out!*' she ordered raspingly.

She heard the door open seconds later, Neil's surprised voice as Lyon was the one to appear and not her, silence as the two men walked down the corridor and back down the stairs.

Her worst fear had come true, her worst nightmare. It had always been like that between her and Lyon, right from the first, but she had hoped she had exorcised Lyon's physical effect on her by showing him for exactly what he was when she based the rake, Leon de Coursey, on him in her book. The man in *Scarlet Lover* had been as selfish and domineering as Lyon; he had also been the demon lover that Lyon had always been, the savagery he often displayed as much a pleasure as his most erotic caress.

If she had thought Leon de Coursey had driven Lyon from her mind as well as her body, his touch just now had shown her that she had been wrong; she might hate Lyon as much as it was possible to hate anyone, but she still burnt at his slightest touch!

From that first night together she had wanted him, the conclusion of their first actual date together something she had desperately tried to put from her mind, embarrassed that Lyon should take her over the plateau of desire, through the storm-tossed sea and then into calm waters, while denying himself the same release. Their second evening together had a much more satisfactory ending for both of them, she had made certain of that.

She had been nervous about going out with him again after the intimacies they had shared, and from the time Lyon called for her he had made her completely aware of his intention to make complete love to her that night. It had been an intent she had no intention of denying him.

When he had invited her back to his apartment after their meal together she had breathlessly agreed, his innuendos and caressing glances during the evening filling her with tense excitement, longing for that aching sweetness he had shown her last time. As soon as the door closed behind

them, encasing them in a world of expectant
silence, they moved into each other's arms,
Shay's mouth open to his, welcoming the deep
thrusts of his rigid tongue.

They didn't even get as far as the bedroom,
pulling off their clothes in heated movements,
falling to the thickly carpeted floor, mouths
searching and finding, hands touching, caressing, clawing, legs entwined, their bodies damp
with perspiration as Lyon delayed a joining between them. His lips and teeth were rough with
pleasure on her breasts, his hand on the moist
core of her before his fingers entered to know her
intimately, introducing a rhythm that made her
arch against him with need.

'Not yet,' he rasped, leaning back. 'Take me in
your hands and know me as I know you, Shay,'
he groaned, his eyes bright with need.

On her knees beside him, her breasts moved
temptingly in front of him, a temptation he
couldn't resist, levering up to take one desire-
tightened nipple into his mouth, pulling on it in
suckling caresses. Red-hot heat surged through
her body as she arched into him, Lyon touching
her in no other way than with his lips and tongue
and, occasionally, teeth.

She took his flesh between loving hands, shyly
caressing him with her fingertips, the rhythm of
her movements causing a constriction of his
stomach muscles, his whole body rigid with
need as he fought release against her velvet-soft
touch.

He pulled her astride him, dragging her down on to him, the tip of his throbbing shaft hitting a gossamer-like barrier before he surged completely inside her, filling her, engulfing her, big and hard as he began to move slowly within her, increasing the tempo as she arched back wildly on top of him, seeking the ultimate sensation he had shown her only once before.

'Next time we'll take it more slowly,' he ground out heatedly. 'Right now I need you too much, need—Oh, Shay!' he groaned dazedly as she began to shudder around him in convulsive movements, his eyes half-closing as he gave in to the warm demand of her.

Shay's fingers bit into his shoulders as pleasure such as she had never known ripped through every particle of her body, her eyes squeezed shut as the heat reached the top of her head, the tips of her fingers, and down to her contracted toes, feeling the heat of Lyon as he flooded her, his pleasure seeming never-ending too as he thrust even deeper inside her, again and again, until finally she collapsed on top of him, too weak to move.

'I never knew virgins could be so damned sexy,' Lyon finally murmured into her hair.

Shay didn't move, unable to gauge his reaction to her inexperience. 'You knew?'

'Of course I knew,' he drawled, his lips against her throat and shoulders. 'Even if I hadn't felt your virginity, I don't usually have to teach my women how to touch me.'

Colour stained her cheeks. 'I'm sorry.' She began to ease herself away from him.

'No.' His arms tightened about her. 'I want to show you every pleasure there is between a man and a woman. You're like a brand new book, and I want to write on every page! No, this was only the start, Shay!'

It had been the beginning of a relationship that rarely saw them out of bed, the merest touch igniting the desire that was never far below the surface. Every day she waited for Lyon to grow bored with her, to reach a satiation point with the lovemaking that could sometimes be so wild they were both bruised and scratched.

But Lyon showed no sign of becoming bored with her, demanding to see her every night, spending so much time together that a lot of her things accumulated at the penthouse apartment he called home when he was staying in London.

The visits they made to the Falconer family home weren't something she enjoyed, Lyon's three brothers always a little sceptical even if they were unfailingly polite. And the presence of Lyon's wife on several occasions made her feel very uncomfortable, the other woman treating her with open contempt. It was at the end of one of those awkward weekends with Lyon's family that she had finally broached the subject of where her own relationship with Lyon would eventually lead. His answer had been enough to almost destroy her!

She couldn't stay on here now, *wouldn't* stay

here, not when Lyon could still touch her in that way and receive only a half-hearted rejection from her.

'I think you should stay on with the Falconers.'

Shay's eyes widened with shock at her grandfather's statement. He had joined her for dinner in her suite, quietly supportive as he ensured that she ate the well-balanced meal that had been brought up on the trolley for them by Patty. She had never imagined he would advise such a thing when he knew how she felt about Ricky's family.

'You have to be joking, Grandy,' she scorned.

His expression remained serious, his blue eyes untwinkling. 'Surely you can see that it's the only sensible thing to do in the circumstances.'

'Sensible!' she choked disbelievingly, standing up to move restlessly about the room, the soft material of her long lilac gown brushing silkily againt her legs. 'Grandy, I don't like being in the same country as Lyon Falconer, let alone the same house! We don't get on, Grandy, and we never will.'

'Think of your child, Shay—'

'I am thinking about it.' Her arms went about her body protectively. 'I think of nothing else,' Shay added softly. 'And I can assure you that staying here will only make me, and consequently the baby too, ill.' She grimaced.

Her grandfather looked worried. 'You don't intend living alone when you leave here?'

'Unless you want to move in with me.' She arched dark brows questioningly.

'Live in London?' The face he pulled answered that question. 'How about your coming back to Ireland with me?' he suggested eagerly. 'It could be like old times.'

She had thought of going back to live with her grandfather for some time, and had sadly dismissed the idea. Except for visits, she hadn't lived in Ireland for over seven years, had lived alone or as Ricky's wife during that time, and she knew she couldn't go back, that she had become too independent for that.

She looked at him pleadingly, wanting him to understand. 'I can't, Grandy.'

The light went out of his eyes as he sighed. 'I didn't think so,' he acknowledged heavily. 'But I don't like to think of you alone in London.'

'In that "den of iniquity"?' she teased.

He looked uncomfortable. 'Do you have to remind me I once called it that?' he grimaced his embarrassment. 'You were only seventeen; I was worried about you. As it turned out, I had reason to be,' he added darkly. 'If I hadn't encouraged you to leave Ireland you would never have met Lyon Falconer—'

'Or Ricky,' Shay put in huskily, squeezing his arm reassuringly. 'And I wouldn't have missed being his wife for anything.'

'Anything?' her grandfather prompted gruffly.

'Grandy, the past is over, I have to think of my baby now. And that means moving to London, setting up a home for us both, and getting on with our lives.'

'Then I'll come down to London and at least help you get settled in,' he insisted stubbornly.

'Grandy, you hate London,' Shay mocked.

'I hate the thought of your being alone there more,' he muttered.

'Oh, Grandy!' She hugged him. 'I'll let you help me set up home and then I insist you go home,' she smiled. 'You're like a wounded bear if you're away from Ireland too long!' she teased.

He gave a rueful smile. 'I'll agree to that only because I know you're right!'

Lyon didn't agree, that was obvious when he stormed into her suite later that evening!

She was already in her nightclothes, the purple of her silk nightgown a perfect match for her eyes, the silken mass of her hair secured back with a ribbon of the same colour. She hadn't been expecting any more company tonight, hadn't said good night to Neil very long ago after he came back to offer his congratulations on the baby. She should have known Lyon wouldn't take the news of her leaving without protest.

His gaze flickered coldly over the case Patty had begun packing for her earlier in the evening, turning to her coldly. 'I asked you not to leave,' he grated.

Shay met his gaze unflinchingly. 'And I told you I couldn't stay here.'

'Because of me?' His eyes narrowed to tawny slits.

'Yes,' she answered with brutal honesty, the time when she had been in awe of him long gone.

'Then I'll leave,' he stated decisively.

Her mouth twisted. 'You think your absence would make any difference?' she scorned, giving him a pitying look. 'This house *is* you, Lyon. Everywhere I look I see you, feel you,' she added with a shudder of distaste. 'I couldn't go through my pregnancy here!'

A pulse throbbed in Lyon's rigid cheek, his hands clenching and unclenching at his sides, the brown shirt he wore moulded to his powerful physique, the brown trousers tailored to the lean length of his legs. 'You really hate me, don't you,' he ground out.

Shay gave a choking laugh of scorn. 'How could you ever doubt that?'

He drew in a harsh breath. 'I remember a time when you felt very differently about living here with me, when you begged me to—' He broke off as she paled dramatically. 'Oh God, I'm sorry,' he groaned self-disgustedly. 'I didn't mean to say that!' He looked at her concernedly.

Shay felt like ice, as if someone were squeezing the life out of her. 'You bastard!' she finally choked. 'I'll admit you once stripped me of my pride.' The memory was as painful to her as all her other memories of Lyon now were. 'But I loved you then, believed, in my innocence, that you felt the same way about me.'

'I—'

'Don't worry, Lyon,' she told him derisively,

'you soon pointed out to me that I was just another affair to you, just a little bit of fun that you and Marilyn could laugh about once it was all over and the two of you felt the inclination to temporarily share your marriage bed again!'

'It wasn't like that—'

'It was *exactly* like that, Lyon,' Shay snapped vehemently.

'I don't know what the hell you're complaining about,' Lyon rasped roughly. 'You were married to my brother within a year! I might have written on all the pages, Shay, but Ricky was the one to read the book from cover to cover!' he added bitterly.

Her eyes glazed with an ice that lightened the purple of her eyes, her face looking as if carved from stone; a beautiful statue without emotion or feeling. 'And he enjoyed every moment of it!' Shay told him defiantly. 'You see how it is between us, Lyon.' Her sigh was weary. 'We resort to insults over the least little thing.'

'I don't happen to consider your staying on here a little thing,' he said tautly.

'Believe me,' she shook her head, 'neither do I. For my own peace of mind, and for the sake of the baby, I have to go.'

'You're so damned stubborn,' Lyon muttered. 'What happens if you have an accident of some sort while alone in London?' he demanded to know.

'Ever heard of telephones?' she quipped.

'This is serious, Shay.'

'I couldn't agree more,' she nodded coldly. 'But I'm a grown woman, well able to support myself—and my baby, if that was going to be your next argument,' she added sharply. 'This baby may be Ricky's heir, but the money will go into a trust until it comes of age.'

Lyon stiffened at the determination in her voice. 'The child should have the best—'

'It will have the best,' she assured him haughtily, her head high. 'The best that *I* can give it.'

'I'm sure you're going to be a very good mother,' Lyon nodded.

Damn him, what was he up to now? All her arguments against him, her resentment, he met with a quiet intensity that unnerved her, his actions very unLyonish. She had been expecting anger from him over the baby, instead he had shown awed wonder for the life growing inside her, and now he was showing his approval of her as the mother of his niece or nephew. She had thought she knew the selfishly harsh man that he was, but something about him had changed. Maybe Marilyn's final rejection of the life they had lived together had shown him that he had given up his own chance to have a normal marriage and children. Whatever the reason, he intended taking extreme interest in the child she was carrying. And she wouldn't allow him to.

She straightened her shoulders determinedly. 'Grandy and I will be leaving for London tomorrow.'

Lyon's mouth thinned. 'You don't intend wasting any time, do you!'

'I can't see the point in that, not when I've made the decision to go.'

'No,' he muttered. 'I remember that from six years ago.'

Her cheeks coloured delicately. 'I'll keep you informed about my plans as best I can, where I shall be, things like that.'

'Thanks!'

'Lyon, I'm not going to be made to feel guilty because I want to bring my child up alone.'

'He'll be a Falconer, damn it!'

'He?' she prompted icily. 'This one and only heir to the Falconer empire could be a girl!'

'I don't care whether it's a boy or a girl; it will be your child!'

Silence hung heavily in the room after Lyon's forceful outburst, Shay barely breathing as she looked at him with wide eyes. She moistened her lips with the tip of her tongue, air entering her lungs in a long-drawn-out breath.

'Oh, to hell with it,' Lyon suddenly exploded. 'Go to London, set up house there, but I'll be watching you every step of the way!'

'You wouldn't dare!' Shay gasped her outrage at his arrogance.

'You know me better than that, Shay,' he reminded her in a softly threatening voice. 'I've always done whatever I had to for my family, and the child you're carrying is a member of it. If you leave here tomorrow I'll have someone watching you!'

'You can go to hell, Lyon Falconer!' She glared at him, had known he was ruthless, but this—! She couldn't believe even Lyon would go to the extreme of having her watched and spied upon.

'I've lived there more years than I care to think about,' he dismissed bitterly. 'I can live there for as long as it takes.'

'Well you can do it without any help from me,' Shay told him furiously. 'And if I do happen to see someone following me, I shall report it to the police. And tell them the name of their employer!'

The derisive smile on Lyon's lips as he left the room wasn't conducive to an easy mind.

Damn him, *damn him*! Even though she was leaving this house Lyon wasn't going to let her go. She was a prisoner of her own body and the life of her child!

CHAPTER FIVE

'ANY calls, Mrs Devon?' Shay smiled at the middle-aged woman who had been her housekeeper for the last two months. Only two weeks after coming to London with her grandfather, he had helped her move into this delightful mews house in a private cobble-stone courtyard, and from the many applicants she had had for the job of housekeeper she had chosen this openly friendly woman. She hadn't been disappointed with the choice, the woman kind and hardworking.

'Did Mr Flanagan's flight leave on time?' The older woman took Shay's jacket, a tiny woman whose movements were birdlike, her light brown hair liberally sprinkled with white, her brown eyes warm. She occupied the upstairs flat to this comfortably spacious house, an ideal arrangement for both of them.

Sadness tinged Shay's smile. Her grandfather had finally returned to Ireland this morning, and she had just come back from seeing him off at the airport. 'Yes,' she nodded. 'He's probably already back in Dublin by now.' She had stopped off on the way back from the airport and had lunch.

'Such a nice man.' Mrs Devon handed her the

list of messages she had taken while Shay was
out. 'The one from Mrs Falconer, Mrs Marilyn
Falconer,' she added with a slight strain in her
voice, 'is urgent.'

Shay stiffened at the mention of Lyon's wife,
and she could tell by the housekeeper's manner
that she hadn't been enamoured of the other
woman from their telephone conversation either.
'Did she say what was—urgent?'

'No.' Mrs Devon frowned. 'And I didn't like to
ask,' she grimaced tellingly.

Shay held back her smile with effort, nodding
dismissively to the other woman. 'I'll have tea in
the other room while I answer some of these
calls.'

She ate the scones that accompanied the pot of
tea, eating well nowadays, her well-rounded
body evidence of how her pregnancy was prog-
ressing, the baby's movements strong and reg-
ular now, all of Shay's dresses loose and flowing.
She had bloomed healthily away from Falconer
House—and Lyon—had enjoyed the last three
months in London with her grandfather, pleased
that he would be coming back for the birth of the
baby. In the mean time she intended resuming
her writing, keeping herself busy until she had
the baby to care for.

Shay kept returning Marilyn's call until last,
impatiently tapping her nails on the telephone
table as she waited to be put through to the
other woman's office, sure Marilyn had deliberately kept her waiting. Or perhaps she was

being paranoid. Although it would be just like Marilyn.

'Shay, how nice of you to get back to me so promptly,' Marilyn greeted smoothly when she did at last come on the line.

Shay was instantly on her guard; the other woman was *never* this pleasant. 'You told my housekeeper it was urgent I do so,' she pointed out distantly.

'Oh yes,' Marilyn laughed. 'Well I do want to see you, but I only stressed the urgency to your housekeeper because I've learnt you just can't rely on the help nowadays,' she drawled dismissively.

'So it isn't really urgent?' Shay snapped, impatient with this woman's snobbery.

'There are certain things I need to talk to you about,' Marilyn said irritably. 'We still have to go over Ricky's will with you.'

'I informed your office that I already know the contents of Ricky's will.'

'Nevertheless—'

'Look, Marilyn,' Shay interrupted, smiling her thanks to Mrs Devon as she came in to remove the tea-tray. 'Why did you really call me?'

'I've just told you—'

'What could just have easily been said in a letter, to my own lawyer, if necessary,' Shay sighed.

'We are still sisters-in-law,' the other woman snapped waspishly. 'I believed, erroneously as it turns out, that this could be handled in a friendly manner. Obviously I was wrong,' she said briskly. 'So could you come to my office some time tomorrow?'

If she hadn't known the other woman better, of the bitchiness that was never far from the surface with Marilyn, Shay might have felt remorse about her cold attitude towards her. But she did know Marilyn, too well as it happened, and she wasn't fooled for a minute. 'Before twelve or after two,' Shay agreed curtly.

'What happens between twelve and two?' Marilyn was curious.

'I rest,' Shay bit out.

'Oh, of course,' the other woman drawled. 'I should imagine you're quite big by now, aren't you?'

'I look like any other woman who's seven months' pregnant,' Shay answered tartly.

'Don't be so sensitive,' Marilyn mocked. 'I only put into words that day what everyone else in the room must have been thinking.'

Shay drew in a deep breath in her resentment. 'Thinking it and saying it are two different things,' she pointed out coldly. 'Besides which it was totally untrue.'

'What do I care whose baby you're carrying,' the other woman stated insultingly. 'I shall soon cease to be a member of the Falconer family anyway.'

'You seemed concerned three months ago,' Shay reminded her tautly, pleating folds absently into the pale peach dress she wore in her agitation, impatiently smoothing the soft material as she realised what she was doing.

'Surprised,' Marilyn corrected. 'We all were. You really foiled poor Lyon's plans this time, you know. But then you seem to have made a habit of that through the years,' she challenged softly.

'Sorry?' prompted Shay sharply.

'No need to apologise, Shay,' the other woman taunted. 'I was used to Lyon's affairs by the time you came along. But he intended keeping you around as his mistress for a long time,' she derided. 'And you spoilt it all by bringing up the subject of marriage.'

'He told you?' she gasped.

'Of course. Lyon and I have never had any secrets from each other. I knew that he always discarded his women when they brought up marriage,' she scorned.

'He married you!'

'Yes, he did,' Marilyn acknowledged softly. 'And it isn't his decision that we divorce now either,' she added with satisfaction.

Shay had already guessed that before Lyon confirmed it three months ago. 'Before twelve or after two, Marilyn?' she prompted curtly.

'Two-thirty?' The other woman wasn't in the least perturbed by Shay's sharpness.

She felt the return of the unease she always felt around the Falconer family as she replaced the receiver. The last three months had been tranquil, a time to gather her defences after the trauma of Ricky's death and funeral. She had felt

almost serene the last few weeks of her pregnancy, had enjoyed preparing the house for the
arrival of the baby. And if Lyon had kept to his
threat about having her watched she hadn't seen
any evidence of it. And if she didn't see it she
wasn't going to worry about it, had told herself
she wasn't going to worry about anything any
more. She cursed Marilyn for destroying her
peace of mind with one telephone call, vividly
reminding her that *she* would never be rid of the
Falconer family.

She shouldn't have tried to shop during the
lunchtime hours, should have stuck to her usual
routine and rested during that time. But she had
thought to perform two chores at the same time,
that of shopping for more maternity clothes before going on to Marilyn's plush legal office.

The shops were crowded, and she felt the pull
of her pregnancy as she tried on a couple of
gowns, feeling hot and sticky by the time she
emerged out of the changing-room with one of
the dresses to buy. She paid for it quickly before
hurrying to the Underground, a few stops away
from Marilyn's office, and not in the mood to
attempt to walk it, or fight for a taxi.

The station was busy too, everyone rushing to
get somewhere, Shay buying her ticket before
being caught up in the crowd heading for the
escalator down to the platform. No sooner had
her foot touched the moving top step than she felt
herself jostled by the crowd behind. She felt her

balance go, and stared with horror down the long length of escalator occupied by only a few people before she pitched forward with a terrified scream.

She tumbled past the people on the stairs, down and down as hands came out to try and stop her, feeling the sharpness of the metal steps cutting into her, fighting for consciousness as she tried to stop herself falling any farther. But she just kept going, going over and over, until she reached the bottom with a sickening lurch, feeling the hot rush of blood down her legs before she passed out.

She had lucid moments during the next half an hour, looking up briefly to see a sea of faces gathered over her as she still lay at the foot of the moving stairs; staring, grotesque faces that suddenly turned to blackness once again. The next thing she was aware of was being in an ambulance, its bell ringing wildly as it weaved in and out of the traffic. She wanted to shout out that it was too late for that, that she knew her baby was gone. But the bell kept ringing, and she was sobbing as the blackness engulfed her once again. The next thing she knew she was in an examining room, hysterically demanding to know what they had done with her baby. Then she knew nothing else as she felt the sharp sting of a needle in her arm.

'Shay.'

She knew that voice, knew that her nemesis

had come to haunt her, and she refused to open her eyes and look at his face. 'Come to gloat, Lyon?' Her bitterness rasped in her throat. 'If you've brought that contract with you now I'll sign it.'

'Shay, damn you, open your eyes!' he ordered through gritted teeth.

She did so reluctantly, her lids feeling heavy. 'How long have I been drugged?'

Lyon looked down at her with dark eyes, his face so pale he looked almost grey, his hair slightly tousled from its usual immaculate style. 'You've been out about six hours; I've been here five of them.'

'Why?' she asked dully, wondering why he was bothering with her now.

'Shay, what the hell is the matter with you?' He thrust his hands savagely into the hip pockets of his trousers, the jacket and waistcoat to the dark suit unbuttoned to be pushed back from his chest. 'You're covered in bruises, have a dozen stitches in several cuts, and as soon as you regain consciousness you attack me because I've gone through hell sitting watching you!' His eyes glittered ominously.

She knew about the bruises, daren't move because of the pain they caused in every part of her body, and she could feel several constrictive bandages on her legs too. 'Didn't you forget something, Lyon?' she said bitterly, staring at the ceiling.

'The fact that I don't understand what you

were doing at that underground station in the first place?' he rasped.

She turned to him with flashing eyes. 'The fact that I've lost my baby!'

A heavy frown settled on his brow. 'Shay, you—'

'Don't tell me I can have other babies.' Her voice rose shrilly at the thought of this man's insincere platitudes. 'I wanted *this* baby! What did they do with it? Oh God, they didn't—'

'Shay, stop this.' Lyon put restraining hands on her arms as they waved about madly. 'You haven't lost your baby. Do you hear me?' His voice rose as she continued to thrash about. 'You-haven't-lost-your-baby!' He grasped her hands. 'Feel, Shay. For God's sake feel it. I have.' His voice steadied as she began to calm a little, looking up at him disbelievingly as she registered what he was saying. 'I've sat beside you with my hand gently resting on the baby. It's moved, Shay. I think it even punched me once,' he added teasingly, his voice gentle now.

'It did?' she said in a hushed voice. 'It really did?' The glow started to come back in her eyes.

'Yes.' Lyon held her hands flat against her stomach. 'It's going to be a tough little boy—or girl,' he added ruefully.

'But I—I felt the blood.' She still wasn't convinced. 'I felt the baby go—'

'No,' Lyon insisted firmly. 'You've cut your leg rather badly, enough to need several stitches,' he frowned, 'but the baby is still there. You aren't usually this fat, Shay.' He mocked the swell of her stomach.

She was afraid to look down, afraid to believe him. 'Some women still look pregnant for a few days after they've given birth.'

'Not you, Shay,' he cajoled. 'You'll have your baby and be as slender as you ever were.'

'No, I—' Her eyes suddenly widened with wonder. 'It moved, Lyon,' she said in an awed voice. 'Lyon, it did move!'

'I told you—'

'Lyon, it *moved*!' She sat up to fling her arms about his neck, crying and laughing at the same time, hugging him so tightly neither of them could breath. Her other aches and pains from the fall were forgotten in the wonder of knowing her baby was safe, her hatred of Lyon too in this mutual bond of relief.

'I know, Shay.' He stroked the silky softness of her hair as he cradled her to his chest. 'I know, my darling.'

Even the endearment went without rebuff, her relief and happiness too extreme at the moment to care that he used the insincerity. 'You're sure everything is all right?' She moved back to look at him anxiously. 'The fall . . . ?' she shuddered at the memory of that fall, of the iron steps cutting into her again and again.

Lyon looked grim as she moved out of his arms completely to lie back against the pillows. 'The doctors here have assured me there will be no repercussions, but I have Peter Dunbar standing by to examine you now that you've regained consciousness. I meant to call him the moment you woke up.' He seemed irritated that he had been diverted from carrying out that decision.

'You have Peter Dunbar, the specialist, waiting for your call?' The obstetrician was world-known, hardly the sort of man to be at anyone's beck and call!

'No,' Lyon answered arrogantly. 'I have him waiting in the staff-room here. I'll go and get him.' He strode over to the door. 'It's about time he started earning the exorbitant fee he will no doubt charge me.'

Even Lyon's arrogance couldn't spoil her happiness, smiling up at the ceiling as her hands rested possessively on the swell of her stomach. The baby was alive, *alive*! She could even like Lyon at a moment like this.

Although he did little to endear himself to anyone during the next half an hour, hovering gloweringly over the doctor as he gently examined her, refusing to leave the room, even when Shay seconded the barely civil request of the harassed doctor that he do so. For her own part she felt no awkwardness in his presence, having known his full examination of her pregnant body weeks before. But Peter Dunbar was obviously agitated by the way Lyon watched his every move with narrowed eyes.

'Thank God only the expectant fathers behave in this way.' He scowled at the younger man as he washed his hands after the examination.

'Expectant mothers, thank goodness, have more sense!'

Shay's sharp gaze flew to Lyon's suddenly pale face, seeing he disliked the idea of the child she carried being his as much as she did. 'My husband is dead, Mr Dunbar,' she announced coldly, immune to the way Lyon flinched.

Peter Dunbar looked totally confused by this revelation. 'But I thought—'

'We're aware of what you thought,' Lyon cut in harshly, his expression savage as his gaze raked over the other man. 'And my relationship to Shay, or lack of it, is none of your damned—'

'Lyon!' she cut in warningly, looking apologetically at the tall distinguished specialist. 'I'm Mr Falconer's sister-in-law,' she explained softly.

'I see,' he nodded, giving the other man a dark look. 'It would have been a simple thing to have explained the relationship. I can understand your concern for your brother's wife—'

'Can you?' Lyon scorned. 'I doubt it!' He turned away to stare sightlessly out of the window.

'I'm really sorry.' Shay was embarrassed at Lyon's lack of courtesy to this highly respected man. 'The baby?' she prompted frowningly, ignoring Lyon.

'Has had a shake up,' the man smiled, 'but otherwise it seems well.'

'Seems?' Lyon turned back sharply. 'What's that supposed to mean?' he grated.

'The baby is reacting—'

'You said seems,' Lyon repeated forcefully.

Peter Dunbar looked at Shay for help—as if she had ever had any influence over Lyon's arrogance!

'Please let the doctor speak, Lyon,' she said with quiet determination.

Gold eyes flickered irritably but his lips remained firmly clamped together.

She turned back to the doctor. 'You were saying?'

The specialist's face softened at how gracefully elegant this woman was even after the trauma she had so recently suffered. He eyed Lyon Falconer warily, instantly banishing his admiration for the lovely Shay from his face; the man across the room looked set to tear him apart if he didn't! A strange relationship, he shook his head, one he wouldn't like to have the misfortune to be in the middle of.

'The baby is moving normally, reacting normally.' His smile was completely professional as he looked at the woman in the bed. 'You seem to have come out of the fall a lot worse than the baby did,' he gently mocked.

'I'll survive.' She gave him a serene look. 'It's the baby who counts.'

She really believed that, Lyon thought savagely. She could have been killed, broken her neck falling down those stairs, could have suffered brain-damage, broken limbs, and none of it

would have mattered as long as they could have
saved Ricky's baby.

As he had sat beside her and gently felt the
baby moving inside her he had felt a special
bonding with it, a oneness with them both. But
no baby would ever take Shay away from him.
Heads were going to roll for what had almost
happened to her today.

'—special care and attention,' he came back in
on the conversation to hear Peter Dunbar advise.
'The baby simply cannot take another upset like
today.'

'Shay will get all the care and attention she
needs at Falconer House,' Lyon told him bluntly,
wishing the other man would stop looking at
Shay the way that he was. She was his patient,
damn it, was seven months' pregnant; he had no
right to be looking at her with desire in his eyes!
Why the hell not; he desired her didn't he, baby
or no baby! 'And I'd like you to attend her at the
birth,' he heard himself add.

Rebellion flared in Shay's eyes. 'I have a
perfectly good obstetrician of my own—'

'Dunbar is the best,' Lyon stated arrogantly.

'Thank you for your confidence,' the other man
smiled, 'but as Mrs Falconer is already satisfied
with the man she has—'

'She doesn't have the best.' Lyon's voice was
steely. 'And I want that for her.'

'And what about what *I* want?' Shay flashed
him a look of intense dislike.

Lyon looked at her steadily. At least he hoped it

was steadily; the way Shay looked at the moment
he could take her to bed for a week and never tire
of making love to her. 'I thought you wanted
what was best for your child?' Bastard, he cursed
himself as she paled once again. But he was
determined that she should be in Peter Dunbar's
care, just as he was determined that she would
move back to the house with him, where he
would make sure she was never out of *his* care.

Shay's head went back with gentle pride as she
turned to Peter Dunbar. 'I should be very grateful
if you would accept me as your patient.'

Lyon dared the man to refuse her, dared anyone to refuse her anything when she asked so
charmingly. He had once wanted to give her the
world, even though he knew he could never give
her what she really wanted—now he knew the
world wouldn't have been enough, none of it
would have been enough for this beautiful gypsy.
Gypsy. It had been the way he always thought of
her, that image no longer his alone when his
brothers also thought of the name with no
prompting from him. Soon his brothers had
taken more than just the name away from him.

'Call my office as soon as you leave here,' the
other man invited smoothly. 'I'm sure we can
arrange something.'

'In future you will call on her at Falconer
House,' Lyon put in softly.

Glacial blue eyes were turned on him. 'If that's
what Mrs Falconer wants, yes.'

'It's what I want.' God, he was acting like a

damned fool, treating this man like a lackey. But he had almost lost Shay today, surely that exonerated his behaving like some power-crazy idiot. But he could see Shay was boiling because of his arrogance, and he absently ran a finger over the scar on his temple. She could be a vixen when roused, and all her protective instincts had been brought to the fore by her pregnancy. There was going to be hell to pay once the doctor left them alone. But Shay angry was much more preferable to the coldly assured witch he had met at the airport in Los Angeles three months ago.

Shay held on to her temper with difficulty, knowing this added distress couldn't be good for the baby. But Lyon wasn't going to have everything his own way. 'I'll call your office,' she smiled at Peter Dunbar. 'Thank you for today.'

The two men were like adversaries as they walked carefully around each other, dramatically, their parting at the door brief in the extreme.

Shay was frowning when Lyon returned to her bedside, her hands folded calmly on top of the sheet. 'Peter Dunbar seems an ideal choice,' she spoke softly. 'And I'll look forward to him visiting me—at *my* home.'

'Your things have already been moved to Falconer House,' Lyon stated firmly.

How could she stay calm, how *could* she when confronted with his damned arrogance! She had thought she had learnt to control her fiery temper long ago, had strived to do so since the time she had physically injured this man. But at this moment she could cheerfully have forgotten that resolve and struck him a second time. Only he had ever had the power to enrage her to this violence by his efforts to take over her life.

'On whose authority?' she demanded tautly.

'Mine,' he stated the obvious.

'Mrs Devon—'

'Was very concerned when informed of your accident.'

'So concerned she let someone into the house to take all my things,' Shay flashed.

'So concerned she could see the sense of moving you somewhere where you would have constant care,' Lyon maintained dismissively.

'I had constant care in my own home!'

'I'm well aware of Mrs Devon's capabilities,' he drawled. 'I was most impressed by her efficiency in packing your things for Jeffrey to collect without asking too many questions.'

'In that case Jeffrey will know exactly where to bring them back to, won't he,' said Shay stubbornly. 'Mr Dunbar told me I can leave in two days' time; I shall expect all my things to be back in their right place by then.'

Lyon shrugged broad shoulders. 'That's your choice, of course.'

Shay's pleasure was short-lived as she saw the look of satisfaction in his eyes, her own suspicion suddenly aroused. Lyon never looked satisfied unless things were going exactly the way he wanted them to. 'What's my choice?' she asked warily.

'If you won't move to Falconer House I'll simply move in with you,' he stated calmly.

'Like hell you will—'

'Remember the baby, Shay,' he warned softly. 'You shouldn't get upset.'

'And who is the one making me upset?' Two spots of colour stood out lividly on her otherwise pale cheeks. 'It's my home, and I will not have you violate it!' She was breathing heavily in her agitation.

'Violate?' repeated Lyon in a steely voice. 'What an odd choice of word.'

'Is it?' Shay scorned. 'You destroy everything you touch, Lyon—and you aren't going to do that to the peace and tranquillity of my home!'

'Neil doesn't seem to have received the same treatment.' Lyon's eyes were narrowed.

Neil had visited her on his way back to Los Angeles ten weeks ago; it didn't surprise her that Lyon knew about that. 'Neil is one Falconer I can tolerate,' she drawled.

A power as dangerous as a volcano about to erupt emanated from Lyon. 'You have your choice, Shay,' he bit out icily. 'But either way, I intend to see that nothing like today happens again.'

'It was an accident—'

'Does that make it any less serious?'

She sighed, feeling as if the ground were being taken from beneath her. But the idea of having

Lyon in the comfortable intimacy of her mews home was unthinkable. Damn it, she was a grown woman, an independent woman, he couldn't do this to her! 'It could have happened at any time—'

'I agree, it could,' he muttered grimly. 'Which is why I think you should have care at all time. You walk about London as if you aren't carrying the Falconer heir! Do you have any idea of the amount of lunatics there are about today who take pleasure in hurting people like us just for the hell of it?'

'You're over-reacting, Lyon—'

'Am I?' he demanded impatiently. 'I don't happen to think so. You didn't even have any identification on you when you were found. *I* telephoned the hospital, they didn't contact me!'

'How did you know?' she gasped. 'How could you have known?'

'You were late for your appointment with Marilyn, so she telephoned the house and was told you had left in plenty of time to get to her office. I was called, and from there we contacted the police and hospitals. I can't risk that happening again, Shay,' he told her grimly. 'I repeat, you either come to Falconer House or I move in with you?'

'I don't have to accept either!' she snapped resentfully.

'You don't *have* to . . .'

'Don't threaten me, Lyon,' she told him

harshly. 'I don't react well to threats.'

'Now who's threatening whom?' he taunted softly.

She gave him a scornful look. 'You don't react to threats at all!'

'No?' he queried softly. 'I remember I once reacted very strongly to a threat you carried out.'

Her eyes glazed over coldly as he reminded her of that scene six years ago. 'And I counter-reacted!'

Once again he unconsciously ran a finger along the scar on his temple. 'Yes,' he acknowledged flatly. 'I'm not threatening you now, Shay, I'm merely concerned for your welfare.'

'I have Mrs Devon to do that.'

'And I repeat, she isn't enough,' he said with barely controlled violence. 'For God's sake, Shay, do I have to beg!'

'Now that would be a novelty, wouldn't it!' she jeered hardly.

'Damn you!' Lyon bit out furiously. 'I'm tired of trying to reason with you; your things are at Falconer House, and once you're discharged that's where you're going too!'

She turned away from him, her face wooden. 'Would you please go.'

'Shay—'

The cold gaze she turned on him silenced him in seconds. 'The next time I'm not even going to ask, Lyon,' she told him flatly. 'I'll just ring for the nurse and tell her you're bothering me. I'm sure they employ someone to deal with people like you.'

His mouth tightened. 'Think of the baby.'

'I think of it constantly,' she assured him stiffly. 'And that's why I'm going to ask that you not be allowed in to see me again.' Her face was emotionless.

'Just having me around contaminates your child, is that it?' Lyon scorned viciously.

'Having you around contaminates *me*,' she corrected evenly.

An angry flush darkened his lean cheeks. 'God damn you!' His voice shook forcefully.

'He did that the moment I set eyes on you,' dismissed Shay coldly. '*Goodbye*, Lyon.'

'The car will be here for you in two days' time,' he told her in a controlled voice. 'Don't embarrass Jeffrey by making a scene.' He wrenched her chin up, purple clashing with tawny. 'You should know by now that I always get what I want!' He gave a disgusted snort as she continued to look at him unblinkingly, flinging away from her to stride over to the door. 'I will see you in two days—at Falconer House,' he warned before closing the door forcefully behind him.

Shay turned as the door was opened again only seconds later, smiling her relief as a middle-aged nurse bustled into the room, crossing to straighten bedclothes that were already perfectly neat as far as Shay could see.

'Your hubby seemed a little—tense, when he left just now.' The woman plumped up the pillows. 'I shouldn't let it bother you, they're all like that when they're worried.'

This friendly nurse was the second person today to assume Lyon was her husband, and this time she didn't bother to correct the assumption. No one, especially this kindly woman, could possibly guess at the savagery of the scene when Lyon had convinced her she would never, ever, be his wife.

They had spent the weekend at Falconer House, a rather unpleasant time for Shay, Marilyn there too with one of her men. She and Lyon had been due to return to London Sunday evening, but at the last moment Lyon had decided they would stay over another night and drive back to London in the morning. The thought of spending yet another night under the same roof as the woman who was still legally Lyon's wife had completely unnerved Shay.

She was agitatedly drinking a cup of coffee brought up to Lyon's rooms by one of the maids when he returned from the adjoining bathroom, affected as she always was by his near-nakedness, only a towel wrapped about his waist after his shower. She knew that soon, very soon, they would be in bed making love with an intensity that always shook her, each time better than the last, each night better than the one before. But at this precise moment she didn't want to think about that, was too disturbed by Marilyn's presence a short distance down the corridor.

She flinched away from him as Lyon bent to

kiss her throat. 'Lyon, I can't go on like this!' she snapped emotionally. 'How much longer before you'll be free of her?'

Lyon became suddenly watchful, straightening slowly. 'Free of whom?'

'Marilyn, of course.' Shay stood up to pace the room. 'I realise that while she's still your wife she has a perfect right to stay here, but once you're divorced—'

'Divorced?' he cut in sharply. 'Who said anything about divorce?'

Shay blinked. 'It's public knowledge—'

'You mean public gossip,' Lyon corrected harshly.

She swallowed convulsively. 'You—you mean it isn't true?'

'No.'

'But I—I love you. And I thought you loved me!'

His mouth was tight, his eyes glacial. 'Did I ever say that I did?'

No, he never had, not even at the height of their intimacy. But they had been together six months now, she had assumed Lyon's emotions were as deeply involved in the relationship as her own were, that it was only a matter of time before he asked her to marry him.

'Is that the reason you had an affair with me, Shay?' he scorned. 'Because you thought I loved you and would eventually marry you?'

An affair? Just another of his temporary women. And she hadn't even guessed!

'You surely didn't think I was going to divorce Marilyn to marry you?' Lyon said disbelievingly. 'My God, Shay, you didn't even know how to touch a man until I taught you!'

And how he had taught her! She suddenly felt like a courtesan who had been tutored by her master.

'Admittedly you're better at it now, but—Shay, put that cup *down*!' he thundered as the article was raised like a weapon, her eyes blazing with anger. 'Shay—' His stern warning was cut off as the cup flew through the air like a missile, landing against his temple, the delicate china smashing into a dozen pieces.

Shay watched in horror as blood spurted from the gash in his temple. She had always had a temper, quite a vicious one as a child, but she had thought she had it under control until Lyon spoke about her performance in his bed as if she were a whore he had hired to entertain him. She was no man's whore, not even the one she loved! But the cut looked quite bad, bleeding profusely, dripping down on to his chest now.

'Lyon, let me—'

'Oh I'll let you, all right,' he ground out, advancing on her menacingly.

'Lyon . . . ? Lyon!' she gasped as he pushed her back on to the bed, ripping aside her robe even as the towel fell from about his own waist, his arousal already hard with need. God, he couldn't want her now!

But he did, grinding his mouth down on hers, not caring that they were both covered in his blood now, not caring whether she was ready for him or not as he pushed her legs apart and thrust inside her. But to her shame she *was* ready for him, the primitive savagery of his lovemaking arousing her as never before. She was moist and hot, taking him deep inside her, arching her hips to meet his thrust, their bodies slicked with perspiration, Lyon biting painfully at her breast, the nipples peaked and hard.

With the pain came the pleasure, again and again, for both of them, Lyon insatiable, allowing no respite between the pleasure they reached together, his body moving constantly over and inside hers until he hardened with desire once again, gritting his teeth as her nails raked down his back and buttocks before once again spilling himself convulsively inside her.

It was wild and primitive, and it went on hour after hour, both intent on pleasuring the other until they could take no more. It was morning before exhaustion claimed them both, Shay packing her things when Lyon finally woke up just before lunchtime.

He sat up on his elbows to look at her. 'What are you doing?'

As that had to be perfectly obvious, she didn't bother to answer him, packing her clothes methodically, her movements slower than usual, every bone in her body seeming to ache from their hours of feverish lovemaking.

'Do that later,' he frowned. 'Let's order lunch and eat it in bed.'

At the mention of food she turned and ran into the adjoining bathroom, instantly bringing up the contents of her stomach, continuing to heave even after that meagre amount had gone. She was aware of Lyon standing in the doorway, and she retched anew. 'Don't touch me.' She flinched away from him as he reached out for her.

'Shay, it's all right,' he soothed, misunderstanding the reason for her aversion. 'You're ill—'

'And *you* make me ill!' She quickly washed her face, rinsing her mouth out. 'It's over between us, Lyon, don't you understand that?'

His mouth twisted. 'It didn't seem that way last night,' he taunted.

'Don't remind me,' she shuddered, moving past him to close her suitcase in agitated movements, shaking as she turned back to face him. 'But it *is* over, Lyon. You love your wife—'

'Nowhere in our conversation last night did I ever say that,' he grated.

'You have to, why else would you stay married to her?' Shay derided.

'There can be many reasons for a marriage, Shay,' he replied scathingly. 'And love is usually the least of them. I respect Marilyn for what she is, and she respects me in the same way. The marriage we have may not be everyone's ideal,' his mouth tightened at Shay's snort of disgust, 'but it suits us.'

'Then it's a pity you don't make that clearer to the people that get involved with you!'

'Shay—'

'I hope you and Marilyn remain suited to each other,' she spat the words at him. 'Because I want no further part of you!'

'You told me that you love me!'

She nodded jerkily. 'And that hasn't changed. Unlike you, I'm not able to control my emotions. But I want my *self*-respect, and I can't have that if I continue to see you.'

'Look—'

'I *said* don't-touch-me!' She froze as he once again reached out for her. 'I'm leaving now—and I think perhaps you ought to see a doctor about that cut on your temple; it's started bleeding again!'

He absently touched the trickle of blood on his cheek. 'That can wait, you can't. For God's sake, Shay, what we have is good—'

'What we have is sex, fantastic sex!'

'And you love it,' he grated.

'It isn't enough!'

'I can't give you any more than that,' Lyon bit out. 'The vows I made to Marilyn—'

'Vows you both constantly break!' she accused.

'They were for a lifetime.' He looked harsh. 'If she ever wants to end our marriage that's a different matter, but I'll never do it.'

She knew that, had known from the finality in

his voice when she asked him about a divorce the night before that Lyon would never seek one, not for any woman.

She had left him that day, had married his brother a year later, and now it was Ricky's child she had to think about, its future.

CHAPTER SIX

'YOUR morning tea, Mrs Falconer.' The quietly soothing voice of Mrs Devon woke her from her deep sleep, the subdued bedside lamp turned on in the darkness, the heavy curtains at the window keeping out the late autumn sun. 'I'll just go and run your bath.'

Shay was sitting up in bed drinking the tea when the housekeeper returned from the adjoining bathroom, giving no indication of the struggle it had been to get into the sitting position. She had found when she got out of the hospital bed yesterday ready to leave that although none of her cuts and bruises were serious they were certainly very painful, especially the cut on her inner thigh.

Jeffrey had duly arrived at the hospital yesterday to take her to Falconer House, only to be told she had already left—for her own London home. When he arrived at the house she had told him she wanted all her things returned; he had promised to pass on the message to Lyon. But as she had gone to bed just after seven last night, her bedside clock telling her she had more than slept the clock round, she had no idea if her clothes had been returned.

Not that it mattered greatly for now, not all of

her things had been taken, and she had enough here to last until she could get out to the shops for more. Which, from the way her body ached, wouldn't be for a few more days yet!

'Did my things come back last night, Mrs Devon?' she asked hopefully, not holding out much hope; Lyon was going to be far from pleased that she had disobeyed him. In fact, she was surprised he wasn't here now, ranting and raving.

'Yes, they did.' The older woman pulled back the curtains slightly now Shay was completely awake. 'I haven't unpacked everything yet because I didn't want to disturb you last night; you seemed so exhausted,' she said in a concerned voice.

'I think I was,' Shay acknowledged. 'But I feel perfectly rested today.'

'I'm glad.' The other woman was genuinely relieved. 'You had us all worried when you took that tumble.'

'I worried myself for a while,' she admitted with a grimace. 'But I feel fine now.'

'That's what I told Mr Falconer—'

'Lyon?' Shay prompted harshly, her fingers clasped tightly around the handle of the cup she held. 'Has he telephoned?'

'No—'

'He hasn't been here?' The thought of him entering the peaceful serenity of her private domain was very disturbing, especially if he did it without her knowledge.

'Mr Falconer was the one to bring your things back.' Mrs Devon frowned as she saw how tense Shay had become. 'Is everything all right, Mrs Falconer?'

She must get control of herself, banish this almost pathological dislike she had of Lyon or be destroyed by it. 'Of course.' She forced herself to relax, although her smile lacked its usual warmth. 'I'm sure you made Mr Falconer very welcome.'

'Well, I tried.' Mrs Devon poured her another cup of tea from the pot. 'But he wouldn't have any dinner last night, and he only had coffee this morning. I don't know how—'

'This morning?' Shay echoed in a hushed voice, her hands beginning to tremble. 'What do you mean?' she demanded shakily—although she had a feeling she already knew. Lyon had dared to carry out his threat without her knowledge! 'Did Mr Falconer stay here overnight?' she asked in a controlled voice.

The housekeeper nodded, seeming unaware of Shay's tension this time. 'I think it's very sensible of you to have him staying here with you. I know I'm only in the flat upstairs, but I really wouldn't be of much help if I'd finished for the day; I can't even hear you up there. I've been a little concerned about that ever since Mr Falconer asked me to take care of you. It was all right while Mr Flanagan was here, I could always be sure he would listen out for you at night, but since he left—'

'Mrs Devon, when did Lyon ask you to take care of me?' Shay asked woodenly, once again having that feeling of losing control of her life that was so common when Lyon was involved. If Lyon had *dared*, my God, if he had dared . . . !

'He called round one day while you were out shopping with your grandfather.' Mrs Devon moved about the room tidying things away. 'He was so concerned about you. Of course, that's very understandable. I assured him that he had no need to worry, that Mr Flanagan and I would look after you.'

My God, he had! Lyon hadn't carried out his threat to have a private detective follow her at all, he had managed to persuade her own house-keeper to spy on her. No wonder he was so aware of Mrs Devon's capabilities! The bastard, the lousy bastard!

'Mrs Devon,' she said in a controlled voice, 'could you please pack everything Mr Falconer brought with him last night and see that it is delivered to his office. I'm sure you know the address,' she added hardly.

'Mrs Falconer . . . ?'

She felt sorry for the poor woman; her face was stricken as she realised all was not well with last night's arrangements. But she didn't relent; she would not have Lyon staying here in her house. And she also intended seeing that Mrs Devon knew she risked losing her job if she took any further instructions from Lyon about her welfare.

'Mr Falconer isn't welcome in my home,' she

told the housekeeper with chilling clarity. 'Neither will I have you spying on me for him—'

'Oh, I didn't do that!' Mrs Devon gasped, shaking her head emphatically. 'I had no idea—It didn't seem such a strange request—Oh, I'm so sorry, Mrs Falconer!'

Shay couldn't help but feel regret for the tears of distress she had caused in the troubled brown eyes. 'I realise that my brother-in-law can be very persuasive,' she sighed. 'And now that you know of the—rift, between us, I'm sure you will deal with him accordingly in future.'

'Well of course I will, Mrs Falconer.' The housekeeper seemed bewildered by her vehemence. 'I'll see that he gets his things immediately.'

'Thank you,' Shay accepted with quiet dignity.

'I really didn't know,' Mrs Devon turned to tell her regretfully as she reached the door.

'I know you didn't,' she assured her gently, realising the woman was genuinely upset. 'Mr Falconer and I have never got along, but unfortunately he now considers his brother's widow his dependant.'

'These family differences can be awful, can't they,' the housekeeper sympathised. 'I know my husband couldn't stand my father; the two of them never did become friends,' she added sadly. 'It can cause a lot of friction.'

Shay nodded dismissively. 'As long as you remember in future that Lyon is not welcome here.'

'I'll remember,' the other woman nodded

vigorously. 'About Mr Falconer's things, how shall I—'

'Put them in a taxi,' Shay told her sharply. 'Or out in the street.' She ignored the housekeeper's shocked expression. 'I really don't care what you do with them as long as you get rid of them,' she said wearily.

Her bath water had cooled somewhat by the time she got into the bathroom, but she was too agitated to do more than take a quick wash anyway, forgoing her usual long soak in the bubbling, scented water. 'Think of the baby' that swine had told her; when did *he* ever think about it! How dare he sneak into her home once she was asleep and take up residence in her guest-room? Guest! She was more likely to invite Attila the Hun to stay than Lyon!

The third draft of her book, polishing all the rough edges, was what saved her sanity, becoming so engrossed in what she had been assured by her editor would be her sixth block-buster, that she even needed Mrs Devon to remind her to eat lunch.

'I dealt with that other matter,' she told Shay when she came to collect the empty tray a short time later.

'Thank you,' Shay accepted stiffly.

'Why don't you go outside for a short walk before your rest?' the housekeeper suggested. 'You're looking a little pale, and some fresh air might put some colour back in your cheeks.'

Shay knew the suggestion was only made out

of concern, and she did feel better as she walked in the brisk autumn wind, feeling invigorated by the crisp air, Lyon briefly forgotten.

She gave the housekeeper a serene smile as she entered through the kitchen, handing her the full blooms she had bought to brighten up her study for the little time they had left to live. 'It worked, Mrs Devon,' she glowed. 'I could go on working for another couple of hours now.'

'Rest,' she was told sternly. 'Oh, I almost forgot, a parcel came while you were out. I left it on your desk in your study.'

'It was delivered?' Shay frowned, knowing the post had come earlier.

'A young boy brought it.' Mrs Devon was busily arranging the roses in a vase.

Shay picked up a freshly baked biscuit that was cooling on a tray, a thoughtful frown to her brow as she went to her study. She didn't remember ordering anything that had to be hand-delivered.

It was a heavy parcel, her frown almost as heavy as she removed the brown wrapping-paper to reveal four of her published books, hardbacked copies for a collector, only one of the books missing. She quickly turned the wrapping-paper back over, recoiling as she saw it was Lyon's name above her address on the hand-written label.

Her first emotions were ones of anger; how dare he take the liberty of actually having things delivered here. The whole of London would

quickly learn that he had taken up residence here!
That was just what she needed.

. After the anger came puzzlement. Why on
earth did Lyon want her books, he hadn't exactly
been over-enthusiastic about their existence in
the past. She didn't want him reading them
either, felt as if he were intruding in something
that was very personal. And she didn't understand why *Scarlet Lover*, the only one of her books
they had ever discussed, was missing from the
collection.

She agitatedly returned to the kitchen, no
longer humming happily to herself. 'There are
some more things of Mr Falconer's in my study,
Mrs Devon,' she told the housekeeper stiltedly.
'Please see that they are delivered to him too. I'll
be in my bedroom if you should need me.'

She slept so long her head ached when she
woke up, a glance at the clock telling her it was
after four-thirty. Mrs Devon was a well-meaning
dear, but she should have woken her. For someone who had always had so much energy, needing only a few hours' rest at night to 'recharge her
batteries', Shay found this habit of sleeping in the
day almost decadent.

She was sitting in the kitchen enjoying a much-
needed cup of tea when she heard the front door
slam shut, and the sound of someone whistling
as they walked down the hallway and up the
stairs.

Mrs Devon gave Shay a startled look.
'Who . . . ?'

She knew very well *who!* Lyon was here in spite of the pointed returning of his clothes.

Her mouth tightened as she heard the sound of water being run upstairs; Lyon always showered as soon as he returned home for the evening. At least, he had done six years ago, and she had no reason to suppose he had changed the habit during that time.

'Excuse me, Mrs Devon.' She left the kitchen in a blaze of fury, too angry to see where she was going, finding herself suddenly in the guest-room, wrenching open the door to the adjoining bathroom. 'Get out of my house, Lyon,' she ordered harshly.

He stood in front of the mirror shaving, steam from the running shower already beginning to fog his reflection, a towel draped about his thighs his only clothing.

He turned calmly to look at her. 'Like this?' he drawled pointedly.

'Stark naked for all I care!' She didn't give a damn about his nakedness, was unmoved by his physical perfection. 'Just get out.'

He turned back to the mirror. 'My case arrived safely, by the way.'

'Good!'

'You don't really mean that,' he sounded amused.

'Oh, but I do,' she assured him forcefully, her eyes blazing deeply purple. 'I want you to take that suitcase now and go.'

'You look very beautiful in that dress,' he

murmured appreciatively, checking his jaw for a smooth shave. 'I think I need a new blade in my razor—'

'Leave the blunt one in,' Shay flared. 'If I'm forced to cutting your throat I'd like it to be as painful as possible!'

Lyon laughed softly. 'Being in an advanced state of pregnancy suits you; it brings out the tigress in you.'

She retained control of her temper with effort, breathing deeply. She would not let him do this to her! 'I'm not supposed to be upset, Lyon—'

'Then don't be,' he shrugged, testing the temperature of the shower water. 'I'd ask you to join me, but I don't think there's room for the three of us.' He looked pointedly at her swollen body.

Shay stepped back with a furious gasp, slamming the bathroom door in his face, the pounding in her head worse, feeling dizzy as she went to her own room, lying down on the bed once she had slipped off her clothes, closing her eyes to shut out the pain. This was supposed to be a euphoric time in her life, and here she was being haunted by the devil himself!

'Mrs Falconer . . . ?'

She lifted heavy lids to look at the house-keeper, smiling wanly. 'I seem to be so tired today.' She had been asleep again for over two hours!

'I didn't think you should be working again so soon after your accident,' the other woman scolded, helping her sit up against the pillows. 'A nice bowl of soup and a steak salad will soon buck you up,' she decided primly.

'Mr Falconer . . . ?'

'Is going out to dinner.'

'You mean he's still here?'

'Now please calm down,' Mrs Devon soothed. 'Mr Falconer said you—'

'I believe we've already had this conversation once today, Mrs Devon,' she reminded her stiltedly. 'Mr Falconer's wishes do not interest me!'

'I accept that,' the housekeeper nodded. 'But when what he says is just plain good sense I don't see the point in opposing him.'

'And just what has he said this time?' she asked with sickly sarcasm.

'That you shouldn't have been working today, that it was silly of you to push yourself in that way, and that you should have dinner in bed tonight.'

'I give the orders in this household, not Mr Falconer—'

'And I'm sure they are very prettily given too.' Lyon strode into the room unannounced, wearing an evening suit now. 'Thank you, Mrs Devon,' he smiled at the older woman. 'I'll deal with Mrs Falconer now.'

Purple eyes spat flames at him as soon as they were alone. 'Isn't it enough that you had that poor woman spying on me without trying to take over here completely?' Shay accused.

'Looking after you and spying are two different things,' he drawled.

'Mrs Devon seemed to think there was a distinction too,' Shay snapped. '*I* don't. What do you think you're doing now?' she gasped as he lifted her arm.

'Checking your pulse.' He studied his wristwatch as he felt her pulse. 'Dunbar mentioned that your blood pressure is up slightly—'

'And just when did he happen to "mention" this?' she demanded indignantly.

'While you were in hospital,' Lyon shrugged.

'You had no right discussing *my* health with *my* doctor,' she muttered resentfully.

'Your pulse appears to be racing.' He looked down at her with questioning gold eyes. 'Because of me?' prompted Lyon huskily.

'Because you *are* you,' she corrected forcefully. 'Because you're arrogant, and bossy, and totally unrelenting, and—and—' To her everlasting consternation she began to cry, deep racking sobs that she had no control over. 'Because I can't fight you and win, because—'

'Shay, stop it!' Lyon ordered harshly.

'I—can't!' she hiccuped.

'Damn it, I swore I wouldn't touch you again,' he rasped in a tormented voice.

'Please—don't.' She shook her head, tears streaming down her cheeks.

'I can't help myself!' He sat down on the bed to take her in his arms, trembling slightly as he did so, cradling her head gently into his chest.

'You've tired yourself into this state, you know,' he admonished. 'Is fame and fortune so important to you?' he added bleakly.

Shay looked up at him with puzzled eyes. 'Fame and fortune . . . ?'

'Shay Flanagan's sixth best-seller,' he derided bitterly. 'Mrs Devon tells me you worked on it most of the morning and then spent the better part of the afternoon sleeping; is it so important to you to finish it before the baby's born? I've read one of your books, and I didn't see anything special in it!'

Scarlet Lover? If that were the book he had read he gave no indication of it. 'Fortunately, millions of other people disagree with your opinion!' she snapped.

Lyon's face hardened, his eyes suddenly cold as she sat away from him. 'You didn't answer my question, is it so important you finish the damned thing now?'

'To my publisher, yes! I'm contracted to finish it by Christmas.'

Lyon's mouth twisted. 'I'm sure you weren't a widow or pregnant at the time!'

'You bastard!' she choked.

'Shay—'

'You'll never change, Lyon, so it's no good thinking you will! I'm finishing the book because I want to, not for any other reason. And if it makes me tired then I'll sleep instead of lying here in the darkness wondering how I can explain to a small child that its father died before it was even born!' She glared at him, hating the complete way she had exposed her feelings to a man to whom she had sworn she would never again show any sign of weakness.

Lyon silently cursed himself for pushing her to this point. God, he knew she hated him, did he have to keep punishing himself by proving it time and time again!

He hadn't meant to belittle her work, had been surprised by the strength of the book he had read. But that was before he saw how tired writing made her! God, she was black and blue all over from the beating she had taken down that escalator, how dare she tire herself out by working the day after she came out of hospital!

'If you don't take better care of yourself there won't be a child to explain to.' He flinched inwardly as she paled even more. 'Don't you realise how lucky you are not to have lost the baby already?' he continued mercilessly.

'Yes, I know.' She stood up, magnificent in the purple nightgown, her breasts full in preparation for her child, that child nestled safely in her body. God, how he wanted her, now, like this, felt as if the child she carried were his own. 'A lot has happened during this pregnancy, and I can assure you that constantly being bullied and pushed about by you is certainly not helping the situation!'

He smiled as the fight came back into her. As long as she kept fighting he knew everything was going to be all right. It was when she became so cold and remote that he floundered. 'I know everything is going to work out for you, Shay.'

She looked at him sharply, suspiciously. 'I don't need your assurances about *my* life,' she finally snapped.

She would be his again one day, he vowed it! He had to have her, had to make her belong to him again, body and soul. And this time there would be no escape!

His smile deepened. 'If you have any trouble sleeping tonight just come along to my room; I'm sure I could find a way to help with your insomnia.' God, she was going to throw something at him in a minute, he knew it by the gleam of fury in her eyes.

'Lyon—'

'Yes?' He raised innocent brows.

She sighed wearily. 'Why don't you spend the night with your dining companion?'

His mouth twisted. 'You, more than anyone else, should know I'm not that way inclined,' he taunted.

Colour heightened her cheeks. 'You're meeting a man this evening?'

He nodded. 'A business acquaintance.' He glanced at his watch. 'And I'm going to be late if I don't leave now.' He looked back at her. 'Now why don't you be a good girl and eat the soup and steak salad Mrs Devon is preparing for you?'

'Because I know that you ordered it!' Her eyes

flashed. 'Because you've walked into my home, made yourself comfortable, and taken over!'

His mouth tightened, and he knew his eyes frosted over. 'You aren't working again tonight.'

'I—'

'If I have to I'll stay in with you this evening and make sure that you don't,' he threatened softly, pain in his chest at the hunted look that came over her beautiful face. He *would* have her. She had loved him once, she would again. Oh he knew that in the past he had destroyed her love with a cruelty she would find hard to forgive, but he had had his reasons. Now that Marilyn had decided she would like to end their marriage, there were no obstacles in the way of his having Shay. Except that she didn't love him. But he could *make* her want him; he had always been able to do that!

God, how she hated the thought of backing down in front of this man, but the thought of spending the evening with him was out of the question. 'I have no intention of working again this evening,' she told him tightly. 'I rarely work in the evenings, Ricky and I—'

'Yes?' Lyon prompted as she broke off abruptly.

She looked at him with defiance. 'Ricky and I liked to spend our evenings together.'

'You were happy with him?' His voice was gruff.

'Extremely so,' Shay nodded challengingly.

'I'm glad.' Lyon's answer was bitten out.

Shay gave a scornful laugh. 'You'll forgive me if I find that hard to believe!'

'Is that why you married Ricky, to spite me?' Lyon grated.

Her eyes darkened angrily. 'Aren't you assuming that you meant something to me?' Her voice was contemptuous.

He nodded curtly. 'I know I did once.'

'That was a very long time ago,' dismissed Shay coldly.

'You still haven't answered my question about why you married my brother,' he prompted.

'I married Ricky because he was the kindest, gentlest man I ever knew. And because I loved him deeply,' she added quietly.

'I see,' Lyon bit out roughly. 'How quickly the love you expressed for me died!' he scorned.

It hadn't died at all, it had been killed. It had been ripped out of her, Ricky the one to pull her back out of the darkness, to care for her in a way Lyon had never even tried to do. Her initial warmth and gratitude to Ricky had slowly turned to love. It hadn't been the volcanic emotion she had felt for his brother, but a much more comfortable love, and one that she had known was more than returned.

'I was very young, Lyon,' she said self-derisively, effecting a bored tone. 'You were the older, much more experienced man. Every young girl should have a fling just like that one. But you certainly aren't the sort of man any sensible woman would try to settle down with; even

Marilyn has had to admit defeat in trying to tame you after eleven years.'

Tawny eyes were hard with anger. '*We* were together six months, a little more than a fling, wouldn't you say?' he challenged tautly.

Shay's poise almost slipped as he reminded her of the most tempestuous six months of her life, but she managed to maintain her smile. 'I was enjoying myself too much to let it end,' she mocked. 'So much so I even fell a little in love with you. But I think we were right to end things when we did.'

'It was not a mutual decision,' he rasped.

'Wasn't it?' she dismissed lightly. 'I forget the exact details now. You know, I think I am hungry, after all,' she said thoughtfully. 'And didn't you say something about being late for your dinner engagement?'

'This conversation is more important than a damned business dinner,' he told her harshly, his eyes narrowed. 'And in my opinion it's also long overdue! You disappeared once you got back to London after that weekend; where did you go?' he demanded to know.

'How dramatic you make it sound, Lyon,' she mocked. 'I went back to Ireland for a few weeks' holiday—which was due to me—'

'Which also turned out to be your notice,' Lyon rasped.

She shrugged. 'I had the chance of a better job and decided to take it.'

'In Ireland?'

'No.' She laughed.

'Then where?'

'For another firm in London, of course,' she chided his denseness in not realising that.

Lyon shook his head. 'I looked for you, I couldn't find you. You even moved out of your flat.'

'How did you know that?' she gasped.

'That was the first place I looked,' he said impatiently.

Shay's eyes widened. 'But why on earth should you want to look for me?'

'You know damn well *why*.' Lyon's voice rose angrily. 'We argued that morning, but we could have worked something out, you didn't have to disappear completely like that.'

'I didn't disappear completely, Ricky was able to find me,' she goaded, disturbed to find that Lyon hadn't just given up on her after that weekend, that despite what had happened he had still wanted to see her.

Lyon drew in a sharp breath. 'Conveniently,' he sneered.

He would never know how 'convenient' Ricky's unexpected visit to her bed-sit had been six years ago, how Ricky had called an ambulance while he tried to stop the life's blood draining out of her. If he hadn't found her she would surely have died that night. But she never intended letting Lyon know how she had almost died because she had loved him. Ricky had been with her constantly after that night, and her liking and gratitude to him had turned to love, a love that had merely deepened and grown during their years of married life together. Surely no two brothers could be as different as Ricky and Lyon!

'I'm going downstairs to have my dinner now, Lyon, you must do what you choose.' She pulled on the silk wrap that matched her nightgown, past feeling awkward with Lyon in whatever state of dress he found her. He didn't seem to mind, so why should she!

'Just answer me one question.' Lyon grasped her arm as she would have left the room. 'Did you and Ricky have an affair while we were still together?'

'An affair implies that we had a relationship of fidelity between us, Lyon,' she scorned. 'And that could hardly be the case when you were married to someone else!'

'*Did you?*' he demanded forcefully.

It would be so easy to say yes, to hurt this man's pride as it deserved to be hurt. But to lie would be to malign Ricky, and she couldn't do that. 'No,' she answered abruptly. 'Your brother was too much of a gentleman for that,' she couldn't resist adding goadingly.

Green sparks flew from tawny eyes. 'But you wanted him?'

Now she felt no hesitation in lying. 'Obviously,' she drawled. 'He was much more my type than you were; young, uncomplicated, fun to be with—'

'Free,' Lyon ground out.

'That too,' Shay nodded mockingly. 'Why are you making all this fuss, Lyon?' she dismissed. 'Is it because *I* was the one to finish things between us? Couldn't your pride take it?'

'My pride has nothing to do with it—'

'Oh, come on, Lyon.' Purple eyes challenged tawny. 'It would have ended between us sooner or later anyway.'

'Would it?'

She frowned at the flatly spoken question. 'If you expected me to go on as we were for the next five years or so you were out of luck!'

'Why?' he grated. 'I could have given you anything you wanted—except marry you.'

'Because you already had a wife!'

'You knew that when we first started seeing each other. The fact that you thought I was divorcing Marilyn didn't alter the fact that she was still my wife when we began our affair. God, I can't believe marriage was so important to you that you threw away what we had!'

'Why not?' she taunted. 'Most women want permanence, a husband and eventually a family.'

He pushed her away from him. 'You've had them both.'

But not together. It would have been wonderful if Ricky had been able to go through this pregnancy with her. He had been so concerned for her, was already proving himself to be an indulgent father-to-be, toys for the baby appearing almost daily in the second bedroom at their apartment that was going to be turned into a nursery. Shay had teased him that if he continued like that the baby wouldn't be able to get in the room! He had just laughed, and so had she, enjoying her pregnancy.

Lyon's eyes were like icy slits as he seemed to read the happy thoughts going through her mind. 'I shouldn't be late back tonight, and Mrs Devon will be upstairs in her apartment if you need her later.'

He sounded just like a concerned husband leaving his pregnant wife alone for the evening— and she wouldn't allow him that privilege. 'You're at liberty to return here whenever you feel like it,' she told him haughtily. 'And I certainly don't need you to tell me how my household runs!'

Instead of the anger she had been expecting, Lyon gave a satisfied smile, touching her cheek gently before leaving the room. He moved with animal grace as he descended the stairs, wishing Mrs Devon a cheery goodnight on his way out.

It was only then that Shay realised why he was so damned pleased with himself; she had just given him permission to stay on here in her house. Unwittingly goaded into doing so, but she *had* given it!

She shouldn't have slept so much today, she told herself as she tossed and turned in the bed, unable to fall asleep despite the hands on her bedside clock telling her it was well after midnight.

But she knew her insomnia wasn't all due to the fact that she had had two lengthy naps today. A lot of it was due to the fact that tonight she was aware of Lyon's presence in the bedroom opposite hers.

He had been back about an hour now; she had heard him moving about the room as he undressed before going into the bathroom to take a shower, and then the slight movement of the bed as he sat on its side. She had been conscious of every sound coming from that room the last hour, couldn't sleep *because* she couldn't stop being aware of Lyon's movement.

She needed a bath to cool off, or calm down. She needed to relax somehow, knew she shouldn't let Lyon's presence here disturb her so much. Heavens, she had lived in the same house as he had for the first two years of her marriage, so why should tonight in her house be any different? Because Ricky wasn't there to protect her! Lyon had felt no compunction about coming to her suite at Falconer House the night of the funeral, so why should he stay away tonight?

The bath did much to calm her, and she dismissed the thought of Lyon across the hall as she repeated the nightly ritual she had of rubbing oil into the taut skin stretched across her swollen body, so far managing to ward off the stretch marks with this little bit of care.

'What are you doing?'

She almost dropped the bottle of oil she held in her agitation at Lyon invading her privacy in this silent way, hastily pulling her robe around her as his dark gaze seemed fixed on her gleaming body. 'How dare you just walk in here?' she spluttered her indignation, feeling very vulnerable in her vanity.

'I heard the water run for your bath,' he spoke absently, moving towards her. 'What were you doing when I came in?' he repeated.

He was standing over her now, and Shay was uncomfortably aware of the fact that her only piece of clothing was clinging to her stickily. She usually rubbed off the excess oil before going to bed, Lyon's intrusion interrupting the ritual, and now she felt very uncomfortable.

She swung her legs to the floor. 'Trying to make sure I don't get stretch marks,' she snapped. 'Haven't you ever heard of knocking before you enter a room?' She marched over to the bathroom to get a towel, closing the door behind her, looking up indignantly as Lyon pushed into the room behind her. 'Lyon, please!' she gasped.

'Let me.' He took the towel from her, taking her back to the bed to lay her gently on the sheet.

'Lyon—'

He parted her robe, revealing her glistening skin, gently patting her dry with the towel. 'I interrupted.' He picked up the bottle of oil, pouring a little into his palm as he gently used both hands to caress the swell of her body.

'Lyon, no!' she protested weakly.

'Oh, *yes!*' he insisted, his hands moving slowly, rhythmically, over her silken flesh.

She shouldn't be letting him do this to her, but as a heated warmth spread through her body, she knew she wasn't going to be able to stop him.

Shay closed her eyes, the oil he was slowly massaging into her body warmed by his hands before he touched her. His hands smoothed oil either side of her stomach, down to her lower body, before moving up again. His movements were soothing even while she felt her senses leap. She became languorous, too comfortable to move as Lyon continued the gentle caresses.

'He should have got the girl, you know,' Lyon suddenly murmured.

She squirmed protestingly as those sensuous hands travelled up the sides of her heavy breasts. 'Hm?' she groaned as her breasts ached in a completely different way from their usual fullness.

'Leon de Coursey.' Lyon's fingers grazed her responsive nipples.

She raised heavy lids. 'You've read the book?'

'Several weeks ago.' He concentrated on gently kneading the oil into her hips.

She closed her eyes again. 'Men like that don't "get the girl",' she told him firmly, desperately searching for the strength to end this. But his hands felt so *good* on her body!

'Page one hundred and twenty-three was our last night together, wasn't it?' One of his hands curved over the mound of her womanhood,

Shay's gasp turning to a groan as that hand slowly began to move. 'Shay?' he prompted persuasively.

'Yes!' she gasped as he increased the pressure, feeling the moist heat begin to take control of her body as he probed her softness with a knowledge that had her writhing against him.

As the reality of what was happening to her washed over her, Shay sat up to push his hand away, clasping her robe to her as she knew she had been on the edge of complete sexual release. Just from Lyon's *touch!*

She was breathing hard in her agitation. 'And at the end of that night I felt the same loathing for you that Adelia felt for de Coursey!'

Lyon straightened as she stood up, wiping the oil from his hands on to the towel. 'The same loathing you felt just now when I touched you?'

She swallowed hard, whimpering softly. How could she deny her arousal of just now; Lyon had *felt* the ready moistness of her, had probed the velvet warmth of that desire.

'This time *I'm* going to "get the girl",' he grated.

'No!' Shay cried her panic.

Lyon's mouth thinned. 'You may be able to control the characters in your books, Shay, make them do what you want them to, but you can't control me. I lost you once, it isn't going to happen a second time.'

'I don't want you!' she gasped at his arrogance.

He shook his head. 'Maybe not me, but now I

know what you do want. I also know you can't stop me. You're going to be mine again, Shay. And this time you'll stay mine!'

CHAPTER SEVEN

FALCONER House looked very beautiful, the surrounding trees an assortment of autumn reds and golds, the smooth lawns still beautifully green, varied flowers still brightly gracing the garden with their blooms.

Shay walked slowly amongst the beauty, strangely at peace, even though she had fought so hard against coming back here. But last night had given her no choice. She couldn't stay alone with Lyon at her mews home, and he wouldn't leave unless she had him physically thrown out. And they all knew that if she did that there would be a great deal of publicity, publicity she no more wanted than Lyon did.

Last night had given her no choice but to pack her bags and drive down to Falconer House. At least here there were other people to blunt Lyon's threatening behaviour. And she did consider him a threat. Lyon had hurt her physically as well as emotionally six years ago, and he could do it again if he were given the opportunity. She had tried to tell herself that last night had happened because of her heightened sensuality due to her pregnancy; it was a well known fact that hormonal changes in a pregnant woman often made her feel sexy. And yet that explanation didn't quite describe her behaviour, not when it had been with a man she hated. And that admission had drawn another one from her; the attraction she had always felt for Lyon couldn't be as dead as she had believed it to be.

And so she had run—for there could be no other explanation for what she had done. After years of seeming almost as much an enemy as Lyon was Falconer House had seemed like her only refuge, a welcoming friend.

Matthew had been pleased to see her, had asked for no explanation of her unexpected arrival, seeming to know it had something to do with his older brother. Her suite was ready as it always was, and the two of them had later lunched together before he returned to the office to work. With a mocking promise not to tell Lyon she was there. Matthew's warped, and often cruel, sense of humour allowed him to see something amusing about the situation. She wished she could see it too!

'He'll find you, you know.'

She turned to face Matthew as he joined her in the garden, the Falconer Estate designed to cater for his wheelchair, a small ramp bringing him down amongst the beauty of the rose garden. 'I don't happen to be hiding,' Shay told him firmly.

'Aren't you?' His mouth twisted. 'Your attraction towards Lyon always resembled that of the rabbit for the snake.'

Shay bristled indignantly. 'I'm no longer an infatuated eighteen-year-old,' she snapped.

'You were never an infatuated anything,' Matthew told her softly. 'You loved Lyon like no other woman ever has or ever will. Even Ricky knew that.'

'You're wrong,' She shook her head. 'Ricky knew just how much I hated Lyon.'

'Ricky knew he was second-best,' Matthew said gently. 'He always knew that.'

'He never was,' denied Shay heatedly. 'I loved him. We had a good marriage.'

'I know that,' he nodded. 'And I'm glad you were able to make my little brother happy. But we all knew that what you and Lyon had together was the sort of love legends are made of, like Cleopatra and Antony.'

'Their relationship ended tragically too,' she dismissed hardly. 'And Ricky wasn't second-best for me. We had five wonderful years together, and if he had lived I hope we would have had fifty more.'

'Have you ever noticed that sometimes things happen, tragic things at times, that work out to be necessary to the ultimate plan of things?' Matthew spoke thoughtfully.

'Ricky's death could never be necessary in the "plan of things",' Shay cried angrily. 'He was twenty-eight years old, a wonderful man, would have made a wonderful father for our child, so how can you even *think* that his death may have been necessary!'

Matthew shrugged. 'Why did Marilyn suddenly decide she wanted a divorce after all this time?'

'Probably because she realised she was sick of being married to a man like Lyon! And also because she fell in love with Derrick.'

'She's worked with Derrick for years; she didn't just suddenly fall in love with him.'

'Then she just decided it was Lyon she was sick of,' Shay dismissed, unwilling to admit that it had been her own sense of the inevitable that had stopped her falling apart after Ricky's death. She wasn't going to encourage Matthew's idea that all of this was some sort of a master plan! 'You aren't going to tell me that it was also necessary in the "plan of things" to put you in that wheelchair!' she challenged.

She hadn't meant to say anything that hurtful, knew he was deeply wounded as his face grew harshly cold, his hazel eyes frosting over.

'My being in this wheelchair is through my own damned stupidity,' he rasped.

'Matthew, I—'

'I thought I knew it all,' he bit out, lost in bitter memories. 'I came down from the top of that mountain as if I were floating on air. And then it all went wrong,' he said flatly. 'I lost control, flew off the side of the mountain at a tremendous speed. When I reached the bottom I couldn't move my legs. I haven't moved them since.'

'Oh, Matthew, I'm sorry!' She went down on her haunches beside his chair, grasping his tensed hands. 'I didn't mean it. I—'

'It's all right, Gypsy.' Hazel eyes had softened compassionately as he gently squeezed her hands in his own. 'I was intruding where I had no right to be.'

'No—'

'Have you ever known me to be wrong?' he mocked with teasing arrogance.

'Matthew, I shouldn't have said what I did,' Shay told him determinedly, tears in her eyes for the way this strong man suffered every day of his life for a youthful impetuosity.

'Neither should I,' he said ruefully. 'By this time I should have learnt to mind my own business.'

She moistened her lips, still crouched down in front of him. 'Did Ricky tell you—did he really think he was second-best?'

Matthew patted her hand. 'It didn't matter to him, all he ever wanted was you.'

'But—'

'Gypsy, you can't change the past, unfortunately that's something that will always be with us.'

Perhaps she had once loved Lyon the way Matthew believed she had, but Ricky, of all people, had to know she had stopped loving him; Matthew just couldn't have realised that.

'I'm only concerned with the future, the future of my baby and me,' she told him firmly.

The man who watched her knew that he was going to be included in that future. She was a magnificent creature, her purple eyes glowing, the black hair cascading down past her shoulders. She was proudly pregnant in the pale lilac dress, a dark-eyed gypsy of a woman burgeoning with her child.

He knew every silken inch of that body beneath the dress, knew that she had run from him because he knew her so well. Last night her body had quivered beneath his hands, had cried out for the release he could give her, a release she had finally denied herself.

But she couldn't go on fighting him for ever, and the relief of finding her here far outweighed the anger he had felt at her disappearance from London. Although he didn't particularly like the way she and Matthew were holding hands.

'We're all concerned about that, Shay.' Lyon stepped out of the house, looking down at them, his mouth tightening at the way Shay was instantly on her guard as she straightened. Perhaps he should go a little slower with her, give her a chance to get used to his being back in her life. If only he didn't want her so much!

'You're early,' Matthew drawled.

Lyon looked coldly at his brother. 'Keeping tabs on me, Matthew?' he rasped.

Matthew's mouth quirked. 'Not particularly. We just weren't expecting you just yet. I don't think Shay was expecting you at all.'

Lyon gave his brother an impatient look before turning to Shay, his mouth thinning at how pale she had become. She was frightened of him! What the hell did she expect him to do, *force* himself on her? He had never needed to use force

on Shay, and he knew he would never need to do
so now either.

'I telephoned the house,' he revealed flatly.
'Mrs Devon told me you had packed your suitcases and gone. She's very worried about you,'
he added reprovingly.

'I told her not to be,' Shay said jerkily.

He gave a scornful snort. 'None of us can
turn our emotions off just because we're told
to!'

Emotions? This man didn't even know what
they were!

She had been grateful to Matthew as he was the
one to answer Lyon's opening comment, not
certain she would have been able to if pressed,
her mouth going suddenly dry. Lyon had looked
dangerous as he stepped out on to the terrace, his
eyes flinty, totally unlike the liquid-eyed man
that had oiled her body the evening before. She
had known he would be angry at her sudden
departure from her mews home, but already
she felt safer from his threats with the cryptic
Matthew as a buffer between them. This man
wasn't going to make an emotional conquest of
her a second time!

'*You* can, Lyon,' she derided haughtily.
'You've always been able to turn your emotions
on and off to suit the occasion.'

Matthew watched them with amusement,
hazel eyes alight with mischief. 'Well?' he
prompted his brother.

Lyon looked at him. 'Well what?' he growled.

A perplexed frown marred Matthew's brow. 'No come-back?' He sounded disappointed.

Lyon's mouth twisted. 'None that I intend making in front of you.'

'You're spoiling my fun,' Matthew drawled.

'Why don't you go and get your own girl and stop interfering in other people's lives?' the other man sighed.

'Don't be so bloody silly!' Matthew exploded angrily, a mulish look to his face as he propelled his wheelchair up the ramp.

'Matthew—'

'Cripples aren't in fashion just now!' Matthew cut icily through Shay's concerned exclamation. 'I won't be joining you for dinner,' he snapped before going inside the house.

Shay turned furiously on Lyon, her eyes deeply purple, almost black. 'You cruel bastard!' she choked.

He didn't even flinch at her unrestrained anger. 'The only cruelty I can see is that there isn't a rose out here to match the colour of your eyes,' he smiled at her warmly, bending to pick a delicately pale pink bloom. 'This will have to do instead.' He tucked the flower behind her ear, a vivid splash of colour against the ebony of her hair.

'Lyon, you've just hurt Matthew unbearably, how can you talk about roses!' she demanded incredulously, impatiently ignoring the tingle in her cheek where his fingers had grazed the skin.

'Matthew isn't hurt—'

'You taunted him in the cruellest way possible,' Shay accused indignantly. 'How do you think he feels being stuck in that chair for the rest of his life?'

'I know how he feels,' Lyon dismissed. 'But he's had lovers in the past.'

'Not for a very long time.' Her heart went out to the younger man, for the almost desperate look in his eyes before it was quickly masked by anger. Matthew was a very self-possessed man, rarely gave in to self-pity about his disability, and for Lyon to have taunted him in that way was the height of cruelty.

'I'll grant you it's been a few years,' Lyon shrugged. 'But that's been his own choice.'

Her eyes widened. 'Are you saying—Is—Can he—'

'Take a woman to bed and give them both satisfaction?' Lyon finished mockingly. 'As I remember it he can do that very well.'

'But he—Even now?' she squeaked. In all the years she had known Matthew she had never seen him with a woman, had believed because of that that he was incapable of a physical relationship.

Lyon nodded. 'It's a little awkward for him, I'm sure, but it is possible.'

'I had no idea,' Shay said dazedly. 'But you told me he would never marry?' she frowned.

'And he won't,' Lyon confirmed tightly. 'He doesn't want to burden any woman by having him as a husband.'

'But any woman that really loved him wouldn't find his disability a burden,' she protested.

Lyon's mouth tightened. 'His fiancée didn't feel that way.'

'He was engaged at the time of the accident?' Shay gasped.

Lyon nodded. 'It isn't something he talks about, and so no one else does either. Everyone has something they would prefer to keep to themselves,' he bit out tautly. 'Don't you?'

Her eyes were suddenly huge in her pale face. 'I—I think I'll go and freshen up before dinner.' She turned away, Lyon's hand on her arm stopping her from leaving.

'Coming here changes nothing, Shay,' he rasped. 'Matthew won't help you.'

She looked at him with glittering eyes. ''I've come here as *you* wanted me to do!'

He smiled, the merest curve of finely sculptured lips. 'I want more than that, and you know it.'

She looked at him coldly. 'All you'll ever get from me is the contempt you deserve!'

The smile stayed confidently in place. 'And a response you can't deny,' he drawled.

She wrenched away from him, breathing hard. 'Is that all you've ever wanted from me, a sexual response?'

'One of the things,' he confirmed softly. 'Lousy sex can deteriorate a relationship quicker than anything else.'

A coldness came over her. 'And sex alone is the

surest end to a relationship,' she challenged.

'We aren't just going to have sex between us, Shay,' he mocked. 'Now tell me, did you take your rest this afternoon?'

She frowned suspiciously. 'Of course. But what does that have to do with you?'

'I'm showing a little natural concern,' he shrugged. 'Just trying to find out if you had a restful and relaxing day.'

Her expression was contemptuous as she suddenly realised what he was doing. 'Am I now supposed to go inside and pour you a drink before we talk over the events of our respective days?' she scorned.

'It would be nice—'

'It would be impossible!' Shay snapped. 'I'm not your wife, Lyon, I'll never be anything to you ever again. Just because your wife has finally decided to kick you out of her life is no reason for you to think I'm interested in taking up where she left off!'

'You know that Marilyn and I haven't had what could be called a marriage for years,' he said icily.

'And whose fault was that?'

Lyon stiffened. 'Mine,' he finally bit out.

'Exactly,' Shay scorned. 'I had a good marriage with Ricky—'

'It was safe,' Lyon corrected harshly. 'That doesn't necessarily mean it was good!'

She gave him a pitiful glance. 'It was good,' she repeated flatly. 'Now you can take your "natural concern" and find some other poor woman to bestow it on.' She made it sound like an insult. 'There must be hundreds of women who would just love to be your mistress!' she derided, pulling the rose from her hair and thrusting it into his hands. 'Gestures like this are wasted on me!' She followed Matthew into the house, no less angry than he.

Hundreds of woman was probably an exaggeration, although the power of money certainly appealed to a lot of women, and the fact that he didn't look like a monster and wasn't nearly in his grave had always helped him attract women too.

Before Shay, he had taken as many of those women as it amused him to, even after Shay he had taken women to his bed. But never more than once; he couldn't bear to see the same woman in his bed more than that.

His life had consisted of before, and after, Shay. And he was determined it would now be *with* Shay. And whatever her child happened to be. It would be *their* child, he was determined on that too.

And he knew Shay was just as determined she would never be his again. She must have forgotten how arrogantly sure of himself he could be when he wanted something badly enough.

He was so arrogantly sure of himself and what he wanted!

He had been the same when she had first met him; but he couldn't get away with it now! Lyon had always wanted what he couldn't have, and at the moment she presented a challenge to him.

'Plotting his downfall?'

Matthew's door stood open as she passed his suite of rooms on the way to her own, Matthew seated at his desk in front of the window. Shay realised, with embarrassment, that this room overlooked the rose garden!

'Murder would be more like it,' she drawled, strolling into the room, casually standing next to the window, a quick glance outside showing her Lyon striding off in the direction of the stables. Her eyes glittered angrily as she turned back to Matthew. 'You voyeur!'

He returned her gaze steadily. 'You didn't look as if you were making love.'

'Far from it,' she snapped, high points of colour in her cheeks. 'In fact, we—' Shay turned as a movement outside caught her eye, a horse and rider coming out of the cobbled stable-yard to ride off towards the woods at the back of the house. Lyon seemed like part of the golden stallion as they moved fluidly together, only Lyon's business shirt and trousers seeming out of place as he still wore the clothes he had been to work in.

'When you and Ricky lived here riding half the night away seemed to be the only way Lyon could get through them,' Matthew told her softly.

She turned to him sharply, Matthew slowly moving from looking at his brother to meet her gaze.

'It's true,' he assured her huskily. 'Sometimes he wouldn't come home until dawn.'

'He was probably meeting a woman,' Shay dismissed scornfully.

Matthew shook his head. 'He couldn't bear to be in the same house as you and Ricky, knowing the two of you were probably making love. But he couldn't stay away from here either.'

Delicate colour flooded her cheeks once again. 'You're crediting Lyon with a sensitivity he just doesn't possess!' she snapped.

'And you're judging him too harshly,' replied Matthew gruffly.

'You have no idea what happened between us,' Shay told him heatedly.

'There are a lot of things I don't know, or even understand. Why Lyon stayed married to a woman he didn't love while the woman he did love married his brother being one of them!' he acknowledged coldly.

'Lyon never loved me!'

'You can't be that stupid!'

'I—' She broke off abruptly, turning back to the window once again, the golden stallion looking wild as it galloped across the grass towards the stable—its rider nowhere in sight! She moistened suddenly dry lips. 'Matthew, you don't think—'

'No, I don't *think*!' He moved to pick up the telephone, dialling quickly. 'Jackson? Wildfire is coming back alone! Yes! The west woods. Right now!' he instructed harshly, slamming down the receiver to join Shay in front of the window, his anxious gaze scanning the fields and woods to the west of the house.

Shay couldn't move, felt the ice creeping over the whole of her body, knew that if she did attempt to move she would break into a thousand pieces. Lyon was an excellent rider, had been riding horses as feisty as Wildfire since long before she had met him. She couldn't believe he had been thrown. Maybe Wildfire had loosened his tether—She jumped nervously as the telephone shrilled loudly in the deathly-quiet room.

'Yes?' Matthew barked into the mouthpiece. 'Hell!' he rasped roughly. 'Yes, get everyone out there looking.' He turned to Shay after replacing the receiver for the second time in minutes, his eyes dark with worry and fear. Fear? Yes, Shay was sure she could see the emotion in those deeply hazel depths.

That same fear gripped her now. She had wanted to do Lyon physical harm six years ago, but she hadn't wanted him dead! 'What is it, Matthew?' she gasped anxiously.

He swallowed convulsively. 'Wildfire came back without a saddle,' he bit out tautly.

Shay frowned; it wasn't like Lyon to be careless. God, could their conversation in the garden have so disturbed him he hadn't been his usual meticulously careful self when he saddled Wildfire? If that were true, and anything serious happened to him—

'Don't let your imagination run wild, Shay,' Matthew ordered abruptly. 'It could turn out that all that's injured is his pride,' he added ruefully.

She knew that Lyon would be furious with himself if it were his carelessness that had been the cause of his fall. But that would be far preferable than for him to have been seriously hurt. 'I'll go downstairs and wait for news,' she told Matthew breathlessly.

'Shay—!'

She turned at the door, her face pale with worry. 'Yes?'

'Don't blame yourself if—if it's bad news.' He looked at her with dark eyes.

'I have nothing to feel guilty about,' she snapped.

He shrugged. 'Tell that to the rose crushed into the ground down there.'

She swallowed hard. 'I'll come back and let you know as soon as there's any news.'

She couldn't wait in the house, walked over to the stables, most of the employees and horses out looking for Lyon. He couldn't have gone far, so what was taking them so long? She hated the man, but this family had suffered enough of a loss when Ricky died.

'Why doesn't someone let us know what's happening?' she demanded of Jackson as he tried to soothe the golden stallion, the muscled body quivering in his distress.

'They will as soon as they find Mr Falconer,' the elderly man assured her calmly, revealing none of his own concern for the man he had sat on his first horse as a young boy, picking him up and putting him back in the saddle if he should fall off. This time there might be no getting back on . . .

'Yes, but—' She turned as one of the stable-hands galloped back into the yard.

'Mr Falconer is only bruised,' he gasped breathlessly. 'Jim's bringing him in on Cinnamon,' he announced before riding off again.

With Shay's relief at the news came anger at her own reaction to the accident. She shouldn't have *cared* if Lyon lived or died!

'It's good news, Mrs Falconer,' Jackson prompted softly as she seemed on the verge of collapse.

'Yes,' she acknowledged jerkily, shaking herself out of her dazed state; she wouldn't be here when Lyon returned! 'I have to go and tell Matthew.' She turned and almost ran back to the house, deliberately blocking all thought from her mind.

Matthew was very open about his own relief, the grey cast to his cheeks seemed to lessen slightly.

'I'm going to my suite,' Shay told him abruptly.

His eyes widened. 'Aren't you going to stay and see Lyon?'

'No,' she rasped.

Matthew shook his head. 'Don't be so hard on yourself, Shay,' he chided softly.

She stiffened. 'I don't know what you mean.'

His mouth twisted. 'This love-hate relationship

you have with Lyon will be the death of someone.'

'Then let's hope that it's Lyon!' she snapped
angrily.

She was shaking uncontrollably by the time she
shut the door to her suite. She *didn't* care whether
Lyon lived or died, she wouldn't let herself care!
The man had almost destroyed her once, she
just wished she had a way of destroying him as
thoroughly.

She looked beautiful when she was asleep, those
hate-filled eyes covered by palely translucent
lids, her mouth soft and inviting.

But she also looked exhausted, and it wasn't
surprising after what Matthew had told him. She
shouldn't be distressed any further in her condition, and Wildfire coming back alone seemed to
have done that.

He had come straight to her suite after leaving
Matthew, only the pain in his leg where Wildfire
had trampled on him in his fright to show he had
fallen from the horse. Shay was sleeping, and he
stood watching her for long, timeless minutes.
The witch did care, he was sure of it. He was also
sure she would fight the emotion with everything
in her. And that was quite a lot.

She moved in her sleep, making one of those
purring sounds in her throat that instantly made
his blood boil, desire surging forward, his hands
itching to touch her. She moved restlessly as
one of his hands lay over the baby inside her,

turning on her side with his hand trapped beneath her. The gentlemanly thing to do would be to extract his hand gently and leave. But his feelings for Shay had never been gentlemanly, lying down at her side to curve his body into the back of hers. God, she felt good. He shuddered against her, his hand moving from the baby to her breast, his heart leaping with exhilaration as she eagerly turned towards him.

'Ricky?' she murmured lovingly, her face aglow.

Lyon froze, continuing to hold her until her movements settled, and then slowly easing away from her to stand up. Even in her sleep she called out for his brother!

His leg hurt unbearably as he swung up on to Wildfire's back for the second time that night, urging him out of the cobbled yard, his expression set grimly as he knew he would probably ride until dawn.

Shay woke slowly. She had been having the most wonderful dream, Ricky had been beside her, holding her, enveloping her in the love he had always shown her. Even once she was awake, and aware he was dead, the feeling of well-being stayed with her, almost as if she had Ricky back.

It wasn't until she returned from the bathroom that she saw the indentation on the pillow beside her own, as if someone had lain beside her on the bed. Even if she believed in ghosts, she knew they didn't leave such a human sign of their presence. Lyon had been here, not Ricky!

She looked up angrily as a knock sounded on the door. 'Yes?' She wrenched open the door, only to find it was Patty and not Lyon who stood outside. She gave an embarrassed grimace for her rudeness. 'I'm sorry, I—' She stopped herself from saying she had thought it was Lyon. 'I'm usually a bit crotchety when I wake up,' she excused.

The other woman nodded, about Shay's own age, perhaps a little older. 'I've brought your dinner up for you,' she explained, placing the tray on the table in front of the window. 'Mr Falconer thought you might prefer that tonight,' she smiled.

'Lyon shouldn't have made such a decision for me,' she snapped. 'He—'

'Oh, not that Mr Falconer.' Patty looked concerned by her anger. 'This was *Matthew* Falconer.'

Shay felt the aggression go out of her. She was picking on this unfortunate woman for no reason! But she had become so used to Lyon trying to interfere in her life that she had just assumed it was him this time. 'That was very thoughtful of Matthew,' she smiled. 'I don't really feel up to a family dinner this evening.'

'Matthew is eating in his rooms too.' The other woman unloaded the tray, attractively arranging the meal on the table. 'And Lyon isn't eating at all.' She straightened, frowning. 'One of the

stable-boys said he's gone out on Wildfire again.'
She sounded censorious.

Shay nodded dismissively to the other woman,
more sure than ever that Lyon left the house in
that way to be with a woman.

He had already left for work when she came
downstairs next morning, even though she had
made an effort to come down earlier than she
usually did just so that she could speak to him.
She didn't even feel safe from him when she was
asleep any more, had half expected to wake up
and find him next to her this morning.

Matthew was scowling when she joined him at
the table, his coffee black, a sure sign that he was
very angry about something—or someone.

'Who's upset you this morning?' she mocked
lightly as she buttered a slice of toast.

Matthew glared at her. 'I'll give you one guess!'

Her mouth quirked. 'Not your dear brother
Lyon?' she taunted.

Matthew crushed his napkin in his hand, as if
he wished it were something more tangible he
could squeeze the life out of. 'He's hardly ever
here any more, and yet he refuses to let me
dismiss a new employee who's turned out to be
incompetent!'

Shay sipped her coffee, looking at him curiously over the rim of her cup. It wasn't like
Matthew to lose his temper over anything, usually shielding his real feelings behind a wall of
mockery. 'I'm sure he must have a reason,' she
shrugged.

'I can't imagine what!' he snapped. 'The woman is obviously not cut out to be a maid!'

Shay's eyes widened. 'You surely aren't talking about Patty?' she frowned.

He glared. 'You aren't going to start defending her too, are you?'

She couldn't understand his vehemence. 'I've always found her very helpful and friendly.'

'But hardly maid material,' Matthew insisted forcefully.

Shay frowned thoughtfully. Patty did her work willingly and well, but now that Matthew mentioned it the other woman did have an air of pride and intelligence that didn't quite fit with the career she had chosen for herself. But perhaps the fact that it was a job without pressure suited the other woman; some people preferred to opt out of the constant competition some careers necessitated.

'You can't sack someone just because they don't look the part,' she chided her brother-in-law. 'I like her.'

'You and Lyon both!' he complained, turning to leave, stopping to look back at her. 'Lyon was out until dawn again last night,' he derided. 'It's just like old times.'

'Surely it's his affair?' Shay said primly, almost groaning at the pun she had made without intending to do so. 'It probably *is* an affair, Matthew,' she scorned.

'You can't really believe that,' he exclaimed.

'Lyon's a little too old to be changing his habits

now,' she said dryly.

He shook his head. 'I'm beginning to wonder if you ever really knew him.'

'Ricky knew him well, and he didn't trust him either!'

'Ricky was biased,' Matthew muttered.

'I beg your pardon?' Her eyes widened.

'Never mind,' he dismissed. 'Have I told you that you look beautiful today?'

'No,' she smiled. 'You haven't.'

'Pregnancy suits you,' he said with sincerity.

She was enjoying being pregnant, the nausea long gone, the tiredness easily dealt with by her short naps in the day. She felt well, and she knew she looked well, the bruises from her fall almost gone now, the stitches in her thigh almost ready to come out, the wound only slightly irritating now.

She was in her suite working when Patty came up to tell her she had a visitor, slightly surprised to learn that it was Derrick Stewartby calling on her. She left her work reluctantly, regretting having to do so when she had been doing so well.

It was the first time she had seen Derrick since the day of the funeral, and away from the overpowering masculinity of the Falconer men, she acknowledged that he was a very handsome man, tall and dark, with distinctive wings of silver at his temples, warm blue eyes, with an attractive rather than strictly good-looking face. She guessed him to be somewhere in his early forties.

'How nice to see you again.' Shay put out her hand in a friendly gesture, liking the firm but brief way he returned the politeness.

His mouth twisted ruefully. 'Although you don't really understand what I'm doing here,' he said self-derisively.

It would be useless to deny that, although now that he was here she felt she probably owed him an apology. 'I'm glad you are,' she smiled. 'I—I think perhaps I wasn't very polite to you the last time we met, and—'

He waved away the apology with a flick of his hand. 'Under the circumstances, I'm surprised you noticed me at all,' he dismissed softly. 'It was your husband's funeral, and you had no idea who I was or what I was doing there.'

'No,' she acknowledged huskily. 'Nevertheless—'

'Shay, I'm going to marry a woman you don't even like very much, you don't owe me any apologies for the distress you felt that day.' He shook his head, smiling tightly. 'Marilyn behaved disgracefully towards you; I can only say that she's finding the experience of the divorce more traumatic than she realised.'

Shay wished she had this man's understanding—or was it a blind spot?—where Marilyn was concerned. But as far as she was concerned the other woman had always been a bitch, the day of Ricky's funeral proving no exception.

'Actually,' Derrick spoke briskly as he saw the scepticism in her face, 'I expected to find Marilyn here with you, but the maid told me she hasn't arrived yet.'

Shay's brows rose in surprise. 'Marilyn is coming to see me?'

He nodded. 'She asked me to meet her here on my way back from an appointment.' He glanced at his watch. 'But I have to get back to the office.' He frowned. 'Perhaps you could explain to her that I couldn't wait?'

'Of course,' Shay assured him absently, wondering why Marilyn could possibly be going to call on her. 'Er—Do you have any idea why she wants to see me?' she asked Derrick.

'Something to do with your husband's will, I believe,' he shrugged.

Her brow cleared. 'Could I offer you something to drink before you leave?'

He smiled his gratitude at this show of friendliness on her part. 'I really don't have the time, but thank you, anyway.' He gave a rueful smile.

Shay felt sorry for him, knew it couldn't be easy loving a woman like Marilyn. But she was grateful to him for giving her warning of Marilyn's visit, even if it had been unintentional, ready for the other woman when she breezed into the lounge a short time later, having been too tense after Derrick's visit to return to her work upstairs, flicking disinterestedly through a magazine as she waited for the other woman. She hadn't had to wait long.

'The maid informed me I've just missed Derrick,' Marilyn greeted waspishly, her red hair a vivid splash of colour against the black severity of the suit she wore with a white blouse beneath, her make-up perfect as usual. The other woman certainly didn't look the thirty-five she must now be.

'Yes, he said he had to get back,' Shay confirmed. 'He's a nice man,' she said tentatively.

'Very,' the other woman snapped, the smile she gave not quite reaching her eyes. 'I've brought those papers that I wanted you to look through,' she explained her presence in what used to be her home.

Shay nodded, Derrick having already told her that, smiling her thanks to Patty as she brought them in a pot of coffee. 'I could have driven up to town,' she told Marilyn lightly.

'Not with Lyon watching over you like some mother-hen,' Marilyn snapped. 'He seems to think you're made out of delicate china!' she scorned.

Shay only skimmed reading the contents of Ricky's will, knew already what it outlined; she and Ricky had had no secrets from each other.

'He's received no encouragement from me,' she snapped resentfully.

'Lyon never needed any where you were concerned,' the other woman sighed. 'He went berserk once he realised you were half an hour late for our appointment last week. Are you feeling better now?' she asked in a bored voice.

Marilyn certainly hadn't changed in the last six years, she had always been interested only in

herself and the things that directly affected her,
and she never tried to make a secret of that fact.

'Almost completely.' Shay handed back the
papers, watching as the other woman put them
away in her briefcase. 'Would you like some
coffee?' she offered politely.

'Thanks,' Marilyn drawled, watching as Shay
stood up to cross the room to the tray of coffee.
'God, aren't you uncomfortable?' she suddenly
exclaimed.

Shay shrugged, knowing how ungainly she
looked at just over seven months' pregnant, often
feeling very uncomfortable indeed. But she
wasn't about to admit that to Marilyn! 'Not really,' she shrugged. 'It's all a question of priorities; I
want this baby.'

Marilyn didn't try to hide her disgust as Shay
eased gingerly down into her chair. 'You and
Lyon both. But aren't I glad I never had to go
through a pregnancy,' she confided. 'Lyon
seemed to think it was very important that we
couldn't have children. I didn't like to tell him
how relieved I've always been.'

Shay stiffened, a frown marring her brow. 'I
didn't realise you couldn't have children,' she
said breathlessly, perhaps better understanding
why the marriage had broken down if there had
been a conflict on the subject.

'I didn't say that,' Marilyn snapped indignantly.

'But—'

'There's nothing wrong with me!' the other

woman asserted quickly. 'I'm sure it isn't going to hurt to tell you this, Lyon is very virile, a fantastic lover, but it just doesn't lead to anything,' she jeered.

Shay swallowed hard, sure she had gone white. 'Are you saying it's Lyon's fault you've never had children?' she croaked. 'That he's sterile?'

'Of course,' Marilyn dismissed.

'Are you sure?' Shay frowned.

'After trying since the beginning of our marriage, we had all the tests done when I hadn't conceived after two years. The specialist told us it was Lyon's fault I hadn't become pregnant.' Marilyn's mouth twisted mockingly. 'The Americans have a deliciously crude way of describing what's wrong with Lyon,' she said with relish. 'Something to do with "shooting—"'

'I've heard it,' Shay cut in absently, her thoughts racing. So Lyon wanted *her*, did he? He was as deceitful as ever, wanted her *baby* not her! She must seem ideal to him now, a very pregnant widow who could give him the child he had always wanted.

But she finally had it, the one weakness in the man she had believed not to have any. She had retribution for what Lyon had done to her six years before, and that retribution was her silence!

CHAPTER EIGHT

THERE was something different about her
tonight. He couldn't put his finger on exactly
what it was, except that she seemed filled with an
inner serenity.

After yesterday, he had expected her to avoid
him at all costs, to continue to eat in her suite. She
had greeted him at the dinner table with a query
about his health after his fall yesterday. Matthew's expression had clearly mocked his stunned
surprise.

She had continued to glow through dinner, to
charm both him and Matthew with her light-
hearted teasing. And he didn't trust this change
in her one little bit!

He turned to Matthew as he realised his
brother was looking at him expectantly. 'Sorry?'

Matthew's mouth twisted derisively, clearly
taunting Lyon's lack of attention to the conversation. 'Maybe if you took a little more interest in
what was being said . . . ?' he mocked.

One of these days he was going to do Matthew
some physical injury! 'I'm listening,' he grated.

Hazel eyes gleamed with the enjoyment of
disconcerting Lyon. 'Shay and I were just discussing Christmas.'

Lyon stiffened warily, sure Shay would want

to spend the holiday with her grandfather in Ireland, and equally sure he couldn't let her travel only days before the baby was due to be born. 'Yes?' he prompted guardedly.

'What do you think to the idea of letting Shay organise the party this year?' Matthew queried.

'Oh no, I couldn't,' she protested. 'I—'

'You aren't going to Ireland!' God, when was he going to learn to hold off on the arrogance with this woman, especially when she was holding a coffee cup in her hand!

She stiffened resentfully, her eyes more purple than ever, but the angry retort he had been expecting didn't materialise, and although it trembled slightly, the cup remained in her hands. 'I do realise it would be too close to having the baby,' she said stiltedly. 'What I was about to say,' her eyes flashed, 'was that I wouldn't feel right organising the party when it's something Marilyn usually does.'

He clamped his lips together to stop himself from pointing out that it would be far from the first time she had performed a duty in his life Marilyn used to do! That would guarantee the cup being thrown in his direction, he was sure of it. 'Marilyn no longer lives here,' he rasped. 'And although I don't want you to tire yourself, as the mistress of the house, the organisation of the party is now up to you.' He looked at her challengingly.

Her gaze met that challenge before she cut into,

him. 'You're right,' she drawled. 'Ricky would have wanted me to do it.'

Bitch, he inwardly groaned, reeling from the blow she had deliberately dealt him.

Shay enjoyed seeing Lyon flinch, intended to make him suffer as she had once suffered. Before she had finished with him Lyon would be as desolate as she had once been.

She had given away none of her elation to Marilyn that morning for her revelation, had even invited the other woman to stay to lunch. She had refused, thank goodness.

But Shay no longer felt as if she were floundering about in the wake of Lyon's much stronger nature, felt confident to deal with him now, no longer even minded giving in to his arrogance at times. She had a secret knowledge that she would keep to herself, knew about Lyon now, and felt comforted by it.

She would enjoy organising the party the family usually gave at Christmas for relatives and friends, knew that as Ricky's widow she had a right to the rôle. 'Yes, I'd like to do it,' she smiled. 'And you can help me, Matthew.'

'Me?' His eyes widened. 'I've never organised a party in my life!'

'Well, you're going to help organise one now,' Shay told him firmly.

'You never used to be as bossy as this,' he muttered.

'This is what happens after living with a man

for five years who totally indulged me,' she teased, looking up enquiringly as she heard Lyon draw in a hissing breath. 'Something wrong, Lyon?' she taunted.

A nerve pulsed in his jaw. 'You're living here with Matthew and me now,' he ground out unsteadily.

'You make it sound almost indecent,' she mocked. 'When really Matthew loves me as a sister, and you—well, you aren't quite the same, are you?' she added huskily.

His eyes were narrowed. 'If you mean I don't think of you as a sister too, the answer is no!'

'But I didn't mean that at all, Lyon,' she said mockingly. 'I meant that you probably have a woman in your life already.'

'There's no other woman,' he bit out.

'"Other" woman, Lyon?' she repeated softly. 'What do you mean?'

His eyes gleamed golden. 'I told you that Matthew being here won't help you, and I meant it,' he jeered harshly. 'There is no other woman in my life because I'm going to have *you*,' he told her bluntly. 'Just as soon as you've had the baby.' He marched out of the room.

'And you can't say clearer than that,' Matthew drawled ruefully.

'Can't you?' Shay looked at him with hard eyes. Matthew couldn't be aware of Lyon's problem, and she could guess why; Lyon's pride would dictate as few people knew about it as possible. But because she knew she was also aware of something else Matthew couldn't even begin to guess. As a pregnant widow, she was considered an ideal candidate for Lyon's second wife, but he was going carefully, not making any definite commitment until he was sure the baby was all right. She was even going to enjoy letting him think she might eventually come round to that idea herself!

'Gypsy, the man is frantic to have you,' Matthew chided.

'Because I'm unattainable,' she snapped.

'Are you?' he mocked. 'Last night when Wildfire came back alone I could have sworn you felt something for my big brother.'

Shay's eyes were cold. 'For a moment I forgot it was Lyon who had been thrown,' she bit out.

'I don't think I believe that.' He shook his head.

'Believe what you like, Matthew,' she dismissed brittly, 'but Lyon will never have me again.'

'Whatever he did—'

'You'll never know what he did,' she cut in. 'Now let's give some thought to this party, shall we?' she suggested brightly.

Matthew, for all that he said he knew nothing about arranging parties, knew the names of the caterers and other people Marilyn had always used in the past, but while Shay wrote them down she wasn't sure she was going to use them; they would expect things to be done the way Marilyn had always had them, and this was going to be *her* party.

Lyon didn't come back into the lounge, she and Matthew playing a game of cards once they had sorted out the details of the party, a smile curving Shay's lips as she walked up the stairs to her bedroom shortly after eleven o'clock.

She almost collided with Patty as the other woman came out of one of the rooms. 'I'm sorry,' she smiled as she steadied the other woman. 'I—' Shay broke off as she realised *which* room Patty was leaving, slowly turning to look in the still open doorway at Lyon sprawled out on his bed wearing only his robe. 'I didn't mean to interrupt,' she drawled scornfully.

Patty looked stricken, a flush to her cheeks. 'Shay—Mrs Falconer, I—'

'There's no need to feel embarrassed,' she dismissed lightly.

'But I was only—'

'It's really none of my business what you were doing,' Shay shrugged. No wonder Lyon refused to have the other woman dismissed; she was *his* latest woman! Pity, she liked Patty.

'What Patty is trying to say, Shay,' Lyon declared heavily, having joined them at the door, 'is that she only came up to bring me some cream for my leg. As you can see, it's badly bruised,' he drawled.

She could imagine the livid purple and black bruising on his shin from his fall off Wildfire was very painful, but that hardly allowed for one of the maids creeping out of his bedroom this time of night. Her expression of contempt clearly told him that.

His mouth tightened. 'You can go now, Patty,' he bit out. 'And thank you for the cream.'

'Really, Lyon,' Shay drawled once Patty had hurried down the stairs. 'She's too nice for you.'

'You—'

'Poor Matthew just thinks you're behaving with your usual arrogance by insisting Patty not be dismissed,' she mused.

'Matthew dislikes Patty only because she's the maid that found him when he fell out of his chair that day,' Lyon told her roughly. 'He's been trying to get rid of her ever since.'

'And, of course, you can't allow that to happen,' Shay mocked knowingly.

'What you saw just now was perfectly innocent,' he claimed angrily.

'Of course it was,' she derided.

'Shay—'

'Shouldn't you go and put some of the cream on that leg?' She raised mocking brows.

'Shay, I won't be called a liar,' declared Lyon tautly.

Her eyes flashed fire. 'Then maybe you should keep your latest bed-companion from the house while you're trying to convince me I'm the only woman you want in your life!'

His mouth tightened. 'It *is* you I want!'

'Of course it is,' she agreed pityingly.

'Shay, you know I want you,' he groaned. 'You know how much I need you!'

'Do you, Lyon?' She looked up at him enticingly. 'How much do you need me?'

He swallowed convulsively. 'Come inside and I'll show you,' he said raggedly.

'The baby . . . ?'

'I'll be gentle,' he promised achingly, his hand on her arm as he pulled her inside his bedroom.

'Peter Dunbar said I shouldn't—'

'I won't make love to you, just—just hold you.' He closed the bedroom door to take her in his arms, shaking with the force of his need. 'Shay, let me take care of you.'

She held herself stiffly in his arms, not able to relax even to cause him pain. 'You are taking care of me by having me at the house.'

'I don't mean that.' He looked down at her with tawny eyes. 'The other night I left you unsatisfied, tonight I want to give you the release you need.'

'No!' She tried to pull away from him, realising this had gone much further than she had intended. She had only meant to tease a little, not let him fire that aching desire again.

'Yes,' he insisted forcefully. 'Shay, you know there's nothing wrong with that sort of lovemaking. It's still me giving you pleasure.'

After their second night together all those years ago she hadn't been ashamed to enjoy that aspect of sensual pleasure with him, she just had no intention of giving this man satisfaction ever again, even that of knowing he had pleasured her.

'I don't think so, Lyon,' she told him coldly, stepping back out of his arms, enjoying the look of bewilderment on his face at this sudden change in her. Too many times, in the past and recent months, she had been the one at the disadvantage.

'Shay?' He eyed her suspiciously. 'A minute ago—'

'You were in your bedroom with one of the maids.' She gave a mocking laugh. 'Really, Lyon,' she chided tauntingly, 'you're getting more like Leon de Coursey every day!'

His mouth tightened. 'What are you trying to do to me, Shay? Tonight when I came home you were the solicitous sister-in-law, then you deliberately caused an argument between us, and just now you were teasingly inviting—'

'I think you're mistaken, Lyon, none of that sounds like me,' she scorned.

Lyon looked impatient, his hands thrust into the pockets of his robe. 'I don't think I know you any more, Shay,' he sighed. 'But I'm going to have you.'

'And the baby,' she prodded tautly.

'You don't think I'd ask you to give it up?' His eyes were angry.

'God, no,' she gave a bitter laugh. 'I know you wouldn't do that.'

He frowned. 'Shay—'

'I have to go, Lyon,' she told him coldly. 'After all, we wouldn't want the staff to start gossiping about the amount of time we spend in each other's bedrooms.' She turned at the door. 'Don't come into my bedroom again like you did last night, Lyon, or I'll scream so loud everyone will think the house is on fire!' With a triumphant smile in his direction she went out into the hallway, leaning back against the door, the scene having taken a lot out of her.

Lyon was being so persistent, so caring, almost loving, and if Marilyn hadn't told her about his sterility she might eventually have begun to believe Lyon's interest in her was genuine.

Retribution could be so sweet!

Sweet, *tormenting* witch! Lyon lay on his bed aching for her, resisting the urge to dress and go down to the stables and saddle Wildfire. Returning at dawn hadn't done him any good last night, he had still prowled his bedroom until he could change and leave for work. Even that had been a disaster, he had done nothing but snap people's heads off all day, wondering if Shay would still be at the house when he returned that evening.

She had been like a drug in his blood since the moment he had first seen her, but now he wouldn't be able to stand the 'withdrawal' symptoms a second time.

But she was playing a game with him—and he had no idea what the rules were!

Shay had always been so open in the past, so candid, even when they met again in Los Angeles this time she had been completely honest—she had plainly shown her hatred of him! But something had happened today to change her from the spitting cat to the contented kitten. The only thing that had happened today that Matthew had told him of was Marilyn's visit, and his wife usually had the effect of alienating Shay from him more than ever. No, he couldn't believe it had been Marilyn's visit that had changed Shay in this way!

Then what was it? God, why couldn't he just accept that she was more amenable towards him and go on from there! But he couldn't, didn't trust the change in Shay, had seen the gleam of satisfaction in her eyes as she had refused his love-making.

Maybe telling her how much he wanted her had been a mistake, had betrayed his one and only weakness; that of needing and wanting Shay so much he would do anything to get her.

The vixen was enjoying this change in rôles that knowledge gave her. But he didn't care, as long as he ultimately got Shay.

He was stifling her, there was no other way to describe the way Lyon was always there!

During the day while he was at work she wasn't allowed to go out except for a gentle walk around the grounds, and the only times she was allowed off the estate was when Lyon himself took her. She was suffocating beneath his constant attention!

This Lyon wasn't the same one she had known six years before, a man who had complained of being harassed if she dared even to telephone him at an unarranged time. Now *he* telephoned her constantly, at least three times a day, and usually at the most inconvenient times.

Matthew thought it was very amusing. 'How many times has he telephoned so far today?' he mocked her at lunch, the two of them usually sharing this meal.

'Three times,' she muttered. 'Once to see if I'd taken my vitamin pills, another time to see if Peter Dunbar had been yet, and another time to see what he had said when he did come,' she sighed. 'As if that's any of his business!'

Matthew shrugged. 'This baby is a family affair, Shay.'

Her eyes frosted over. 'The baby is mine,' she told him flatly.

He gave her a sympathetic look. 'Lyon's only concerned for you.'

'So much so that he insists his latest mistress take care of me,' she snapped.

Matthew stiffened, his eyes narrowed. 'What are you talking about?'

'Patty!' She bit savagely into the apple she was having for dessert, still furious at the way Lyon had informed her a week ago that he was making the other woman her personal maid. Of course she had refused, and of course he had ignored the refusal. Not that she didn't still like the other woman, she did. But knowing what she did about Patty and Lyon made it seem as if he were taking her for a fool a second time.

'You're wrong about that,' Matthew protested. 'They aren't having an affair.'

'Matthew, I know how you always defend Lyon,' she mocked, 'but I actually saw Patty leaving his bedroom late one night.'

'That doesn't prove anything,' he bit out tautly, a nerve pulsing in his cheek.

'She was looking flushed and embarrassed, and Lyon was only wearing his robe,' Shay taunted.

His mouth thinned. 'The bastard!'

'Matthew—'

'I have to get back to work.' He turned his chair and left the room.

Shay frowned after him before shrugging. Lyon *was* a bastard. He also believed he had a place in her life now that she was no longer openly antagonistic to him. But she didn't need to be, hugging to herself what Lyon had no knowledge of, anticipating the day when she would tell him he would have no part in the life of her baby.

She and Matthew had done very well organising the party for Christmas, and she spent the afternoon addressing invitations, not surprised to find Lyon had added Marilyn and Derrick to the already extensive list; he and the other woman may be getting a divorce, but Marilyn was still very much a part of the family. It would greatly surprise Shay if the other woman actually married the innocuous Derrick when she still seemed to care so much for Lyon.

'I thought you had finished your book,' Lyon

rasped as he entered the library shortly after five to find her sitting at the desk in front of the window, a fire burning in the hearth adding to the warmth of the centrally-heated room.

She looked at him with cool eyes. 'I have, it went off to my publisher last week. I'm addressing invitations to the party.'

'Still?' He frowned, standing beside the desk now, a scowl darkening his brow.

He hadn't bothered to shower and change after returning from work before searching her out, still wearing the grey business suit and gleaming white shirt, his tan from the summer having faded now, until sometimes he almost looked white.

'You only telephoned me an hour ago, Lyon,' she mocked.

He looked irritated. 'Couldn't you have asked one of the staff to do them?'

She quirked black brows, her face glowing healthily, the silk dress that was the same colour as her eyes feeling comfortably loose in her eighth month of pregnancy. 'Patty, perhaps?' she derided.

'If I didn't know how ludicrous the idea was I would think you were jealous of her,' Lyon challenged harshly.

Her expression remained bland. 'As you said, the idea is ludicrous.'

He drew in a ragged breath. 'Shay—'

'Lyon, I really would like to finish these invitations tonight.' She pointedly turned away from him, becoming engrossed in the pages of names of the people to be invited to the Christmas party. She and Ricky had given several parties in Los Angeles, but nothing like the scale this guest-list implied!

'Shay, I want to—'

'Ah, there you are.' Matthew was at the door, his expression censorious as he glared at his older brother. 'I called the office and they said you had already left; working part-time now, are you, Lyon?' he sneered.

Lyon looked surprised by the attack, and Shay could understand why. Matthew could often be cryptic and rude, but she had never known him to be this cutting to Lyon before.

Lyon's face darkened even more. 'If I choose to leave a few minutes early I don't feel I have to justify myself to you!'

Hazel eyes met his coldly. '*Excuse me*,' Matthew snapped with sarcasm, 'I believed we were running a business!'

'What the hell is the matter with you, Matthew?' Lyon demanded impatiently.

'If you feel that your—other commitments, prevent you from doing your job properly as Chairman of Falconer Enterprises, then perhaps you ought to resign!'

Shay gasped at the anger and resentment emanating from the younger man. He seemed so—so *bitter*, and it wasn't an emotion she normally associated with him. 'Matthew, if I've done anything—'

'I wasn't talking about you, Shay; you're family.' He still glared at Lyon. 'Well?'

'Well what?' Lyon frowned. 'I'm not resigning, if that's what you mean.'

Matthew looked at the older man with coldly angry eyes. 'Then maybe you ought to think about it!' He turned to leave.

'Matthew!' Lyon's instruction for him to stop sounded like a whip cracking. He strode across the room to join the younger man. 'Maybe we should talk about this—'

'There's nothing to talk about,' Matthew told him harshly.

'I agree you seem to have said it all,' Lyon drawled derisively. 'But I'd like to know *why* you said it at all.'

'It isn't important.' Matthew seemed to be regretting his outburst now.

'I disagree,' his brother frowned. 'We'll go to your office. Excuse us, Shay?'

'Of course,' she nodded absently, as disturbed by Matthew's behaviour as Lyon seemed to be. Matthew always gave the impression of being too coldly cynical to lose his temper in the way that he had. And although he had assured her it had nothing to do with her, Shay couldn't help feeling partly responsible for his anger, knowing full well that she was the reason Lyon kept leaving work early. Not that she encouraged him to do so, but he did it anyway. And she had to admit she hadn't done too much to stop him, not averse to letting Lyon believe he was making some ground with her. But she hadn't meant to upset Matthew in the process.

She didn't see either of the men again until dinner, and then it was only Lyon.

'Matthew has decided to eat in his suite,' he told her tersely.

She frowned her concern. 'What's wrong with him, do you know?'

'How the hell should I know what's wrong with him?' Lyon poured himself a drink before swallowing it down, knowing Shay would have refused if he had offered her one.

'You talked to him earlier—'

'Much good it did me,' he said bleakly. 'I've never seen him like this before.'

'Maybe it has something to do with my being here—'

'You heard him say it wasn't,' Lyon snapped. 'God, I'm sorry.' He was instantly contrite, sitting down beside her on the sofa to take her hand in his, seeming pleased when she didn't instantly flinch away from him. 'I'm not used to sharing my problems with anyone,' he admitted ruefully.

If he were hoping to appeal to her sympathy, he was out of luck; she didn't have any where this man was concerned. 'I don't want to share your problems either, Lyon,' she told him callously. 'But I am concerned about the way Matthew is behaving.'

Lyon sprang to his feet, his face a mask of anger. 'You're concerned about every damned member of this family except *me*!' His eyes were cold.

'Yes,' she agreed bluntly. 'But I wouldn't worry about it, Lyon, there are plenty of other women who do care,' she taunted.

'I want *you*.'

'Poor Lyon,' she drawled unsympathetically.

'God, what made you so hard?' he rasped. 'I can't believe it was just me.'

'No,' she admitted harshly. 'It wasn't just you.'

'Then why blame me for it all?' he reasoned. 'Once my divorce from Marilyn is made final we could get married, and then—'

'I don't think so, Lyon.' Her voice was scornful, knowing her theory of him wanting to marry her for the baby was correct; it hadn't taken him long to get round to suggesting marriage—once his divorce was final, of course, and her baby had been born! 'I don't love you, and I never could,' she added coldly.

'The baby is going to need a father—'

'It has a father!'

'He's dead!'

'Then maybe later on I'll find some nice, kind man who will care for my baby and me,' she challenged.

Lyon's eyes glowed like liquid gold. 'You aren't marrying anyone but me!'

She drew in a controlling breath. 'I only said maybe, Lyon. As it happens I don't intend marrying again—ever. And neither will I be dictated to by you, or let you even *think* you're making any of the decisions in my life. Now, is it convenient for me to drive up to town with you tomorrow, or shall I ask Jeffrey to take me?' she arched haughty brows.

'You aren't going up to town tomorrow.'

'I am.'

'Shay, you only have five weeks to go before the baby is due—'

'And Peter Dunbar said today that it was perfectly safe for me to do a morning's shopping, as long as I rested in the afternoon.'

'The man's an idiot!'

Her mouth twisted. 'You said he was the best in the country,' she reminded mockingly.

'It's just plain stupidity for you to wander about London on your own,' he insisted adamantly.

'Frightened I'll have the baby in Harrods?' Shay jeered.

He shook his head. 'Just frightened you'll have the baby; it wouldn't matter where it was.'

'Then come with me,' she invited lightly. 'As long as you don't think Matthew will accuse you of shirking your work again.'

'I told you that has nothing to do with the time I spend with you,' Lyon dismissed absently. 'Why this sudden desire to go shopping tomorrow?'

'It isn't sudden,' she protested. 'I still have some things to get for the baby, and I haven't done any of my Christmas shopping yet either,' she added dryly.

Lyon's eyes darkened. 'I'd like an Irish pixie

with purple eyes under my tree,' he said gruffly.

All the colour drained out of her face as he reminded her of that Christmas six years ago, a time when she hadn't yet learnt of his cruelty and selfishness, his need to have affairs constantly to prove his masculinity because he couldn't prove his manhood by having a child of his own. It wasn't surprising that Marilyn had also turned to other men!

'I thought of buying you a box of cigars,' she told him woodenly.

'I don't smoke,' he frowned.

'I know,' she nodded.

His mouth twisted ruefully. 'I suppose I could always smoke one the night the baby is born!'

'That's the father's privilege,' she gasped indignantly.

He drew in a harsh breath. 'Ricky has been dead over six months!' he rasped savagely.

She stood up. 'I know he's dead without your constant reminder of it,' she bit out forcefully. 'I think I knew it the moment his plane went down, but I wouldn't admit it to myself! But you'll never take his place. *Never*, do you hear?' she glared at him heatedly.

'I believe you've made yourself clear,' he muttered between gritted teeth, pouring himself another drink.

'I hope so.' She looked at him contemptuously. 'Now, I think I'll leave you to enjoy your liquid dinner while I have mine sent up to my room!'

'Shay!'

She turned to look at him, her breasts rising and falling as she tried to calm her breathing. 'Yes?' she answered coldly.

'Do you still want to go shopping tomorrow?' he asked huskily.

'I'll get Jeffrey to drive me in.'

'I'll take you,' he grated.

She gave a shrug, turning her back on him. 'Whatever you want.'

Whatever he wanted! He wanted her, all of her, and she damn well knew it.

His 'liquid dinner' had left him with a mammoth headache, and the last thing he felt like doing was talking, but he would have preferred that to Shay's silence as they drove up to London together the next day. It was far from being a companionable silence, only two words exchanged between them from the time Shay had joined him at the breakfast table; and they both knew she *didn't* wish him a 'good morning'! If those words had been daggers they would have been stuck between his shoulder blades!

'Where do you want to go first?' He had to break the silence, could feel the tension down his spine. Not that Shay looked tense, very beautiful in a bright red dress that proudly displayed her pregnant state. God, how he wished it were his child nestled in her body! But it would never be, even if she did finally give in to his marriage demands. Which he doubted.

'I really don't mind,' she uttered in a bored voice.

The shopping was carried out with none of the spontaneity of that Christmas night so many years ago, when Shay had seemed to glow brighter than any of the lights around them. He had been entranced by her that night, but he had in no way guessed at the impact she was to have on his life.

She chose her gifts for the family with care, some golf clubs for the addicted Neil, an antique clock for collector Matthew, a set of handcarved pipes for her grandfather, several smaller gifts for members of the staff. He hadn't expected her to buy anything for him, although that hadn't stopped his commission several weeks ago of an exquisite necklace designed especially for her; he hoped she would understand the message it conveyed.

Shopping for the baby turned out to be more fun than he had anticipated, getting totally caught up in the toys and furniture necessary for the nursery once the shop assistant had assumed he was Shay's husband.

'Lyon, I won't let you do this,' she protested as the assistant went to ask the manager if the white and gold furniture Lyon had picked out for the nursery at Falconer House could be delivered straight away. 'I have the nursery arranged at my own house, I don't need this other furniture,' she muttered.

'You'll need it for when you stay at the house,' Lyon dismissed.

'The baby and I will not be staying at the house.' She looked at him coldly.

His mouth tightened. 'With you or without you, Shay, the baby will occasionally visit with us.'

Her gaze continued to challenge him, but she was finally the one to look away. 'As you don't seem to need me here, I think I'll go into the shop across the road,' she snapped resentfully.

'I don't want you going off alone.' Lyon grasped her arm.

Her eyes shot purple flames at him. 'I am merely going into the shop over the road, not running amok through London!'

'I'll only be a minute longer here—'

'Lyon,' she warned softly. 'If you don't let me go right now—'

'You'll start screaming,' he grimaced, still holding on to her.

She shook her head. 'I'll have the assistant call the police to stop you harassing me.'

'She wouldn't believe that,' he scorned. 'Not since we've obviously been shopping together.'

'I know that,' Shay nodded. 'But I could cause quite a scene, why not save yourself the embarrassment?'

His mouth twisted before he began to smile, glancing out of the shop window to the shops opposite.

'I promise to look both ways before crossing the road,' Shay mocked.

His humour faded. 'Make sure that you do.' He released her, turning back to the assistant as she returned from the manager's office, beaming as she told him that of course the furniture could be delivered today.

Shay had known what the answer would be; when had anyone dared to refuse Lyon Falconer anything he wanted! The resentment he incited wasn't conducive to shopping for his Christmas present, but once she had seen the painting she couldn't resist buying it.

'Didn't you buy anything?' Lyon met up with her on the pavement outside.

'Does it look as if I did?' she derided her empty hands, having the painting delivered to the house tomorrow while Lyon was at work. 'I think I'd like to go back to my house for lunch now, and I'm sure you should be getting to work.'

'I'd rather stay and have lunch with you,' he drawled.

'You weren't invited,' Shay said bluntly.

He laughed softly. 'You're consistent, anyway.'

Mrs Devon was at the house keeping it clean and warm in Shay's absence, very pleased to see Shay, providing her with an appetising lunch before the younger woman went up to her bedroom to rest.

Shay woke up with a feeling of foreboding, rather as if she had had a bad dream. But she was sure she hadn't dreamt, had slept too deeply for that. She forced the blanket of sleep from her, wanting the oppression to go away too, turning into welcoming arms as cool lips blocked out those feelings to ignite desire.

'Oh, Gypsy!' he gasped, his lips feverish in her hair. 'Gypsy, I want you so damned much!'

'Ricky?' It had to be he who called her Gypsy, and yet it couldn't be, Ricky was dead!

'Do you have to keep throwing his name in my face?' It was Lyon who pushed away from her, standing up to glare down at her with golden eyes. 'Every time I touch you it's his name I hear on your lips!'

Shay was completely awake now, blinking up at him owlishly. 'How long have I been asleep?' she frowned dazedly.

'It's almost six—'

'Four hours? But I never sleep for four hours!' She shook her head. 'I—' She gasped as a pain shot through her back, paling as she realised it wasn't the first pain she had known in quite this peculiar way, that it was these pains that had caused the feelings of oppression even while she slept. 'Lyon!' Her hand came out desperately, Lyon immediately taking it into his own.

'What is it?' He came down on his knees beside the bed, his expression anxious at her obvious discomfort. 'Shay, I didn't mean to hurt you just now. I—'

'It wasn't you.' She shook her head.

'The shopping was too much for you. I knew it would be. You—'

'Lyon, it wasn't that either.' She swung her legs to the floor. 'I think it's the baby.'

'What's wrong with it?' One of his hands moved protectively to the swell of her body, coming to rest over the nightgown she wore. 'It hasn't stopped moving?'

She gave a rueful smile. 'The opposite, I think.' She gasped as another griping pain washed over her in a wave, making her feel nauseous.

'The op—! Shay, you can't be in labour, it's too soon,' he protested.

'Tell that to the baby!' She knew it was too soon, didn't need him to remind her of that fact, her fears all for her baby right now.

'Shall I ask the doctor to come here, or drive you straight to the hospital?' Lyon asked worriedly. 'What—'

Shay stared at him in amazement; Lyon Falconer in a complete panic?

CHAPTER NINE

DURING the next half an hour Lyon proved just how much of a panic he could get into!

It took him two dials to get the right telephone number for Peter Dunbar, swearing audibly when, after describing her contractions and the timing of them, the other man told him he thought it would be best if he met them at the hospital. Lyon helped her down the stairs as if she were a piece of delicate porcelain, snapping at Mrs Devon as she came out of the kitchen to ask if there were anything wrong, literally shouting at the midwife who met them at the hospital and assured them it was probably just a false alarm.

The doctor on duty, who examined her just as casually, assured her that it wasn't, that she was well into the first stage of labour, the injection they gave her to stop the contractions doing nothing at all, as they continued to come with sickening regularity.

Besides the fact that Shay was sure it was too early for the baby to be born without complications, she was also aware that having Lyon here with her was far from ideal too. Her grandfather, who was coming over for Christmas and had intended staying on for the baby's birth, was supposed to be the one at her side now, not Lyon!

Things became a little calmer once Peter Dunbar arrived, examining her quickly. 'Well, young lady,' he straightened, 'this little one seems to be in a hurry to be born.' He took off his mask, smiling reassuringly.

'It can't be born yet,' Lyon told him frantically. 'It's too soon. Can't you stop it?'

The other man shook his head, obviously a little disconcerted to have Lyon there at all. And considering their last meeting, Shay couldn't altogether blame him! 'We've tried to do that, it isn't working. No, I'm afraid the only thing to do now is let it be born. Five weeks premature isn't so bad, and the baby seems a good size—'

'There you go again with the "seems",' Lyon snapped. 'What if it isn't a good size?'

'We have an excellent staff here especially trained to deal with premature babies that—'

'What if he's too small? Can't you see how much Shay wants this baby?'

'I'm fully conversant with Mrs Falconer's feelings concerning her unborn child,' Peter Dunbar told him coldly. 'Can't you see how *you're* upsetting her?' he added censoriously.

Lyon flushed uncomfortably, not a man to appreciate having his faults pointed out to him.

Shay looked at the doctor. 'Do you really think it will be all right?'

He squeezed her hand. 'We'll do everything that we can. Now I'm going to ask the midwife to come back in and get you ready. Mr Falconer?'

'I'm staying with Shay,' Lyon told him flatly.

'You can come back as soon as Mrs Falconer has been prepared for the birth.' Peter Dunbar had obviously given up arguing with a man whose strength of will far outweighed his own.

'Please, Lyon,' Shay encouraged as he seemed about to argue once again. 'You can call Matthew and tell him what's going on.'

'I'm staying with you during the birth,' he insisted stubbornly.

She had already guessed that, and while she would rather have shared this moment with any other man *but* Lyon, she didn't think anyone here had the power to stop him doing exactly what he wanted to do. 'Could you telephone Grandy too?' she requested huskily. 'He'll want to know.'

'Your brother-in-law is a very determined man,' Peter Dunbar drawled once Lyon had gone to make the telephone calls. 'I got the feeling that if you had said no to him staying with you he would have fought off anyone who tried to prevent him.'

'Yes,' she agreed ruefully. 'Peter, I—I want—'

'I'm sure everything is going to be fine, Shay,' he said softly. 'And this baby is going to be born before the night is over too, if I'm not mistaken,' he teased. 'Once you've been prepared for labour, the midwife is going to put you on a monitor. It's nothing to worry about it, it just tells us how quickly your contractions are coming and how the baby is bearing up to them. All right?' he prompted gently.

She nodded, not needing the monitor to tell her

of the steady regularity of the cramping across her stomach as the midwife helped her undress and shower. The young woman looked astounded when Lyon strode arrogantly back into the room as she was helping Shay into her hospital gown.

She stepped protectively in front of Shay. 'Sir, I believe you have the wrong room.'

Cold tawny eyes pierced through her. 'I have the right room. How are you now, Shay?' His voice gentled from harshness as he spoke to her.

'Fine,' she nodded warily, a little apprehensive now that the birth was so imminent.

'I'm sorry, sir, I didn't realise—'

'I'm Lyon Falconer,' he supplied tersely, walking over to Shay. 'Are you really all right?' His eyes were dark with concern.

The midwife still looked confused. 'But I thought . . .' She glanced down at Shay's notes which she now held in her hand.

Shay knew what was puzzling the young woman; under 'marital status' it would read 'widowed'. 'Mr Falconer is my—'

'Fiancé,' he put in firmly.

Shay turned to him angrily as the midwife looked satisfied with this explanation. 'Lyon, you—'

'Darling, shouldn't you be lying down or something?' he cut in determinedly. 'I'm sure you aren't supposed to be walking about like this.'

'It feels more comfortable when I do.' She

pulled on her own robe taken from the small suitcase Lyon had somehow remembered to bring with them in their mad rush from the house.

'It won't hurt until I get back,' the young midwife assured him. 'I'll be back in a few minutes to put you on the monitor, Mrs Falconer.'

'What sort of monitor?' Lyon demanded as the young woman prepared to leave.

'Please don't worry, Mr Falconer, I'll only be gone a short time.' She smiled at Shay before leaving.

'Just what I need,' Lyon muttered. 'Condescension from a girl almost half my age!'

Shay coped with the cramping pains as she moved restlessly about the room. 'She's been through this hundreds of times before,' she excused distractedly. 'Why did you have to lie about being my fiancé, Lyon?' she demanded to know.

'I've heard about these places,' he scowled. 'They throw out anyone who isn't closely related to the expectant mother!'

'No one would have dared to throw you out, whatever the circumstances,' she scorned.

'I was just making sure no one tried,' he rasped.

She shrugged, knowing it was no good to argue; the damage was done now. 'Did you talk to Matthew and Grandy?'

'Yes. Look, isn't something supposed to be happening?' he sounded harassed.

She smiled. 'Probably not for hours yet.'

He sank down into a chair, looking slightly dazed. 'You're sure about that?' he asked doubtingly.

'Very.' Her smile deepened. 'Don't you know anything about childbirth?'

'Only what I've read in books the last few months,' he scowled. 'The way they described the stages of labour it all just—happened.'

She wasn't surprised that he had gone to the trouble of reading about childbirth; Lyon wouldn't like to let anything defeat him, even something he believed he would never actively be involved in. 'It takes a little longer than that, I'm afraid,' she mocked.

'I don't—Shay, what is it?' He stood up anxiously as she was suddenly bent double with pain. 'Shay!' he prompted desperately.

'I think you had better get the midwife back in here,' she told him as he helped her get on to the delivery table. 'It seems to be happening a little faster than it should.'

'Oh God,' he paled again. 'Oh God!'

If she weren't in so much pain Lyon's uncharacteristic behaviour would be laughable. But the pain had been building steadily since they had got there, feeling quite separate from the crampings of labour. She hadn't mentioned it before because she hadn't wanted to seem as if she were making a fuss over nothing, but the pain really was excruciating now.

It was Peter Dunbar who came back with Lyon,

bringing calmness back to the proceedings, his smile gently reassuring. The smile didn't quite seem to reach his eyes when he straightened from examining her once again.

'What is it?' Shay demanded sharply.

He shrugged. 'The baby wants to be born—is determined to be born,' he amended dryly. 'But he or she has also decided it would like to make its entrance into the world feet first!'

'Breech?' she gasped, her eyes widening with shock—and fear.

'Don't look so worried.' The doctor patted her hand. 'It's what I suspected earlier. It isn't so unusual.'

'Breech?' Lyon stood on the other side of the delivery table. 'What the hell is that?'

Peter Dunbar looked at him reprovingly. 'Could we talk outside?' he grated, his expression softening as he looked down at Shay. 'I'll send in Nurse Stevens to sit with you. And please don't worry, this breech birth is exactly what I've been expecting.'

He sounded so confident, and yet Shay knew it was his job to sound that way; he didn't necessarily feel as confident as he sounded. So many things seemed to have gone wrong during this pregnancy: Ricky's death, her fall, and now this breech birth. Maybe she wasn't meant to have this baby.

It *was* going to live, she was determined it would. This was Ricky's child, and she wanted it!

Lyon was more subdued when he came back

into the room after talking to Peter Dunbar. 'I'm sorry,' he bit out. 'I'm behaving like a fool.'

She gave a wan smile. 'I'm sure Peter didn't tell you that.' She didn't think the other man dare!

'No,' he admitted ruefully. 'But it came across during the conversation.'

She smiled at him, closing her eyes weakly. 'If anyone can make this come out right it's Peter.'

God, she looked so fragile lying there, her face pale, her lids translucent!

If he could have taken the pain as his own he would, but now it was too late to do anything but pray. For both her and her child. And he was doing a lot of that.

He watched emotionlessly as the midwife put two straps about Shay's swollen body before switching on the monitor, the steady beep beep telling them that the baby's heartbeat was strong at the moment.

But would it remain that way? Peter Dunbar had been brutally honest with him outside in the corridor—Shay could die, the baby could die, or they could both die. Much as he hated what the other man was telling him, Lyon appreciated his honesty, needed to know.

Shay lifted those pale lids to look at him with eyes darkened with pain. 'If anything should happen to me I want—'

Pain ripped through his chest like a knife. 'Nothing is going to happen to you!'

She gave a wan smile, her eyes dull with the

pain now. 'I read *all* the books, Lyon, including the one on complications during childbirth.'

'You heard Dunbar,' he dismissed lightly. 'Nothing is going to go wrong.'

She gave him a sympathetic smile, as if pitying his confidence. 'My grandfather is too old to take care of another child the way he had to me, even with the help of a nanny, so it will be up to you, Matthew, and Neil to take care of—'

'Shay, stop talking as if you're going to die!' He couldn't control the shudder of emotion that ran down his spine.

'If it's a boy it's to be called Richard Patrick, after Ricky and my grandfather,' she continued as if he hadn't interrupted. 'And if it's a girl—'

'Shay Elizabeth,' he put in harshly. 'After its mother and grandmother.'

'I chose Elizabeth Anne, after both its grandmothers,' she chided. 'Beth for short.'

'This conversation is unnecessary, Shay.' He frowned as the young midwife hurried from the room. 'You'll be able to name your baby yourself very shortly.' He stood up as Peter Dunbar entered the room, knowing that things were happening much faster than the other man had expected—or wanted—them to.

After the other man's entrance he lost all track of time as Shay became convulsed with the contractions, her grip on his hands excruciating at times. But that was all right, as long as it helped take away some of her own pain. And what she was going through sickened him. So much pain and suffering just to bring another baby into the world. He had wanted children when he first married Marilyn, he thanked God now that he had never put any woman through such agony because he wanted a child. And if Shay survived this—*when* she survived it—he intended seeing that nothing ever hurt her again.

He was told that Matthew had arrived at the hospital some time during the ordeal, but he couldn't leave Shay to speak to him, in this with her to the end, no matter what the outcome might be.

He mopped her brow, spoke to her soothingly when it seemed she couldn't take the pain any more, and all the time he cursed the baby inside her for doing this to her.

'Here it comes, Shay,' Peter Dunbar finally shouted excitedly from behind his mask, both men bathed in sweat after hours of battling to bring the baby into the world. 'Leg first,' he said dryly. 'But it is coming,' he told her triumphantly.

'Is it moving?' Shay was exhausted, her hair clinging damply to her brow, her face pale from the hours of struggle. But she wasn't about to give in to the exhaustion she felt until she knew her baby had been safely delivered.

'I have a black eye to prove it!' Peter teased.

Lyon could see the leg that had emerged, sure there couldn't be life in that purple-blotched body, no matter what Dunbar said. And then the body and head appeared, showing a shock of hair as black as its mother's. The baby looked to be perfectly formed in every way.

Shay seemed to know that the birth was over, pushing away from him.

Lyon gazed in awe at the tiniest scrap of humanity he had ever seen, still covered in the blood and body fluid from the birth as its cry filled the air.

'A son, Shay,' he choked. 'You have a son!'

Life seemed to be revived in her body as Peter Dunbar lay the screaming baby on her chest, looking down at her son with rapt wonder. Lyon knew he had never seen anything as beautiful as Shay with her small indignant son.

It was over. They had both survived! She hadn't thought they would, had been prepared to die as long as her baby lived.

But she was so glad she hadn't died as she looked down at Richard, knew she would never tire of looking at his beautiful face. He had thick black hair, a small rounded face with unfocusing blue eyes that could either remain that colour like his father's, or go the deeper purple of her own. His body was tiny but perfect. She knew, because she had immediately counted all of his fingers and toes!

She looked up tearfully at the tawny-eyed man who had stayed at her side the whole time, who had shared the pain with her. 'He's beautiful, isn't he,' she said huskily.

'As he looks exactly like you, he has to be,'

Lyon nodded, looking at her, not the baby.

'You ought to go outside and tell Matthew.' She watched the nurse as she took Richard away to wash him. 'He'll be worried.'

'Go right ahead,' Peter Dunbar said at his questioning look. 'I just have to check on this young lady and her son and then they can go to their room.'

Lyon left reluctantly while Shay learnt that Richard weighed five pounds twelve ounces and was twenty-one inches long. He also didn't like water, letting out a yell as he was washed.

'You did well, Shay.' Peter Dunbar came to stand beside her, smiling tiredly.

'Richard's well?' She couldn't hide the anxiety she still felt.

He glanced ruefully over at the baby as he continued to cry while he was dressed. 'Probably wishing now that he had waited the other five weeks,' he smiled, 'but otherwise he's healthy. A nice weight, a nice colour. You're the one who's going to feel the effects of his early birth the most.'

'I don't mind.' She held her son in her arms. 'I don't know how to thank you,' she choked.

'You owe as much to your brother-in-law as to me,' he told her softly. 'He *willed* you to get through it.'

She had known how much she owed to Lyon for Richard's safe delivery, but she was afraid to let that gratitude blind her to all that she hated about him. 'Yes.' She turned away abruptly, her expression softening as she saw Richard had fallen asleep now that he was clean and warm.

Matthew was with Lyon when they came into her hospital room a short time later, Richard down in the nursery now so that she could get a good night's rest.

'You're a very clever girl,' Matthew told her proudly.

'You've seen Richard?' She couldn't seem to look at Lyon now it was all over.

Matthew nodded. 'We've just come back from the nursery. Of course Lyon demanded to hold him.' He derided his brother's arrogance.

Shay looked up sharply at the rigid-faced man. 'You've held Richard?'

His eyes hardened. 'Shouldn't I have done?'

'I—'

'I'm afraid Mrs Falconer must rest now,' the young midwife came in to tell them sternly.

'We'll be back tomorrow.' Matthew squeezed her hand. 'Your grandfather will be here then, too.' He glanced at Lyon. 'I'll wait for you outside,' he muttered.

She felt even more uncomfortable once she was alone with Lyon, aware of the midwife in the room as she filled in the chart at the bottom of Shay's bed. Even though her resentment had returned for Lyon's intrusion into a private moment she couldn't let what he had done for her go unmentioned. 'Thank you,' she said stiltedly. 'I don't know how I would have managed without you.'

His mouth was tight. 'You would have done, I'm sure.'

'No, I—' She broke off as she looked up to meet his gaze, hastily looking away again from that molten gold. 'I'm grateful for what you did,' she told him abruptly.

'Don't worry, Shay,' his mouth twisted, 'I'm not about to try and collect on that gratitude by repeating my offer of marriage,' he rasped. 'Goodnight!'

Shay sensed the young midwife looking at them curiously, and she deliberately kept her face averted until she was alone.

She had a son, a beautiful baby boy, and she wasn't going to let anything spoil that—and especially not Lyon!

Shay looked down in wonder at the dark head resting against her breast, the greedy mouth sucking determinedly on the nipple she had placed between his eager lips. The nurse had shown her how to do it, and while it had felt strange at first, it also filled her with overwhelming love for her son.

He fell asleep halfway through feeding on the other breast, his tiny mouth still open as she placed him back in his crib beside her bed after holding him for several more minutes, having kept him beside her since the nurse had brought him in to her early this morning. He had been asleep most of the time, only waking up for the occasional feed, and Shay had spent most of her time just looking at him as he slept. She hadn't believed the day would ever come when she would hold her own baby in her arms.

Luckily he didn't seem allergic to pollen because her room looked like a florists', half a dozen assorted coloured roses from Lyon in as many vases, carnations from Matthew, violets from Neil, an assorted arrangement in a lace crib from her grandfather, a bouquet that had been divided into four vases from her publisher, and even an arrangement in a china-blue train from Marilyn and Derrick.

Shay still felt very tired, had dozed a little during the morning, but she had showered and washed her hair in preparation of seeing her visitors this afternoon, feeling quite refreshed after she had, applying only a light make-up to her flushed cheeks.

Her grandfather was so excited about the baby that he completely forgot he had an aversion to hospitals of any kind, shaking the rattle he had bought Richard in front of the baby's face. Richard didn't seem at all impressed by all the new people looking down to admire him, and promptly fell asleep again!

'Neil is flying home at the weekend,' Matthew told her.

'He didn't have to do that.' Shay tried not to be aware of the brooding man standing at the back of the room, Lyon not having said a word since his arrival with the other two men.

'Of course he did,' Matthew chided. 'We're

all very excited about the newest member of our family. Of course I'm a little upset that he doesn't look like me, but he couldn't have everything . . .' he teased.

'He's perfect!' Lyon suddenly rasped.

Everyone in the room turned to look at him: Shay's grandfather in puzzlement, Matthew with censure, and Shay with fear. She had known he would feel this way, as if Richard were partly his because he had been with her at the delivery. He was acting like the doting father she would never allow him to be, and which she knew he was going to demand to be!

'Of course he's perfect,' she snapped. 'He's Ricky's son!'

Black anger darkened his face. 'Damn you!' he cried hoarsely before striding from the room.

Shay had a rebellious flush to her cheeks as she looked challengingly at the two men left in the room. 'He asked for that!' she defended.

'Right between the eyes, I would say,' Matthew grimaced.

'I was only stating a fact,' she said resentfully.

'Because you knew it would make Lyon as mad as hell,' he taunted.

'Because it was the truth!' Her eyes flashed.

'You didn't have to throw it in his face,' Matthew reproved. 'By the way,' he changed the subject as her expression set mutinously, 'a mysterious package arrived at the house for you yesterday morning; I put it in your suite.'

Lyon's Christmas present, she had forgotten

all about it in the excitement. 'Thank you,' she nodded stiffly.

'Also the nursery looks like something out of a toy shop,' he derided. 'Didn't you think anyone would buy him anything?'

'The toys were Lyon's idea,' she snapped.

'I'm sure you told him how unnecessary they were,' Matthew sighed.

'I don't intend for Richard to be spoilt!'

'The way we were?' Matthew taunted, shaking his head. 'Our father was a disciplinarian, hardest of all on Lyon because he was the oldest. You should have indulged him about the toys, Shay,' he reproved.

'Matthew—'

'Okay, I accept that now isn't the time for this discussion.' He held up his hands defensively. 'But just try and remember, Lyon only gives the impression of being a self-sufficient bastard. In his own way he's as vulnerable as the rest of us.'

Her mouth was tight. 'I don't want to start an argument either,' she told him stiffly. 'So we'll talk about something else. I hope Mrs Devon made you comfortable, Grandy,' she smiled at her grandfather.

'I'm sure she would have done if I'd been at the house,' he nodded. 'But I'm—'

'Staying at Falconer House,' she finished with inevitability.

'Darlin', enjoy the baby and stop fussing so much about what everyone else is doing, hmm?' he reproved.

She flushed guiltily. 'I'm sorry. I—I'll stop fussing,' she agreed ruefully. 'Would you hand Richard to me?' she requested as the baby began to wake up.

'Your mother always said you should never pick up a baby as soon as it cries,' her grandfather teased as he instantly picked Richard up, the surprised baby struggling to open his eyes.

'And that's the reason I was so spoilt as a child?' Shay mocked as she took her son in her arms.

'You weren't spoilt,' he defended, turning slightly as a stone-faced Lyon came back into the room. 'I think I'll just go outside for a breath of air,' he excused.

'I think I'll join you,' Matthew muttered, following the older man from the room.

Shay was very much aware of Lyon standing across the room from her, and she pointedly ignored him as she spoke softly to Richard, entranced with her tiny son.

'I didn't ask them to leave,' Lyon finally rasped.

Her smile slowly faded as her gaze reluctantly left Richard to look at Lyon. 'Sorry?'

'I didn't ask your grandfather and Matthew to leave,' he bit out, moving to stand next to the bed, looking down at her and the baby.

'You didn't need to,' she shrugged, turning back to her son.

'Shay, I—' He thrust his hands in his pockets, his shoulders hunched over, a haggard look to his face. 'I don't mean to seem so damned moody, but I—God, you know how I feel!' he glared.

Yes, she knew how he felt, and her arms tightened protectively about Richard, who instantly let out a protesting wail.

'I don't want to take him from you, Shay,' Lyon told her softly. 'I just want to share him.'

'No!'

'Shay—'

'Would you please leave, Lyon.' Her eyes were coldly dismissive. 'Richard wants feeding now.' Her expression dared him to mock her request for privacy.

He let out a ragged sigh. 'Don't resent me because I was there, Shay.' He shook his head. 'If I hadn't been—'

'It won't work, Lyon,' she snapped harshly. 'I owe you nothing!'

'I didn't mean—'

'You meant exactly that!' she bit out forcefully. 'I'm well aware of what you did for Richard and me yesterday, but it was no more than you owed me.'

Lyon frowned. 'What do you mean?'

She was breathing heavily in her agitation. 'Six years ago you tried to destroy me, helping me give birth to Richard only gave back what you tried to take from me then; a reason for living.'

'I thought marrying Ricky gave you that!' Lyon said with bitterness.

She looked at him coldly. 'And now Ricky's son will continue to do that.'

She wasn't in the least surprised when he turned on his heel and walked out of the room for the second time that day.

'Where is Lyon?' she demanded of Matthew.

He was her only visitor this morning, her grandfather and Neil coming this afternoon. Peter Dunbar had insisted she had to stay in hospital for at least a week, that it had been a difficult and tiring birth for her, and although Richard was a good weight he wanted to keep an eye on him for several days longer. After only three days Shay was chafing to leave.

Matthew raised mocking brows. 'Don't tell me you've missed him?'

'Don't worry,' she shook her head, feeling more like her old self now, doing nothing but rest and caring for Richard. 'I won't ever do that,' she added hardly.

His mouth twisted. 'Then why the curiosity about where he is?'

'I need to see him,' she announced stiffly.

'Need?' Matthew taunted.

'Want, then,' she amended sharply, glaring at him. 'Don't be so damned patronising, Matthew!'

He shrugged. 'Now what could you possibly want to see my big brother for?' he drawled.

'Where is he, Matthew?'

'Away.'

She grimaced her displeasure at the abrupt disclosure. 'For how long?'

'Who knows?' he dismissed dryly. 'Lyon has always been his own master.'

'And everyone else's if he gets the opportunity,' she muttered tautly.

'Yes,' Matthew grinned. 'What's he done wrong this time?'

'It isn't funny, Matthew,' she snapped. 'Even if I did feel like running, I don't know where he thinks I would run to so that he couldn't find me!'

Matthew sobered, frowning his puzzlement. 'What are you talking about?'

She sighed. 'Did you see the man sitting outside in the corridor? A short way down,' she explained at the appearance of his frown. 'A plump man with a receding hairline,' she described with distaste.

'I remember him now,' Matthew nodded slowly. 'An innocuous-looking chap. What about him?'

'*He*'s what Lyon's done wrong this time!' she cried angrily.

'Shay, I've never believed you to be lacking in eloquence,' Matthew told her steadily. 'In fact, the opposite at times,' he added dryly. 'But this certainly isn't one of them!'

'The man sitting outside,' she snapped, 'the "innocuous-looking chap", is another of Lyon's spies!' She breathed heavily in her agitation, hadn't been able to believe it this morning when the young midwife had told her about the man in the corridor being here to watch her.

'Shay—'

'It's true, Matthew,' she sharply interrupted his reasoning voice. 'I've actually asked him.'

'Asked him what?' he frowned.

'If he works for Lyon.' She sighed her impatience. 'The nurse that brought my medicine this morning seemed very agitated,' she revealed hardly. 'And when I asked her if everything was all right she said she hadn't ever been questioned as if she were a criminal before. It seems that "innocuous-looking chap" gave her the third degree before letting her in here!'

'That doesn't sound as if he's spying on you,' Matthew said slowly.

'Of course it does,' she raged bitterly. 'He probably thought the poor woman was trying to smuggle me in some clothes for the great escape! I'm telling you, Matthew, he's gone too far this time.' Her expression was mutinous. 'I'm going to have that man kicked out of here.'

He looked at his wrist-watch. 'It's about seven o'clock in the morning in New York,' he said thoughtfully. 'Not too early to call Lyon.'

'Call him from here,' she invited tightly. 'Then I can tell him what I think of him too!'

Matthew smiled hardly. 'I think I'll make the call from home. I wouldn't want to get *you* kicked out of here for using obscene language in front of Richard!'

Some of her tension left her as she gave a rueful grimace. 'Lyon just infuriates me,' she sighed. 'I've told him from the beginning that I'll never try to keep Richard away from you all, but that doesn't seem to be enough for him.'

'I'm sure there must have been some sort of mistake—'

'Lyon doesn't make mistakes, he only has set-backs,' Shay dismissed hardly.

'As usual, you're misjudging him,' Matthew reproved. 'I'm sure there's a perfectly good explanation for—'

'Donaldson,' she put in harshly. 'He said his name is Eric Donaldson,' she told him disgustedly.

'I'm sure Lyon can easily explain the man's presence here,' Matthew frowned.

'I wish you looked, and sounded, more convincing,' Shay condemned his obvious confusion.

'I'll get back to you later,' he promised.

He hadn't contacted her by the time Neil and her grandfather arrived later that afternoon, although Neil did happen to mention that Matthew had been on the telephone most of the day trying to contact Lyon in New York.

That didn't placate Shay at all, wanting to know what Lyon's explanation was for Eric Donaldson. By seven o'clock that evening she had had enough of waiting, putting a call through to the house, ringing off impatiently when the line was engaged, jumping nervously when her own telephone began ringing as soon as she had replaced the receiver.

'Matthew, you scared the life out of me!' she

accused as soon as he had identified himself as the caller.

'Why, what's happened?' he demanded sharply.

'I just put the receiver down from trying to reach you, and obviously you were just calling me. And—Never mind all that,' she continued impatiently. 'Have you managed to contact Lyon?'

'Are you sure you're all right?' he persisted.

'Of course I'm all right. Matthew—What did you say?' she frowned, sure he had said something like 'he's got me at it too now'. It didn't make any sense to her if he had. 'Matthew?' she prompted again.

'Look, I know it will be late when I get there,' he told her briskly, 'but I have to talk to you.'

She swallowed hard at the seriousness of his tone. Matthew was either sarcastic, mocking, derisive, or just plain cruel, he was never this gravely serious. 'If it's bad news, Matthew, I'd rather you told me now,' she said abruptly.

'It isn't bad news.' His voice was hoarse. 'It's— Look, I'll be there in about an hour, we can talk then,' he told her firmly before ringing off.

Shay immediately rang him back, only to be told he had already left the house. Something was wrong, badly wrong, and she couldn't think what it could be. Unless something had happened to Lyon, and that was the reason Matthew had had such difficulty trying to reach him. But she couldn't believe that was it—Lyon was invincible!

Matthew looked pale and haggard when he arrived shortly after eight o'clock, and Shay knew she was right to be so concerned when he told her he thought it would be better if she sat down while they talked.

'What is it?' she demanded sharply. 'Matthew, you're just making things worse!'

'I'm not sure they can be any worse than they already are,' he frowned.

'Just tell me!'

'Donaldson isn't spying on you for Lyon,' he stated flatly.

Her expression was scornful. 'Lyon was sure to tell you that, but I told you, I've spoken to the man, and he definitely works for Lyon.'

Matthew looked angry. 'I don't care what your personal differences are,' he bit out tautly. 'Lyon is not a liar!'

She blushed uncomfortably. 'I'm sorry,' she mumbled.

He nodded acceptance of the apology. 'Donaldson has been hired as a body-guard by Lyon,' he stated flatly.

Shay frowned her puzzlement. 'A body-guard? But—He's guarding *me*?' she said disbelievingly.

Hazel eyes met hers steadily. 'Yes.'

Her mouth quirked. 'I know Lyon doesn't like my books, but he can't seriously think anyone would want to hurt me because of them!'

'This isn't a time for levity, Shay!' Green flecks

flashed angrily in Matthew's hazel eyes. 'There have been several attempts on the lives of members of this family during recent months, and although I don't agree with the secretive way Lyon has tried to protect us all, I do agree that it had to be done.'

'You have to be joking, Matthew!' she dismissed.

'No,' he said in deadly earnest.

'But why would someone want to hurt anyone in the family?' she gasped.

He shrugged. 'In business you sometimes make enemies you don't even know you have.'

Fantastic as it might sound, she could no longer doubt he was completely serious about this. And with her acceptance that he was telling the truth came something else. 'Ricky?' she choked.

'We don't know if his death was an accident or not, Shay,' he said huskily. 'We just don't know,' he repeated heavily.

CHAPTER TEN

SHAY stared at him blankly, not even aware that she had stopped breathing until she sucked air into her starved lungs. Matthew couldn't really have just said there was a possibility that Ricky's death hadn't been an accident after all.

'Drink this,' Matthew ordered her to swallow the water he had poured, watching her closely as she numbly did so. 'I said we don't know, Shay.' He took the empty glass from her trembling fingers. 'And we don't. The initial report in Los Angeles wasn't extensive, so we're waiting for a more detailed report on the plane from the people Lyon hired.'

She swallowed hard. 'I—You—Lyon—' She couldn't articulate, too choked with emotion.

'Neil was the first one to be involved in an accident.' Matthew held her hand as he gently began to talk. 'His hang-glider nosedived from a couple of hundred feet in the air. He was only concussed, luckily; it was surprising he wasn't killed. The people at the workshop told him one of the supports had worn away.'

'Oh God, oh *God*,' Shay cried, burying her face in her hands, tears streaming down her face.

'We can talk about this some other time if it's upsetting you too much—'

'No!' she looked at him wildly. 'I want to know it all now.'

Matthew frowned. 'I only meant to explain to you why Donaldson was so necessary outside. Lyon will be back tomorrow to tell you the rest.'

'I have to know now.' She shook her head desperately. 'I *have* to know, Matthew,' she pleaded, clutching at his hand.

He sighed raggedly. 'I know you do, I felt the same way earlier when Lyon finally told me what's been going on. But obviously he still knows more than I do—'

'Just tell me what you know!'

He nodded abruptly. 'We all dismissed Neil's accident as the stupidity of the sport,' he rasped. 'Then Lyon had an accident in the Porsche. At least, he told us it was an accident at the time. Actually his brakes failed and he had to drive into an embankment rather than go over a bridge.' Matthew revealed grimly.

'Was he hurt?'

'His pride took a beating,' Matthew attempted to mock. 'And it knocked his lifetime no-claims bonus for six!'

'Matthew!'

He gave a rueful shrug. 'He had a nasty bump on his head for several days, but nothing more than that. Then Ricky had his accident—As far as we know there's no connection, Shay,' he put in quickly as she paled even more.

'But Lyon suspects there is?'

'He—isn't sure.' Matthew watched her closely. 'And that's the truth.'

'But if it wasn't an accident, then there—there's a murderer out there somewhere.' She felt sick at the thought of her beloved Ricky being deliberately killed. 'Why hasn't Lyon gone to the police?'

'He has,' Matthew sighed. 'But so far we only have a string of unrelated accidents—'

'Three members of the same family isn't *unrelated*—'

'Five,' Matthew put in softly.

'What?' she gasped.

'Six if you count Richard,' he added grimly.

Shay's face was stricken. 'Richard . . . ?'

'I could have been badly hurt when the electronics on my chair went haywire, and both you and Richard could have died when you went down the escalator.'

'That was an accident—'

'Was it?' Matthew prompted softly. 'It was a crowded station, everyone rushing for the train due in, couldn't you have been *pushed*?'

'No, I—' She broke off as she remembered the jostling at the back of her as she prepared to step on to the escalator. Someone *could* have pushed her. 'I can't believe this, Matthew.' She shook her head. 'It can't be real.'

'That's the way the police feel about it too. Lyon can't give them a motive for anyone wanting to hurt all of us in this way, and so they dismiss it as several accidents that have happened over quite a period of months.'

'Lyon's sure it couldn't just be that?'

'Yes. At first he wasn't sure, but the night he came off Wildfire his saddle had been tampered with.'

She drew in a ragged breath. 'Why didn't he tell any of us about this?'

Matthew shrugged. 'He didn't tell *you* because of the baby, and he didn't tell the rest of us because at the beginning he just *wasn't* sure.'

'We had a right to know!' Shay claimed bitterly.

'Lyon was frightened you might lose the baby if he told you.'

Her mouth twisted. 'Of course,' she derided harshly, sighing deeply. 'He'll be back tomorrow, you said?' Her eyes were narrowed.

'Yes.'

'Tell him as soon as he gets back that I would like to see him,' she instructed hardly.

'Shay, it's no good being like this, none of this is Lyon's fault—'

'I know that,' she nodded. 'I just have to know if he's found out any more about Ricky.'

'Even if he has, it won't bring Ricky back,' Matthew told her quietly.

Shay's eyes took on a haunted quality. 'I know that. But accepting that the plane crashed and Ricky died is one thing, knowing that someone deliberately caused that accident is something else entirely.'

Matthew squeezed her hand comfortingly. 'I'm sure it was an accident, Shay.'

Shay wasn't, and just the thought that it might

not have been kept her awake all night just looking at Richard as he slept between feeds, insisting
he stay in with her even though the night nurse
had offered to take him so that she could have a
peaceful night. The thought that someone, some
faceless person, might try to take him away from
her filled her with apprehension and fear.

Who could want to do such a thing? *Why*, that
was what she didn't understand? Could what
Matthew said be true, that someone had a grudge
against the whole family because of business? If
that were so why did it have to be Ricky who was
the one to die?

'Shay, I don't have any more answers,' Lyon told
her wearily.

He had come straight to the hospital from the
airport, looked tired and haggard, his tailored
brown suit still slightly creased from the flight.

Shay knew she looked no less tired, dark circles
under her shadowed eyes, the rest of her face
very pale in comparison. 'Matthew said you're
waiting for a second report on Ricky's crash?'

He shrugged broad shoulders. 'It will be
several more weeks.'

'Lyon—'

'Shay!' he said with patient sternness. 'I had
Matthew tell you what was going on because he
said you were all set to have Donaldson removed
from the hospital.' His eyes were narrowed. 'I'm
sure you can understand now why I couldn't let
you do that. But nothing else has changed—'

'Nothing has changed?' she echoed incredulously. 'There's some lunatic out there trying to do every member of this family harm, and you say *nothing has changed!*' She shook her head disbelievingly. 'Lyon, you amaze me!'

'Except for a couple of slip-ups, you have been protected from the moment Ricky's plane went down—'

'You had me watched even then?' she demanded sharply.

'I had you guarded,' corrected Lyon harshly.

'So that was the reason you didn't doubt Richard's parentage.' Her eyes flashed. 'You knew I hadn't seen another man since Ricky's crash!'

Lyon's mouth thinned. 'I didn't doubt your baby's parentage because I know *you!*' he bit out. 'I never, ever doubted it was Ricky's child you carried. I had you guarded for your own safety, and it was made easier by the man you yourself hired to keep the press away from you. But your stubbornness in insisting on finding your own home when you came back to England complicated matters slightly, especially after the threat you made about going to the police if you saw anyone following you,' he added grimly.

'So you had Mrs Devon watch me instead!'

He shook his head. 'Not at first, no.'

'Then—Grandy,' she realised with dismay. 'He knows, doesn't he?' she said flatly, sure that she finally had the answer to her grandfather's unexpected advice that it would be better if she stayed at Falconer House. It had been so unlike him, considering that he knew how she felt about Lyon, but now it was easier—if not more pleasant!—to understand his concern.

'I had to tell him,' Lyon nodded abruptly, 'so that he knew what to look out for.'

'He went everywhere with me,' she realised bitterly, feeling a little like an overprotected child.

'We daren't risk your being upset in any way, Shay,' Lyon sighed.

'No wonder Grandy didn't want to go home.' She frowned as she recalled her grandfather's reluctance to go back to Ireland.

'We realised that his delay was arousing your suspicions, and so Mrs Devon was persuaded to watch over you at the house, and I hired a private detective to follow you if you went out, on the supposition that after all that time you wouldn't suspect me of having you watched.'

'The day on the escalator—'

'Donaldson's predecessor lost you during your shopping expedition,' Lyon recalled harshly. 'I almost strangled him when I found out what had happened, even more so once I discovered you hadn't arrived for your appointment with Marilyn. The man was lucky he just got off with a dismissal,' he recalled savagely.

'Then all these months have told you nothing?' Shay frowned.

'All these months,' he bit out, 'have shown me that someone has a grudge against the family.

I've been trying to protect its members as best I could.'

She blushed at the reproof in his tone. 'Maybe if you hadn't treated us all like children it wouldn't have been so difficult,' she snapped resentfully.

'If it hadn't been for your child maybe I wouldn't have done.' His eyes glittered angrily.

'Don't keep using Richard as the excuse for everything, Lyon,' she dismissed scornfully.

'Your doctor told me that any more distress could bring on a miscarriage,' he told her coldly.

Shay became suddenly still, very pale as she looked at him with stunned eyes. 'You spoke to Andrew Fitzroy about me?' Her voice was very faint.

'Yes,' he instantly admitted talking to Peter Dunbar's predecessor.

'I—And what did he tell you?' She moistened stiff lips.

'Nothing detailed,' Lyon assured her derisively. 'After all, he had a patient's confidence to think of.'

'It sounds very much to me as if he forgot all about that!' she returned angrily.

'He understood that the family were concerned about you—'

'You *are* the family!' she glared.

'God, Shay, I'm not going to keep arguing with you about everything and nothing!' he rasped. 'Your doctor, quite rightly, warned of the possibility of miscarriage. And because of that possibility I didn't tell you about the attempts on the lives of members of the family. Now you can say what you like about the rights and wrongs of that decision, but it will ultimately make no difference to the outcome. If you want to argue choose some other time,' he snapped. 'I've had enough for one day!'

She had become so used to his arrogant determination where she was concerned, his mockery, his anger, that his coldness now came as something of a shock to her. It was also evidence of just how weary he was.

'I'm sorry,' she said abruptly. 'But you must realise what a shock all this has been to me.'

'I'd like to sympathise with you, Shay,' he sighed. 'But I've been worried by it and shocked by it for months, not hours!'

She blushed at his intended rebuke. 'Maybe you should learn to share your problems, Lyon,' she bit out scornfully.

His mouth twisted. 'Maybe when the woman I want to share them with stops acting like a spoilt little child, I will! Now if that's all, I'm going home,' Lyon said forcefully. 'I feel as if I could sleep for a week!'

'That isn't all!' She stopped him at the door. 'What about Ricky?'

'What about him?' Tawny eyes were narrowed.

'Someone could have murdered him!'

'Someone could have murdered all of us by now if all the attempts had been successful,' he blazed. 'But a series of accidents don't make a crime!'

'You sound like a policeman yourself now!'

'None of it can be *proved*!'

She knew that, but somehow she had expected Lyon to be able to do *something*.

Lyon looked at that beautiful face so vulnerable and raw and he could have wept. He knew what she expected of him, and there was nothing he could do. He had already done everything humanly possible to protect her and her baby. Except stay with her constantly himself. And he knew she wouldn't allow that.

He hadn't seen Richard since the day after his birth, and as the baby had stayed hidden in his crib the whole of his visit he had no reason to suppose Shay wanted him to see her son now either. He hesitated about leaving. 'Shay, could I look at Richard?' he requested huskily, expecting her to say no.

Wide purple eyes looked at him fearfully, and he knew the reason for that fear. But he wasn't about to deny the tenuous claim being present at Richard's birth gave him with the baby.

She avoided his gaze now. 'As you can see, he's asleep.'

'I only want to look at him, Shay,' he prompted gently.

As if on cue, the baby in the crib began to move restlessly, letting out a tiny grunt of displeasure, as if he knew someone wanted to disturb his rest.

Lyon's throat closed emotionally as Shay bent over the crib to take out the baby, handing Richard to him. Wide blue eyes looked up at him seriously, eyes that held none of the fear and apprehension of his mother. Lyon's throat closed with emotion.

'Thank you.' He gave Richard back to Shay, nodding curtly to her before leaving, a frown marring his brow as the man outside stood up expectantly. 'She knows all there is to know now, Patrick,' he told her grandfather, the elderly man the one to meet him at the airport, the two of them coming to the hospital together after Patrick told him of Shay's wish to see him.

'How is she?' Patrick showed his deep concern.

Lyon's mouth twisted. 'Angry. And as usual, it's mainly directed at me.'

The older man grimaced. 'She's never been able to forgive you for making her love you.'

A heavy weight pressed down on Lyon's chest. 'I couldn't give her what she deserved then,' he said dully. 'And now she doesn't want what I *can* give her.' He shook his head at the other man's gasp of surprise at this revelation. 'She'll probably be angry all over again because I've told you that,' he acknowledged ruefully. 'Nothing I do is right for her. But I want to marry her, Patrick, and I'm not going to pretend otherwise.'

'You've got a battle on your hands, lad,' Patrick agreed sympathetically.

'But you don't object?'

'I've never objected to anything or anyone that

could make my Shay happy,' Patrick assured him softly. 'And I believe you've learnt by past mistakes and truly want to make her happy.'

'Ricky has only been dead six months,' he reminded.

'Time is irrelevant. And I'm sure Ricky would have approved,' he nodded.

'I'm not!' Lyon declared ruefully. 'And I know Shay doesn't.'

'Where you're concerned Shay has always only seen what she wanted to see,' her grandfather said indulgently. 'When you were together six years ago she loved you as if you were a cardboard hero, and when you let her down she couldn't forgive you—'

'She still hasn't,' Lyon said with regret.

'Give her time, lad,' the other man advised. 'She'll come round.'

Lyon didn't agree with him; six years hadn't softened Shay's feelings towards him, probably another six years wouldn't either!

Much as he loved Shay, he had something much more pressing on his mind now; when the next 'accident' would occur, and who its victim would be!

'Not late at all, Shay,' Marilyn drawled mockingly, 'but early.'

Shay had been deeply shocked when this woman had arrived during afternoon visiting, sweeping into the rooms with her usual arrogance, making herself comfortable in the bedside chair. Her flowers the other day had come as something of a surprise, the woman herself was totally unexpected.

'Now I suppose I'll have to withdraw the remark I made about an "overdue" baby,' she grimaced delicately.

'You don't have to do anything,' Shay told her dazedly, feeling at a disadvantage in her nightgown and robe, although her hair was neat and clean, her light make-up perfect.

Marilyn's gaze returned from looking critically around the hospital room. 'Oh, but I must,' she drawled. 'Lyon would never forgive me if I didn't.'

'And is that important to you?' Shay said dryly, sceptical of this woman's needing anyone's approval, especially Lyon's.

Anger flared briefly in blue eyes before it was quickly masked. 'Yes, it is,' Marilyn snapped. 'Did you think it wouldn't be?'

As that was exactly what she had been thinking, it would be useless to deny it. Surely it was a natural assumption to make considering the other couple were obtaining a divorce. Now she realised that perhaps Marilyn's decision to end the marriage wasn't all that it appeared to be; she certainly seemed to want and need her husband's approval still.

'Marilyn, why are you divorcing Lyon when you still love him?' Shay frowned.

Colour came and went in the other woman's

face. 'I don't believe that is any of your business!' she finally bit out coldly.

Shay sighed. 'No, possibly not—'

'Or is it?' Marilyn looked at her suspiciously. 'I've heard that he's in hot pursuit of you again.'

'I don't know who your informant is, Marilyn,' she said indignantly, 'but I can assure you I have no interest in Lyon.'

'I didn't say that you had,' she replied in a tight voice. 'I said he was after you.'

'Lyon's *fantasies* have nothing to do with me,' Shay dismissed.

Marilyn looked at her steadily for several minutes before looking away. 'Now that I'm here I might as well take a look at the baby everyone is talking about . . .'

Yet another shock. Marilyn had never given the impression of being the baby-holding type! 'He's occasionally sick,' Shay delayed. 'He makes a pig of himself and then brings up the excess.' The dress Marilyn was wearing looked like cashmere!

'It will clean, Shay.' The other woman correctly read the reason for her concern. 'Or don't you *want* me to hold him?' Her eyes were narrowed.

She had to admit to an inner suspicion of everyone now that she knew of the attempt on the lives of the Falconer family. Although she couldn't think what Marilyn's motive could be! Now that she knew how the other woman still felt about Lyon, she couldn't believe she would want to harm him, seriously, as he could have been in the car crash or falling off Wildfire's back.

'Of course,' she smiled, bending to pick up the sleeping baby and hand him to the other woman.

Marilyn's expression softened as she looked at the downy softness of black hair, the cherubic beauty of the pink rounded face. Tears glistened in her eyes as she looked up at Shay. 'He's beautiful.' Her voice was husky. 'You must be very proud of him.'

'Yes.' Shay frowned at the other woman as her attention returned to the baby she gently held.

Marilyn acted so hard, had mocked her pregnant state even as she said she was glad Lyon had never been able to give her children, and yet the awed wonder in her face as she looked down at four-day-old Richard gave lie to the claim. Marilyn was a fraud, had become as hard as Lyon over the years, and just as adept at hiding her real feeings. Until she held a small baby in her arms! But things like sterility didn't break up marriages any more, the constant breakthroughs in such fields enabling lots of couples who previously hadn't been able to have a child of their own to achieve that dream. And there was always adoption. No, if Marilyn and Lyon had really loved each other they would have made their marriage work regardless.

'Marilyn—'

'Here, you had better take him.' The other woman thrust Richard back into her arms. 'He feels as if he might be wet!' She grimaced her distaste. 'I have to be going now, anyway. I have to change before seeing a client; I don't want to smell of babies!'

If Shay hadn't seen the tenderness in the other woman's face as she held Richard she would have bristled angrily after having warned the other woman of the 'baby smell'. But she *had* seen the tenderness, and she also knew of Marilyn's love for Lyon. Marilyn hid behind a wall of bored disdain for everyone and everything, her real emotions masked and unreadable.

'I'm sure the client won't mind,' she smiled, gently placing the still sleeping baby back in his crib.

'I wouldn't want them to think it was my baby!' Marilyn snapped.

'Why not?' Shay asked. 'I think you would make a good mother, Marilyn.'

Dark colour tinged the other woman's cheeks. 'Don't be ridiculous!'

'Marilyn, there's no shame in wanting children—'

'I don't want them!' the older woman glared. 'I may have done once, but I'm too old now.'

'That's silly,' Shay dismissed. 'A lot of women are having children later in life nowadays.'

'By the time Derrick and I get married I'll be thirty-six; that's too old,' Marilyn insisted.

'I don't think so.' Shay shook her head.

'Then *you* have some more,' Marilyn scorned. 'Although that isn't going to be possible if you marry Lyon,' she taunted.

'I have no intention of ever marrying Lyon,' she snapped.

'But he wants you,' Marilyn mocked. 'At least, he wants your son! Within a year he would make sure you didn't even remember Richard is Ricky's son!'

'I'll never forget that,' Shay bit out coldly, all compassion for this woman gone in the face of her taunts.

'As Lyon's wife you would,' Marilyn assured her firmly.

'I am not marrying, Lyon,' she said with slow emphasis. 'I wish you would believe that.'

'I don't have to,' the other woman shrugged. 'It's Lyon you have to convince.'

'Lyon already knows exactly how I feel about him,' Shay's reply was firm.

'We're all aware of that.' Matthew came into the room. 'But it doesn't mean a hell of a lot, does it, Marilyn?' he taunted his sister-in-law.

She turned cold blue eyes on him. 'Lyon has always done exactly as he pleased,' she snapped.

'Then why did he stay married to you for so many years?' Matthew scorned.

The older woman's face flushed with anger. 'Obviously because he wanted to,' she dismissed. 'Now if you'll both excuse me, I have to go and change out of these sicky clothes!'

Shay was smiling as the other woman left. 'Marilyn will never change.' She shook her head ruefully. 'She insisted on holding Richard even though I warned her against it, and then proceeded to complain about it!'

'What was she doing here at all?' Matthew's
eyes were narrowed. 'She's never come across as
the nursery-orientated type.'

Shay shrugged. 'She said she came to apologise
about the "overdue" baby insult. And to see
Richard.'

'And did she?'

'Apologise or see Richard?'

'Either!'

'Both,' Shay nodded.

'Why?' he asked suspiciously.

'Because she was wrong,' Shay shrugged.

Matthew's mouth twisted. 'When you've
known Marilyn as long as I have you'll know that
wasn't the only reason for her visit,' he derided
sceptically.

'Oh, she also wanted to find out if I intended
marrying Lyon once she's divorced him,' Shay
mocked him.

'We would all be interested to know that,' he
drawled.

'The answer is no!' Shay flared.

'Really?' he mused. 'Have you told Lyon that?'

'Repeatedly!'

'Then why has he moved from his suite of
rooms into the ones the other side of Richard's
nursery?'

'He hasn't.' Shay gasped.

'Hasn't he?' Matthew frowned. 'I thought he
had.'

'Matthew!'

'Shay?' he taunted, repaying her for her earlier mockery.

'Don't tease, Matthew,' she chided. 'Not about something like this.'

'I wasn't teasing, Shay,' he told her with quiet sincerity.

'You mean Lyon has changed suites?' she gasped again. 'But what will the servants think?'

'*Are* thinking,' he corrected, shrugging. 'He was with you during the birth, now he's moved next to the baby's room, I would say that gives them enough scope to think just about anything!'

'If he doesn't care about himself or me he might at least think of Richard!'

'I'm sure he does that, all the time.' Matthew sobered. 'The baby means a lot to him.'

Her mouth twisted bitterly. 'I'm well aware of what Richard means to him.'

'Are you?' Matthew frowned.

She nodded abruptly. 'Yes. But he isn't taking Richard over.' She looked at Matthew challengingly.

'Shay, he wanted you again long before he knew there was going to be a baby.'

'Matthew, you don't have to lie for him,' she scorned. 'He can do that very well for himself.'

'I told you, Lyon never lies!'

'He lies by omission, by deception, and by seduction,' Shay accused heatedly. 'From the day he found out about the baby, he's tried to insinuate himself into our lives. He can move back into his own suite,' she stated determinedly.

'I think you had better discuss that with him yourself,' Matthew shrugged. 'And as he isn't due back until the day you're due to come out of hospital, that could prove a little difficult.'

Shay frowned. 'He's gone away again?'

'He was always the one to do the travelling, you know that,' Matthew replied.

'Where has he gone to this time?'

'Los Angeles,' he revealed reluctantly.

'Why?' she asked sharply. 'Does he have new information about Ricky's crash?'

Matthew shook his head. 'He's just gone over to see Neil.'

'Oh.' She turned away as Richard began to fret for his tea.

'Shay, he's left instructions that he'll be the one to come and collect you and Richard once you're discharged,' Matthew told her quietly.

She wasn't surprised by that, and didn't pretend to be. 'Neil hasn't been involved in an—accident, has he?' she asked anxiously, suddenly realising there could be another, more dangerous, reason for Lyon's sudden departure to Los Angeles.

'There have been no more accidents since the night Lyon came off Wildfire,' Matthew assured her. 'It's like waiting for an axe to fall!'

'But at least we now know it's probably going to!'

'Shay, stop being so bloody-minded,' he rasped. 'What good has knowing done you?

Don't you look at everyone now and suspect them?' he derided.

'With four possible exceptions,' she nodded.

'Four?' he prompted frowningly. 'I can only count three.'

'There's you, Neil and Lyon—for obvious reasons. And Marilyn, because I know she would never harm Lyon. She respects him too much ever to want to hurt him.'

It wasn't until she was on her own later that evening that she realised Marilyn was perhaps the *only* exception she could make!

Matthew, Neil and Lyon had all *claimed* to have had accidents, but they had each been alone at the time of those supposed accidents, and none of them had received serious injuries. She was the one who seemed to have been hurt the most, almost losing the baby. God, she had to suspect everyone, could trust only her grandfather!

Leaving the hospital with Richard seemed very strange after being cocooned in such a safe environment for over a week. Once she stepped out the front doors she was on her own. Nervousness was mixed with exhilaration at finally having Richard in her sole care. Luckily he had remained jaundice-free, that yellow tinge to his skin that Peter Dunbar had warned her about never materialising, and now that Richard was ten days old they were both being allowed home.

The only dampener to her pleasure was Lyon gloweringly watching her every move as she packed her own and Richard's things now that they were both dressed in their outdoor clothes, the woollen suit a little big on Richard still, although he was gaining weight nicely.

'Let me.' Lyon took over as she closed the small case ready for fastening.

She stepped back silently; the only noises in the room since Lyon's arrival half an hour ago had been Richard's contented grunts and her movements as she packed.

Lyon closed and locked the case, turning to Shay with a heavy sigh. 'What is it?'

She looked at him coldly. 'I don't know what you're talking about.'

He gave a sceptical grimace. 'You've hardly spoken since I got here, so what have I done wrong this time?'

'Didn't Matthew tell you?'

'Matthew and I don't talk much lately either!'

She had forgotten the argument the two men had had the day before Richard was born. Surely they weren't still at odds because of that?

'You tell me?' Lyon frowned as she seemed lost in thought.

She had noticed a harsh bitterness emanating from Matthew whenever the two men were in the same room together, but she had felt sure Matthew would have told his brother of the displeasure she felt over the new sleeping arrangements at the house. Matthew would probably have enjoyed it, knowing his warped sense of humour!

But it seemed that he hadn't, so it was up to her. 'I want you to move back into your own suite,' she told Lyon bluntly. 'It isn't necessary for you to be near Richard.'

'I want to be.'

'And I *don't* want you to be,' she glared at him. 'Richard has me, he doesn't need anyone else. I had expected you to insist he had a nanny, but not this—!'

'I wouldn't dream of suggesting you had a nanny, but a night-nurse may not be a bad idea—'

'I don't need one of those either,' Shay informed him coldly.

'You'll tire yourself out.'

'I'll cope.'

'What about your writing?'

'What about it?' she frowned.

'You'll be too tired to do any if you take complete care of Richard,' he warned harshly.

Her eyes widened. 'Don't tell me you're waiting with bated breath for my next publication?' she scorned.

'No,' denied Lyon predictably. 'But I thought it might bother you if you can't work.'

She shook her head. 'I'm taking six months off to spend with the baby now that my sixth book has been accepted.' Her publisher had visited her in hospital and told her of their delight with the latest book she had submitted. 'I hope by the end of that time Richard will be sleeping through the night.'

'You'll still be tired,' Lyon insisted.

'Most new mothers are,' she dismissed. 'Now about your suite—'

'I'm staying where I am—'

'The staff will talk!' Two bright spots of angry colour heightened her cheeks.

'Let them,' he bit out. 'I want to be close to you and Richard.'

'But especially Richard,' she scorned. 'You feel as if he's yours, don't you, Lyon?' she taunted, knowing she had hit target when he flinched.

'Why are you doing this to me, Shay?' he asked her dazedly.

If she told him the reason for that she would have to tell him everything. And she had no intention of ever doing that!

'I'm sorry if you think I was being offensive,' she replied woodenly.

'Are you?' Lyon still looked puzzled.

'Yes.' She turned to pick up Richard as the nurse came in with the wheelchair that was dictated by the hospital regulations as being necessary to take her to her waiting car at the front doors. 'Would you take my case, Lyon?' she requested coolly, turning away dismissively as he did so.

She had expected Lyon to be the one driving them back to Falconer House, but instead of that he got in the back of the Rolls with her and Richard, Jeffrey at the wheel on the other side of the glass partition.

'I want to talk to you about the Christmas party before we get home,' Lyon said after several minutes, very close to her on the seat, although the length of it made his proximity unnecessary.

Shay frowned. 'Matthew's been bringing in my mail, and almost everyone seems to have already accepted. And all the arrangements had been made before I went into hospital.'

'It isn't that.' He absently tucked Richard's hand back inside the shawl he was wrapped in. 'Now that you all know of the circumstances, I think it would be madness to go ahead with the party. It would be an ideal opportunity for the person who is trying to harm us to strike again, to get all of us if necessary.'

'Maybe they don't want all of us,' she frowned.

'It would still be too much like asking for trouble.'

'Are you saying we should cancel the party?' demanded Shay incredulously.

'I'm saying we should think about it,' Lyon nodded.

'I disagree,' she shook her head. 'I'm not going to be forced into living my life in fear because of some nut-case who seems to be making a lousy job of it if he wants to harm any one of us!'

Lyon smiled. 'I had a feeling you would say that.' He sat back with satisfaction. 'It was Matthew's suggestion that we cancel the party, but I felt sure you would feel the same way about it that I do.'

Shay stared at him helplessly as she realised

she had been tricked into doing what he had wanted from the beginning of the conversation. She would never have done it voluntarily.

CHAPTER ELEVEN

LYON watched Shay as she moved easily and confidently among the hundred or so guests gathered in the reception area and main lounge, the purple of her gown a perfect match for her sparkling eyes, her face glowing with health and happiness.

It was just a month since Richard's birth, and already Shay was looking more beautiful than ever before, her body more slender than he had ever seen it, her hair glowingly ebony. She was a wonderful mother to Richard, and that she was enjoying the rôle showed in her inner air of contentment.

There had been a few clashes of wills between them since she had returned home, the first one being the following morning when he had carried Richard into her bedroom for his early-morning feed. She had protested at his intrusion the next morning too, and the morning after that, and then she had given up protesting and accepted that he intended doing it whether she wanted him to or not.

A week later he had lingered in the room as Richard yelled loudly for his food, shaking his head when Shay asked him to leave. Her request had turned to anger, but as Richard became more and more upset at the delay in his breakfast, she had had no choice but to feed him. Lyon's heart leapt as she unbuttoned the front of her nightgown to reveal one brown-tipped breast, Richard latching greedily on to the nipple as it was placed in his mouth, the other breast unwittingly bared as Shay became engrossed in feeding her son. Lyon hadn't been able to look away from the beauty of mother and child so intimately together.

'Jealous, Lyon?' Shay had suddenly looked up to taunt.

'Insanely,' he answered instantly. Watching Richard suckling from her breast was the most moving experience of his life; it also gave him the deepest surge of passion he had ever known! He had watched mother and child a lot the last three weeks, and he still got that same aching rush of warm desire every time he saw them together.

He was aroused now as he watched her circulate among their guests, her breasts only slightly heavier from feeding Richard, her waist so thin he could span it with both hands, her hips swaying provocatively. She was the most beautiful woman he had ever seen!

'Lovely, isn't she?' mused Matthew mockingly at his side.

'Very.' Lyon didn't rise to the taunt, still following Shay's progress with his eyes.

'You should have married her, Lyon, while you had the chance,' his brother continued heartlessly.

Lyon looked at him with narrowed eyes. 'I already had a wife, remember.'

The two men turned simultaneously to look at the glittering Marilyn, the silver dress she wore held up only by thin shoulder-straps, the style of the dress almost indecent. She easily outshone the handsome man standing amiably at her side.

'You shouldn't have invited her here tonight, Lyon,' Matthew bit out curtly. 'Three of your women in the house at the same time is two too many!'

'Three?' Lyon frowned, looking at the many beautiful women in the room; he had touched none of them. 'What are you—' His brow cleared as he saw the way Matthew was looking at Patty as she moved about the room with a tray of drinks. 'Don't be ridiculous, Matthew,' he snapped. 'Just because you don't like the girl doesn't mean I have to be having an affair with her!'

'It wasn't my idea,' Matthew snapped.

Lyon's frown returned, and then he gave a weary sigh. 'Shay seems to think I have affairs with every young woman I meet.'

'Does that mean you aren't involved with Patty?' his brother rasped.

'Of course I'm not.' Lyon took two glasses of champagne off a tray as Hopkins passed him, handing one to Matthew. 'I haven't so much as looked at another woman since I brought Shay back from Los Angeles. I want *her* every time I look at her,' he admitted ruefully, the evidence of that desire hidden beneath his dinner jacket.

'So I see,' Matthew drawled. 'Well I wish you luck; I think you're going to need it.'

Lyon watched his brother move smoothly away, frowning heavily. Matthew really was the damnedest man! A few minutes ago he had been ready to rip out his throat, had been acting like a wounded animal for weeks, snapping and snarling at him at every opportunity, and now he acted as if nothing had happened, his good wishes concerning Shay genuine, if cryptically given.

He didn't have the time right now to probe Matthew's unpredictability, filled with a new tension as his gaze darted restlessly about the room. Was it one of these people, friends for years most of them, deliberately trying to hurt members of this family?

She might have acted unconcerned when Lyon had suggested there could be another accident, but now that the night of the party had actually arrived, Shay couldn't help suspecting everyone there. Maybe if they knew the *reason* for the 'accidents' it wouldn't be so difficult to know who was doing them. Obviously the person responsible thought that too, no explanation given for what had already happened, no threats made, just the coincidence of possible-fatal accidents to all of them. Or so each of them said; she was still wary of trusting anyone other than her grandfather.

'Would you care to dance, Shay?'

She turned to smile warmly at Derrick Stewartby, had been at Lyon's side when they greeted the other couple on their arrival a short time ago, Derrick looking a little strained now. 'I'd love to.' She moved gracefully into his arms as they stepped on to the dance-floor, looking up at him with a grimace as they both caught the fiercely angry face of his fiancée as she glared at them.

'Marilyn looks a little annoyed,' Shay commented as she turned away.

'She is,' Derrick nodded grimly.

Shay's eyes widened. 'With you?' If she were it would explain the worry-lines beside this man's eyes.

Derrick gave a tight smile. 'I merely remarked what a good party this is, and—'

'Oh dear.' Shay couldn't hold back her smile. 'Not the most tactful of things to have said, I'm afraid.' Marilyn had been giving her venomous looks ever since she arrived because Shay was so obviously the hostess tonight instead of her.

'So I gathered,' he groaned. 'It's difficult for her,' he frowned. 'Realising she's—no longer a part of all this.'

Shay would have liked to have pointed out that it was even more difficult for him, constantly being thrust into the company of Marilyn's estranged husband and his family. But she didn't say it, knew Derrick must love the other woman very much to put up with the things he did.

She patted his arm understandingly. 'Go and

tell her how beautiful she looks,' she smiled. 'No woman can resist a genuine compliment.'

'Marilyn can,' Derrick sighed. 'It is a good party, Shay,' he told her softly. 'And you're a beautiful hostess.'

Colour highlighted her cheeks. 'You see.' She gave an embarrassed laugh at this unexpected praise. 'I told you no woman can resist a genuine compliment.' She stepped back from him as the music ended.

He returned her smile. 'I'll go back to Marilyn and try it.'

She squeezed his hand, really liking this man who had unwittingly placed himself in the unenviable position of loving a woman who wasn't prepared to let go completely of her ex-husband.

She watched as he approached Marilyn, the other woman giving him a cold look, thawing a little as Derrick bent to whisper something in her ear, the two of them moving to the adjoining room, Marilyn laughing throatily as Derrick took her in his arms and they began to dance.

'Like something to eat?' Neil joined her, having arrived for the holidays only that afternoon.

'Not for me, thanks,' she smiled. 'But you go ahead.'

'It's a successful party, Shay.' He helped himself to a pastry stuffed with turkey from the buffet table, several other people helping themselves to the sumptuous array of food.

'I hope you'll save me a dance for later,' she teased. 'I've noticed all the single women here giving you inviting looks.'

'But of course,' he mocked, 'I'm the most eligible Falconer here. Matthew isn't interested, and Lyon—'

'Yes?' prompted Shay tautly.

'Look, I'm sorry if I've put my two left feet in it,' Neil grimaced. 'But it's obvious to everyone in the room that Lyon can't see anyone but you.'

She had been aware of the golden-eyed man across the room for the last hour, knew he was watching her, devouring her with his eyes, making silent love to her. It dismayed her to realise everyone else here was aware of Lyon's preoccupation with her too!

'Damn him!' She turned to glare at Lyon furiously, satisfied by the stunned surprise he showed at her vehemence.

'He damned himself a long time ago,' Neil chided, taking her hand in his. 'Come on, let's give the gossips something else to talk about; we'll have the next half a dozen dances together and have everyone guessing!'

'Which Falconer I'm after next,' she finished wearily, following him into the adjoining room where the band was playing, several couples dancing to the slow, romantic music. 'Most of them know I knew Lyon before Ricky.'

'What difference does it make?' Neil teased as he held her close as they danced. 'Every one of the men in the room would marry you if you would have them—even the ones that are already married!'

'Don't be ridiculous!' She blushed at the compliment.

'It's true,' he shrugged.

'I've just had my husband's baby!'

'So?'

'So I'm not on the look-out for another husband,' Shay told him firmly. 'And especially another Falconer.'

Neil grimaced. 'I wish you wouldn't make us sound like some sort of disease!'

She laughed softly. 'If you were you would be a fatal one!'

'Don't look now but we're being stared at,' Neil bent to whisper conspiratorially in her ear.

She instantly stiffened. 'Lyon?'

'How on earth did you guess?' Neil drawled with sarcasm.

Despite the fact that it was obvious who their observer was, she also felt a tingling at the nape of her neck every time Lyon looked at her. She could feel it now, had been aware of it all evening. She stepped back from Neil. 'Would you please go and tell him to stop this,' she said forcefully. 'Before I cause a scene he'll never forget!'

'I think you must have become more of a Falconer than I realised,' he derided. 'And I must be more of one than I realised too,' he added ruefully. 'Because I would love to see you cause a scene.'

'Neil!'

'All right,' he soothed. 'I'll go and talk to him. Not that it will do any good, Lyon's never listened to anyone but himself!'

'He's making fools out of all of us,' Shay said between stiff lips, knowing they were the cause of amusement among a lot of the guests. They were certainly the cynosure of all eyes!

'Come outside for a walk,' Matthew invited softly as Neil approached Lyon. 'Before the sparks start to fly,' he added dryly.

She took her wrap from Hopkins as she and Matthew went outside, the air feeling crisp enough for snow. 'Do you think we'll have a white Christmas?' She snuggled down into her white velvet jacket.

Matthew looked up at the dark cloudy sky. 'Who knows?' he shrugged.

'Or cares?' she teased, looking down at him as they moved across the brightly-lit yard towards the stables.

'Or cares,' he acknowledged disinterestedly. 'It certainly daren't snow before Lyon finishes for the holidays at five o'clock tomorrow.'

That bitterness again! 'Matthew, what's been wrong with you lately?' she prompted concernedly. 'You seem to have lost interest in everything.' And she had missed his cryptic humour the last few weeks.

'It's the time of year,' he revealed abruptly, as if he instantly regretted revealing even that much. 'It was Christmas when I had my accident and put myself in this chair,' he added harshly.

'I didn't realise,' Shay apologised. 'No one mentioned it . . .'

'I've never felt it as much before as I am this year,' he shrugged.

'Has something happened to upset you?' she frowned.

'No,' he rasped. 'And it isn't going to either!'

'Matthew—'

'Let's go back to the house,' he suggested abruptly.

'Matthew, please—'

'Now!' he insisted harshly.

She shook her head. 'I'm not ready to go back inside yet.'

He frowned. 'You know staying out here on your own isn't a good idea.'

Her mouth twisted. 'I'm sure Donaldson is about protecting me somewhere.' The other man had become almost like her shadow lately!

'I'm sure you're right,' Matthew derided. 'But don't stay out here too long, we don't want you to catch a chill.'

'I have to come in and feed Richard soon anyway,' Shay nodded.

'With Lyon as your audience!' He chuckled as she blushed. 'Don't look so upset, love,' he chided. 'I only know about it because I saw him follow you into the nursery when it was time for Richard's feed one evening. He didn't come out again until you did.'

'He just won't go away,' she muttered uncomfortably. 'Even though I've repeatedly asked him to.'

'Don't feel you have to apologise for Lyon's

actions, Shay,' Matthew soothed. 'I'm sure he would consider it unnecessary.'

'Lyon is a law unto himself!' she agreed resentfully.

Lyon had become even more insistent since she had come out of hospital, invading her life on every level. She had been outraged the first time he insisted on witnessing the intimacy of her feeding Richard, but her distress only upset Richard, and so after that first time she had just ignored Lyon's presence in the room as he watched them heatedly.

His divorce was only weeks away, and although he no longer mentioned marriage between them, she knew he considered it a foregone conclusion.

Thoughts of Lyon continued to plague her. Every time he looked at her he smouldered with a sexual hunger that made the heat come and go in her own body. And that bothered her almost as much as his continued presence. She was no longer pregnant, her body was almost back to normal, Peter telling her it would only be a matter of time now before she was completely back to normal health. She couldn't help wondering what was going to happen the next time Lyon tried to make love to her. Twice now she had burned with a need to know his full possession; she didn't seem to have the will to say no where he was concerned.

She turned sharply as she heard a noise behind her, able to see a shadowy shape several feet away, a shadow that was slowly approaching her. 'I had a feeling you wouldn't be far away, Eric,' she greeted the man who constantly watched over her, the two of them having become friends. 'I—Eric?' she questioned suspiciously as he didn't answer her. Come to think of it, it didn't look like Eric at all. Who—

The blow to the side of her head sent rockets shooting through her brain before darkness engulfed her.

She was a vivid splash of colour lying on the cold grey stone floor, and Lyon felt afraid to approach her, could see the stain of red on the concrete beneath her head. If she were dead—

'For God's sake, Lyon,' Matthew snapped, breaking him out of the fear that had gripped him. 'Don't just stand there, do something!'

Lyon moved woodenly towards the body of the woman whom he loved beyond life. Body? A body implied that she was dead—and he wouldn't believe that! No, she *wasn't* dead, he could see the rise and fall of her breasts as she breathed, very shallowly, but she was alive!

'Don't move her!' Peter Dunbar came up behind him, going down on one knee to feel her pulse gently.

Lyon hadn't been too thrilled at the idea when Shay had insisted the specialist be invited to the party, but now he was glad that she had.

'Don't hurt her!' he rasped as the other man made her moan with pain as he carefully moved her head so that he could examine the wound on her temple.

God, she looked so fragile lying there. If anything happened to her—!

'Call an ambulance,' Peter Dunbar instructed calmly.

'Is she—'

The other man shook his head. 'It's a nasty-looking cut, and the bump she has is enough to cause concern; I want to get her X-rayed straight away.'

God, he was falling apart, down on his knees beside Shay as someone else—he wasn't sure who!—went to telephone for the requested ambulance.

He stood over her as the men got her into the ambulance, held her hand all the way to the hospital, pain racking his body for the agony in purple depths as her lids finally fluttered open.

'Richard?' she croaked raggedly.

It was natural that her first concern should be for her son, but nevertheless it angered him that it was. *She* was the one who needed medical attention!

'Being taken care of—'

'Who by?'

'Patty,' he dismissed harshly. 'Shay, did you— did you see who hit you.' He looked at her anxiously.

She closed her eyes as a slight shaking of her head seemed to increase the pain she was feeling. 'He was—was tall,' she muttered. 'I think. Or it could have been a trick of the light.' She tried to concentrate. 'It was very dark over there.'

'He?' Lyon latched on to the only part that was really important.

'Yes,' she confirmed on a sigh. 'At least, I thought it was a man, but it could just as easily have been a woman,' she frowned. 'I don't know,' she groaned her frustration. 'Someone just hit me with something.'

'A shovel.' Lyon shuddered at the thought of what that metal tool could have done to her.

'Was it?' Shay grimaced with the effort of trying to remember. 'I don't know. I—'

'We're taking Mrs Falconer into X-ray now,' the young nurse told them gently.

The next time he was allowed to see Shay her grandfather was at his side. Shay was sleeping now, a bandage wrapped about her temple, her face almost as white as the gauze.

'At least the X-ray showed there's no internal injury,' Patrick murmured huskily.

Lyon couldn't feel quite so grateful, knew that if he ever got his hands on the person who had done this to Shay that he would rip them apart. The police *had* to believe him now!

Resting on a couch in her suite wasn't the way Shay had envisaged spending the day before Christmas, but it was the only way the doctors at the hospital would agree to her discharge. She had to admit that her head still ached abominably, but she couldn't stay away from Richard any longer. From the way he had latched on to her breast when she fed him this morning, it was obvious he had missed her as much as she had missed him—that he wasn't overly fond of the bottle feeds he had been subjected to in her absence, anyway!

She had dozed the rest of the morning away, eaten only a light lunch, very aware of all the things she still had to do for Christmas—and which she couldn't now do.

Lyon had driven her home this morning, but he seemed to have gone to work this afternoon. He had been so furious at Donaldson for not being there to stop her being injured this second time that the poor man had been dismissed, another of his associates taking his place. Lyon had been furious at Matthew too for leaving her alone out there, but Shay knew she had to take the blame for that, that she had been the one to insist on staying outside. But she had thought Donaldson would be watching over her, protecting her. Apparently he had been delayed by one of the guests. The police were 'investigating'— whatever that meant!

She turned from her contemplation of the log fire in the hearth in her lounge to see what all the noise was about as she could hear several people talking outside her door. Lyon walked in, directing the two men behind him as they carried in an enormous Christmas tree.

'What—?'

Lyon grinned at her stunned surprise. '"A real

fire, a real Christmas tree—pine-needles and all!—and thee'',' he misquoted triumphantly.

'You forgot the cottage,' she drawled to hide her truly overwhelming emotion that he should have done this, watching as he directed the men to stand the tree to one side of the fireplace, the fire blazing brightly.

'Couldn't get it in here, I'm afraid,' he shrugged. 'Thank you.' Lyon handed the two men a tip that would probably buy *six* Christmas trees. 'Well, what do you think?' He stood back to admire the tree.

'I think it needs some decorations,' Shay said dryly, shielding her confusion with derision.

'Be back in a minute,' Lyon told her lightly.

Tears clouded her vision as she looked up at the tree. It had to be eight feet high, almost touched the ceiling, its lush green branches pointing proudly upwards. The fresh smell of pine filled the room.

Lyon staggered in seconds later with two big boxes, putting them down on the sofa. 'Now, do you have a star, a fairy, or a Father Christmas on top of the tree? I bought all three.' He held up the decorations for her inspection.

She swallowed hard. 'Lyon, did you do all this for me?' she choked with emotion.

'Of course.' He sounded affronted that she should doubt that.

'But—'

'Star, fairy, or Father Christmas?' he prompted determinedly.

'Star,' Shay answered dismissively. 'What else do you have in the boxes?' she frowned.

'Wait and see,' he teased.

'Can I help?' she offered eagerly.

'Only until you tire,' said Lyon sternly. 'The doctor said you weren't to over-exert yourself or it could affect your milk. And Richard wants a Christmas dinner of Mother's milk, not the powdered kind!'

Her mouth quirked, all hostility forgotten in the face of Lyon's infectious festivity.

There were so many decorations in the boxes she felt sure Lyon had bought out a whole shop! But by the time they had attached all the ornaments to the tree, wound on the lights, it looked truly beautiful. They stood back side by side to admire their handiwork.

'I think the star is crooked,' Lyon frowned, stepping forward to straighten it.

'Leave it,' Shay pleaded huskily, full of emotion as she looked at the beautiful tree. 'I think it looks just right as it is.'

Lyon turned to her concernedly as her voice broke, his arm moving companionably about her shoulders. 'What is it, Shay?' he prompted softly.

She blinked back the tears, turning her face into his chest. 'It's my first Christmas with Richard, and my first Christmas *without* Ricky!' she choked.

Lyon's arms closed about her convulsively as reaction washed over her. She cried quietly in his arms as he continued to hold her, at last regaining

control of her emotions as she looked up at
him.

'I'm sorry,' she sighed raggedly, wiping the
tears from her cheeks.

'Shay!' The kiss was inevitable, she had known
that from the moment he had come into her suite
with the tree—and she had put off the moment
until it could be delayed no more!

Her lips opened to his like a rose to the sun,
their bodies moving together with a dizzying
intensity as Lyon moulded her to him.

'At last I can get close to you again,' he teased
as his lips travelled the length of her throat.
'Richard is a lovely baby, but he did have a way of
keeping us apart.'

Shay stiffened at the reminder that it was her
son he wanted, but her indignation faded as his
mouth returned to hers. She was starving for
what only he could give her, for what she had
burned for for so long. The gentle touch of his
hand, the fiery caresses, even the pain they had
occasionally inflicted on each other. She needed
Lyon more at this moment than she had needed
him for a very long time, at last knew her reaction
to 'the next time he tried to make love to her'!

Her mouth widened to his as she gave herself
fully into his arms, pressing against him as her
arms entwined about his neck, her fingers
tempted by the thick dark blond hair curling at his
nape.

His lips left hers to trail moistly down her
throat, his teeth nipping her earlobes, a quiver of

reaction gripping her body, warmth instantly filling her.

Lyon suddenly pulled back. 'You're tired—'

'Not *that* tired.' She pulled his head back down to hers, running her tongue in a tingling caress across his lower lip before she initiated the explosive meeting of their mouths.

'Shay, don't!' Lyon gasped, his forehead resting on hers. 'I don't know if I have the strength to be gentle with you.'

'I don't care.' She kissed the strength of his jaw. 'I don't want you to be gentle.'

'It's too soon after the baby—'

'I only have another week or so to go before Peter okays me,' she dismissed. 'And I won't magically be all right at six weeks after Richard's birth,' she derided, a fever of need in her dark eyes. 'Peter said I was very well when I saw him a couple of days ago.'

'That was before your accident, before you got that bump on your head—'

'It hasn't affected my thinking process,' she assured him impatiently. 'I'm beginning to think you don't *want* me, Lyon,' she taunted.

A shudder ran through his body. 'Of course I want you,' he denied harshly. 'I just don't think I can cope with the regret afterwards. And there would be regret, Shay, I'm sure of it.'

She recoiled as if he had struck her. 'I didn't mean to force you into something you would rather not—'

'Not me, Shay,' he rasped. 'It's you. I can't

cope with your self-recrimination, or your accusations that I've seduced you.' He took her hand in his, pressing it against his thighs. 'I want you, Shay,' he derided his own blatant need. 'I want to make love to you until you can see and feel only me. I want to be inside you, gently stroking your desire, to know again those tiny convulsions your tightness around me gives before you completely engulf me. I want it all, Shay.' He gently touched her heated cheek. 'But I don't want any of it if there's going to be regret afterwards.' Deep lines were grooved into his cheeks.

There would be no regret for her because this didn't mean to her what it would mean to him. She wanted all that he wanted, knew and recognised that need for what it was, and there could be no regret for a mere physical gratification, a few brief moments of forgetfulness in the arms of a man she knew to be a wonderful lover. Her emotions weren't involved.

'I'm not going to regret a thing, Lyon,' she told him confidently.

'You're sure?' He still looked uncertain.

In answer she moved out of his arms to pull the heavy brocade curtains across the window, the late afternoon light instantly blocked out, only the cheerful flames from the fire giving the room a warm red glow. Tiny lights shone on the huge Christmas tree, the decorations shimmering and glistening with promise.

She undressed in front of the fire, its glow

licking her body as she stood naked before him, her breasts thrusting proudly, her waist slim and flat, her hips gently curving, her legs long and creamy. With her black hair loose about her shoulders, she looked like a naked gypsy standing before a camp-fire.

Lyon's eyes glowed golden as he feasted optically on her, slowly moving to lock the door. 'I'd throw away the key if I thought it would keep you in here with me,' he grated, pulling off his own clothes.

Shay looked at him beneath lowered lashes, their ebony darkness a heavy curtain over the desire in her eyes. 'I don't think Richard would like that,' she mused huskily.

'Do you know how I feel when I see him suckling at your breasts?' Lyon groaned, throwing off the last of his clothing, his chest deeply muscled, the hair darker on his body, his hard arousal drawing her passionate gaze, seeming to harden even more as she continued to look at him.

She moved slowly across the room, touching him, her hand closing about him. 'Like this?' She began to move, feeling him tremble convulsively.

'*Exactly* like this.' He didn't try to stop her intimate exploration. 'By the time I leave the room I'm usually at exploding point!'

She could feel his moistness now, reluctantly releasing him, kissing his chest languidly, her tongue flicking slowly over the brown nubs that quickly hardened.

'Shay, is this what it feels like?' His legs almost buckled beneath him as she gently suckled him.

'Yes.' Her mouth returned moistly to his.

'How do you stop yourself from—'

'Richard is my son,' she gently chided. 'It isn't quite the same. I feel—protective towards him as I give him the nourishment that helps him live.'

'And how will you feel about your lover receiving the same nourishment?'

'It's so long since I've known the touch of a man's lips . . .'

'Can I?' He lowered his head to her breasts, looking up at her heatedly.

'Please!' She gently held him to her, the soft kisses and barely discernible movements of his tongue not enough to cause her milk to flow. But the pleasure—Oh, the pleasure was almost enough to make her convulse with release right then and there!

She fell to her knees in front of the fire, taking Lyon with her, their bodies moulded together now as their mouths met in painful demand. Despite the difference in their heights she and Lyon had always fitted together perfectly when they lay together like this, and today was no exception, Lyon hard where she was soft, that softness now welcoming the slow invasion of his hardness.

'Am I hurting you?' He looked down at her anxiously.

'Exquisitely,' she groaned, moving beneath

him. 'Wonderfully. Beautifully. Oh Lyon, so *beautifully*!' she cried as the dizzying pleasure began to explode around and inside her before she was ready for it, her body more sensitive than it had ever been before.

'Shay?' Lyon looked stunned by the speed of her approaching release.

'Yes, Lyon. Yes!' she groaned demandingly as he stilled above her. 'Don't stop now!' She almost cried her frustration. 'Lyon, *please*!' she choked desperately, poised on the edge but denied the aching satisfaction.

Confusion flickered in his eyes, and then he began that slow stroking inside her. Shay arched up to meet those thrusts, wanting deeper penetration, *needing* it as the heat built up inside her again, reaching its end this time, her nails digging painfully into Lyon's back as she felt the aching heat flow through the whole of her body, spasm after spasm convulsing her as she cried out with the intensity of her release.

She continued to move beneath him even after her own shudders of satisfaction had ceased, gripping Lyon's buttocks as she held him in to her, feeling the sudden tautening beneath her hands before Lyon's own release shot warmly into her, his powerful explosion seeming to go on and on.

Shay lay silently beneath him, feeling weak now, so heavily tired. But no regret for using Lyon as he had once used her. Never regret.

*　　*　　*

Beautiful. The most beautiful experience of his entire life. He had never known such a prolonged climax in his life before, feeling as if he could go on for ever, could spill himself inside her until he was empty, all of himself given to Shay.

He shifted slightly so that he shouldn't crush her, his expression tender as he looked down at her flushed face, her eyes closed in exhaustion.

Shay had come alive for him as never before, had been the aggressor while he felt like the ravished. And when she had reached the very pinnacle of her desire he had felt her flow around him, had known her unreserved response to her desire.

His expression softened indulgently as he saw by her heavy lids and steady breathing that she had fallen asleep. He had known it would be too much for her, he just hadn't had the strength to stop it when he wanted her so much.

He had expected her to be different somehow after having the baby, but she had been just as tightly erotic as she had ever been, so that he only had to rock gently inside her almost to explode. When she had demanded he hadn't been able to hold back for either of them.

He lay beside her for long timeless minutes, just holding her as she slept, trembling with the knowledge that she belonged to him again now. They would soon be a family, he, Shay—and Richard.

*　　*　　*

Shay woke slowly, disorientated for several minutes as she lay in the bed, the ivory silk nightgown soft against her skin, the small bedside lamp the only illumination in the room.

It was the red rose lying on the pillow next to hers that alerted her to what had happened that afternoon. She threw back the bedclothes, rushing into the adjoining room. The fire still burned, the decorated tree still glittered, and her earlier discarded mauve nightdress had been folded neatly and placed in one of the armchairs.

Her stricken gaze returned to the rug in front of the fireplace. She and Lyon had made love there—she gave a hasty look at her wrist-watch—two hours ago! God, Richard would want feeding any moment!

A knock sounded on the door, and she went to unlock it, suddenly realising Lyon must have done that to leave the room. She looked about the room guiltily, searching for any sign of what had happened there not long ago, giving a nervous start as the door opened after the second knock, Patty entering with a tray of tea.

'Mr Falconer—Mr Lyon Falconer,' she explained softly, 'thought you might like some tea after your afternoon rest.'

Rest? She had been almost unconscious! 'Thank you,' she accepted abruptly. 'That was— thoughtful, of him.'

Patty smiled. 'Can I get you anything else?'

'No—thank you,' Shay added to soften her harshly given refusal.

The tea remained untouched long after Patty had left. Shay found it hard to believe she had actually undressed and made love with Lyon! If she had been seduced—or forced!—that would have been different, but *she* had been the one to initiate their lovemaking.

No regrets, she had said! And she wouldn't have any. She had wanted Lyon, badly, and no matter what he might think, she hadn't pretended it meant anything more to her than that. She had nothing to reproach herself with, had used Lyon as he had used her and other women in the past, to assuage a physical need. That need had been satisfied now, and she had no further use of him. God, what had she become—

'Somebody said something about—Good Lord, so it's true.' Matthew grinned up at the Christmas tree. 'We haven't had a real Christmas tree in the house since Mother died.'

He didn't exactly look as if having one now displeased him. 'Lyon bought it,' answered Shay flatly.

'Where is my big brother?'

'I—'

'He had to go out for a while,' Neil absently answered Matthew as he too came into the suite to look at the tree everyone seemed to be talking about.

'He said something about seeing you later, Shay,' her grandfather added as he came in too.

She knew what Lyon meant by that, and she had no intention of leaving him with the impression that he could now come into her bedroom any time he felt the impulse. She would soon disabuse him of that fact, and as cruelly and bluntly as he had once told her *she* had no part of *his* life.

Lyon hadn't returned to the house by the time they had dinner, a hilarious affair that Shay insisted on joining the other men for, although she didn't put up too much of a fight when her grandfather suggested it was time for bed, even her sleep this afternoon not alleviating the weariness she felt since the blow to her head.

She had just settled Richard down in his cot when she heard Lyon moving about in the room next door. The sooner she informed him that this afternoon wasn't a permanent arrangement the better!

She could hear him singing as he took his shower, and it wasn't too difficult to guess the reason for his light-hearted mood. She would be waiting here in his bedroom for him as he had once waited for her.

But not on the bed, as he had done. She had come here to tell him there would be no further physical relationship between them, not encourage him to believe otherwise!

She wandered over to the window, gazing out at the strategically-lit grounds, one of the big fir-trees at the front of the house seasonally draped with huge coloured lights. They had had a light sprinkling of snow earlier in the day, and everywhere looked very beautiful. It was difficult to believe there was so much ugliness surrounding them when everywhere looked so clean and bright, but someone was definitely trying to harm the family, and the hate she felt for Lyon hadn't diminished even as she shuddered to satisfaction in his arms. Was it possible to love and hate a person at the same time? She knew she hated Lyon, but she didn't think she was the type of woman to sleep with a man if she didn't feel some genuine affection for him. The only two men she had ever made love with were Lyon and Ricky, and she had loved both of them. She didn't believe she could love Lyon now—

Her thoughts came to an abrupt end as the papers lying on top of the table in front of her caught her eye. Ricky's name leapt up at her from the print, and she couldn't stop herself from picking up the top sheet of paper. It was a report on Ricky's accident, and from the date at the top of the letter attached, she knew this had to be the report Lyon had personally commissioned. And he hadn't even told them of its arrival!

Her mouth set angrily as she began to read what she had a perfect right to know, her face having paled dramatically by the time she reached the end of the report.

CHAPTER TWELVE

LYON froze in the act of towelling dry his hair as he emerged from the bathroom, his attention all on the sickeningly pale woman who stood across the room from him. Shay looked so vulnerable, as if she couldn't take any more blows without cracking. Which was precisely the reason he hadn't told her about the report straight away! It hadn't even occurred to him that she would come to his room in this way, although after this afternoon he didn't see why it should be such a surprise to him to find her here.

She had been more fiery that afternoon, more responsive than he had ever known her. His body still tingled from the passion he had known with her, and he still ached to have her again. He had wanted to make love to her again for such a long time, years it seemed, that it had come as a shock to him when she had finally been the one to give herself to him.

But if she gave completely with her body then he knew she held back just as completely with her mind and emotions. What they had shared this afternoon had been physical—and it wasn't enough, not for him.

He straightened his shoulders as if for a fight, his mouth setting determinedly before he smiled.

'Hello, darling,' he greeted the shocked woman lightly, bending to kiss her lingeringly on the lips, hers too numb to do anything else but move pliantly beneath his. 'You're looking beautiful.' She couldn't know how beautiful she looked in the clinging black dress! 'Sorry I had to leave you like that.' He ignored the dullness of her eyes as he began to towel his hair once again, glad of something to do with his hands, sure they were shaking. If she didn't say something soon—! 'I had to put in an appearance at the impromptu company party. Obligatory.' And he would have gladly missed a hundred such dull parties to be with Shay if he hadn't been unsure of how she would feel if she woke up to find him beside her in her bed. So he had gently carried her into the other room, helped her into her nightgown, before leaving her alone in her bed, only the red rose on the adjoining pillow to show her his thoughts would all be of her.

And now he knew he was never likely to know what her reaction had been when she woke up to realise what had happened between them, the report she held in her hand blocking anything else from her mind—but especially any idea of a continued relationship with him!

'When did you get this?' she asked between stiff lips, not even looking at him directly but at some point over his right shoulder.

'Shay—'

'When?' she bit out tautly, the coldness of her voice like a whip cracking across his bare back.

'It came this morning,' he sighed. 'But I already knew what it contained.'

'You knew! Why didn't you—'

'Shay,' he reasoned at her anger. 'It's only a report confirming that Ricky's crash was a genuine accident and not—'

'*Only?*' Fury glittered in deeply purple eyes as she looked at him fully at last. ' "Only confirms it was a genuine accident"!' she repeated with icy accusation. 'I've been worried out of my mind that Ricky might have been a victim of this senseless vendetta, and you have in your possession the means to alleviate that terror and yet you do nothing!'

'The written report only arrived this morning—'

'But you've known about it for days, haven't you?' she accused heatedly.

'I—'

'You have!' she flared. 'And yet you've said nothing to any of us.' She shook with anger. 'You arrogant bastard,' she stated coldly. 'You—'

'Shay, I was going to tell you!'

'When?' she demanded icily, her eyes the only colour in her face now, deep pained pools of despair.

'This afternoon. I—'

'Oh no, Lyon,' she scorned with distaste. 'I'm not accepting that.'

'It's true,' he rasped, hating her distrust of everything he said. 'Even though it was good news—in a way—I knew the report would upset you, so I got the tree and decorations to divert you.'

'Except that we decorated the tree and you *still* didn't tell me,' she dismissed hardly.

He grimaced at the truth of the accusation. 'You got upset about Ricky, and I—Well, you know what happened next.' He watched her anxiously.

'Yes,' Shay confirmed with self-disgust. 'Instead of *you* telling me about the report *I* made love to you.'

'It wasn't one-sided—'

'I know what it was, Lyon!' She held herself proudly. 'And above all it was a mistake.'

'You said there would be no regrets,' he reminded her harshly.

'I didn't say I regretted it, Lyon.' Her eyes flashed. 'Only that it was an unrepeatable mistake.'

He had known this would be her reaction, had known it was too soon for her, that even though she had wanted him she had hated him too.

When he spoke to the expert in Los Angeles a couple of days ago and the man had told him what the report he had sent off contained, Lyon had been filled with relief to know Ricky hadn't been killed because of this senseless vendetta against the family. The report clearly stated, without doubt, that the small plane had gone down because it had been struck by lightning. But although the report was a relief, he hadn't known how to break the news to Shay; she had already been through so much the last few months. And it wasn't the sort of thing you just blurted out over the breakfast table, and so he had gone out and bought the tree in the hope of somehow softening the blow. He realised now it had been a stupid thing to do, that it would have been kinder just to have told her what he knew as soon as he had known it.

'Shay, whatever the report contained, it wouldn't have altered the fact that Ricky is dead, no matter how quickly you had been informed,' he pointed out gently.

'It might have stopped me from making a fool of myself with you this afternoon!' she replied hoarsely.

He didn't say it, didn't think she could take it right now, but they both knew it; telling her of the report and its conclusions might have had exactly the same effect as not telling her had done.

'I'd like a copy of this report for myself.' She flung it down on the table. 'Merry Christmas, Lyon!' she said with obvious insincerity as she turned and walked away.

He let her go, knew there was nothing he could do—or say—to stop her.

The family tradition of opening Christmas presents after lunch was broken the next day when Shay insisted Richard couldn't possibly wait until then before seeing what was in his many, and varied-shaped, parcels beneath and beside the tree. Neil and Matthew indulgently agreed it

wasn't fair, while Lyon remained silently brooding, as he had been most of the day. Shay
pointedly ignored him, was determined to enjoy
Richard's first Christmas in spite of Lyon's
presence.

As Richard was only just focusing, and
occasionally giving a windy smile, he showed
little or no interest in the numerous toys Shay
unwrapped for him. A big car and trailer from
Matthew that he wouldn't be able to peddle for at
least another year! A teddy-bear six times his size
from Neil, and a rocking-horse from Lyon. Considering Lyon had already stocked the nursery
there with enough toys for a toyshop, she hadn't
expected him to get Richard anything else. Her
own gifts to her son were a little more practical;
toys for him to play with in the bath in a couple of
months' time, safe toys that he could chew on
during the painful time of teething—and a train-
set.

'Ricky said the first thing he was going to buy
for the baby was a train-set—whether it was a boy
or a girl,' she explained gruffly at Matthew's
mocking raise of eyebrows after she had teased
the men about the impracticality of their gifts.

'So that he could play with it,' Neil nodded,
setting it up on the dining-room table.

'I expect so,' she acknowledged softly. 'I think
all men must be little boys at heart,' she derided
as Matthew, Neil, and her grandfather worked
on setting up the track so they could have the
train running. 'With the odd exception.' She

looked hardly at Lyon before trying to gain Richard's waning attention with the squeaky duck Mrs Devon had sent him; Richard just lay on the floor and blew bubbles at her.

'Your Christmas present.'

She gave a startled jump as Lyon spoke quietly beside her, turning to him resentfully. 'Do you have to creep about in that awful way?' she snapped.

His mouth twisted. 'I wasn't creeping. It must be a guilty conscience, Shay,' he taunted.

'Not mine!' she bit out.

'Your present.' He held out a flat package to her from beneath the tree, gaily wrapped in Christmas-tree decorated paper with a pretty silver bow in one corner.

'Yours,' she returned abruptly as she placed the big flat parcel in front of him, feeling as if they were in a private cocoon, the other three men now arguing about whether the track for the train would be more effective round or oval. If she had known it would give them this much pleasure to play with trains she would have bought them all a set, it would certainly have saved on arguments! Although she didn't doubt that all three would deny wanting one if she suggested it!

Lyon looked at her with compelling gold eyes. 'Open yours first; I have a feeling that after I've seen mine we may not be on good enough terms for me to sit and watch you open yours!'

She blushed at the truth of that, ripping off the

bow and paper to her present, groaning inwardly as she saw it contained a jewellery box, the jeweller's name more than familiar to her. Lyon had always bought her jewellery in the past, and although she had returned it after they broke up, Ricky had continued to spoil her in the same extravagant way. The last thing she needed—or wanted—was more jewellery.

'It isn't what you think it is,' Lyon encouraged throatily.

She gave him a quick glance before gingerly opening the velvet lid. Her breath caught in her throat as she looked at the necklace nestled against the blue velvet. She had expected the usual jewels, but this—! It had obviously been especially made, gold moulded into the shape of a book, a diamond set in engraving in the shape of a star decorating its front.

'If you open it there's an inscription,' Lyon prompted softly.

She lifted the gold book and chain from the box, gently separating the folds of the book. 'My talented woman', it read, signed 'Lyon'. And it did actually look like his signature! It was the most thoughtful and beautiful gift she had ever received.

'I wanted you to know that I'm very proud of your writing,' Lyon told her sincerely.

Shay frowned up at him. 'But I thought you hated it.'

He grimaced. 'I thought I did too. But I read all the books, and you have a gift with words, Shay.

You make your characters come alive, make them real.'

She swallowed hard at this unexpected praise. 'Thank you.'

He nodded abruptly, looking down at the huge flat parcel that lay beside him. 'I suppose I had better open this now, hadn't I?' he said ruefully.

She didn't regret buying the painting, but she also knew it would have the effect Lyon had predicted it would. It was a pity to cause this dissension at Christmas, but it couldn't be helped.

She watched his face closely as the last of the wrapping-paper fell away, but she could read nothing from his expression, not anger, not frustration at the message it conveyed, not even appreciation for what was also a work of art.

At last he looked up at her, compassion in his eyes. *Compassion?* It was the last emotion she had expected!

'I know what you're telling me with this, Shay,' he told her huskily. 'I understand it—'

'You can't!' she denied dazedly, shaking her head.

He smiled a gentle smile. 'I can. But I also know that after yesterday you belong to me—'

'No!'

'Against your will,' he acknowledged. 'But you do belong to me, because we both know I could make yesterday happen all over again any time I want to.'

Her mouth twisted. 'Perhaps you could, but it wouldn't get you what you really want.'

'No,' he agreed heavily. 'It wouldn't do that.' He looked down at the painting once again. 'You're telling me this is the only "purple-eyed pixie" I'll ever have, right?'

'Yes,' she bit out. The painting wasn't exactly of a pixie, more a mischievous-looking fairy as she sheltered from the rain beneath a mushroom. Predominant in the heart-shaped face were deep purple eyes. As soon as Shay had spotted the painting at the back of the shop she had known she had to buy it and give it to Lyon.

'I'll hang it in my bedroom,' he told her huskily. 'Over my bed.'

'Lyon—'

'Come and look at this, you two,' Neil called to them excitedly as the train was finally set up and running; Richard had fallen asleep in his great-grandfather's arms long ago.

'Thank you for the necklace, Lyon,' she told him stiltedly as they stood up.

'Will you wear it?'

'I—'

'Now,' he prompted softly.

Shay was about to refuse when she saw the determination in his face. Why not wear it; it was a beautiful piece of jewellery, a compliment to her writing. As long as no one looked inside and read the inscription!

Marilyn asked to look inside the gold book after dinner that evening.

The small family dinner party was another Falconer tradition on Christmas day, and as Marilyn was still a member of it, she and Derrick had been invited for the evening too. Shay felt a little sorry for the other woman's fiancé, knew that he must feel very uncomfortable spending so much time in the company of Marilyn's soon-to-be ex-husband. But he seemed to take it in his stride, very friendly with all the Falconer men.

'New necklace, Shay?' Marilyn drawled as they enjoyed an after-dinner drink in the lounge.

Her eyes flashed warily as everyone turned to admire the necklace she had left beneath the high neckline of the black dress she wore, but which had somehow slipped on top of the silky material.

'Does it open?' Marilyn stood up to take a better look at the necklace, not waiting for confirmation or denial but flicking the book open, her eyes narrowing as she read the inscription. 'Santa has been busy, hasn't he?' she snapped the book closed so forcibly that Shay winced. 'How is your head now, Shay?' Marilyn was in control again now, only the hardness of her eyes showing how much she resented the gift Lyon had given Shay.

She frowned. Was that a threat in the other woman's voice? Surely it couldn't be Marilyn after all—

'Shay?' the other woman prompted hardly.

'Better,' she answered abruptly. 'It just aches a bit.'

'Good.' Marilyn gave a tinkling laugh of derision. 'I meant, of course, that I'm glad you're feeling better,' she explained challengingly.

'We're all glad about that,' Shay's grandfather put in curtly, his eyes narrowed on the other woman.

'Yes, indeed,' Derrick agreed with enthusiasm, ignoring the glare he received from his fiancée for his trouble—unless he just didn't see it. 'Lyon was in a terrible state when he realised you had gone missing from the party.'

'You do seem—accident-prone, lately,' Marilyn drawled uninterestedly, obviously bored with the conversation she had introduced.

'It must be a terrible thing if you are,' Derrick nodded. 'You never know what's going to happen next.'

'Shay isn't accident-prone,' Lyon rasped.

'She isn't?' Derrick looked surprised by the firm assertion.

'No,' the other man bit out.

'Oh.'

Shay felt sorry for the older man, and not just because of Lyon's terseness with him just now. Derrick was obviously not up to matching Lyon, in any way, not if Marilyn's often derogatory treatment of him was anything to go by!

'Have you seen Matthew's collection of antique clocks, Derrick?' Shay asked conversationally.

He frowned. 'I didn't know he had a collection of clocks.'

'I'm sure he would love to show them to you. Wouldn't you, Matthew?' she added pointedly.

'Um? Oh—oh yes,' he nodded, looking at her questioningly.

'I'll come with you,' she decided, ignoring Lyon's scowl, Marilyn's scorn, Neil's amusement, and her grandfather's surprise, as she stood up gracefully.

'Count me out,' Neil drawled. 'I'm too stuffed to move!'

'You made an absolute pig of yourself,' Marilyn agreed with disgust.

'Don't nag, Marilyn,' he said easily, looking very comfortable as he lounged in the chair.

'Lyon, are you going to let him—'

'Do stop nagging, Marilyn,' Matthew groaned. 'And if you want to appeal to anyone to come to your rescue then use Derrick here; he is the man you're going to marry. Isn't he?' he challenged.

Marilyn gave him a blazing look of anger before turning away. 'Lyon, I have something I need to discuss with you. In private.' She looked pointedly at the lounging Neil.

'I'm not moving,' Neil told her lazily.

'We'll go into one of the other rooms,' Lyon bit out. 'If it's really important.'

'Why don't you take her upstairs and show her your new suite of rooms?' Matthew jeered.

Marilyn's eyes widened. 'What new suite of rooms?'

'We'll leave you to tell her.' Matthew looked mockingly at his brother. 'Come on, Shay, Derrick. Patrick?'

He shook his head. 'I think I'll stay here and keep Neil company.'

Shay felt even more sorry for Derrick as they went to the room put aside for Matthew's clocks, the one she had bought him for Christmas already added to the collection. Didn't the poor man realise that if he wanted to hold on to Marilyn he was going to have to be a lot stronger than he was?

He had obviously only come with them now to view the clocks out of politeness, and Matthew did his best to bore him as he went into detail about each clock. Shay wasn't in the least surprised when the man made his excuses as soon as it was possible and escaped back to the lounge, Matthew's boring monologue having droned on for over half an hour.

'That was cruel,' she chided as Matthew chuckled once the other man had left.

He shrugged unrepentantly. 'If he wants to survive in this family he'll have to toughen up.'

'He won't be in this family.'

'You think not?' Matthew replaced the Victorian clock on the shelf that he had been reverently holding. 'Has it seemed as if Marilyn has actually made a move to leave the family completely?'

'No, but—She and Lyon are getting a divorce!'

'Yes, I finally think they are.' He sounded surprised. 'But I wonder if Marilyn will actually marry Derrick.'

'Of course she will; they're engaged.'

'So they are,' he mused.

'Matthew, stop being evasive. If you have something to say, then say it!'

He shook his head. 'I don't have anything to say.'

'Then why don't you leave that poor man alone?' she chided. 'It can't be easy for him.'

'No, I pity any man who intends marrying Marilyn.'

'That isn't the problem.'

'No?' He raised blond brows.

'No.' Shay shook her head thoughtfully. 'It's following Lyon that's so difficult. Marilyn is obviously still very fond of him.' She wouldn't embarrass the other woman by telling Matthew Marilyn was still in love with her husband. 'And any woman who's been that close to Lyon must find it difficult to accept another man in her life.'

She was so lost in thought that she didn't even notice the way Matthew was looking at her, but when she did notice she didn't like the speculative look in his eyes.

'Do you realise what you just said?' he asked slowly.

She frowned. 'We were talking about Marilyn and Lyon.'

'Were we?'

'Of course we—Matthew, why do you keep looking at me like that?'

'When you first came back here I told you I didn't think you were ready to talk just yet,' he spoke gently. 'Well, I think you're ready now.'

'We have guests—'

'Later then, after they've gone. I have to tell you a few things about Lyon—and Ricky,' he added softly, his gaze searching.

'Ricky?' Her eyes widened. 'What—'

'Later, Shay,' he promised. 'We'll talk later.'

Marilyn appeared to be in no hurry to leave, Shay finally hearing the other couple go as she was feeding Richard shortly after one o'clock, having excused herself so that she could go up to him.

Lyon came into the room just as she was tucking the sleeping baby back into his cot, self-conscious of her unbuttoned dress, her breasts bared.

She gasped as Lyon came up to her to cup her breasts inside the dress, heat instantly coursing through her body. 'No, Lyon!' She swung away from him, hastily adjusting her dress, her eyes bright as she looked up at him.

He walked silently from the nursery into her bedroom, and Shay followed him, closing the door to Richard's room quietly behind her.

'Since when did you have such an interest in Matthew's clocks?' he rasped.

She gave a start of surprise. 'I haven't.' She shook her head.

'You stayed with him for about ten minutes after Derrick came back to the lounge,' he scowled.

She relaxed a little. 'Ten minutes, Lyon?' she derided.

'Nine minutes and twenty-five seconds,' he said gruffly.

'I'm flattered that you timed us, Lyon, but it wasn't necessary. Matthew and I were just talking, about you, in fact.'

'Me?' He looked taken aback.

'And Marilyn,' she taunted.

'Don't make fun of me, Shay,' he warned softly. 'Not now. I'm not in the mood to be amused.'

'Threats, Lyon?'

His eyes darkened. 'You know I would never willingly hurt you.'

'Then leave me alone.'

His mouth tightened. 'One day you're going to have to admit how you really feel.'

'About you?' she taunted. 'I already know how I feel,' she scorned. 'Disgusted, most of the time.'

'And what about the rest of the time?'

'Hatred, Lyon,' she told him softly. 'I feel intense hatred.'

'Even that's better than nothing at all,' he declared. 'And there's a very thin line between love and hate.'

'And between sanity and insanity, so they tell me!' she snapped.

Lyon smiled without humour. 'I'm not mad, Shay.'

'No,' she conceded heavily. 'Just arrogantly determined.'

'Thank you for the painting, Shay.' He touched her cheek. 'It will do until I have the real thing in my bed.'

If it weren't for Richard she would leave right now and never come back. But even if Lyon wouldn't bother to come after her, she knew he would never let Richard go. And after yesterday she got an uneasy feeling in her stomach whenever Lyon was near. No regrets, she had decided when she had taken what he so blatantly offered. But how could she *not* regret the fact that she had given in return!

She was too disturbed to be able to sleep just yet, and surely this was the 'later' Matthew had spoken of.

She left her room quietly, pressing back against the wall as she saw the figure moving stealthily up the hallway, holding her breath as Patty stopped outside Matthew's bedroom door. What on earth was the other woman doing here this time of night? The staff had been given the evening off after dinner had been served. Patty obviously wasn't working, wearing tight denims and a pale blue sweater, looking younger out of uniform. *But what was she doing creeping about the house in the early hours of the morning?*

Shay was about to call out to the other woman when she suddenly knocked softly on Matthew's door instead of quietly entering as Shay had expected her to. The person who had been causing all the 'accidents' to the family hadn't shown themselves so far, surely knocking on a door for entry wasn't characteristic of that elusive person?

Matthew had obviously been preparing for bed, partly undressed as he opened the door to

Patty's knock, not looking surprised to see her standing there.

Shay couldn't hear what was being said, although Matthew did sound angry. Patty was calmer, more reasoning, suddenly stepping fully into the room and closing the door firmly behind her.

Shay didn't know how long she stood there, but it must have been ten minutes or so, and still Patty hadn't left Matthew's room. She had even heard the other woman giggle once! Matthew and Patty . . . ?

Matthew and Patty *what*? Matthew acted as if he hated the other woman, had even asked for her dismissal, so what was going on? Only Matthew or Patty could answer that question—and neither of them seemed in a hurry to leave Matthew's bedroom!

'Why do you keep frowning at me like that?' Matthew demanded tersely.

Shay's eyes widened at his show of temper, the five of them—the three Falconer men, her grandfather and herself—sitting down to breakfast together. 'I didn't realise I was,' she told him truthfully.

'I feel as if I've suddenly grown two heads,' he snapped.

'I'm sorry. I—'

'Leave her alone, Matthew,' Lyon rasped, scowling heavily. 'Take your bad temper elsewhere.'

Matthew slammed down his coffee cup. 'I think I will!'

'Matthew!' Shay gave Lyon a reproving glance before following him. 'Matthew, I want to talk to you—'

'I'm going to the office!'

'Then I'll come with you. Matthew, I wasn't staring at you, it's just that I came to your room last night, and—'

Lyon stiffened as the rest of the conversation was shut off to him as the couple went into the office and closed the door after them. Shay going to *Matthew's* bedroom?

'What's going on?' Neil looked puzzled by the whole incident.

'Certainly not what it sounded like,' Patrick told them sternly.

It could have been funny if it weren't so damned *devastating*! Lyon wasn't about to lose Shay to another of his brothers. 'Excuse me.' He stood up. 'I have some things to do.'

'Lyon.'

He turned at Patrick's softly spoken plea.

'It isn't what it sounded like,' Patrick repeated firmly.

Lyon's mouth twisted. 'I hope you're right, Patrick,' he ground out. 'Because if you aren't, I'm likely to commit murder!' He strode out of the room after Shay and Matthew.

*　　　*　　　*

'You did *what*?' Matthew turned on her as soon as they were in the privacy of his office.

'Came to your room,' she repeated with a grimace, not having meant to burst out with that the way that she had.

'And?' Matthew's eyes were narrowed defensively.

She moistened her lips. 'And I was too late to talk to you,' she shrugged.

Green sparks shot from hazel eyes. 'You mean Patty got there first,' he snapped.

'Matthew—'

'Just what did you see, Shay?' he demanded angrily. 'Or thought you saw?'

She didn't *think* she had seen anything, she knew exactly what had happened—before Patty entered Matthew's bedroom and closed the door. After that, she didn't even want to guess. But whatever had transpired between those two it hadn't made either of them happy; Matthew's temper could attest to his own disturbed state, and when Patty had brought her coffee up this morning her eyes were shadowed with pain.

'I wasn't spying on you, Matthew—'

'No?' he scorned. 'Forgive me, it sounds very much like it to me!'

'Well I wasn't.' Her own temper rose at his unreasonable tone. 'You said we were going to talk—'

'It was after one o'clock in the morning when Patty came to my room!'

She looked at him with calm eyes. 'I know,' she confirmed softly.

For a moment his gaze challenged hers, and then he gave a disgusted snort and turned away. 'And as it was after one, what was she doing in my bedroom,' he acknowledged harshly.

'She could have been bringing you a late-night drink—'

'We both know she wasn't.' He looked up at Shay with tortured eyes. 'Patty spent the night with me,' he admitted.

'And?' She looked at him expectantly.

'And nothing,' he dismissed coldly.

'Matthew—'

'My relationship with Patty is none of your business,' he told her heatedly.

'I know that—'

'But you want to know anyway!' he rasped. 'What do you want to know, Shay? How I managed to—'

'Matthew!' she cried her dismay.

'Yes—Matthew!' Lyon stepped into the room. 'That's enough! Shay is aware of the fact that your disability doesn't incapacitate you in a sexual sense.'

'And I wonder just who told her that?' his brother challenged, furiously angry.

Tawny eyes darkened even more. 'Matthew—'

'Matthew, I only told you I knew about last night because I don't want you to get hurt,' Shay spoke gently. 'We have to—'

'I never care enough about any woman to be hurt by one.' His reply was bitter.

In Patty's case that was a lie, and they both knew it; Matthew was in love with the other woman. 'That wasn't the sort of hurt I was talking about, Matthew,' she gently rebuked. 'We're all in danger until we find out who is trying to harm us, can trust no one—'

'You can both trust Patty,' Lyon put in hardly. 'Implicitly.'

Shay knew that Matthew looked as surprised by the unequivocal claim as she felt. Just how could Lyon be so sure—'Oh, my God,' she breathed raggedly. 'She's another one of them, isn't she? One of your spies!' she accused disbelievingly. Not a *mistress*, another bodyguard!

Lyon looked at her coldly. 'Patty works for the same firm Donaldson and Grieg do, yes. Luckily she's a damn sight more efficient than both of them!' he declared fiercely.

'My God!' Matthew gasped dazedly.

Shay turned to him with concern, worried by the grey cast to his cheeks. 'You didn't know, did you?' she groaned.

'Patty had instructions not to tell *anyone* who or what she is,' Lyon told them arrogantly.

Hazel eyes blazed with fury, and Shay was sure that if Matthew could have he would have knocked Lyon off his feet and not let him up again until he had beaten him to a pulp! Instead, he used every verbal weapon he had to beat his brother into the ground!

'"Who and what she is"?' Matthew repeated icily. 'Why don't we concentrate on what you are, Lyon. You're a cold-hearted, calculating bastard,' he accused with dislike. 'You manipulate and use people at your will. But you couldn't manipulate Ricky into staying here, could you?' he goaded with derision. 'He married the woman you wanted, had the nerve to keep her, to eventually take her away from here.'

'Ricky married me because he loved me,' Shay claimed forcefully.

'Of course he loved you,' Matthew acknowledged. 'That was why once he knew about Lyon he knew he had to get you away from here.'

'What are you talking about?' she frowned.

'He guessed that Lyon's noble gesture where you were concerned couldn't last for ever,' Matthew scorned. 'Saw, as we all did, the hungry looks Lyon gave you whenever he saw you. Ricky couldn't risk the two of you being here if Lyon got over his scruples where you were concerned and decided to forget all about his ste—'

'Matthew, don't!' Lyon's protest came out as a strangulated cry.

Matthew looked at him, and so did Shay, shocked by his pallor, the almost feverish look to his eyes, his hands clenching and unclenching at his sides.

'Doesn't she have a right to know?' Matthew challenged cruelly.

'I'll tell her in my own good time!' Lyon grated between stiff lips, tense as if waiting for a blow.

'After you've married her, Lyon?' his brother taunted. 'After her child becomes yours?'

'Damn you, Matthew!' he cried in a tormented voice.

'And damn you for putting at risk the life of the woman I love,' Matthew's eyes glittered dangerously. 'You have no right to endanger an innocent—'

'If you're going to tell Shay, Matthew, then do it now,' Lyon ground out bitterly. 'We can discuss Patty later.'

'*All right*, I'll tell her,' Matthew said heatedly, turning to Shay with fevered eyes. 'Lyon takes such an interest in your child, Shay, because he knows he can never have any of his own,' he revealed harshly. 'Because he's sterile!'

She had already guessed this was what Lyon so dreaded her knowing, it was the things Matthew had said about Ricky that disturbed her the most.

'Ricky had the good sense to leave here before the two of you had a child of your own,' Matthew grated. 'After Lyon told us of his sterility, Ricky knew any child the two of you had would be dominated by Lyon if you stayed here. The poor bastard couldn't know it was going to happen anyway!'

'Ricky asked for the Los Angeles office after he was told of Lyon's sterility?' she croaked, her throat dry, her hands suddenly clammy.

'Yes!'

'Are you sure it was after he knew?' Shay breathed heavily, feeling faint.

'Lyon told all of us at the same time,' Matthew dismissed. 'Almost four years ago.'

'I thought you had a right to know,' Lyon bit out harshly. 'I had no idea you were going to use it as a stick to beat me with!'

Shay looked at him dazedly, feeling faint, sick, hot, cold, all at the same time. 'Lyon—Lyon—'

'It's all right, Shay,' he scorned bitterly, 'I've got used to the reaction I get when I tell people I can't father a child.' He turned to his brother. 'Thank you, Matthew,' he said with icy control. 'If you ever want anyone to kill you slowly just give me a call; I'd be glad to do it!' He strode from the room, his shoulders stiffly back.

'Shay—'

'Shut up, Matthew,' she ordered sharply. 'Just shut up!'

'What—'

'Tell me you were mistaken.' She turned to him with blazing eyes. 'Tell me Lyon's sterility had nothing to do with Ricky's and my leaving here.'

'I can't tell you that, Shay,' he frowned. 'It was only a matter of days after Lyon talked to us all that Ricky asked for an office abroad, any office, he just wanted out. Shay?' he frowned as she made no response.

'I have to go and see to Richard,' she told Matthew jerkily. 'I—Excuse me.'

'Shay!'

'What is it?' She gave an irritated frown, just wanting to be alone, needing to work out what she should do.

'I only meant to hurt Lyon.' He looked at her worriedly. 'I shouldn't have involved you. My temper got the better of me—'

'Matthew,' she gently interrupted him, 'we both know you don't *have* a temper. If you love Patty you should marry her.'

'I don't—It isn't as simple as that,' he muttered at her sceptical expression.

'Loving someone never is,' she said bitterly. 'Now I really do have to go.'

She almost ran up the stairs to her room, leaning back against the door, shaking so hard she thought she was going to collapse.

Oh Ricky, my *God*, Ricky!

CHAPTER THIRTEEN

THE look on her face when Matthew told her he was sterile! First the stunned shock, and then the disgust.

He would have told her himself eventually—it wasn't something he would have been able to keep secret from her for ever! But he had intended waiting until she was his wife and he was more sure of her. He knew now he would never get the chance.

'Lyon?'

His body tensed before he turned to face Matthew, pain etched into his face. 'Come to make another few stab wounds, Matthew?' he returned harshly. 'I shouldn't bother if I were you, the wounds you've already made will eventually be fatal. Slowly but surely.'

'Hell, Lyon.' Matthew propelled himself fully into the bedroom, closing the door behind him. 'Sometimes you make me so damned angry I could—'

'You already did,' he drawled. 'Can't you see the blood?'

He knew Shay would never consider marrying him now, that she believed he only wanted her so that he could make Richard his own. Maybe that was true in a way, but not the way—

'It was because of Patty,' Matthew reasoned. 'She could get killed defending us. How would you feel if it were Shay?'

Lyon had been sure he couldn't feel any worse than he did right now, but the renewed thought of Shay being dead filled him with cold dread. 'Matthew, until a few minutes ago I had no idea you were in love with Patty—'

'I'm not,' Matthew denied heatedly.

'You forgot yourself earlier, Matthew,' Lyon told him huskily, 'and admitted that you did. But I hired Patty to do a job; I had no idea your boorish temper where she was concerned hid much deeper feelings.'

'You and Shay think you're so damned smart, don't you!' he glared. '*Yes*, I love Patty. But I'm not going to do a thing about it.'

'I thought you already had,' his brother drawled.

Matthew flushed angrily. 'It isn't funny, Lyon,' he rasped resentfully.

'I couldn't agree more,' Lyon sobered. 'But do you really want to live the way I have the past six years, loving a woman you had denied yourself, seeing her married to someone else?'

'God, no!' Matthew groaned at the thought.

'Then marry her yourself,' he advised heavily. 'Before someone else does.'

'Lyon . . .' Matthew said slowly. 'Lyon, six years ago, why did you—'

'Go and see Patty now,' he instructed harshly.

'And don't worry about Shay and me. I was never meant to have her.'

'Lyon—'

'Matthew, for God's sake go!' he rasped forcefully. 'Unless you would enjoy seeing a grown man cry?'

Matthew looked at him searchingly for several minutes before turning his chair and leaving.

Cry? God, he wasn't going to—

At that moment Lyon did something he hadn't done since he fell off his bicycle at six years old, and no one was more surprised than he to feel the dampness on his cheeks.

'Shay?'

She turned to look at Patty, sitting up on the bed to push the hair from her face. 'Yes?' she asked sharply, not feeling in the mood to make polite conversation.

The other woman looked uncomfortable. 'Matthew was worried about you—'

'So he sent you,' Shay sighed. 'Why didn't he come himself?'

'I think he's gone to look for Lyon,' Patty grimaced. 'I understand the two of them argued.'

'That's an understatement.' She stood up to check her appearance in the mirror, dampening a tissue to cool her heated cheeks. 'Why don't the two of you get married, it's obvious you love each other?'

'Yes,' Patty sighed. 'But he has the idea that he mustn't burden any woman by marrying her. I

would marry him tomorrow if he would let me.'
Her voice broke slightly.

'Oh God, I'm sorry I pried.' Shay was instantly
contrite. 'I shouldn't take my confusion out on
you. Come and sit down and we'll talk,' she
invited.

'Is this a private party or can anyone join in?'

Shay and Patty were sitting in the lounge
drinking sherry, the two of them having been
talking for the last twenty minutes or so. And
Shay could cheerfully have hit Matthew for what
amounted to his stubbornness in keeping himself
and Patty apart, last night a lapse on his part he
had assured Patty he didn't intend repeating.

'You can come in,' she told him abruptly,
'as long as you don't mention Lyon and you
ask Patty to marry you.' She looked at him
challengingly.

'Shay!' Patty groaned her awkwardness as
colour darkened her cheeks, avoiding looking at
Matthew.

'The only thing keeping you apart is Matthew's
misguided pride,' insisted Shay forcefully. 'It's a
trait all of the Falconer men have.'

'And none of us more so than Lyon,' Matthew
taunted.

'You just broke the first condition,' she snapped, her mouth tight.

'One out of two isn't too bad,' he drawled.

'I don't—Did you just say what I thought you
said?' Shay gasped.

He was looking at Patty now. 'I still think you

would be a fool to marry me, but if you want me—'

'Oh, I want you,' Patty assured him eagerly.

He shrugged. 'Oh well, at least I'll have my own personal bodyguard now!'

'You really mean it, Matthew?' Shay said excitedly, thrilled that there was at least to be a happy ending for these two people she liked so much.

He nodded. 'I've just seen a man I like and respect very much, totally broken because he let the woman he loves get away from him.'

'If you're talking about Lyon,' Shay derided, 'I'm sure Marilyn would—'

'Not Marilyn, you fool,' Matthew cried.

'Matthew!' Patty gasped.

His expression softened. 'Don't worry, Shay has heard much worse from me.'

'That doesn't make it any more acceptable now,' she reproved.

'Looks like I'm going to have a nagging wife,' Matthew grimaced.

'Considering you haven't even asked her yet, you may find you aren't going to have any sort of wife,' Shay teased. 'I'll leave you two alone; I'm going to spend time with Richard.'

'Shay!'

'Yes?' She looked at Matthew challengingly.

'I'd like to talk to you some time soon.' He held her gaze intently.

'Not today, Matthew,' she told him harshly. 'I can't take any more today.'

'It's important, Shay,' he insisted.

'So is my sanity,' she snapped. 'But I think I'm in danger of losing it!'

As she lay awake long into the night, haunted by thoughts she couldn't even admit to herself, she knew she would have been wiser to talk to Matthew.

He and Patty had celebrated their engagement that evening, and Lyon had been conspicuous by his absence. But Matthew and Patty looked ecstatically happy, and Neil and her grandfather could have no idea of the trauma that had taken place earlier that day.

She had joined in the celebrations, making her excuses as soon as she was politely able, accepting Patty's request that she be her Matron of Honour at the New Year wedding she and Matthew were busily planning.

If it weren't for the fact that she suspected Patty was with Matthew in his suite again tonight she would have gone and spoken to him now, knew she wasn't going to be able to sleep.

And she knew that wherever Lyon had gone to tonight he hadn't returned, that his suite was empty.

'He's in town,' Matthew told her at breakfast the next morning.

'Who is?' She feigned puzzlement at the announcement.

He gave her a derisive look. 'Lyon.'

'Oh?' she dismissed without interest. 'Grandy,

do you feel like taking a walk this morning? We could—'

'Lyon hasn't returned to work, has he?' Her grandfather frowned at Matthew. 'He's been looking so tired lately.'

Matthew shook his head. 'He had business in town, private business.'

'Oh?' Shay's query was sceptical now.

'Patrick, was Shay ever beaten as a child?' Matthew asked him conversationally.

'Not that I can ever remember,' her grandfather replied thoughtfully. 'I thought she deserved it a few times, but—'

'Grandy!' She gave him an indignant frown.

'She looked at you with those huge purple eyes and your heart melted, right?' Matthew mocked.

'Something like that.' Her grandfather nodded.

'Luckily, I'm immune to those limpid dark pools,' Matthew drawled.

'And just what is that supposed to mean?' she challenged.

'That it's time you listened for a change,' he told her firmly. 'That you might learn something if you did that instead of stubbornly drawing your own conclusions.'

'Just because I assumed that Lyon's "private business" meant the same as it always has—'

'He's gone to see Marilyn,' Matthew cut in bluntly.

Her eyes widened with shock, and then she shrugged. 'It was only a matter of time,' she rasped.

'What was?' Matthew looked at her with narrowed eyes.

'Until she realised her mistake, as you said she would, and tried to get him back!'

'And do you think she'll succeed?'

'Do you?' she returned brittly.

'She might,' he shrugged. 'Lyon is very vulnerable right now.'

'Lyon has never been vulnerable in his life,' she snapped.

'He is now,' Matthew snapped back. 'It isn't every day the woman he loves is told he's sterile. He—' He broke off concernedly as Shay's grandfather suddenly choked over his coffee.

'Grandy, are you all right?' Shay patted him on the back as he continued to splutter.

'Yes, I—' He began coughing again. 'Matthew, you're mistaken about Lyon.' He shook his head.

'I realise it's a shock, Patrick—'

'It's also untrue,' the older man stated firmly.

Shay looked at him as if she had never seen him before. Her grandfather knew. She didn't know how, when, or why, but he *knew*!

'He had all the tests done, Patrick.' Neil handed him the glass of water he had poured for him.

'There's only one true test,' her grandfather insisted.

'He was married to Marilyn for eleven years,' Matthew drawled. 'That's test enough.'

All the laughter had gone from her grandfather's twinkling blue eyes when he turned to look at her. 'Shay?' he prompted hardly.

Her breath came in short gasps, as if someone had pushed her in the chest and she was recoiling from the blow. Her grandfather *knew* she had miscarried Lyon's baby six years ago!

'Shay!' he said again, this time with impatient anger, as if he couldn't believe she was just going to sit there and say nothing.

'I—I have to go upstairs.' She stood up noisily.

'Shay!'

His voice thundered across the room, and when he spoke in that tone she knew better than to move another step. It was true her grandfather had never hit her when she was a child, his disappointment in her actions had always been enough to stop her doing something she knew he would disapprove of. He was more than disappointed in her silence; he was disgusted!

'I didn't realise he thought that,' she told him pleadingly. 'I had no idea—'

'Until?' he prompted tightly.

'Marilyn told me several weeks ago,' she admitted heavily. 'Grandy, how long have you known?'

'Since you came to spend that holiday with me after you and Lyon broke up,' he told her gently. 'I know the signs, had watched your grandmother and mother in the same condition.'

'My God,' Matthew gasped incredulously. 'My God!' he said again even more dazedly.

She turned defensively to him and Neil. 'He didn't want me—'

'Shay, how could you have kept something like
that from him?' Matthew groaned.

'How?' Her eyes were feverish. 'I'll tell you
how, I'll tell you *all* how! Lyon told me I was just
another affair to him. I now know I was also just
another woman to give him faith in his ability to
be a lover if not a father. I lost my baby and almost
my own life because of him,' she bit out raggedly.
'You see, I still loved him more than life itself, had
thought that I would have his baby if not him,
and when the baby rejected me too, I almost bled
to death. I *wanted* to die. But Ricky saved me,
cared for me, *loved* me. And eventually I loved
him too. I *hated* Lyon with everything in me,' she
told them vehemently.

'And Ricky fostered that hate,' Matthew said
dully. 'Shay, you must realise by now that Ricky
knew three years ago, knew it wasn't true about
Lyon—'

'He hated him too,' she cried harshly. 'For
what he had done to me.'

'Shay—'

'Leave me alone,' she cried desperately. 'All of
you, just leave me alone!' She ran from the room
to the sanctuary of her suite.

She fell across the bed, her face buried in the
pillows as she sobbed her pain. She had known
yesterday when Matthew told her that Ricky
knew three years ago about Lyon's belief that he
was sterile, that Ricky had deliberately kept the
truth from his brother. And she didn't need to
question why he had done it, she knew. Even

after all that they had shared, all the years they had been together, Ricky had still been frightened of what she once felt for Lyon. Oh Ricky, darling, I loved *you*, she cried silently.

That last weekend with Lyon she had intended telling him about the baby they were going to have. But when they arrived at Falconer House it was to find that Marilyn intended to stay for the weekend too. Shay had hugged the knowledge of their child to herself, little dreaming of Lyon's intention to remain married to Marilyn, no matter what. She had felt sick when he told her that she was just another affair to him. She had also known she would never tell him about their baby.

The last night she shared with him had been primitive and savage, when she had wanted to hurt him as he hurt her, only succeeding in arousing them both to fever pitch. But mixed in with the savagery had been the knowledge that she would never see Lyon again after that night, her responses all the deeper because of it. But when Lyon had expected her to continue with their relationship as if nothing had happened, she hadn't been able to stop herself from being physically sick.

After her visit to her grandfather in Ireland, Shay felt London to be hostile and alien. But the baby was her problem, she couldn't burden her grandfather with it. So she had moved from her flat to a small bedsit, leaving Falconers without having another job to go to, finally managing to find work in a department store which was taking people on for the summer.

It hadn't mattered then that she was so alone, cherishing the baby even as she hated its father. That baby should have been a Christmas baby too, but she was only into her fourteenth week when the cramping pains began in the base of her spine, moving round to her stomach as the day progressed, making her scream with agony by the time she got home from work, her face grey, her brow damp from the effort of not being sick with the pain.

She had climbed into bed, too weak to make the effort to try and telephone a doctor. And some time during the evening the pain had stopped, and then there was only the warm stickiness between her legs, a warmth that didn't stop, until finally she fell into a fevered unconsciousness.

She had fought against the hands that tried to wake her, murmured protestingly at the strangulated cry as the bedclothes were ripped back. But Ricky wouldn't let her die as she so wanted to do, was with her when she came round at the hospital, sitting with her through the night when the doctors tried to stop the haemorrhaging.

When the bleeding finally stopped she had lost so much blood the doctors feared for her life. And still Ricky had stayed with her, hour after hour as they pumped the blood back into her—and then day after day as she slowly regained her strength.

But she had lost Lyon's baby.

Once she had strength enough, she begged

Ricky never to tell Lyon about the baby, had told him how Lyon wanted no part of her. Ricky had promised.

He had been the one to take her home from the hospital, to look after her until her strength was fully recovered, to help her find another job, the summer over now, to help her move into a new apartment once she was earning more money, refusing his offer to help with the rent before that.

He had been the first guest she had invited to dinner at her new apartment, the man to share her celebration as she quickly gained promotion in the small advertising company she worked for. He was also the person who sat with her and held her hand during the long dark depressions that had gripped her since the miscarriage. To Shay, that had been the most devastating experience of her life. She had wanted the baby, hadn't cared about the complications it was sure to cause in her life, and when she lost it she felt as if it had rejected her too.

Ricky's anger towards Lyon for what he had done to her was enough to make him move out of the home he had always shared with his three brothers. Shay had been dismayed when she learnt that, hadn't wanted to be the cause of a rift between the two men. But Ricky had been adamant, and with his permanent move up to London, the two of them had seen even more of each other.

Rarely a day went by during the next year

when they didn't see each other at least once. And somewhere during that time Shay learnt to love the man who was responsible for her being alive, found in him a reason for cherishing that life. His proposal of marriage and her acceptance came as naturally as day follows night. She loved him, and he loved her, so what other conclusion could there be than for them to become husband and wife.

Their wedding had been the first time she had seen Lyon in almost a year. He had looked the same, and for once he and Marilyn had attended a social function together, sitting next to each other in the church. Shay had looked at him as if he were a stranger, remembering that if it hadn't been for him their child would probably still be alive, the doctors having told her too much stress and strain had caused her miscarriage.

She had hated Lyon then, and she continued to hate him even when she suggested to Ricky that there was no earthly reason why they shouldn't move back to his family home as she knew he now wanted to do. There was no *earthly* reason why they shouldn't because all of them belonged to the hell she wanted to send Lyon to!

For the two years she and Ricky had lived at Falconer House, she and Lyon had acted like strangers, never speaking unless they absolutely had to, Shay always leaving a room if Lyon should happen to join her in it while she was alone.

But her relationship with Ricky flourished in

spite of the tension she felt about Lyon. Or at least she had thought it had. Now she wasn't so sure. She had believed Ricky knew how much she loved him, that their marriage, in spite of the unhappy beginning to their relationship, was a good one.

She could think of no other reason than insecurity in her feelings for him for Ricky to take her away to Los Angeles once Lyon had told him of his sterility. Did he think she would have left him, gone to Lyon and told him she had carried his child? He couldn't have thought that! Could he . . . ?

'Shay, love, please don't do this to yourself,' Matthew encouraged softly.

She rolled over reluctantly to look at him. 'I loved Ricky,' she choked.

'I know you did,' he soothed gently. 'And so did Ricky love you. But he also knew it wasn't the sort of love you had once had for Lyon.'

'I—'

'Listen to me, Shay,' he instructed firmly. 'I want to tell you a story.'

'Matthew, I don't—'

'About four brothers,' he continued determinedly, holding her attention this time. 'The oldest brother was invincible, strong, and women found him deeply attractive. Then came the cynic,' he said derisively. 'Then the kind one, and finally the baby of the family. A pleasant enough boy, if a bit overshadowed by his older brothers. Everyone liked him, but it wasn't enough for him, he wanted to be like the eldest brother—'

'No, you're wrong,' she protested. 'Ricky was gentle, he wasn't—'

'This is my story, Shay,' he softly reprimanded. 'If you don't like the way I'm telling it you can change it at the end. The baby of the family wanted what the eldest brother had, his power, his attraction to women. And then one day the eldest brother brought a gypsy into their midst, a beautiful black-haired, purple-eyed vixen. Of course, like all the other women, the gypsy loved the powerful older brother. But the youngest brother wanted her too, at first just *because* she belonged to the older brother—'

'No!' she protested again.

'I said at first, Shay,' he sighed. 'That want soon turned to a possessive love, but still the gypsy belonged to the older brother. Then one day she just disappeared from their lives. The eldest brother was like a wounded lion—forgive the pun!' Matthew mocked. 'But the youngest brother was determined to find the gypsy and make her his own. Within a year he had married his gypsy and brought her to his home. They should have lived happily ever after—'

'We were happy!'

'I know that,' Matthew nodded. 'And maybe in a way it was a more rewarding happiness than you had known with Lyon; it was certainly more comfortable! But Ricky was never able to forget you had once loved Lyon, although he knew

Lyon had no intention at that time of renewing the relationship. But when you suggested it, he couldn't resist the idea of the two of you living here right under Lyon's nose—'

'Ricky wasn't a vindictive person!' she defended forcefully.

'He didn't intend to be vindictive. He did it to prove to Lyon that you no longer wanted him, that you belonged to him now. Then, I believe, he finally discovered the reason Lyon had let you go, and he panicked,' Matthew frowned.

'What do you mean?' she gasped.

'Well, as I know Lyon still loves you, believe he has never stopped loving you, I can only come to the conclusion that by giving you up the way he did he believed he was being noble—' He broke off as Shay gave a scornful snort. 'Shay,' he chided, 'no matter what you think, Lyon does love you. He had to have a reason for giving you up the way he did without a fight.'

'He did—his *wife!*' she derided hardly.

Matthew shook his head. 'I haven't spoken to Lyon about this, so I can't be sure, but I believe I finally have the answer to the puzzle of why Lyon stayed with Marilyn and let you go. I think it was because he knew he couldn't give you children.'

'When we were together I only wanted him,' she protested. 'Nothing else mattered.'

'And when you realised you were expecting his child, how did you feel then?' he prompted gently.

Her eyes became moist as she once again re-
lived the sheer ecstasy of knowing Lyon's child
was nestling in her body. She had been over-
whelmed, enthralled, and so very proud—until
he destroyed that pride by making a mockery of
her love.

'No, don't think of that part,' Matthew dismissed impatiently, as bitterness controlled her.
'Just think how it felt to carry Lyon's child.'

Serenity once again lit her deep purple eyes. 'It
was beautiful. But—'

'No buts, Shay,' he said gently. 'Tell me, do
you think Marilyn was always the brittle bitch
that she is now?'

She gave him a startled look. 'Marilyn? But—'

'I said no buts, Shay,' he smiled encouragingly.
'When they were first married Marilyn was vivacious and fun to be with, and deeply in love with
Lyon. I think he was a bit bowled over by her at
first, had always had to be the responsible one of
the family, and suddenly this glowingly lovely
lady took over his life and made him have fun
too.'

It caused an ache in her chest she didn't want
to acknowledge to think of Marilyn and Lyon
happily married.

'Inevitably they decided the next step was to
have children. At first it was just another game,
but as time went on and nothing happened you
could see the tension growing between them.
Lyon blamed everything, from their demanding
careers to their busy social life. Marilyn, quite

rightly, refused to give up her career because of it, and that caused a lot of friction between them. Eventually they went to a specialist. Lyon was found to be the one responsible for Marilyn's not conceiving. He changed after that, he and Marilyn drifted apart, and finally there were other people for both of them.'

'They could have adopted.'

'Lyon wouldn't hear of it.' Matthew shook his head. 'He wanted his own child, conceived naturally, or none at all.'

'It could have saved his marriage,' Shay protested.

'By that time I don't think anything could have saved it,' Matthew dismissed. 'They were two people living separate lives while still remaining married. And then Lyon met you,' he sighed. 'The first time I saw you I thought you were too young for him, that you wouldn't last the month most of his women did. You lasted six, and from Lyon's behaviour after the break-up it was obvious you had been the one to end it.'

'It was a mutual decision.'

'It was not, Shay,' he gently rebuked.

'I was eighteen, pregnant by a man who had made it clear he intended remaining with his wife,' she defended. 'I had to go.'

'And do you know how different things would have turned out if you had just *told* Lyon about the baby?' Matthew groaned for all the wasted years.

'He didn't love me.' She shook her head. 'He told me he didn't.'

'And that's why your marriage to Ricky almost killed him?' Matthew scorned.

'Matthew, since I've known that Lyon believes himself to be sterile I've thought about what would have happened if I had told him about the baby six years ago,' she said softly. 'And maybe he would have married me just so that he could have his child. But do you know what that sort of marriage would have done to me? He can be told the truth now,' she said harshly. 'And then maybe he'll find someone else to marry and have children with. He may even decide to try again with Marilyn.'

'And what if he still wants you?'

She gave Matthew a startled look. 'You can't be serious?'

He gave a short laugh. 'I'd bet the rest of my life on his still wanting you, no matter what.'

She swallowed hard. 'Because of Richard.'

'Shay, you have just admitted he could have children of his own. He loves *you*.'

'No—'

'And you love him, you always have.'

'That isn't true!' Her eyes flashed.

'Ricky knew it,' he told her softly.

'No!'

'Yes, Shay,' he insisted firmly. 'He told me himself that he knew he only had you "on loan", but that he loved you too much to care. I didn't understand what he meant at the time, but now I do. He was frightened of your knowing about Lyon because he thought you might return to him.'

As that was what she had already decided herself she couldn't refute that claim, knew it had to be true. 'I never would have done, you know,' she said sadly.

'I do know,' he nodded. 'I think it was just Ricky's insecurity over Lyon surfacing again.'

'It was so unnecessary.'

'Was it? You may have stayed with Ricky, but if what I think about the reason Lyon couldn't make a commitment to you is true, it may have been Lyon you loved.'

What if it *were* true? Could it possibly be that Lyon had seen his sterility—or what he thought was his sterility—destroy one marriage, and that he daren't take the risk on another one?

But it was all supposition on Matthew's part, her own version of what happened could be the correct one!

'Shay—' He broke off as a knock sounded on the door before her grandfather walked in.

'Sorry to interrupt,' he grimaced, 'but Marilyn is downstairs, and Neil doesn't know how to cope with her. He sent me up for reinforcements.'

Matthew's mouth twisted. 'What does she want? And where's Lyon? I thought he was in London with her.'

'He was,' Shay's grandfather nodded. 'Apparently he's sent her down here for a few days.'

'Great,' Matthew groaned. 'She's alone, I take it?'

'Lyon still has business in town,' Patrick confirmed dryly.

'I'll bet he has,' Matthew muttered. 'Thanks, Patrick, I'd better go and deal with her. Think about what I've said, Shay,' he advised softly.

Shay looked uncertainly at her grandfather once they were alone. His disgust with her earlier had been all too obvious.

'Darlin', don't look at me like that,' he gently chided. 'You know you've done wrong; I'm not about to start berating you.'

'Oh, Grandy.' She flew into his arms. 'I'm sorry. So sorry!'

'I think you're saying that to the wrong man, Shay-me-love,' he soothed.

'Lyon?' Her voice was muffled against his chest.

'What do you think?'

'I've hated him *so* much, Grandy.' She shook her head, not seeming to realise she had used the past tense. But the man holding her did, his eyes very gentle. 'And when his baby didn't seem to want me either—Grandy, you never thought that I'd . . . well, when I suddenly wasn't pregnant any more, you didn't think I'd got rid of the baby?' She looked at him anxiously.

'Never,' he assured her without hesitation.

'Then—'

'Ricky called me after your miscarriage,' he explained. 'But he said you were in such an emotional state that he thought your realising I knew would make you worse. It was hard to do, but I stayed away. As you've never talked about it, neither have I.'

'Until now.'

'Shay, I couldn't stay silent when I realised what it must have done to Lyon over the years to believe he couldn't have children.'

'I know,' she accepted tearfully. 'I think I would have told him eventually—'

'Flung it at him, you mean,' Grandy derided ruefully. 'Once you had finished punishing him by letting him think there might eventually be a place for him in your and Richard's lives.'

'It—it sounds so *awful* when you put it like that,' she choked.

He nodded slowly. 'I'm not going to pretend otherwise; it *was* awful.'

'But I felt—so *used* once I realised what Lyon really wanted from me,' she defended.

'And how do you think Lyon's felt all these years? There now, and I said I wouldn't berate you,' he grimaced. 'There's just one more thing I want to say, and then I won't mention the subject again.'

She tensed. 'Yes?'

'Do you still believe that Lyon only wanted you because he also wanted Richard, and you came in a package?' he probed softly.

'Yes,' she murmured.

'And what would you say if you were told that the night Richard was born your doctor told Lyon that both you and the baby could die, that it might even come to a choice between you?' Her grandfather watched intently for her reaction.

She paled. 'The breech birth . . . ?' Shay gasped.

He nodded. 'Peter Dunbar told me Lyon didn't even hesitate.'

She couldn't breathe, felt hot and cold at one and the same time. 'Didn't hesitate to what?' she prompted desperately, her eyes feverish.

'In telling him to save you at all costs, to take the baby from you now before it got to that point, even though it probably meant death for the baby,' her grandfather related simply.

She still couldn't breathe, her eyes black pools in her white face.

'Now, tell me, does that sound like the action of a man interested only in the baby you carried?' he asked softly.

It had to be true, she knew her grandfather wouldn't lie to her. It wasn't Richard Lyon wanted at all, he *did* love her!

CHAPTER FOURTEEN

SHE found Marilyn in the suite the other woman once used to share with Lyon, before they had gone their separate ways within the confines of their marriage. The other woman looked pale, moving restlessly about the room once she had let Shay inside.

Shay watched her with puzzled eyes. 'Is there anything wrong?'

'Wrong?' the other woman repeated sharply. 'What do you mean?'

'You seem upset,' Shay shrugged, not wanting to get into an argument with Marilyn, just wanting to talk to her.

'I'm perfectly well, thank you,' Marilyn dismissed hardly. 'Now what can I do for you?'

'Tell me where Lyon is.'

Irritation flickered in hard blue eyes. 'Why do you want to know?'

'Where is he, Marilyn?' she demanded firmly.

'I've already told the others, he's in town,' Marilyn snapped.

'Could you be more precise?'

'No!'

Shay sighed. 'Then do you have any idea when he will be back?'

'None at all,' the other woman answered scornfully.

She should have known Marilyn wouldn't be very helpful; she never had been in the past, Shay had no reason to suppose she would suddenly change now! 'I'm sorry I bothered you,' she said curtly.

'Shay?' Anxiety edged the other woman's voice. 'Why do you want to see him?'

'It's personal,' she evaded. 'And private.'

'I see.' Marilyn bristled resentfully.

'I very much doubt it, Marilyn,' the younger woman sighed wearily.

'He was with me last night, you know,' the other woman told her bitchily.

'Yes, I do know.' She met Marilyn's gaze challengingly, sure that whatever had happened last night Lyon had *not* slept with this woman. Lyon loved *her*.

Marilyn continued to look at her defiantly— and then she crumpled, her resentment gone, leaving only an emotionally-disturbed woman. 'I love Lyon, you know,' she said brokenly.

'Yes.' Marilyn had confirmed what Shay already knew.

'But I'm not *in* love with him,' she added shakily. 'I don't think I ever was.'

Shay frowned. 'I'm sorry, I don't understand?'

'I love him too much to lie just so that I can hurt you. I don't even dislike you, I just resent you because Lyon loves you in a way he never did me.' The beautiful face was ravaged with emotion.

'Marilyn—'

'Listen to me, damn you!' The other woman raised her voice. 'Lyon did stay with me last night, but only because I asked him to, and not in the same bedroom.' Her mouth twisted bitterly. 'We haven't shared a bed, even occasionally, since *you*.'

Shay swallowed hard. 'I'm sorry—'

'Oh, believe me, so am I!' Marilyn said self-derisively. 'He's the most fantastic lover I've ever known—or ever likely to know,' she added regretfully.

'Then why—'

'Have affairs?' Marilyn finished dryly. 'Because I wasn't enough for Lyon, couldn't be what he wanted, or give him what he needed. And I don't just mean children.' Her voice was hard. 'I didn't fulfil him emotionally either. But you did. He would never have married you, but I think he would have stayed with you for the rest of his life. But *you* left *him*,' she frowned. 'I could never understand that when you obviously loved him so much.'

Shay moistened dry lips. 'Marilyn, I think there's something you should know about six years ago, something that happened.'

The other woman frowned at her grave tone. 'Don't tell me he used to beat you because I won't believe it,' she scorned. 'He's arrogant and strong, but he's also the gentlest man I know.'

Shay chewed on her bottom lip, not wanting to hurt this woman any more when she was obviously hurting so badly already. 'Marilyn, I—I think you had better sit down,' she advised gently.

'Don't be ridiculous. I—' She halted at the compassion in Shay's face, sitting down abruptly. 'Go ahead,' she invited raggedly.

Blue eyes darkened with pain and tears as Shay told Marilyn about the baby she had lost. She hadn't wanted to hurt the other woman, but if she didn't tell her, someone else would.

'Oh God. It's—I—It's incredible!' Marilyn finally gasped shakily. 'I suppose there's no doubt that it was Lyon's—No,' she dismissed woodenly, 'it would have been Lyon's baby; you never even looked at anyone else.'

Shay wasn't shocked, or even insulted that such a thought should have occurred to Marilyn; in fact, she had half expected it.

'That was uncalled-for.' Marilyn looked up at her ruefully, catching the humour in Shay's eyes, giving a reluctant smile herself. 'I'm sorry,' she offered, 'I'm just—dazed, I think.' She shrugged incredulously. 'And happy. For Lyon's sake.' She frowned. 'But he seemed the same yesterday?'

'Because he doesn't know yet,' Shay confirmed heavily.

'Which is why you want to see him,' realised Marilyn dryly.

Shay felt she at least owed it to Lyon to be the one to tell him the truth. If he chose to throw her and Richard out of his life afterwards perhaps that would be best for all of them.

'He—um—He's doing something for me.' Marilyn avoided looking at her directly. 'But he should be back later. Lord, I'd like to see the look on his face when you tell him.' She sounded awed. 'It's what he's always wanted.'

'Yes,' Shay acknowledged flatly.

'But it isn't all he's wanted,' Marilyn hastened to tell her. 'He wants a woman who will love him for himself, and not the Falconer name, who will spend time on him. I'm afraid when I married Lyon I wanted the Falconer name as much as I wanted him,' she grimaced. 'He knew that, of course, but he didn't mind. And being a Falconer hasn't done my career any harm at all.'

'No woman should be expected to give up her career nowadays to devote all of her time to a man,' Shay frowned. 'It's archaic!'

Marilyn shook her head. 'You misunderstood me. He didn't want me to give it up, but he did think he should mean more to me than my career. He was right, of course, but I've always been very ambitious.'

She nodded. 'I'm sure that as Derrick is also a lawyer he'll be more understanding about your career.'

'Probably,' the other woman bit out. 'We—' She glanced irritably at the door as Matthew knocked briefly before entering. 'It's usual to wait until you're invited,' she snapped.

'You know, Marilyn,' he drawled, 'if you ever

stopped being a shrew you just might become a nice person.'

'The same goes for you being a bastard,' she derided dryly. 'Now would you mind explaining what you're doing in here?'

Hazel eyes hardened. 'I don't have to explain anything, Marilyn, I *live* here.'

'You—'

'It was a little rude of you to just burst in, Matthew,' Shay cut in, seeing that the original query was going to be buried beneath the usual abuse these two generated when together. And without an audience Marilyn had been less brittle, less the bored cynic, and more a caring human being. It was a pity to see that quality disappear beneath her usual bitchiness.

'Might I remind you that you're a guest here too, Shay,' he replied viciously.

'Oh dear,' Marilyn mused. 'Who's been rattling your cage, Matthew?' she taunted.

'Mind your own damned business!' he snapped. 'Shay, the police are downstairs waiting to see you,' he told her hardly.

'Police?' Marilyn gasped, paling. 'Nothing has happened to Lyon?' she demanded anxiously.

'It's about your accident at Christmas,' Matthew spoke to Shay, ignoring the other woman. 'They want to walk to you about it again.'

Two policemen had visited her in hospital the day after the accident. They had seemed faintly sceptical at the time, more or less implying that, in their own words, 'it was a party, drink flowing freely, you could have been mistaken in what happened'. Shay hadn't expected to see them again, and her surprise must have shown in her face.

'Patty and Lyon have managed to convince them that it wasn't an accident after all,' Matthew scowled.

'What's going on?' Marilyn demanded to know.

'Don't you know?' Matthew taunted.

'Of course I don't.' Marilyn was angry now, tired of their game.

'You stay here and explain to her, Matthew,' Shay put in hastily, anxious to escape before this developed into a full-scale argument.

'I'd rather come with you,' he returned quickly.

'And I want to know what's going on,' Marilyn insisted, her eyes hard.

'Stay, Matthew,' Shay encouraged. 'After all, I have to go down and see the police.' She hurried from the room before he could stop her, slowing her pace as she approached the lounge, apprehension and nervousness making her palms sweaty.

She needn't have worried, the same two policemen only came to tell her they were now treating their investigation seriously, and did she remember anything else about the night in question. As she didn't, it seemed to her to be a wasted trip for them.

Matthew frowned a few minutes later when he came into the room to find that Shay was alone.

'Have they gone?' He sounded incredulous.

She grimaced. 'I'm afraid so.'

'Hardly worth the damned effort,' he scowled.

'At least they believe us now,' she shrugged.

'They could have telephoned and told us that,' Matthew growled.

'Yes.' Shay looked at him worriedly; he certainly no longer seemed to be the happily engaged man of last night. 'Who *has* been rattling your cage, Matthew?' she prompted gently.

He glanced at her with resentment. 'What makes you think anyone has?' he challenged.

'Well, I realise this is the way you usually are,' she taunted, 'but I thought now that you're going to be married—'

'I'm not,' he rasped.

Purple eyes widened with dismay. 'Matthew, I thought we had settled the question of your ridiculous pride yesterday—'

'We did,' he agreed harshly. 'But we forgot to "settle the matter" of Patty's job.'

'Career,' Shay put in instantly.

Matthew gave her a scathing look. 'What's the matter with women nowadays?' he said disgustedly. 'Why do they have constantly to prove they're as good as men—if not better!'

'They don't,' she teased him. 'But that isn't to say we aren't entitled to a career.'

'Patty risks her life—'

'We all do, every morning, after we get out of bed!'

'This isn't funny, Shay,' he bit out coldly. 'Patty

has just told me that she intends carrying on with her job after we're married.'

'And why not? You don't intend starting a family straight away, do you?'

He gave her an impatient look as she deliberately misunderstood. 'I can't let her do it, Shay,' he said in a tormented voice. 'If anything should happen to her . . . !'

'Matthew,' she spoke gently, 'just because Patty loves you and wants to marry you doesn't mean she belongs to you body and soul, that your wishes instantly become her own. She's twenty-eight years old,' Shay reasoned. 'Besides loving you and being your wife she has plans and dreams of her own. Would you give up your career for her?'

'If I had to, *yes!*' he glared.

Shay sighed. 'You can say that because you know you'll never *have* to!'

He flushed at the truth of that. 'Shay, her job is dangerous!'

'And if the two of you talked maybe you could compromise. Is not being with her, married to her, going to stop you worrying about her, going to stop you loving her?' she challenged.

'No. But—'

'No buts, Matthew,' she told him firmly. 'You have to talk to Patty, not just decide you can't marry her because you risk being hurt if something did happen to her. Another fault of the Falconer men,' she derided. 'You're all too arrogant.'

'And we seem to fall in love with women that are too damned stubborn and independent for their own good!' he rasped.

She smiled. 'But you love us anyway.'

'Yes,' he acknowledged heavily.

'You will talk to Patty before making any firm decisions?' she prompted.

'I—I'll talk to her,' he nodded. 'Now tell me what you were doing with Marilyn; I thought she was your least favourite person?'

'She was,' Shay agreed. 'But I think you're misjudging her, Matthew. She really does care for Lyon.'

'Not enough to make him happy,' Matthew scowled.

Shay sighed at his implacability where Marilyn was concerned. She would once have had to agree with him about Marilyn's hardness, now she wasn't so sure. 'I told her about Lyon,' she revealed.

'That was brave of you.' He sounded slightly surprised that she had dared to speak to the other woman about such a potentially explosive subject.

'I wanted her to tell me where Lyon is,' she shrugged. 'She naturally wanted to know why I was interested.'

'He's doing her dirty work for her,' Matthew scowled. 'As usual. How did she take the news about Lyon?'

'Very well,' Shay nodded. 'Matthew, you were a bit hard on her earlier.'

'I'm still not certain she isn't involved in these "accidents" we all keep having. After all, she's still a Falconer, and nothing has happened to her.'

That was true, and yet she somehow no longer felt in the least suspicious of the other woman. The police were now taking seriously all the other near-fatal accidents that had befallen the family the last year, and Shay was still convinced Marilyn would never knowingly hurt Lyon.

'You're wrong, Matthew,' she dismissed.

'I wish I could be as sure.'

'I think *you* should go and talk to Patty straight away,' she told him firmly. 'She's probably very upset.'

'I doubt it,' Matthew drawled. 'I hadn't gotten around to telling her yet that the wedding was off!'

'Oh, Matthew!' she hugged him, laughing softly. 'Male chauvinists are very out of date nowadays,' she chided.

'Tell that to Lyon,' he taunted. 'On second thoughts, don't bother,' he said dryly. 'He's always given in to exactly what you want.'

'He accepts my writing now, yes,' she acknowledged guardedly, knowing the necklace he had given her symbolised that.

'He would accept it if you decided to jump off the top of the Eiffel Tower wearing a parachute!' Matthew smiled wryly.

'Matthew—'

'Go and see Patty, right?' he mocked. 'Okay, I'll go,' he sighed.

With Richard fed and asleep once more, and no knowledge of when Lyon would return, Shay wandered through to his suite. After only a few weeks he had made his stamp upon the rooms: what had once just been a comfortable guest-room now as much Lyon as the suite he had occupied most of the last twenty-five years.

She idly picked up the book from the coffee-table, the only thing out of place in the tidy room, left lying open, as if Lyon had left in a hurry. Her brows raised as she looked at the front of the book and saw it was one of her own, *Scarlet Lover*. What on earth—!

Shay turned to the pages that had so interested Lyon, frowning as she quickly read them. She couldn't see what—Her heart seemed to stop beating as she read the answer to the riddle of who was trying to harm them in her very own book! She had to find Marilyn, and quickly!

Marilyn was soaking in the bath, and she didn't look overjoyed at the interruption as Shay burst into the room, sinking below the bubbled surface. 'Really, Shay,' she drawled. 'I would have had more privacy if I'd stayed in London!'

Shay didn't have the time to worry about the other woman's modesty. 'Lyon,' she said breath-lessly. 'What is it he's doing for you in London?'

'I don't think that's any of your—'

'Marilyn!' she interrupted harshly. 'This is very important.'

Marilyn looked no less stubborn. 'It's personal,' she snapped.

'Marilyn, someone is going to get killed if you don't tell me right now where Lyon is!' She was becoming desperate, knew there was no time to lose, not if Lyon were where she thought he was. Oh Lyon, you fool!

'Don't be hysterical, Shay,' the other woman scorned. 'You surely aren't encouraging this ridiculous idea Matthew has that someone is deliberately out to hurt the family?'

'I don't think it is ridiculous.' Even less so now! 'And neither do the police.'

Marilyn paled. 'They don't?'

'No. Now tell me where Lyon is?'

She swallowed hard. 'I broke off my engagement to Derrick yesterday,' she revealed stiffly. 'He didn't take it very well. Lyon has gone to reason with him.'

It was worse than she had thought! 'Tell me Derrick's address!' she demanded.

'Not until you explain what all this is about,' Marilyn told her stubbornly. 'Why is it so desperate that you find Lyon now?'

'You either tell me the address,' Shay told her menacingly, too worried to mince her words, 'or be arrested as an accomplice to murder.'

'Shay, you can't be serious!' she protested indignantly.

'Very,' she assured her tensely. 'Now tell me!'

'All right.' The other woman sounded flustered as she did so. 'I'll come with you,' she decided. 'I can take you straight there,' she explained as Shay seemed about to protest.

'All right,' Shay accepted impatiently, seeing the logic in that. 'But hurry up. I'm leaving in a few minutes, with you or without you.'

She couldn't find Patty or Matthew anywhere in the house, but she eventually found her grandfather and Neil in the library, Neil once again dozing in a chair.

'Have you seen Matthew or Patty?' she demanded without preamble.

Her grandfather looked surprised by her aggressive tone. 'They went out for a drive; I think they had something they needed to talk about in private. Shay, what is it?' He frowned his concern at how pale she was.

'Grandy, I want you to call the local police, explain who you are, and ask them to get someone to this address as soon as possible,' she told him breathlessly, writing down Derrick's address on a piece of paper and handing it to him. 'Neil, you're coming with me,' she told him firmly.

'What—? I—Shay, let go of my arm!' he protested irritably as she tried to pull him up out of his chair.

'Someone is going to be hurt if we don't get up to London straight away,' she told him desperately. 'And it could be Lyon.'

Neil woke up completely at that. 'Lyon? But—'

'Neil, will you move yourself!' she ordered in a coldly threatening voice. 'Marilyn,' she greeted the other woman with some relief as she appeared fully dressed in the doorway. 'Let's go. Neil is going to drive us up to London.'

'Am I?' he blinked. 'I mean, I am?' he amended at Shay's fierce look.

'Grandy, please call the police,' she repeated as she dragged Marilyn and Neil towards the door. 'And take care of Richard for me,' she added shakily.

'Shay, I don't understand—'

'Just drive, Neil,' she instructed as she pushed him in behind the wheel of the Porsche, getting in beside him as Marilyn climbed in the back. 'I'll explain as we go along.'

'I certainly hope so,' he said grimly.

'Forget the speed limits, Neil,' she ordered as he drove carefully from the driveway out on to the road. 'If we pick up a couple of police cars on the way, all the better!'

'Shay—'

'Put your foot down, Neil,' she said flatly. 'Lyon is the one who could die!'

She finally knew who had been the cause of all those dreadful accidents. She was also sure she knew why!

CHAPTER FIFTEEN

IT would have been like a scene from a farcical film if it weren't so real!

But it was real, Derrick and Lyon out on the balcony of Derrick's eighth-floor apartment, Lyon bent back precariously as the other man tried to force him over the railing. It was worse than Shay had expected, more than she had hoped for; Lyon still alive even if his life was threatened. She knew she had no time to lose!

'Lyon!' she cried out to him. 'Lyon, don't let him do it. Lyon—darling, I love you!' she choked. 'Don't let him take away our chance of happiness together.'

For a moment the scene remained frozen as Derrick realised he had an audience, and then everything changed. Lyon was suddenly the aggressor, forcing the other man's hands from his throat as he threw him back against the wall.

But Derrick, placid, *innocuous* Derrick, seemed to have the strength of ten men, grasping Lyon in a death-grip once again.

'Don't!' he grated harshly as Neil would have stepped forward. 'Unless you want me to toss your brother over this balcony like a piece of bad meat!' he snarled.

'Derrick . . . ?' Marilyn gasped faintly, disbelievingly.

With a growl of fury Lyon thrust the other man away from him again. But suddenly Derrick had wrestled him to the floor, his knee against his windpipe.

'Lyon, you can't die,' Shay groaned, tears in her eyes as she heard the life begin to choke out of him. 'Lyon, please don't leave me like your child did. Yes, Lyon, we had a child,' she encouraged desperately as he gave a strangulated cry. 'I can give you other children, half a dozen if you like. Lyon, please, *please* don't let him take you from me!' She fell to her knees, too weak to stand any more, knowing she loved this man more than life itself, no matter what the truth was about the past. 'Neil, go to him,' she begged brokenly. 'Help him!'

'Come any further and I'll snap his neck in half,' Derrick told them coldly. 'And don't think I can't do it; I've been training in martial arts.'

Shay looked pleadingly at Marilyn, biting her lip to stop herself from crying out, her face white, as Marilyn could only nod confirmation.

'You shouldn't lie to a man just before he's about to die, Shay,' Derrick taunted. 'I'm sure it can't be good for his soul.'

'Derrick, it will do no good to kill him now,' she choked, the tears streaming down her face. 'Not unless you mean to kill us all, and that would be defeating the object.'

'My object has already been defeated,' he spat

out, glaring at Marilyn with hatred in his eyes. 'She decided not to marry me, after all,' he snarled. 'Decided I couldn't measure up to Lyon.' He looked down at the other man scornfully. 'Well, who's the victor now?' he jeered.

'Derrick, we just had a disagreement,' Marilyn spoke to him soothingly. 'It has nothing to do with Lyon. We can still get married. Darling, let him go, and we can—'

'You stupid bitch,' he said with contempt. 'You still don't realise, do you?'

'Derrick—'

'Marilyn, it's no good.' Shay put a hand on the other woman's arm. 'Derrick is the person responsible for all the "accidents" that occurred to the family. But he wasn't after all of us as it seemed he was, only one of us. Lyon,' she said flatly.

'That's very clever, Shay,' he sneered, increasing the pressure on Lyon's neck so that he groaned weakly. 'What else do you think you know?'

'That at first it wasn't so urgent, but as you continued to be unsuccessful you became more desperate.' She held his gaze. 'That you only had a few weeks left before Marilyn's divorce from Lyon became final and she would no longer be a rich widow, just an ex-wife.'

For that was what she had learnt from *Scarlet Lover*, where Leon de Coursey was almost killed by his wife's lover in an effort to marry her himself and so claim her fortune for his own. The answer to the whole puzzle had been in her own book!

Lyon had decided he was going to give the bastard above him just enough 'rope to hang himself' and then he was going to pulverise him into the ground!

Shay, Marilyn, and Neil obviously weren't aware of the fact that the police had come in the opened door shortly after them, that they were even now listening to the conversation as they stood hidden outside the room! Derrick was going to confess to it all before he showed him that he was far from beaten, as Derrick thought he was, that he was merely biding his time.

He had almost lost control and taken the other man when Shay spoke of their having a baby. But he knew it was a lie as much as Derrick did, as much as they all did. But she did love him, she wouldn't have lied about that, and as soon as this mess was over he was going to make sure she married him.

He had been getting ready to subdue Derrick when the other three arrived, closely followed by the police. He didn't know how they came to be there, but he was glad that they were, that it was all going to be over soon.

'The esteemed Falconer family,' Derrick sneered above him, not seeming to notice the slackening of pressure on Lyon's windpipe. 'You were all so damned self-satisfied,' he scorned. 'So self-righteous, so damned sure you were invincible. You weren't so invincible after all, were you?' he said with pleasure. 'And the potential in having Lyon dead was enormous,' he told them conversationally. 'The settlement Marilyn was asking off him wouldn't have kept me in shirts for a year,' he derided.

'Silk, aren't they?' Neil asked interestedly.

'Hand-made,' the other man confirmed with pride.

Clever Neil, he had caught on to the waiting game he was playing! Neil knew Lyon was capable of taking this man any time he felt like it, and was now trying to draw him out. He hated what this was doing to Shay, could see her anguish as she continued to cry, but he was determined Derrick would be known for all his crimes, that he wouldn't try to claim today as a fit of jealousy because Marilyn had decided not to marry him.

'They're very nice,' Neil enthused. 'You'll have to give me the name of your tailor.'

Too far, Neil, Lyon groaned inwardly. Too far!

'Don't take me for a fool, Falconer,' Derrick predictably blew up. 'I know exactly what you're trying to do, and it won't work. It's a pity you weren't a little higher off the ground when your hang-glider went down,' he scorned angrily.

'You did that?' Neil said admiringly. 'I'd be interested to know how?'

That's it, Neil, Lyon silently encouraged, draw him out *slowly*. He just hoped he could stay down here long enough for Neil to get the whole confession out of him; Derrick seemed to have realised he hadn't been pressing down hard enough, the pressure on his windpipe now unbearable!

'You surely aren't expecting me to go into methods and means?' Derrick derided mockingly, shaking his head. 'I never could understand why the villain in old films always confessed and explained his crimes just before the hero managed to escape and tell the police everything!'

'Derrick, we've *all* heard you,' Marilyn reasoned.

'Heard me what?' he scoffed. 'I only said it was a pity Neil wasn't higher when his hang-glider went down, I didn't say I had anything to do with it.'

'You said the potential of Lyon being dead before our divorce was enormous—My God, you haven't admitted a thing, have you!' Marilyn realised dazedly.

'Not a thing,' he acknowledged conceitedly. 'And that's why I'm a better lawyer than you are, why you'll never be any damned good.'

'Why you—!' Marilyn lunged for him, her fingers like talons in his hair.

'Let go of me, you bitch.' He was momentarily diverted from pinning Lyon to the ground as he tried to fight Marilyn off, giving Lyon chance to breathe again.

'Maybe you should have killed me yesterday when you hit me instead of trying to kill members of the Falconer family all these months,' Marilyn taunted. 'But I suppose you would have been as inefficient at that as you were with them!'

'I wasn't *trying* to kill them,' Derrick snarled.
'Only Lyon. Although if one of them had died too
I wouldn't have been too upset. Even Shay. And I
liked her. But she proved to be a problem once it
became obvious she wouldn't sell Ricky's shares
to Lyon now that she was pregnant with Ricky's
child. Getting rid of the baby seemed to be the
best way to deal with that.'

'But you didn't, did you?' Marilyn sneered.
'Even though you pushed her down an escalator.'

'She turned out to be as indestructible as the
rest of them,' he said with disgust. 'I—'

'All right, sir.' A plainclothes policeman stepped into the room, followed by another officer.
'We've heard enough to arrest you for attempted
murder on Mrs Shay Falconer and Mr Lyon
Falconer. We—'

Lyon didn't hear any more, realising that at last
his chance had come, throwing a stunned Derrick
to the floor, blow after blow landing on the other
man's face.

'Sir! Mr Falconer—'

He paid no attention to the two policemen as
they tried to pull him off Derrick.

'Lyon, please.'

The gentle voice was enough to stop him, to
bring him to his senses, to see the mess he had
made of the other man's face.

'Lyon, it's over,' Shay continued to soothe.
'Lyon, I love you,' she told him for everyone to
hear. 'Darling, it's all over.' Her voice broke
emotionally.

He looked at her with pained eyes, the nightmare of the past year still with him. But it *was* over, and he was going to have Shay. 'Shay!' He gathered her close against his chest as he rested his head on hers.

'I ought to be very angry with you.' Shay looked up at him sternly. 'I really thought Derrick was killing you.'

He put a hand up to the plaster over his eye. 'I didn't get this cut at a tea-party!'

'No,' she acknowledged shakily.

They were back at Falconer House, Derrick safely arrested, all the statements given, all the explanations made, Matthew and Patty annoyed that they had missed all the action, her grandfather just grateful it was all over and they were all back safely.

Now that they knew the truth it was so easy to see that Derrick had believed he could hide his real objective behind a number of unrelated accidents to the family, when Marilyn, still legally Lyon's wife—and consequently his widow—would inherit all his wealth. Shay had also offered him a temptation he couldn't resist when it became obvious only her unborn child prevented her from selling her shares to Lyon. As each planned 'accident' failed, Derrick had become more and more desperate, and consequently more inept.

He was insane, of course, and would probably undergo psychiatric treatment rather than imprisonment, but that didn't make his crimes any less frightening.

'It's Marilyn I feel sorry for,' she frowned. 'She has no one now.'

'I think she may have gained a friend,' Lyon looked at her admiringly.

Shay shrugged. 'I know she's a bitch most of the time, but she isn't as hard and uncaring as she likes to make out she is.'

'No,' he agreed softly.

They were in Shay's suite, sitting side by side on the sofa as they stared at the glowing fire, the lights dimmed, the Christmas tree still glittering in the corner. It all looked so normal—and yet it was far from that.

As she had seen Lyon's life threatened, envisaged a life without him, she had known she couldn't live without him, that she loved him. It had taken her a long time to admit it, but now that she had she was determined to try and salvage something from the mess they had made of things, to make them into a happy family if she could. But first they had a lot of misunderstandings to talk out.

'I shouldn't worry about Marilyn if I were you,' Lyon mused. 'Not from the way the police inspector was looking at her, and she was looking right back!'

Shay's eyes widened. Then she remembered the darkly handsome policeman, and the way he had been so considerate of Marilyn at the police station. 'Do you think—'

'Too soon to tell,' Lyon shrugged. 'But I have a feeling she isn't going to be alone for long.'

'She'll probably be furious with you once she realises she risked herself like that for nothing,' Shay chided. 'That there was no risk to you at all.'

'Marilyn knew it all along,' Lyon said confidently. 'She was just trying to get a confession out of Derrick.' His arms tightened about her. 'Isn't it time you told me you love me?' he encouraged throatily. 'Or did you just say that in the heat of the moment?' He looked down at her with narrowed eyes.

'Of course I didn't,' she blushed.

'Well?'

'Lyon, we have to talk.'

'Why?'

'Well—Because—I told you something else today.' She looked at him frowningly. 'Something you've made no comment about at all.'

He frowned. 'What—? Oh. Yes,' he nodded. 'Well, I realise why you did that Shay; you thought it would make me fight back. It doesn't matter.'

'What do you mean, it *doesn't matter*?' She stared at him incredulously. 'Of course it matters!'

'I'm not angry, if that's what you think,' he dismissed. 'I'll try never to be angry with you again.' He looked at her indulgently.

'Why *should* you be angry?' she asked dazedly. 'It wasn't intentional. I would have done anything to stop it.'

'It was wonderful of you to try, darling—'

'Lyon, what are you talking about?' she demanded impatiently, sure they had to be talking at cross purposes.

'I've just told you, the fact that you tried to make me fight back, even by taunting me with the children we can never have.'

'But—Lyon, when you had your tests what did the doctor tell you about them?' she probed anxiously.

'Do we have to talk about this now?' he bit out.

'Yes.'

He sighed, obviously not liking the subject at all. 'Because of a deficiency in my sperm the chances of any woman ever conceiving from me are about a million to one,' he rasped. 'Satisfied?' He was slightly resentful of her probing into something he was still so sensitive about.

'A million to one,' she repeated thoughtfully. 'Well, we've done it once, I'm sure we can do it again.'

'I would like to bring Richard up as much mine as you'll let me—'

'Lyon, will you listen to what I'm telling you,' she interrupted reprovingly. 'We, *you* and I, conceived a baby, six years ago. I lost it in the fourth month, but—'

'Shay . . . ?' Lyon grated, very pale, his eyes like pools of gold.

'It's true.' She looked deep into his eyes, all of her love for him in hers. 'I carried your baby, Lyon,' she told him softly.

He swallowed hard, the breath ragged in his throat. '*My* baby?' he repeated breathlessly.

'Yes. Lyon, I didn't know you believe yourself to be sterile, not then. I—'

'Tell me about it,' he pleaded gruffly.

She did tell him, all of it, about their baby, about Ricky, everything. He grew greyer and greyer, more and more still, his hands icily cold despite the heat in the room.

'I hated Ricky at times,' Lyon finally said dully. 'I had no idea how much I had to be grateful to him for.'

She couldn't dispute that, knew that if it weren't for Ricky that she would have been dead. 'Don't reproach yourself, Lyon,' she pleaded. 'If I had only told you about the baby at the time none of this would have happened.'

'How could you tell me after I had just told you I only wanted to continue my affair with you?' he said self-disgustedly. 'Dear God, so many years wasted, so much pain. When Ricky brought you back home as *his* wife I thought I was going to die from the agony of knowing you belonged to him and not me.'

'Matthew said you used to take Wildfire out and ride all night.' She knew now that was exactly what he had done, that there had been no woman involved in those all-night rides. Lyon had always loved her, she was sure of it. Finally.

'Yes. Shay, I never meant to hurt you, you have to believe that. I just didn't feel I could marry another woman and put her through the same torment as I did Marilyn. She may act as if she dislikes children, but really she's very good with them.'

She had seen that herself when Marilyn held Richard at the hospital.

'I watched her grow from a beautiful butterfly to an embittered woman intent on using my name to further her career if she couldn't get anything else from the marriage. I felt I owed her that much at least, that if she wanted to keep the marriage it was the least I could do for her. I certainly never intended marrying again,' he recalled flatly. 'When I met you you were like a bright shining star I was afraid to touch in case you disappeared, a vivacious gypsy who danced her way into my heart. But I couldn't marry you and watch you become like Marilyn. I had no idea my million to one chance of ever having a child had come—and that I lost it.'

'Or that I kept the truth from you even when I found out that you believed yourself incapable of fathering a child,' Shay groaned. 'I wanted to hurt you as I had been hurt, even though it was a silent retribution.'

'It was the least I deserved for what I did to—'

'No,' she disagreed heatedly. 'It was a warped part of the sickness of believing I hated you. But when I thought that Derrick was going to kill you today—!' She shuddered at the memory. 'I wanted to die too.'

'Shay!' he moaned.

'Lyon, I know you did what you thought was

best six years ago, but you had no right to make that decision for me, even if there had never been a baby,' she told him urgently. 'It was my decision to make, not yours. Not having children wasn't what changed Marilyn, it was *your* reaction to it that did that.'

'Maybe you're right, I don't know.' He shook his head wearily. 'I just knew I couldn't put you through that, see the love turn to contempt, and finally to hate.'

'But you made me hate you anyway,' she groaned. 'After that I would have done anything to make you pay for what I suffered, and keeping the truth to myself didn't seem such a difficult thing to do. After all, you had believed for years that you were sterile, why shouldn't you go on believing it!' She shook her head in self-disgust. 'I think I must have been slightly insane.'

'You couldn't really think I wanted you for any other reason than because I wanted Richard when you only knew half the facts,' he sighed. 'God, I broke down and cried after Matthew told you about my sterility that day!'

'I already knew what you believed,' she admitted huskily. 'Marilyn told me before I had Richard.'

'I knew something was different about you after her visit to you,' he gasped. 'You changed, and it certainly wasn't for the better. I've always been able to deal with your fiery temper, but your coldness has always left me defeated. You became alternately pliant and cold after that day, not my fiery Shay at all. On my way over to Derrick's today I decided a lot of things, sort of like my life flashing before me,' he said wryly. 'Shay, I was only joking!' he assured her as she paled to a sickly white. 'I was going to come back tonight and tell you everything, to throw myself on your mercy. I've done so many things wrong in my life, staying married to Marilyn being one of them. I should have made her divorce me years ago, make a new life for herself. She always insisted it wasn't what she wanted, that she was happy the way things were, but I should have *made* her make the break.'

'I don't think any other man has ever mattered as much to her as you have,' she told him.

'I care about her too,' Lyon grated. 'I always will,' he added hesitantly, watching her closely.

Shay smiled at him reassuringly. 'I know that; I'm not asking you ever to forget that affection you have for Marilyn. Just as I don't think you'll ever begrudge what Ricky meant to me.'

'I owe him so much!' Lyon trembled as he once again realised how close he had come to losing Shay for ever.

She squeezed his hand. 'We both do.'

'If you had died—'

'But I didn't, Lyon,' she told him firmly. 'I lived. And it's all over now.'

'Not for us,' he told her fiercely. 'Please marry me, Shay. Complete me!'

'Yes,' she answered simply, knowing she had only been half alive without him.

'But?' He sensed the hesitation in her.

She shook her head. 'I—Now that you know you can have children of your own, how are you going to feel about Richard?' she asked anxiously.

'I love him,' he told her instantly.

'Enough?' She couldn't take her own happiness at the expense of her son's, wanted him to grow up loved and loving.

'More than enough,' Lyon assured her gently. 'Didn't I help you bring him into the world? Shay, I don't want to take anything away from Ricky, I'll tell Richard all about him when the time is right, but I want to bring him up as my own son.'

'Lyon!' She moved into his arms. 'Make love to me!' she pleaded, needing that closeness with him now. 'Let's share our love as we never have before.'

'Shay, there may never be any more babies,' he frowned. 'We've had our one million to one chance.'

She looked up at him unblinkingly. 'We will have another child, Lyon.'

'Shay—'

'Trust me, Lyon,' she said softly.

'I don't care about a child of my own any more, all I want is you and Richard,' he grated fiercely.

'You have us,' she assured him huskily. 'You'll always have us.'

'Always is a long time.' He looked at her intently.

'Not long enough.' She took his hand and led him into the bedroom.

Their lovemaking was beautiful, each touch a caress, each glance a promise of their love, burning for each other, needing, wanting, reaching the very pinnacle of their desire at the same moment, only to have that desire instantly renewed, making love again and again, unable to get enough of each other.

Lyon didn't sleep as Shay dozed beside him, her head on his shoulder. Today he had begun to live again after feeling as if he were alone in his living hell, and now he just wanted to hold Shay, to look at her, to take in the knowledge that she was really his, at last loving him again as he loved her. What they had been through had only strengthened the love they had for each other.

'Lyon?' She stirred sleepily, worn out from their lovemaking.

'Yes, darling?' He smiled down at her gently, knew she would never mistake him for any other man again.

'I'm going to write a follow-up to *Scarlet Lover*,' she murmured.

'You are?' he frowned.

'Mm,' she smiled, 'and this time Leon will get Adelia. After all, it was because of that book that I was able to find you today.'

He swallowed hard, his arms tightening about her. 'I think—I think it's only fair Leon should get his love too, don't you?' He knew what she was telling him, his emotions full.

'Oh yes.' She turned and nestled into his body.

'I'll always be here at your side now, Shay,' he told her intently.

'I know that.' She purred like a contented kitten as she fell asleep in his arms.

He hoped she purred like that for the rest of her life!

CHAPTER SIXTEEN

LYON stood in the driveway after parking the car, his sense of well-being increasing as he paused to look up at the house. But it was no longer just a house but a home. Shay had made it that the past five years, Falconer House now drawing people into its warmth instead of being an elegant shell.

Shay.

He still shook at the knowledge that she was his wife, knew he would never be complacent about the fact that she was his, that he cherished that knowledge every moment of his life.

The years had been kind to them both, Shay more beautiful than ever, only the added grey at his temples to show that he was approaching his forty-fifth year. Not that he felt his age, Shay's eternal youth enveloping him in her enjoyment of life, rarely a night passing when they didn't share that exquisite lovemaking that still shook him to his very soul.

Shay had continued to write through the years, had written her follow-up to *Scarlet Lover* as she had promised to do, *Purple Glory* a fitting sequel. The two books continued to be reprinted each year, a powerful story of love lost and refound.

'Darling?'

His eyes glowed as he looked at the woman he

loved more than life itself, her beauty framed in the doorway as she looked at him questioningly. His pulse quickened as it did every time he looked at the beautiful woman who was his wife.

'I know birthday parties are something to be dreaded, especially for a five-year-old,' she teased as she walked down the steps to meet him. 'But that's no reason to try and escape it by standing out here.' She kissed him lingeringly on the mouth, and he couldn't stop his arms from enveloping her convulsively as he buried his face in her scented hair. 'Darling, what is it?' She sounded concerned.

'I love you.' He choked with the emotion.

'Oh, Lyon, I love you too.' She cuddled into him, purring gently.

'When you two have quite finished, perhaps you would like to come and see what your terrible child is doing now?' Matthew derided from the doorway.

With his arm still possessively about Shay's waist, Lyon guided her up the steps to join his brother. 'Wait until the twins are born.' He mocked the fact that Matthew and Patty had just been told that the baby they were expecting in four months was plural. 'You'll be glad to snatch a few private moments when you can too!'

The noise from the party in the dining-room could be heard out in the hallway, and Lyon looked down at Shay indulgently. Richard's 'fifteen or so' guests seemed to be more like fifty!

'It's a little disorganised,' Shay grimaced.

'Marilyn had offered to help out but decided that
number three couldn't wait any longer, and
Michael only had time to drop off Melissa and
Mandy before rushing back to the hospital. So I'm
afraid we have the two girls staying with us a few
weeks earlier than expected.'

Marilyn had married her policeman only three
months after Lyon and Shay were married, and
after coveting the Falconer name so long they had
all realised how much Marilyn must love him
when she changed her name to Marilyn *O'Malley*!
The fact that she had instantly given up her career
to present Michael with two girls, one after the
other, had left no doubt in anyone's mind of
Marilyn's love for him. After the two girls she and
Michael were hoping for a boy this time.

Neil and Patrick were the only ones missing
from the family group today; Neil in the States
with his American wife Robyn and their small
son, Patrick due to come to them in a couple of
weeks for Christmas, the elderly man still living
in his beloved Ireland.

'It doesn't matter,' he answered Shay. 'It will
be company for—' He broke off as they entered
the dining-room to 'see what their terrible child
was doing now.' Five-year-old Richard, with his
mother's purple eyes and the Falconer build,
was standing protectively beside Beth as she
precariously walked unaided.

Despite Shay's insistence that she would give
him a child, he hadn't really expected it to happen, his life already complete with Shay and

Richard. But ten months ago Shay had presented him with this tiny miracle, her black curls and golden eyes making her impossible to resist. With Shay as his wife and Richard as his son Lyon hadn't believed it was possible to be any happier, but Beth completed the family, Richard openly adoring of his small sister. As Shay had often complained, before she became pregnant with Beth, that Lyon was in danger of spoiling Richard, the little boy had adjusted very well to having a little sister. Beth was Lyon's child, but Richard would always be special to him, his child through love if not through birth.

'Isn't she clever, Daddy?' Richard looked up proudly, those purple eyes as heart-stoppingly lovely as his mother's.

'Yes, she is.' But it was to Shay he turned, not Beth. 'Very clever.'

Shay understood and echoed Lyon's choked emotions. Life was good for them, so very very good.

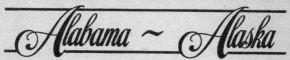